A FEAST OF FRIGHTS
FROM THE HORROR ZINE

Edited by Jeani Rector
With a Foreword by Ramsey Campbell

Published by The Horror Zine Books

SELENE
Artwork by Ignacio Bernácer Alpera

THE
HORROR ZINE

The Horror Zine's mission is to provide a venue in which writers, poets, and artists can exhibit their work. The Horror Zine is an e-zine, spotlighting the works of talented people, and displaying their deliciously dark delights for the world to enjoy.

The Horror Zine is accepting submissions of fiction, poetry and art from morbidly creative people.

Visit The Horror Zine at
www.thehorrorzine.com

Staff:
Jeani Rector, Editor
Dean H. Wild, Assistant Editor
Christian A. Larsen, Media Director

Bat art created by Riaan Marais

Cover and Interior Design By
Stephen James Price
www.BookLooksDesign.com

PRAISE FOR A FEAST OF FRIGHTS

"I have seen the future of horror—and so has Jeani Rector. In fact, she's publishing it. The Horror Zine books are not only fantastic reads, but they provide a valuable public service, exposing the world to up-and-coming talent in fiction, poetry, and art. Amazing stuff."
— Bentley Little, author of *The Disappearance* and *The Haunted*

"*A Feast of Frights from The Horror Zine* is a rare gem within the genre as it strives to cultivate only the finest selection of dark literary genius from the corners of the earth. These are twisted tales from some of the greatest masterminds of our time to poetry fit for a gothic dream; this is one publication that proves its commitment to the world of horror with every turn of the page."
— Gabrielle Faust, author of *Revenge* and *Eternal Vigilance*

"*A Feast of Frights from the Horror Zine* is much more than an anthology. It is an eclectic compilation of dark writings from some of the most talented authors the genre has to offer."
— Cyrus Wraith Walker, *Dark Discoveries Magazine*

"This book from The Horror Zine is a wonderful feast of dark delights. Enjoyable from cover to cover, I recommend it for any horror fan."
— Larry Green, *Death Head Grin Magazine*

SCORPION FLOWER
Artwork by Ester Durães

A FEAST OF FRIGHTS
FROM THE HORROR ZINE

**THE
HORROR ZINE**

-2012-

WHISPERED WORDS
Artwork by Lauren Nash

Table of Contents

FOREWORD BY RAMSEY CAMPBELL

Welcome to the groaning board! You don't have to choose from this feast—it's a buffet. Consume all you like at a sitting and then come back for more. You'll be glad you did. Let me sample the offerings (an unorthodox approach from a host, I know) and then leave you to savour them.

First, the tales. In "Scratchings" Matt Leyshon conducts us through an ominously lively wood to the site of a hideous transformation. In Britain the titular word may refer to pork rind, but we aren't at that kind of feast, believe me. Simon Clark takes us even further underground, and finds a spectral presence that glows with its own dark illumination. Shaun Meeks begins with gruesomeness—this meat is raw, by gum— and then builds on it, image by grislier image. This kind of approach can easily sprawl into excess, but here I think it's under control. By contrast, Graham Masterton conjures up the kind of childhood terror I for one remember all too well, and then extends it into adulthood by way of an ingenuously insidious explanation reminiscent of M. R. James. Philip Roberts starts with crime and sorts it out monstrously, leaving an ominous image to haunt us. As for Joe R. Lansdale, there aren't many who can beat him for spare narration and intense suspense; no wonder his tale here led off the *Masters of Horror* television series.

David M. Buhajla brings us a relentless spectre all the more unnerving for its blindness (physical as much as moral). Eric J. Guignard gives voice to a paranoid vision that's all too believable— indeed, I can readily imagine that his protagonist exists somewhere at this moment—while Mike Goddard graces his grotesque with weird wit and surrealism. As for the video library clerk in Stewart Horn's tale, he might be surrounded by film, but is it too thin? You'll find there's more than one dark joke in the title. And Christian A. Larsen has another graveyard story for us! The dead are restless here for a different reason—they have many, after all.

xiii

FOREWORD

John Forth endows a forest with uncanny life and brings some of it home, morally as well—we may feel we weren't responsible for what we did as children, but suppose something disagrees? Scott Nicholson tells of a folksy haunting, by which I don't mean to belittle the chill it brings—its special eeriness reminds me of Manly Wade Wellman in his country mode. Brian G. Murray evokes the ghost of many a fogbound movie and the landscape of Jersey (the Channel Island, dear reader, not the New York state or the Georgia town). Jason Reynolds conducts us through another kind of spectral terrain—the kind we may come to discover we're afraid to recognise. Cheryl Kaye Tardif reveals the kind of haunting that may disturb us most—the kind that hides inside us, waiting to be conjured forth—while Paul Edwards' protagonist discovers that self-harm bodies forth not just her psychological state but something even more lethal.

Joe McKinney sets a monster loose in his spare narrative—decide for yourself what's on the rampage, but be suitably unnerved that he knows whereof he writes. Christopher Nadeau has a Halloween tale for us; some of the prose echoes the cadences of Bradbury—the man who has made the date his own—and this vision is as dark as any that Ray ever brought us. Susie Moloney reminds us that menaces surround us, as banal as they are all-powerful, and then she turns them into nightmare and indeed a comedy of paranoia. Martin Shelby takes the oldest struggle in the universe into a Texaco convenience station, and one of those present will depart all the better for it. Chris Castle prompts us to recall how school could be a place of dread, and he ought to know, being a teacher. Teachers can be fearful too and, by heaven, some deserve to be (as here).

David A. Hernandez's tale conveys a clammy vividness and steeps its ghastly gourmandising in the gravy of its prose. Tom Piccirilli seizes the reader by the throat and perhaps other portions of their anatomy—just be glad it's only his prose that does, not his characters in person. You may squirm, but I suspect you'll sit still enough to discover where it inexorably leads. Is it the Internet that sets loose the demons in Taylor Grant's tale? After all, that medium has called them forth from within many folk who may very well be timid in everyday life. However you interpret them, his demons ring grimly true. But this anthology may remind us there is no safe place in the world, not even K. A. Opperman's idyllic golden landscape. His hoary rustic would be in good company with several of Lovecraft's old men.

Ed Gorman casts a clear but not cold eye on the process of growing up as a video geek and how damaging obsession can be, but his conclusion is poignant, perhaps even redemptive. In Christian Riley's story, he proves that love is not always what it seems. Like Chris Castle, Sandra Crook roots her tale in teaching. Anyone who suffered bullying at school might have liked to have a playmate such as the one with which she graces her lonely child—even the thought may be satisfying enough. Trevor Denyer offers comfort, but it has to be reached by a disturbing route; perhaps it wouldn't be worth having if it were easier to reach. As for Jeff Strand's terse piece, it isn't just an exercise in grisly humour. See how you feel at the end!

Michael Wolf's story reappears under his name, having previously been credited to a plagiarist. It's more than worthy of revival, and Wolf deserves recognition for his inventiveness (the very quality plagiarists lack). Alva J. Roberts offers us not one monster but a brace of lethal species, and the throats they're at don't belong to each other. And James Strauss shares his nightmare with us. Wake up! You can do it! Just scream, strain to scream...

You'll find a final pair of tales later on, by our good editor Jeani Rector, a famous legend retold with muscular spareness and a classical ghost story that manages to come up with a new species of haunted house. Bravo, Jeani! Assistant Editor Dean H. Wild tells a mortuary tale and finds a new reason for the dead to live before laying them gently to rest.

There's non-fiction here too. John Gilmore gives us many bleak facts in a reminiscence of Hollywood, and the glancing reference to Barbara La Marr seems all the more ominous for being left unexpanded—by all means look her name up. By contrast, Earl Hamner's memories of working on *The Twilight Zone* are as nostalgic as we could want. Joe Lansdale remembers the gestation of his considerable talent and celebrates his greatest influence, while his and Karen's daughter Kasey proves as articulate as she is talented (that is, highly).

Graham Masterton contributes a moving memoir of his much-missed wife Wiescka—I am sure none of us who met her will forget her. Deborah LeBlanc shares a glimpse beyond the grave, and Paul Dale Roberts takes us through the processes of paranormal investigation. As for the excellent Tim Lebbon, he offers many insights for authors; you won't hear much disagreement from me.

xv

FOREWORD

And there's poetry. G. O. Clark's contributions range from dark wit to gentle eeriness. Dennis Bagwell can be bracingly acerbic and also just plain hilarious. Ian Hunter starts in the grave but shows us that worse is available at the touch of a button. Wesley Dylan Gray's poems are vivid enough to make your flesh crawl—a traditional image, I know, but brought to life here. Jorge Baldomero Valdes Jr says a great deal in a very few words; they're sharp as razors. Andrea Laham shows us childhood terrors grown up, and they're only the preamble to her apocalypse. Benjamin Blake relishes funereal lyricism with a spice of surrealism, while Elise R. Hopkins brings visions of the plague but also a sensitive evocation. It's good to see macabre poetry has so much vigour still.

Nor must I forget the art. We all know how many words a picture is worth, so let me offer just a few of mine. Paula McDonald shows how the gruesome can be beautiful in *Apophobia* and conveys a subtler menace in *Despair*. John Richardson's *Straw Man* might have rustled his way out of a minatory folk tale or ghost story. At first sight John Frazee seems to have given us a portrait of old age, but does the image hint at a darker shadow? Esther Durães' haunting portrait is Gothic in more than one sense, and Ignacio Bernacer's *Selene* shows us wistfulness within a machine that may be human. Lauren Nash presents us with a series of avian enigmas, each one more evocative as they accumulate resonance.

And now let me stand aside! Fall upon the feast!

Ramsey Campbell
Wallasey, Merseyside
8 February 2012

FICTION

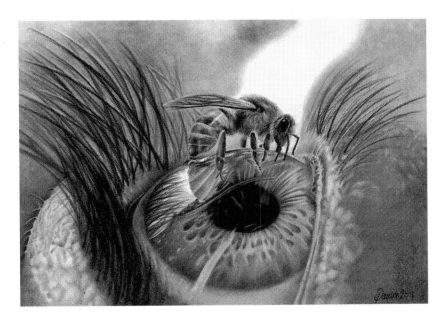

APIPHOBIA
Artwork by Paula McDonald

THE BLANK QUEEN
Artwork by Larkin

SCRATCHINGS

by Matt Leyshon

"Soon it'll be Maisy's last feed before bedtime," Eliza said, looking thoughtfully at the clock over the pub's fireplace.

"She'll be fine. Maisy isn't one to go hungry quietly," George said, picking a wiry pig bristle from his teeth.

She waited as George downed the last of his pint and finished off his pork scratchings, and then she buttoned up her coat, ready to leave. He pulled on his jacket and gave his new white trainers a quick buff with his jacket sleeve. Finally he led her out from the cozy warmth of The Red Lion and into the autumn night.

"The babysitter knows what she's doing. This is a rare evening out without baby Maisy so I want to make the most of it," George told her.

They cut through the car park at the back of the pub and headed for the illuminated byroad that bisected the gloaming like a scalpel of cold white light. The night air was chill and their breath mushroomed wraith-like before them as they crossed the footbridge over the river.

"But it's cold, and I don't want to muddy my shoes. I would have worn my boots if I had known where you are taking me," she said.

"It hasn't rained for weeks," he said, "and I wouldn't be doing this if I thought I was going to ruin my lovely new trainers, would I? Come on, walk a bit quicker and it'll warm you up."

With his free hand, George swung the carrier bag of super-strength cider in time with his long strides and urged her across the road to the gate opposite. "Perfect," he said as he pulled an old newspaper from the hedge and tucked it inside his jacket before climbing over the rusted metal gate.

He helped her over the gate and she brushed away the rust that colored her palms like lily pollen in the moon's glow. The long grass pulled at their feet and ahead of them, the dense clusters of shadowed trees anchored the charcoal sky.

They continued walking, their passage through the still night occasionally pierced with the needling screeches of rutting foxes, each one making Eliza jump a little. They followed a dog walker's path that ran parallel with the river embroidering the edge of the field with a gloomy cross hatch of reeds and rushes.

"We were too young to drink in Leddenton's pubs back then, so we used to make this journey in all weathers, you know," said George. "We'd go to this off-license on the High Street where the guy would serve us, and then through sleet, gales, and pouring rain, we would head for the railway bridge. I remember once crossing this field under a lunar eclipse; the moon was blood red above us. I'll never forget that."

"How much further?" Eliza said, her annoyance showing.

"Not far."

George's enthusiasm was met with a frown but it did nothing to dampen his fine mood and he carried on swinging his bag happily at his side and pulling Eliza along behind him.

Suddenly Eliza sidestepped a little, startled, as a heron set off from the dark of the riverbank. They watched as it lolled heavily through the air above, the full moon glistening off its wings, its head hanging low like an unsightly cyst beneath its silhouetted body. Then he began pulling her again, and when they reached the other side of the field, George climbed the stile and pointed down the narrow lane to the railway bridge. "There it is," he said.

"This is why you brought me here? It looks overgrown," she said as she descended the narrow steps of rotting wood. "And it smells funny down here."

"That's fresh country air," George replied.

"Oh, whatever."

The round moon hung heavy overhead, its smooth geometry contrasting with the jagged silhouettes of dark bony branches arthritically probing the twilight sky around the impenetrable pitch of the tunnel mouth. Bats darted back and forth overhead like fleeting thoughts. Undaunted by the possibility of the tunnel being inaccessible by the advance of nature, George took Eliza's hand once more.

"When Maisy is a bit older I really want her to experience the countryside, you know. It'll be good for her," George said as he breathed in the cloying scent of hawthorn and dew.

"I never left the city until I met you," Eliza told him.

"Exactly. And look how you turned out," he said with a wink.

"I managed to give birth to our perfect daughter, didn't I?"

"You did indeed. I take it all back."

The cracked tarmac petered out into a dwindling mud path that became lost in tangled overgrowth. The blackberry bushes stretched almost up to Eliza's shoulders and blocked their way to the tunnel entrance.

"I guess that's it then," Eliza said.

"It seems nobody comes down here anymore," he said. "But hang on, I'm not giving up that easily."

He began kicking around at the foot of the hedgerows until eventually his toe lifted a thick dead branch. A hedgehog woke from its disturbed slumber and waddled into the dark depths of a prickly shrub with a rustle and a snort.

"I didn't know hedgehogs had long tails," Eliza said.

"They don't."

"Well, that one did. It had a pink tail like a rat."

"It must have been a rat then," George said as he gauged the weight of the big stick in his hands.

"Whatever."

"Watch and learn," he said to Eliza, grinning. "Now stand back."

George passed the cider for Eliza to hold and then swung his stick into the thorny branches. Soon a clearing began to emerge as he thrashed the overhanging twigs back onto themselves. He edged forwards, stamping his feet as he worked, clearing a pathway to the tunnel by flattening the nettles underfoot.

Eliza opened the cider and took a swig. She watched an owl, glowing spectral in the moonlight, on top of a telegraph pole. Its head jerked left and right as it scanned for prey in the neighboring field, and for a second it stopped, seeming then to look right at her.

She started a little when George re-emerged from the thicket.

"Did I just catch you admiring the countryside?" he said.

"Very funny. I was watching an owl. I'd never seen one like that before," she said, but when she turned back to point it out, it had gone.

"Follow me, and watch your feet or you'll trip on the stingers," he said.

The tunnel curved gently and was long enough to conceal the moonlit woods at the other end. When they reached the middle, George stopped, took out the old newspaper from his pocket, and dropped it to the floor and piled some twigs on top.

"We're trespassing, you know. What if somebody comes?" Eliza asked.

"We scarper," said George, chortling contently as he rummaged through his pockets for a lighter.

The crumbling brickwork of the tunnel flashed orange as George crouched, struck the lighter, and held the flame to the newspaper. The wails of more foxes in heat ran through the tunnel, prickling their chilly skin like a lover's caress before fading out behind them.

"George, the tunnel is just going to fill up with smoke and my clothes are going to stink," Eliza whined.

"No it won't," he said, pointing upwards. "The smoke goes out through that crack up there. Perfect, eh?"

"Yes, perfect," Eliza said with a pantomime of boredom as she watched the paper take and the flames begin to lap upwards over the dry sticks.

George rose to his feet and took a gulp of hard cider as he admired his handiwork. The flames made their shadows stretch up darkly upon the curved tunnel walls, becoming elongated until their heads met directly above them. They stood in silence for a while and took turns to drink from the bottle of cider. The tendrils of yellow smoke billowed upwards to swell like feeding leeches before they snaked through the narrow crack above.

"Did you hear that?" George suddenly asked.

"Hear what?"

"A rustling sound, like scratching or something."

"Are you trying to scare me?"

"No, listen," prompted George. "Come and stand next to me."

Eliza sighed and stood on the other side of George so that she was now nearer to the woods on the other side. Neither of them spoke for a long moment as they both stood still and listened.

"There," George said. "Did you hear it just now?"

"That rumbling noise?"

"Not that," George admonished. "That's just a generator from the chemical factory on the other side of the river."

"Strange place for a chemical factory," Eliza said.

"Maybe, but they do stuff for the military, I think. This is Ministry of Defense land. Do you remember those protesters we passed when we drove through Salisbury Plain?"

"What about them?"

"That was outside a military laboratory. They were Animal Welfare campaigners. I saw their placards."

"Anyway," said Eliza, "I don't care about the protesters. Apart from the generator, all I can hear is the fire and your silly new trainers squeaking."

"It might be a badger. Or your pink-tailed hedgehog."

"And it might be a soldier with his gun, more like?"

"Nah, don't be daft," George said. "Have you been watching my Rambo box-set again?"

He pulled up a handful of dead grass and held it into the fire until it caught. Then he went to the opposite end of the tunnel and held the light aloft. "The noise is coming from just over there," he called back. "You coming?"

"No way," Eliza said, and she turned to watch the fire with a stubborn swing of the hips.

Sheltered by the leaves above, the undergrowth leading out of the tunnel and into the wood was less wild, and by stepping high and pushing back the occasional vine of poison ivy, George was able to advance in the direction of the peculiar sounds. He followed an animal track that curved along the edge of the river and then angled abruptly to the left which led him up a gentle incline at the foot of the terraced clay embankment. The flames from his torch ate down the grass and he soon felt their warmth upon his hand so he dropped it and stamped out the embers.

He waited until his eyes grew accustomed to the milky light of the moon and then walked towards the noises that continued ahead. He thought that if he were quiet enough in his approach, he would maybe see badger cubs playing at the mouth of a sett.

He carefully grabbed a sapling and pulled himself quietly onto the first terrace and peered over the thistles and thorns that grew on the edge. He spotted a clearing glowing faintly grey but it was flat and there was no sign of any badgers. He went forward, listening carefully and determined that the noise was coming from the next terrace. George pulled his sleeve over his hand to hold back the thorns and pushed himself up onto the level and scanned the trees and bushes for a gap that he might be able to climb through.

The tunnel was just a little below him now, a short distance to the left through dense and overgrown brambles. It dawned on him that he was away from Eliza longer than he had intended and that she might be worried about him, but the sounds continued to arouse his curiosity. The crackles of twigs were snapping like wishbones, and he could not fight his desire to see what it could be.

He spotted a track leading low through the thicket and figured that if he got to his knees then he would to be able to crawl through without ruining his trainers, and so he continued towards the scratching sounds. Brambles pulled painfully at his hair and clawed at his jacket but he was almost right upon the source of the noises now.

Suddenly a blur of creamy whiteness dart across the ground ahead, something small and fleshy and as milky white in the moonlight as baby Maisy in her bathtub.

"What the...?" he whispered to himself. Although he knew badgers were born without fur, he also knew that if he saw one the size of what he had just seen then it really ought not to be bald.

He crawled forwards and emerged at a clearing with a sunken crater about five feet across before him. At one end there was a large hole at the foot of a mound. He smelled the unmistakable musk of animal, but the sounds had stopped and there were no badgers to be seen.

He rose, kicked weeds from his ankles and frowned at the dirt smeared across the toes of his trainers. He moved silently towards the sett entrance. The opening was big, much bigger than those he remembered seeing in his youth, but he figured maybe a dog had been digging at it, trying to get at the badgers inside. He dropped to his knees and peered into the darkness.

A few roots hung from the roof of the sett inside but a wall of absolute darkness blocked his vision like a blindfold. He rested upon one elbow, his head half inside, and reached for the lighter in his trouser pocket. Then, stretching his arm in as deep as he could, he flicked the flint.

In a flash of amber he saw before him a cavernous space, then a blurred glimpse of pinky-whiteness rushing towards him. Then darkness again, this time wet and warm, and tempered by pain. He managed to open his eyes to see that he was peering down the gullet of a ravenous pig, its jaw snapping over his face, it's teeth plunging into his forehead and chin.

His scream echoed briefly in the pig's skull before his head was torn from his shoulders with a whistle from his severed windpipe. Blood sprayed out behind him as the pig shook him and for a moment the moonlight at the opening of the sett reddened behind a wave of black gore. His feet kicked spasmodically at the ground, tossing a trainer high into the air as squealing piglets gathered around him, seizing his jeans and jacket in their teeth and pulling him down into the depths of the sett.

«« — »»

At the sound of a scream, Eliza jumped and dropped the cider to her feet.

"George!" she shouted.

There was no reply; instead she heard a squealing noise and a thrashing sound, but it suddenly stopped almost as abruptly as it had started. She rushed to the end of the tunnel and peered into the gloom of the woods. As her irises widened, the trees took form and the pale flat mud of an animal track glimmered a muted grey before her.

"George!" she called again. "Come on, you're scaring me!"

She knew he wouldn't carry a joke this far. Was he in trouble? Did he need her?

Cautiously she stepped out from the tunnel and began to follow the track. She heard the river rippling gently through gullies nearby and the generator across the way. She began to progress upwards to where the squeals and frantic scratching had carried down from the embankment just moments ago.

She spotted something white caught high in a bush halfway up the ridge and as she got nearer she saw that it was a trainer that looked very much like George's. Very fearful now, she called his name again but her cry was met with a sudden terrible crescendo of squeals.

"George!" she screamed as she began to crawl upwards. Thorns lashed her temples and knotted weeds gripped her ankles like bony fingers. Mossy branches dragged green tracks over her jacket and dirt greased her shoes like mildew. Kicking up earth and clawing at the cold soil, she scrambled upwards to where George's white trainer hung overhead like an amputated foot.

Emerging into the clearing, Eliza glimpsed George's socked heel disappear into the dripping mouth of a hole and she dashed forwards to try and grab it, but she was too late; it was gone. All she could see was a thick darkness, alive with dust dancing in the moonlight like interference upon a television screen. Clumps of disturbed earth fell from the top of the sett's mouth into puddles of black liquid.

She reached into the darkness and waved her hand around to clutch his foot, but her fingers were met only with hanging roots and clammy air. She took a breath and leaned inside, and then she began to crawl into the small dark cavern.

Suddenly she felt the roof at the entrance of the sett collapse and encase her ankles in soil. She screamed and tried desperately to kick her feet free. She fought to turn back on herself but the sett's walls held her firmly at the hips.

She felt the hot breath of an animal upon her brow and she screamed again as another creature sniffed at her knotted and filthy hair. Then more arrived, grunting hungrily and dripping warm spittle upon her face. She felt them pulling at her jacket and then wiry bristles scratched at the cold flesh of her belly as her blouse was shredded by hungry teeth.

Wet mouths searched her skin, and moving upwards, the teeth set to work again, this time tearing at her brassiere as more and more creatures pushed past her face in the musty gloom as she writhed. She screamed again as scrambling piglets, with tiny trotters kicking against her, cocooned her, and filthy teeth pulled at the tattered remains of her clothes. She felt a tiny hot mouth close with a wet slurp over her breast and begin to suckle.

As she ceased struggling, she thought that the country was no place for her daughter. Her final scream was Maisy's name, and it careered through the woods, sending a murder of crows erupting upwards to eclipse the moon.

About Matt Leyshon

Matt Leyshon is a British writer living in the seaside town of Blackpool, Lancashire. His work can be found in *Lovecraft's Disciples, Midnight Street, Morpheus Tales*, and *Paraphilia*.

GHOST PIT

by Simon Clark

The man spoke in a whisper. "Listen... I mean *really* listen. Can you hear it? That *hiss...shush*. It sounds like lungs, doesn't it? We're down here at the bottom of the pit. A thousand feet below ground, and there it goes: *hiss...shush*. It sounds like someone breathing...some *thing* breathing. Something huge..."

Her guide in the coal mine was a hard, muscular man. Tufts of black hair stuck out from beneath his bright yellow helmet. Up there on the surface John Stryker had been cocky. He strode round the mine like he owned the place. John Stryker loved the sound of his own voice. Yet down here, at the bottom of the shaft, it was a different story. The man was scared.

In the light of the helmet lamp she saw the sweat on his face. Yes, absolutely, the place terrified him. It fascinated him, too.

Jenny Brown suspected he dared himself to come down here into the coal mine. A test of his manhood. Fear was his fix of choice. Then there was something uncanny about these miles of tunnels. The abandoned machinery. The inky blackness. The solitude.

His voice was gruff. "Come on, then. You'll want to get your filming done, so you can get out of here." He tried to smile. It looked like a desperate snarl. Fear was eating into him. "You won't be used to pits like this—no doubt you're scared. That's only natural."

"I'm not scared, Mr. Stryker."

"Uh. Trying to put on a brave face, are we?"

"You promised to show me an unusual feature of the coal mine, Mr. Stryker. It's my job to film it for the Industrial Heritage Archive."

"That's a flipping mouthful, isn't it?" He tried to cover his fright with contempt. "Industrial Heritage Archive. Waste of money, if you ask me."

"If you'd rather not come, I can go by myself."

"Go by yourself? Ha. You wouldn't last two minutes down here, Miss Brown. Not two minutes."

"Then show me what I've come to see."

"Follow me, then. Don't bang your head on the pit props. All right?"

"I'll take care of my head, Mr. Stryker. You look after yours."

As her guide turned away, he grunted something she didn't quite catch. A something that was clearly insulting about the young woman with the video camera.

"What was that you said, Mr. Stryker?"

He bluffed his way out with a lecture about the pit, like Jenny was some dim-witted school girl. "There used to be hundreds of coal mines in Britain. This is one of the last. It was mothballed ten years ago, because it's cheaper to import coal than dig it from under our feet. Mind you don't trip over the cables. I don't want to have to carry you out with a broken leg. Now where was I? Ah. The name of this pit is Capstone Luck. Despite the name it was never a lucky pit. In 1896 two hundred men were killed in a methane blast. And two hundred coffins were paraded through the village to the graveyard. There wasn't a single body in the coffins. No. They're all still down here, lass."

Clearly, he wanted Jenny to feel the fear he felt, so he continued, "They're all lying in the muck and the dark two levels below this one." He decided two hundred deaths weren't enough. "Lots more died, since. Explosions, rock falls, machinery accidents. When the pit was being mothballed, six engineers fell a thousand feet when the lift cable snapped. They hit the bottom of the shaft pretty much where you're standing. Now then…hurry up. Otherwise you'll miss filming Capstone Luck's big mystery." Then his voice acquired a dark sarcasm. "We don't want the Industrial Heritage Archive wasting their pennies, do we now?"

They walked along the tunnel. Its walls had been cut from living coal. Beneath the harsh light those seams of coal shone a glossy, lustrous black. Like black gemstones.

Then Jenny heard the sound again. *Hiss…shush…*

"You don't want to be late lass," he told her. "It's coming!"

"What is it?" she asked. "What's making that noise?"

"You're just about to find out, Miss. Stand at the edge of that shaft and look down."

28

She peered into the shaft. The light revealed smooth flanks of rock that plunged downward. A rusty iron ladder was bolted to one side of the shaft. The phrase 'bottomless pit' came to mind.

John Stryker took a deep breath. "Every twenty-eight days the lower mine workings flood. Water rises up the shaft as far as that steel beam there. Do you see it? About thirty feet down. The L-shaped one next to the ladder?"

*Hiss...shush...*that sound again.

Jenny switched on the camera. "Why does it flood on such a regular basis?"

"Nobody knows. We're miles from the sea. But every twenty-eight days the water comes back. It's like a tide. It rises three hundred feet up the shaft, then stops. Just stops right there at the beam."

Hiss...shush. The sound grew louder. *HISS. SHUSH.* Like a huge animal breathing.

"You know something, Miss?" The man's voice was like the echo ghosting from the shaft. "The truth is, I can't get Capstone Luck out of my mind. It's all I ever think about. Locals call it 'the ghost pit.' And now I know why. I can see all those men that died here. Burnt, suffocated, blown apart...cremated alive. And I know it's those dead men. They make this happen. They do it...the ghosts...they bring the water. They want to drown the fires...they need to stop the pain. The ghosts pull the water into the mine to quench that awful, searing heat. Even though the fires went out a long time ago, there are still fires burning inside their souls."

She stared at him in shock. "You can't really believe that!"

"Oh, but I do, Miss. I see them. All the miners that died...their ghosts are down there."

"I'm going back, Mr. Stryker. You're not well."

"You can't go yet."

"Why not?"

"It's starting. Look." He pointed downwards. His finger trembled and his eyes bulged. "Here it comes. The flood!"

Despite her alarm at his talk of ghosts, she pressed the camera's record button. In the light of the helmet lamps, she saw a pool of silver appear at the bottom of the shaft. A long way down. A very long way down. Strangely, it resembled the glint of an eye. Silvery. Wet.

And then it came. The water rose up the shaft.

Hiss...shush. It flowed upwards. Swirling, turbulent. *Hiss...shush...*

The water stops at the L-shaped beam, she told herself. *It always stops there. The flood never rises higher. That's what Stryker said. The water will stop.*

She watched the rising levels. The flood touched the steel beam. Then the water swirled past it. The liquid surged higher and higher. She saw it racing toward them. A fluid piston remorselessly surging up from the black depths.

She cried out, "You said it would never rise higher than the beam!"

A strange smile appeared on Stryker's face. "The mine needs more ghosts. The faces told me. We will stay here forever and ever."

With that, the man stepped over the edge. When he struck the water it swallowed him without a splash.

Jenny turned and ran.

That was the moment the electricity failed. The sudden death of the lights startled her so much she stumbled. The safety helmet flew from her head. When it struck the floor the lamp went out.

Darkness. Absolute darkness. Jenny held her breath. She could see nothing. There was nothing but black.

She heard, though. *Hiss...shush...*the sound grew louder. *Hiss...shush...*then the sound of pouring.

I know what that is, she thought in horror. *That's the sound of water rising out of the shaft.* A cold wind blew along the tunnel. The air being displaced by the flood. Soon the water would reach her.

Her heart pounded, her chest grew tight; so tight she could hardly breathe.

Move, she told herself. *Get out of here!* But which way? She couldn't see. Yet she knew that the water gushed into the tunnel.

To drown in the dark? Here, deep underground; to die alone. Her heart slammed against her ribs. Arctic shivers ran down her spine. Already she imagined the water's cold touch.

She scrambled to her feet, then reached out for the tunnel wall. As soon as her fingers met the rock she began to walk, using the wall to guide her.

Then she ran, because something was happening. Something worse than the flood. Worse than darkness.

The water behind her began to glow with a faint silver light...a glow like moonlight. Eerie...haunting...a cold, cold glow that was not natural, nor even earthly.

She glanced back. The water pursued her...it wanted her...then she knew why.

Faces...the water consisted of liquid faces. Dozens...hundreds of them...faces with wide, staring eyes. Eyes of men that had been dead for decades...but something in the mine wouldn't let them be properly dead...not dead and gone...these were the spirits of the dead miners, She glimpsed the face of John Stryker in the water.

His lips moved. *Jenny...Jenny, stay...* The liquid souls wanted her. They had to possess her.

The glowing water gave her enough light to see by, so she ran faster. Just then her toe caught a cable. She went sprawling to the floor. The water rushed toward her.

Then she was on her feet again. Running hard. Running faster than she'd ever done before.

At last she reached the lift cage, jumped in and slammed the grill shut. Punched the red button. And kept punching that big red button: the emergency call. The one that told them on the surface to haul up the lift.

Where are they? Why don't they pull me up? Oh, no...oh my God...here it comes!

Hiss...shush. The flood swept toward her.

《《—》》

Jenny must have blacked out. She didn't remember the return journey to the surface. All she knew was that hands carried her out of the lift. *Where's Stryker,* they asked. *What happened to Stryker?*

《《—》》

Jenny Reed was much better now. The nightmares had stopped. No more hallucinations, touch wood. Whatever happened in the coal mine was a terrible accident. Or so they told her. A freak flood, that's all.

Even so, she changed her life entirely. Now she worked for a TV station in Saudi. The sun shone. In the desert, there wasn't so much as a drop of water. She liked it that way. This arid land made her feel safe.

31

Because these days even a jug of water at the dinner table made her shudder. And as for taking a bath...

And then a year later, on the anniversary of her escape, Jenny woke all of a sudden. She was alone in her Saudi apartment. A warm breeze blew through the open window. At first she thought it was the breeze making the sound.

Then she heard it properly. And her blood turned cold.

Hiss...shush...

Jenny turned on the light. A shadow crept under the apartment door. *No, not a shadow...this is water.* A large pool of water, spreading out across the floor toward her bed.

And that sound again...the one from the Ghost Pit.

Hiss shush... Yes. That sound. *Hiss...shush.*

The last sound she would ever hear.

About Simon Clark

Simon Clark lives in Doncaster, England with his family. When his first novel, *Nailed by the Heart*, made it through the slush pile in 1994, he banked the advance and embarked upon his dream of becoming a full-time writer. Many dreams and nightmares later he wrote *Blood Crazy*, *Darkness Demands*, *This Rage of Echoes*, *Whitby Vampyrrhic* and *The Night of the Triffids*, which continues the story of Wyndham's classic *The Day of the Triffids*. His revival of the wickedly ambulatory plants won the British Fantasy Society's award for best novel.

Simon also experiments in short film, one of which, *Dear Simon, Where Do You Get Your Ideas From?* has been featured in the UK's Channel 4 ShortDoc series, and earned the accolade 'the ultimate in TV democracy.' He also created Winter Chills for BBC TV.

More films, with tips on writing horror fiction, plus articles, and news can be accessed at his website http://www.nailedbytheheart.com

THE SOLDIER

by Shaun Meeks

There was smoke coming from his gun, though he hadn't fired it in well over two days. He glanced away from it, out the glassless window at dark clouds that rolled overhead. He wondered what time it was.

It was stupid, thinking on such banality while he lay motionless in a room above rubble-filled streets, the screams of the dying floating to him, though they seemed to be fading every second. He refused to join their chorus because he didn't want to admit that he might be dying as well.

It was highly possible that his mind was wandering to such useless concerns to keep him from looking at himself and seeing the blood pooling under his once pristine uniform, intestines lying on the dirty floor like tentacles. They would probably be covered in flies, laying eggs at that very moment so that they could hatch and his soon-to-be rotting guts would be food for the young maggots.

Wilhelm looked away from the window and back to the still-smoking gun that was laying less than three feet from where he was, right next to an American soldier who was missing the lower left side of his face. He wanted to reach for the gun, maybe figure out why there was smoke coming from the barrel, but just as he tried to move his hand to grasp it, he found he couldn't.

He liked it even less that the gun was close to the American who had shot him. Wilhelm knew that he would feel better if he could just reach over and take hold of his MP40. The feel of it in his hand would give him a sense, even if it was false, that everything would be fine.

His mind drifted to how this had all happened.

As Wilhelm had stepped in the room, gun raised, the American spun towards him, fear and surprise clearly in his eyes, and Wilhelm fired quickly. His bullet found a home in the lower left side of the American's face, disintegrating the flesh and bone in a mist of red that seemed to glow in the light from outside. Wilhelm felt an instant moment of joy, knowing that he had served his country so well, getting the drop on the unsuspecting solider, but the joy was short-lived.

As the American fell sideways, his eyes rolled back in his head, his body tensed like someone that had just been delivered a knockout punch, all the muscles clenched, including those in his hand. The American's gun discharged, echoing in the small room, and Wilhelm felt a hot punch to his stomach. He looked down at himself and saw the impossible.

He realized that dark water was spreading across his shirt, getting bigger with each passing second. His gun fell to the ground as his hands reached for the wound. He lifted his shirt and that only made things worse as the hole made by the bullet must have ricocheted off a bone and found its escape through the area just above his belly button, allowing a place for his intestines to try to evacuate.

Wilhelm reached down as the bluish ropes began to slide out of him in a slow, sickening way, his hands meeting his intestines in an attempt to stop the escape. As he grasped them, trying to keep them from falling to the ground, they felt like his wife's freshly made lamb sausages, all warm, wet and slimy. As he looked down and saw them in his now blood-soaked hands, he felt all the strength leave his legs and they gave out. He crashed to the dirty floor where he still was, two days later, and the hope of survival seemed to be fading like the light outside the window.

He knew he must be dying, was amazed that he wasn't dead yet, though deep in his own mind a voice asked him if he was so sure about that. He pushed that thought away each time it tried to bubble up, not wanting to even consider that he was already dead, that he would never kiss his kids goodnight again, never feel the warm embrace of his loving Hannah. He had to hold on.

Wilhelm sighed and looked away from the gun lost to him. He could hear the sound of tanks crunching their way through the streets below him. He wondered if they were Americans, the English, or his own German brothers down there. If they were German soldiers, there was still a chance for him to make it out of this, to get fixed up and find his way back home where his wife Hannah and his two boys who would be waiting proudly for his return.

He knew that the doctors would be able to fix him up and that he would be sitting by the fire with his wife beside him and his boys at his feet, a thick beer in his hand, telling stories of how he had helped

Germany win the war. He knew his country was so close to winning. He would tell them how he had met Hitler, although that would be stretching the truth a bit. The closest he had ever come to meeting the Fuhrer was being at an assembly hall where he was giving a speech in front of over a hundred thousand other soldiers.

Wilhelm finally found the courage to look down at himself. He saw a pooled mess that smelled of feces and spoiled meat. He saw parts if his insides laying on the outside, covered in dirt from the floor and wondered if that would be a problem when the doctors tried to put him back together.

He licked his dry lips and looked back to the window, hearing the tanks outside coming to a halt, followed by voices. He tried to distinguish in what language they were speaking, hoping that they were his fellow brothers, but he couldn't tell. Wilhelm tried to call out to them, but found the words refused to be formed; all that left his dried lips was a soft sigh.

His eyes moved away from the window again, back to the dead American in time to see a rat scurry over to him and tentatively test the hole in his face. Wilhelm watched as the rat bit into the blackened flesh, burned from the heat of the bullets that tore away skin, muscle and bone. The rat pulled back on the meat with its teeth, then moved backwards quickly as though expecting to be attacked, not realizing that the man he had just tasted was dead.

The rat chewed on the small piece of flesh that it held in its paws and watched the American to see if he would move. When there was no attack and the food was eaten, the rat went in for a second morsel, this time biting off a larger piece. Wilhelm watched with a mix of disgust and fascination; the soft sound of the skin popping and crunching in the rodent's mouth was the worst part of it for him.

What if the rat became bored with the flesh of the dead American and turned his attention to him instead? What if the rat decide to come pick at his intestines that were laying out on the ground under him, joining the flies that were there and the maggots that would soon hatch from the eggs the flies had laid?

Again, Wilhelm tried to move his arms, wanting to make some sort of movement so that the rat would not try its luck with him before he was found and rescued by his countrymen. He hoped the dead American in the room was enough to keep the rodent busy. The rat didn't seem to notice him as it went in for what Wilhelm thought was going to be a third helping of American pie, but instead it suddenly disappeared into the gaping hole that Wilhelm's own machine gun had made in the dead man's face.

He watched as the rat bit and clawed its way inside, the hairless tail wiggling back and forth, the dead man's head moving slightly as it did, causing grey matter to fall from the open wound to the ground with a wet slap. Wilhelm closed his eyes, not wanting to watch the unnatural movements of the dead American's head as the rat continued to move inside his face.

He turned his attention to his own memories, ignoring the sounds of the rat and of the soldiers still outside the building where he lay. He was thinking of his beautiful wife, Hannah, the way her face would glow in the early morning light while they sat on their porch, sipping some tea that she had wanted him to try. They had been married for six years, but it had felt as though he was seeing her for the first time each and every time he looked at her.

He opened his eyes; no tears as he had nothing in him to spare, and saw that there were now more rats in the room, following the lead of the first. One rat sat on its back haunches, seeming to call for others with its strange, high pitched squeaks. Three others went into the opened face wound, then a fourth, a fifth; and Wilhelm began to wonder how many more would be able to fit in there.

The American's body moved about with false life as the rats crawled around inside of him. The biggest of them continued to look as though it were orchestrating the entire scene. He could hear the wet sounds of the animals moving into the rotting flesh and eating...and eating.

He turned his attention back to the window. Rain was now falling and the voices of the soldiers seemed to be changing directions, moving into the building. At least he hoped it was so. He knew he was running out of blood, and therefore running out of time.

He looked back to the American and his eyes opened wide at the sight. Once again he wished that he was within reach of his gun as the body of the man Wilhelm had shot in the face was now bloated and moving.

It wasn't just the rats any more. Could he believe what he was seeing? Wilhelm felt his heart go cold as the icy hands of fear closed around it.

The dead man was trying to rise!

36

Wilhelm felt panic grip him as he watched the American's body lift upwards on stiff arms. The dead man quivered as he moved, looking as though he was trying to do pushups on what should have been lifeless arms. How could this be?

In terror, Wilhelm tried to push his own body away from the scene, and to will his still limbs into motion so that he could escape. He felt like crying out at his own body's disobedience, wanting to yell at himself for failing as he stared unwillingly at the American.

Rising to his feet, the dead man slowly turned his head towards him. If Wilhelm could have gasped or cried out, he would have. The dead man's lifeless eyes, which were partially rolled back in his head, looked towards him.

Wilhelm watched in horror as a smile spread on the remains of the dead man's lower face, the only part that was still intact after Wilhelm's own bullet had torn away the rest, but where the skin and bone was missing, he could see rats still moving, the fleshy tails falling out of the hole now and again as the dead man continued to move.

Wilhelm begged to God, not even caring that he had never believed in any God before, had never even stepped into a church in his entire life, yet prayed nonetheless to Him that this was a dream, a delusional state caused by his own loss of blood and impending death. He prayed that the sight of the dead man moving were hallucinations caused by his own injuries; by the pool of intestines and coagulating blood.

The dead American opened the remains of his mouth as though to speak, his bloated body quivering with unnatural movement. There was a sound like a moan that came from him, and then the body fell back to the ground, hitting hard, a thump followed by a wet tearing sound. The body exploded.

The rats were now covered with gore from the insides of the man Wilhelm had killed. They exited the dead man and scurried back to the holes in the filthy room from where they had first come.

And now what lay on the floor was a ravaged body and Wilhelm started to believe that the impossible events had never happened; that they were mere hallucinations because of his severe wounds. There had never been any rats, and the American had never moved.

Because if it had really happened...no, it was too horrible to imagine.

And suddenly he wondered where the soldiers were; the ones he had heard pull up in the tank and entered the building. He hadn't heard any footsteps coming up the stairs, but then again his concentration had been fully on the re-animated corpse, so for all he knew, they were merely steps away from him. He stopped and listened for any sounds that were close by. Where were the soldiers? He needed to be found or he would die.

Then outside, something exploded. The building shook from the force and felt as though the structure was unsure if it wanted to continue to stand. Wilhelm closed his eyes, feeling the building sway, then it began to settle. He breathed a sigh of relief.

Voices! He heard voices. They were close, nearly outside the room. He would be saved!

"That was too close for comfort," an unknown male said with a strange accent. Again he tried to shift his body, move enough to look outside the room and see if he could get a glimpse of who had spoken, but there was no such luck. He was trapped as though glued to the floor by his own drying blood.

"Let this world shake, brother. It's for the best. I like it better when it shakes with destruction. Better for all of us." A second voice; this one had a strange wet sound to it, as though it were the sea itself speaking; green rotted seaweed and deep dark waters.

"I smell something here. Little less than fresh, but I'm sure it will do." The first voice said and was followed by a creaking door directly behind Wilhelm's back.

Footsteps entered the room. "Here we go, brother. That one over there looks a little unpleasant."

"Looks as though Grentle and his little rat brothers were here ahead of us. Scavenger bastards."

Wilhelm saw two pairs of black boots step into view with grey pants that bloomed above and again he felt a wave of hope. They were wearing German-issued boots and the pants were those of the SS. He still wasn't too sure on the language these soldiers were speaking, but he pushed that down and away as he had those dark thoughts about his own death, holding on to the hope that he was about to be saved.

"What about this one?" said the owner if the first voice. "He looks a little messy. Is he still alive?"

Wilhelm saw one of the group approach and felt the force of a boot slide under his left shoulder. It pushed him onto his back. Wilhelm wanted to wince at the pain he was expecting, but there was little to none at all, only a cold numbness that seemed to tingle down his entire body. His back hit the floor with mild force and his view changed to the cracked, water-stained ceiling above him.

"Looks like we have a winner here," said the owner of the second, wet voice. "Shall we then?"

The two soldiers stepped into Wilhelm's line of sight and he felt his world shake with another explosion. This one was not from a bullet, grenade or mortar, but from the simple sight of what stood before him.

The two men were dressed in German uniforms, but these were no soldiers that Wilhelm had even seen before. They were things from a nightmare.

They had called each other "brother" and perhaps they were, perhaps some monstrous creature had given birth to them, these things that walked like men, and wore the clothing of a man, but were far from human in every way. They seemed more closely related to dogs, their hairless snouts surrounded by wiry black hair that seemed to have clumps of dirt and some sort of meat matted in it. They opened their mouths and smiled at Wilhelm, revealing a nest of barb-like teeth.

Wilhelm looked directly at the creatures' faces, and both looked like his father's old boat when it was infested with barnacles. Black and green growths that seemed to be constantly leaking some sort of yellowish fluid that obscured any real features. Wilhelm wanted to cry out and look away, but one of the monsters grabbed him by the face, its fingers more like the arms of an octopus than actual fingers, and began turning Wilhelm's head back and forth as though inspecting it.

"Help yourselves, brother. He is ours now," the owner of the wet voice spoke. "You just sit back and relax, German. You're fight is over, little man."

Wilhelm tried to shake his head; made an attempt to will himself to call out *no*, that he was not done, that he had plenty of fight in him, but there was no use. He was unable to do anything but look from the face of the creature holding him to the other that was lowering itself to his open gut.

He wanted to plead with them, beg them to save him, to take him to get help so that he could return to his family and pretend the war had never happened. He wanted to be the man that he always knew he should have been, the father and husband that he knew he was. Instead he saw one of the dog brothers bury its hairless muzzle into the open wound, its head moving in frenzied, unnatural movements.

THE SOLDIER

There was no pain there, just a cold numbness and pressure, but Wilhelm was still horrified and wanted to cry out to Heaven. The dog-faced soldier lifted its head up, jerking it as it fought with the muscle that was hanging between its unusual teeth, trying its best to pull the meat loose from Wilhelm's body.

Not able to look at the monster mauling the lower half of his body, Wilhelm looked up and into the other face that looked on above him. Liquid from bulbous growths was leaking out from the crustaceous lesions, and it seemed to boil out from his face and pour down. The thick pus touched his own face, smelling of dead fish rotting on a beach. Wilhelm didn't turn away; instead he looked into the formless face and tried to plead with his eyes, knowing that his voice was pretty much useless.

He thought of Hannah, of his young sons, of his house. He thought of sitting on his porch with his wife smiling together as they watched their kids chasing their pig Greta around, trying to ride her like a pony. He filled his mind with memories of meals, of laughter, of sex, of trips to Berlin and all the things that made him happy, hoping that this creature that loomed above him would see all this and feel some sort of empathy for him and release him, possibly even help him. He looked up, feeling tears that finally welled up in his eyes and he opened his mouth and spoke.

"Home," he whispered, almost inaudibly.

"What was that?" the creature spoke with his moldy voice, a strange grayish tongue poking out between his lips as he spoke. "Did you say home? You want to go home?"

Wilhelm did his best to nod his head, hardly able to believe that he had spoken even a single word and that this monster in a German soldier uniform was able to hear him and understand him.

"Don't be silly, little man. You can't go to your old home. This is your home now."

The dog-faced soldiers began to laugh at that, momentarily ignoring the feast of flesh before them, then one of the dripping-faced creatures lowered its lips to Wilhelm's now silent mouth.

Wilhelm closed his eyes, not wanting to see what came next, thinking only about all he had lost in life, all the regrets, and if the war crimes he had committed for the SS were responsible for his going to Hell.

About Shaun Meeks

Shaun Meeks currently lives in Toronto, Ontario with his partner, Mina and their dog, Lily. He works in the law enforcement field, which has helped inspire some of his darker stories. He has written numerous short stories, his latest, "All Things End Terminal," appeared in *Haunted Path* magazine. He is currently working on his latest novel, *Shutdown* as well as a collection of short fiction, *Dark Recesses*. You can visit his website at www.shaunmeeks.com for updates.

WHAT THE DARK DOES

by Graham Masterton

"Mummy—please don't close the door."

His mother smiled at him, her face half lit by the landing light, the other half in shadow, so that she looked as if she were wearing a Venetian carnival mask.

"All right. But I can't leave the light on all night. Honestly, David, there's nothing to be scared of. You remember what Granpa used to say—dark is only the same stuff that's behind your eyelids, only more of it."

David shivered. He remembered his Granpa lying in his open coffin at the undertakers, his face gray and half-collapsed. He had thought then that Granpa would never see anything else, ever again, but the darkness behind his eyelids, and that *was* scary.

Darkness is only benign if you know that you can open your eyes whenever you want to, and it will have fled away.

He snuggled down under his patchwork quilt and closed *his* eyes. Almost immediately he opened them again. The door was still open and the landing light was still shining. On the back of his chair he could see his black school blazer, ready for tomorrow, and his neatly-folded shorts.

In the corner of his room, lying sprawled on the floor, he could see Sticky Man, which was a puppet that his Granpa had made for him. Sticky Man was nearly two feet tall, made of double-jointed sticks painted gray. His spine and his head were a long wooden spoon, with staring eyes and a gappy grin painted onto it. Granpa used to tell him that during the war, when he and his fellow soldiers were pinned down for days on end under enemy fire at Monte Cassino, they had made Sticky Men to entertain themselves, as many as ten or twelve of them. Granpa said that the Sticky Men all came to life at night and did little dances for them. Sometimes, when the enemy shelling was particularly heavy, they used to send Sticky Men to carry messages to other units, because it was too dangerous to do it themselves.

David didn't like Sticky Man at all, and twice he had tried to throw him away. But his father had always rescued him—once from the dustbin and once from a shallow leaf-covered grave at the end of the garden—because his father thought that Granpa's story about Sticky Men was so amusing, and part of family history. "Granpa used to tell me that story when I was your age, but he never made *me* a Sticky Man. So you should count yourself privileged."

David had never actually seen Sticky Man come to life, but he was sure that he had heard him dancing in the darkness on the wooden floorboards at the edge of his bedside mat: *clickety, clackety, clickety, clackety*. When he had heard that sound, he had buried himself even deeper under the covers, until he was almost suffocating.

What really frightened David, though, was the brown dressing-gown hanging on the back of his bedroom door. Even during the day, it looked like a monk's habit, but when his father switched off the landing light at night, and David's bedroom was filled up with darkness, the dressing-gown changed, and began to fill out, as if somebody were rising up from the floor to slide inside it.

He was sure that when the house was very quiet, and there was no traffic in the street outside, he could hear the dressing-gown *breathing*, in and out, with just the faintest hint of harshness in its lungs. It was infinitely patient. It wasn't going to drop down from its hook immediately and go for him. It was going to wait until he was so paralyzed with terror that he was incapable of defending himself, or of crying out for help.

He had tried to hide the dressing-gown by stuffing it into his wardrobe, but that had been even more frightening. He could still hear it breathing but he had no longer been able to see it, so that he had never known when it might ease open the wardrobe door and then rush across the bedroom and clamber up onto his bed.

Next he had tried hanging the dressing-gown behind the curtains, but that had been worse still, because he was sure that he could hear the curtain-rings scraping back along the brass curtain-pole. Once and once only he had tried cramming it under the bed. When he had done that, however, he had been able to lie there for less than ten minutes, because he had been straining to hear the dressing-gown dragging itself out from underneath him, so that it could come rearing up beside him and drag his blankets off.

His school blazer was almost as frightening. When it was dark, it sat hunched on his chair, headless but malevolent, like the stories that early Spanish explorers had brought back from South America of natives with no heads but their faces on their chests. David had seen pictures of them in his schoolbooks, and even though he knew they were only stories, like Sticky Men were only stories, he also knew that things were very different in the dark.

In the dark, stories come to life, just like puppets and dressing-gowns.

«« —»»

He didn't hear the clock in the hallway downstairs chime eleven. He was asleep by then. His father came into his room and straightened his bedcover and affectionately scruffed up his hair. "Sleep well, trouble." He left his door open a little, but he switched off the landing light, so that his room was plunged into darkness.

Another hour went by. The clock chimed twelve, very slowly, as if it needed winding. David slept and dreamed that he was walking through a wood, and that something white was following him, keeping pace with him, but darting behind the trees whenever he turned around to see what it was.

He stopped, and waited for the white thing to come out into the open, but it remained hidden, even though he knew it was still there. He breathed deeply, and stirred, and said out loud, "*Who are you?*"

Another hour passed, and then, without warning, his dressing-gown dropped off the back of his bedroom door.

He didn't hear it. He had stopped dreaming that he was walking through the wood, and now he was deeply unconscious. His door was already ajar, but now it opened a little more, and a hunched brown shape dragged its way out of his bedroom.

A few moments later, there was a soft click, as the door to his parents' bedroom was opened.

Five minutes passed. Ten. David was rising slowly out of his very deep sleep, as if he were gradually floating to the surface of a lake. He was almost awake when something suddenly jumped on top of him, something that clattered.

He screamed and sprang upright, both arms flailing. The clattery thing fell to the floor. Moaning with fear, he fumbled around in the darkness until he found his bedside lamp, and switched it on.

Lying on the rug next to his bed was Sticky Man, staring up at him with those round, unblinking eyes.

Trembling, David pushed back the covers and crawled down to the end of the bed so that he wouldn't have to step onto the rug next to Sticky Man. What if it sprang at him again, and clung to his ankle?

As he reached the end of the bed, and was about to climb off it, he saw that his dressing-gown had gone. The hook on the back of his bedroom door had nothing hanging on it except for his red-and-white football scarf.

His moaning became a soft, subdued mewling in the back of his throat. He was so frightened that he squirted a little warm pee into his pajama trousers. He looked over the end of the bed but his dressing-gown wasn't lying in a heap on the floor as he would have expected.

Perhaps Mummy had at last understood that it scared him, hanging up on the back of the door like that, and she had taken it down when he was asleep. Perhaps she had taken it away to wash it. He had spilled a spoonful of tomato soup on it yesterday evening, when he was sitting on the sofa watching television—not that he had told her.

He didn't know what to do. He knelt on the end of the bed, biting at his thumbnail, not mewling now but breathing very quickly, as if he had been running. He turned around and looked down at Sticky Man but Sticky Man hadn't moved—he was still lying on his back on the rug, his arms and legs all splayed out, glaring balefully at nothing at all.

Whatever David did, he would have to change his wet pajama trousers, and that would mean going to the airing-cupboard on the landing. Mummy always liked to keep his clean pajamas warm.

Very cautiously, he climbed off the bed and went across to his bedroom door. He looked around it. The landing was in darkness, although the faintest of green lights was coming up the stairs from the hallway, from the illuminated timer on the burglar alarm, and that was enough for David to see that his parents' bedroom door was open, too.

He frowned. His parents *never* left their door open, not at night. He hesitated for a few long moments, but then he hurried as quietly as he could along the landing until he reached his parents' bedroom, and peered inside. It was completely dark in there, although he could just make out the luminous spots on the dial of his father's bedside alarm clock.

He listened. Very far away, he could hear a train squealing as it made its way to the nearest station, to be ready for the morning's commuters. But when that sound had faded away, he could hear nothing at all. He couldn't even hear his parents breathing, even though his father usually snored.

"Mummy?" he called, as quietly as he could.

No answer. He waited in the doorway, with his wet pants beginning to feel chilly.

"*Mummy?*" A little louder this time.

Still no answer.

He crept into his parents' bedroom, feeling his way round the end of the bed to his mother's side. He reached out and felt her bare arm lying on top of the quilted bedcover. He took hold of her hand and shook it and said, hoarsely, "Mummy, wake up! I've had an accident!"

But still she didn't answer. David groped for the dangly cord that switched on her bedside reading light and tugged it.

"*Mummy! Daddy!*"

Both of them were lying on their backs, staring up at the ceiling with eyes so bloodshot that it looked as if somebody had taken out their eyeballs and replaced them with crimson grapes. Not only that, both of them had black moustaches of congealing blood on their upper lips, and their mouths were dragged grotesquely downward. Two dead clowns.

David stumbled backward. He heard somebody let out a piercing, high-pitched scream, which frightened him even more. He didn't realize that it was him.

He scrabbled his way back around the end of the bed, and as he did so he caught his foot and almost tripped over. His brown dressing-gown was lying tangled on the floor, with its cord coiled on top of it.

He didn't scream again, but marched stiffly downstairs like a clockwork soldier, his arms and legs rigid with shock. He picked up the phone and dialled 911.

"Emergency, which service please?"

"Ambulance," he said, his lower lip juddering. "No, no, I don't need an ambulance. I don't know what I need. They're dead."

«《—》》

The red-haired lady detective brought him the mug of milky tea that he had asked for, with two sugars. She sat down at the table next to him and gave him a smile. She was young and quite pretty, with a scattering of freckles across the bridge of her nose.

"You didn't hear anything, then?" she asked him.

"No," David whispered.

"We're finding it very difficult to work out what happened," she said. "There was no sign that anybody broke into your house. The burglar alarm was on. And yet somebody attacked your daddy and mummy, and whoever it was, they were very strong."

"It wasn't me," said David. He was wearing the purple hooded top that his uncle and aunt had given him for his last birthday, and he looked very pale.

"Of course it wasn't you," said the detective. "We just need to know if you saw anything or heard anything. Anything at all."

David looked down into his tea. He felt like bursting into tears but he swallowed and swallowed and tried very hard not to. He was too young to know that there was no shame in crying.

"I didn't hear anything," he said. "I don't know who did it. I just want them to be alive again."

The detective reached across the table and squeezed his hand. She couldn't think of anything to say to him except, "I know you do, David. I know."

«« — »»

Rufus said, "Did they ever find out how your parents died?"

David shook his head. "The coroner returned a verdict of unlawful killing by person or persons unknown. That's all he could do."

"You must *wonder*, though, mate. You know—who could have done it, and why. And *how*, for Christ's sake!"

David took a swig from his bottle of Corona. The Woolpack was crowded, even for a Friday evening, and they were lucky to have found somewhere to sit, in the corner. An enormously fat man sitting next to them was laughing so loudly that they could hardly hear themselves speak.

Rufus and David had been friends ever since David had started work at Amberlight, selling IT equipment. He had been there seven months now, and last month he had been voted top salesman in his team. Rufus was easy-going and funny, with a shaven head to pre-empt the onset of pattern baldness and a sharp line in gray three-piece suits.

David heard himself saying, "Actually…I *do* know who did it."

"Really?" said Rufus. "You really *do* know? Like—have you known all along, right from when it happened? Or did you find out later? Hang on, mate—why didn't you tell the police? Why don't you tell them now? It's never too late!"

David thought, *Shit, now I wish I hadn't said anything. Why did I say anything? I've kept this to myself for seventeen years, why did I have to come out with it now? It's going to sound just as insane now as it would have back then.*

"I didn't tell the police because they would never have believed me. Just like you won't believe me, either."

"Well, you could try me. I'm famous for my gullibility. Do you want another beer?"

"Yes, thanks."

Rufus went to the bar and came back with two more bottles. "Right, then," he said, smacking his hands together. "Who's the guilty party?"

"My dressing-gown."

Rufus had his bottle of beer poised in front of his mouth, his lips in an O shape ready to drink, but now he slowly put the bottle down.

"Did I hear that right? Your dressing-gown?"

Trying to sound as matter-of-fact as possible, David said, "My dressing-gown. I had a brown dressing-gown that used to hang on the back of my bedroom door and it looked like a monk. I always used to think that when it was dark it might come alive. Well, one night it did, and it went into my parents' bedroom and it strangled them. In fact it garrotted them, according to the police report. It strangled them so hard it almost took off their heads."

"Your dressing-gown," Rufus repeated.

"That's right. Sounds bonkers, doesn't it? But there is absolutely no other explanation. Unlawful killing by night attire. And there was something else, too. I had a puppet that my grandfather made for me, like it was all made out of gray sticks, with a wooden spoon for a head. Sticky Man, I used to call it. When my dressing-gown went to murder my parents, Sticky Man jumped on me and I think he was trying to warn me what was going to happen."

48

Rufus bent his head forward until his forehead was pressed against the table. He stayed like that for almost ten seconds. Then he sat up straight again and said, "Your puppet warned you that your dressing-gown was going to kill your mum and dad."

"There—I told you that you wouldn't believe me. Thanks for the beer, anyway."

"You know who you need to talk to, don't you?" asked Rufus.

"A shrink, I suppose you're going to say."

"Unh-hunh. You need to talk to Alice in accounts."

"Alice? That freaky-looking woman with the white hair and all of those bracelets?"

"That's the one. Actually she's a very interesting lady. I had a long chat with her once at one of the firm's bonding weekends. It was down somewhere near Hailsham, I think. Anyway, Alice is great believer in crustaceous automation, I think she called it."

"What? Crustaceous? That's like crabs and lobsters, isn't it?"

"Well, she said something that sounded like that, anyway. What it means is, things coming to life when it gets dark. She really, really believes in it. Like your dressing-gown, I suppose. One of the things she told me about was this armchair that came to life when anybody fell asleep in it, and it squeezed them so hard that it crushed their ribcage. It took forever before somebody worked out what was killing all these people."

"So what was killing them?"

"What she said was, it's the dark that does it. The actual darkness. It changes things."

David looked at Rufus narrowly. "You're not taking the piss, are you?"

"Why would I?"

"Well, I know you. Always playing tricks on people. I don't want to go up to this Alice and tell her about my dressing-gown if she's going to think that I'm some kind of loony."

"No, mate," said Rufus. "Cross my heart. I promise you. I'm not saying that *she's* not loony, but I don't think you're any loonier than she is, so I doubt if she'll notice."

《《—》》

They met in their lunch break at their local Pizza Hut, which was almost empty except for two plump teenage mothers and their

49

screaming children. David ordered a pepperoni pizza and a beer while Alice stayed with a green salad and a cup of black tea.

When he started talking to her, David realized that Alice was much less freaky than he had imagined. She had a short, severe, silvery-white bob, and he had assumed that she was middle-aged, but now he saw that her hair was bleached and highlighted and she couldn't have been older than thirty-one or thirty-two. She had a sharp, feline face, with green eyes to match, and she wore a tight black T-shirt and at least half-a-dozen elaborate silver bangles on each wrist.

"So, what did Rufus say when you told him?" she asked, lifting up her cup of tea with both hands and blowing on it.

"He was all right about it, actually, when you consider that he could have laughed his head off. Most of the rest of the team would have done."

"Rufus has his own story," said Alice. David raised an eyebrow, expecting her to tell him what it was, but she was obviously not going to be drawn any further.

"You know the word 'shoddy'?" she said.

"Of course."

"Most people think it means something that's been badly made. You know, something inferior. But it can also mean a woollen yarn made out of used clothes. They rip up old coats and sweaters to shreds and then they re-spin them, with just a bit of new wool included. Most new clothes are made out of that."

David said, "I didn't know that, no."

"In Victorian times, these guys used to go around the streets ringing a bell and collecting used clothes. They called them 'shoddy-men.' These days it's mainly Lithuanians who pinch all of those bags of clothes that people leave out for charities. They ship them all back to Lithuania, turn them into new clothes and then sell them back to us."

"I'm not too sure what you're getting at."

Alice sipped her tea, and then she said, "Sometimes, those second-hand clothes have belonged to some very violent people. Murderers, even. And clothes take on their owners' personalities. You know what it's like when you try on another man's jacket. It makes you feel as if you're *him*."

"So what are you trying to tell me? My dressing-gown might have had wool in it that once belonged in some murderer's clothes?"

Alice nodded. "Exactly."

"But it's not like *I* put it on and killed my parents. The dressing-gown came alive. The dressing-gown did it on its own!"

David suddenly realized that he was talking too loudly, and that the two teenage mothers were staring at him.

He lowered his voice and said, "How did it come alive on its own? I mean, how is that possible?"

Alice said, "The scientific name for it is 'crepuscular animation.' It means inanimate objects that come alive when it begins to get dark. Most people don't understand that darkness isn't just the absence of light. Darkness is an element in itself, and darkness goes looking for more darkness to feed itself."

She continued, "That night, when your light was switched off, the darkness in your room found whatever darkness that was hidden in your dressing-gown, and filled it up with more of its own dark energy, and that brought it to life."

"I'm sorry, Alice. I'm finding this really hard to follow."

Alice laid her cool, long-fingered hand on top of his. Her green eyes were unblinking. "What else could have happened, David? You said yourself that nobody broke into the house, and that you didn't do it. You *couldn't* have done it, you simply weren't strong enough. And your puppet man came alive, too, didn't he? How do you think that happened?"

David shrugged. "I haven't a clue. And why should my dressing-gown have come to life *then*, on that particular night? It was hanging there for *months* before that. My mother bought it for me in October, so that I could wear it on fireworks night."

"Well, I don't know the answer to that. But it could have been some anniversary. Perhaps it was a year to the day that somebody was murdered, by whoever wore the wool that was woven into your dressing-gown. There's no way of telling for certain."

David sat for a long time saying nothing. Alice continued to fork up her salad and sip her tea but he didn't touch his pizza.

"How do you know all this?" he asked her. "All about this—what did you call it—screspusular stuff?"

"Crepuscular animation. 'Crepuscular' only means 'twilight.' My great-grandmother told me. Something happened to one of her sons, during the war. There was a lot of darkness during the blackouts. So much darkness everywhere. She said there used to be a statue in their local park, a weeping woman, on a First World War memorial.

Apparently her son and one his friends took a shortcut through the park at night, and the statue came to life and came after them. Her son's head was crushed against the metal railings and his neck was broken.

"Of course nobody believed the other little boy, but my great-grandmother did, because she knew him and she knew that he always told the truth. She made a study of inanimate objects coming to life when it begins to get dark, and she wrote it all down in an exercise book and that exercise book got passed down to me. Nobody else in the family wanted it. They thought it was all cuckoo."

To emphasize the point, she twirled her index finger around at the side of her head.

"I don't know what to think," David told her.

"Just beware of the darkness," said Alice. "Treat it with respect. That's all I can say. And if you see a dressing-gown that looks as if might come alive, then believe me, it probably will."

«« — »»

He returned home late that night. The bulb had gone in the hallway and he had to grope his way to the living-room.

The living-room was dimly lit from the nearby main road. He lived on the ground floor of what had once been a large family house, but which was now divided into eight different flats. His was one of the smallest, but he was very fastidious, and he always kept it tidy. Up until the end of last year, he had shared a large flat with two colleagues from work, and that had been horrendous, with dirty plates stacked in the kitchen sink and the coffee table crowded with overflowing ashtrays and empty Stella cans. Worst of all had been the clothes that were heaped on the floor, or draped over the backs of chairs, or hanging from hooks on the back of every door.

He switched on the two side lamps and the television, although he pressed the mute button. On the left-hand wall stood a bookcase, with all of his books arranged in alphabetical order, according to author. In front of them stood two silver shields for playing squash and several framed photographs of his father and mother, smiling. And then, of course, there was Sticky Man, perched on the edge of the shelf, staring at him with those circular, slightly mad eyes.

When Sticky Man had jumped on David the night that his parents had been murdered, he had terrified him, but David had come to believe that he had been trying to warn him, and that was why he had kept him all these years. Hadn't Sticky Men always been helpers and facilitators—entertaining the troops in Italy during the war, and carrying messages under shellfire? When David was little, Sticky Man may have frightened him by coming alive during the night, but he had only been dancing, after all.

"Hey, Sticks," he said, but Sticky Man continued to stare at him and said nothing.

《《——》》

Although he had eaten only one slice of his pizza at lunchtime, David didn't feel particularly hungry, so he opened a can of Heinz vegetable soup, heated it up in the microwave and ate it in front of the television, watching *Newsnight.*

Afterward he showered and brushed his teeth and climbed into bed. He tried to read *The Girl With The Dragon Tattoo* for a while, but he couldn't stop thinking about Alice, and what she had said about inanimate objects coming to life when darkness fell. He still couldn't remember exactly what it was called. Was it Crispucular automation?

Just beware of the darkness. Treat it with respect. That's all I can say. And if you see a dressing-gown that looks as if might come alive, then believe me, it probably will.

After his parents' murder David had been brought up by his Aunt Joanie and his Uncle Ted. They had bought him a new dressing-gown, a tartan one, but on the day that he had left home he had thrown it in the dustbin and he had never bought himself another one since. He never hung any clothes from the hook on his bedroom door, not even a scarf. Even before he had talked to Alice, he had always kept his clothes shut up in closets and wardrobes, out of sight. No jackets were hunched over the back of his chair. No shirts hung drip-drying in the bathroom, like ghosts.

He switched off the light, and closed his eyes. He felt very tired for some reason. Alice had disturbed him quite a lot, even though he found it very hard to believe everything that she had told him. The statue of the weeping woman he found quite unsettling. And he wondered what Ray's story was? Ray was so pragmatic, and so straightforward. What on earth had appeared out of the dark to frighten Ray?

He slept deeply for over an hour, but then he abruptly woke. He was sure that he had heard a clicking noise. His bedroom was unusually dark, and when he lifted his head from the pillow he realized that the digital clock beside his bed was no longer glowing. There were no streetlights shining outside, either. There must have been a power-cut, which might explain the clicking noise that had woke him up: the sound of the central-heating pipes contracting as they cooled down.

As he laid his head back down on the pillow, he heard more clicking. More like clattering this time. He strained his ears and listened. There was a lengthy silence, and then a quick, sharp rattling sound. He thought he heard a door opening.

He sat up. Something was outside his bedroom, in the hallway. Something that made a soft, dragging noise. It sounded as if it was coming closer and closer, and then it bumped into his bedroom door. Not loudly, but enough to give him the impression that it was big and bulky.

His heart was hammering against his ribcage. "Who's there?" he called out. "Is anybody out there?"

There was no answer. Nearly half a minute went by. Then suddenly there was another clatter, and he heard his door-handle pulled down. His door swung open with the faintest whisper, almost like a sigh of satisfaction.

He waited, listening, his fingers gripping the bedcovers. What had somebody once said about bedcovers? Why do we pull them up to protect ourselves when we're scared? Do we think a murderer with a ten-inch knife is going to be deterred by a quilt?

"Who's there?" he called out again, sounding hoarse to his own ears.

No answer.

"For God's sake, who's there?"

It was then that the power came back on again, and his digital bedside clock started flashing green, and the central heating began to tick into life again, and he saw what it was that was standing in his bedroom doorway.

It was his navy-blue duffel coat, with its hood up. It looked like a dead Antarctic explorer, somebody whose body had been found in the snow a hundred years after they had died.

Beside it, tilting this way and that, as if it couldn't get its balance right, was Sticky Man. Sticky Man must have opened the door to the closet in the hallway, so that the duffel coat could shuffle out, and Sticky Man had opened his bedroom door, too. There was nobody else in the flat, so who else could it have been?

It was then that he realized that on the night his parents had been killed Sticky Man hadn't been trying to warn him. Sticky Man had been probably trying to wake him up, so that he too would go into parents' bedroom, to be garrotted along with them.

"*You traitor, Sticks*," he whispered, but of course Sticky Man wasn't a traitor, because Sticky Man was a creature of the dark, just as much as his dressing-gown and his duffel-coat. It wasn't *them*, in themselves. They were only inanimate objects.

It was the dark.

David's duffel coat rushed across his bedroom floor toward him. He lunged sideways across to the other side of the bed, trying to reach his phone.

"Emergency, which service please?"

"—*dark*—!"

Then a struggling sound, and a thin, reedy gasp, followed by a long continuous tone.

It was what the dark does.

About Graham Masterton

Graham Masterton has published over one hundred novels, including thrillers, horror novels, disaster epics, and sweeping historical romances.

He was editor of the British edition of Penthouse magazine before writing his debut horror novel *The Manitou* in 1975, which was subsequently filmed with Tony Curtis, Susan Strasberg, Burgess Meredith and Stella Stevens.

After the initial success of *The Manitou*, Graham continued to write horror novels and supernatural thrillers, for which he has won international acclaim, especially in Poland, France, Germany, Greece and Australia.

His historical romances *Rich* (Simon & Schuster) and *Maiden Voyage* (St Martins) both featured in The New York Times Bestseller List. He has twice been awarded a Special Edgar by Mystery Writers of America (for *Charnel House*, and more recently *Trauma*, which was also named by Publishers Weekly as one of the hundred best novels of the year).

He has won numerous other awards, including two Silver Medals from the West Coast Review of Books, a tombstone award from the Horror Writers Network, another gravestone from the International Horror Writers Guild, and was the first non-French winner of the prestigious Prix Julia Verlanger for bestselling horror novel. *The Chosen Child* (set in Poland) was nominated best horror novel of the year by the British Fantasy Society.

Several of Graham's short stories have been adapted for TV, including three for Tony Scott's *Hunger* series. Jason Scott Lee starred in the Stoker-nominated *Secret Shih-Tan.*

Apart from continuing with some of most popular horror series, Graham is now writing novels that have some suggestion of a supernatural element in them, but are intended to reach a wider market than genre horror.

This story, "What the Dark Does," was written by Graham exclusively for this book, *A Feast of Frights from The Horror Zine.*

You can visit Graham Masterton at www.grahammasterton.co.uk

PROPER PAYMENTS

by Philip Roberts

No other complex in the city could match either the price or squalor of Roy's apartments. The people who streamed through his door had arms riddled with both tattoos and crusted over scars. They were gamblers, prostitutes, thieves, or the poor souls who had their lives ripped out from under them.

Roy assumed the man stepping through the door with a three-year-old boy by his side fit the last category. The man wrinkled his nose at a stink he clearly wasn't accustomed to, forehead slick from lack of air conditioning and nervous tension. Though Roy himself was used to poverty, he still recognized the cost of the rumpled suit the man wore as well as the remains of a manicure.

"I need a one-bedroom apartment," the man said.

"What's your name?" Roy asked.

"Quinn Hadley," he said, the answer a little too jittery; nervously rehearsed. *Fine then,* Roy thought, and slid the form over for Quinn to fill out. As he did, Roy hefted his bulk from the seat and searched through his files for the rest of the forms, eyeing the boy as he did. The child stared curiously around the room, aware, even at such a young age, of how beneath him this room was. Roy didn't like the way the eyes lingered on him, on his balding head, bulging gut, and stained clothing.

Hunched low, he pretended he didn't hear the boy lean in close to his father, whisper, "That man smells," only to be hushed immediately.

"Here are the rest of them," Roy said and set the forms down. "Need down payment and first month's rent upfront. When are you moving in?"

"Tonight, if possible," Quinn said.

"Sure."

Roy watched the elegant print Quinn put down on the forms, and tried to figure out just what Mr. Hadley was running from.

«««—»»»

Empty wrappers, crushed beer cans, and yellowed tissues surrounded the glowing computer Roy leaned close to. Quinn Hadley had died two years prior from a heart attack at the age of seventy-two. The wealthy man had been a CEO of a company Roy had never heard of, but he didn't care about the dead Mr. Hadley. He stared instead at the photos of Hadley standing next to a slightly younger image of the man who had passed through Roy's door just four hours earlier.

"Not much for fake names, eh?" he laughed to himself. Charles Ortner had worked for Quinn, according to the information Roy could find, not that there was very much. By most standards Charles appeared to be quite a wealthy man, but that didn't mean he was a famous man, and the only information Roy could find about him came from a business article detailing Charles's rise to CEO after Quinn died.

He left his computer and his cluttered apartment, trudging through the dark parking lot towards the C building where Charles had taken up residence. Inside the laundry room he locked the door and pulled open a hidden panel in the wall leading to a space between the apartments.

Climbing up the ladder hadn't been easy in his youth, and certainly wasn't pleasant after ten years and fifty additional pounds, but he made his way as silently as he could to the platform next to number C6. He pulled loose a panel and stared into the dimly lit apartment, just barely able to see through the wallpaper. He'd originally used this little secret to spy on the prettier prostitutes and their clients, until age had made the effort too much to bother with.

Charles's son slept calmly in a sleeping bag while Charles himself sat hunched before his laptop on the only table in the room.

Roy didn't bother looking at the man; his attention was drawn to the walls which were covered with chalk. Charles had done up the whole room, symbols everywhere, and most of them looked like Egyptian hieroglyphs to Roy, though he didn't think they literally were.

For over an hour the man worked before finally shutting the computer down and stretching out across the floor. Roy waited until the man slept to put the panel back and climb down. "Some kind of crazy," he whispered on his way back to his apartment.

《《——》》

Roy didn't ignore the idea that the man could be wealthy, no matter how crazy he appeared to be. Charles rarely left his apartment, and Roy never saw the boy leave. For over a week Roy spent the majority of his time within the walls watching the boy pace and complain while Charles remained on his computer, sometimes touching up the markings on the walls, always nervous.

Everything about the man seemed worn out and defeated; his efforts like a dying man clinging to a life that was already over, but Roy couldn't pull himself away. His own research on the company for which Charles was supposedly still a CEO implied nothing but wealth, even if there was no actual sign of it.

He had to admit as well that an odd chill that ran through him each time he got close to the apartment and pulled loose the panel, his hair prickling and his nerves on edge. He wrote it off as nothing but the weird glyphs, though he didn't know why they would affect him so severely.

But finally the moment came, and Roy overhead the conversation he had been waiting for.

"I know I haven't been around," Charles said as he paced the room with his cell phone; his son perched along the wall, occupied with a game. "I've been doing as much as I can from here, but I need you to do something for me. I want a million freed up and put in my account by tomorrow. I'm going to…I won't be here for much longer. Just a few more days and I should be finished with this. Can you do that for me? Yeah, okay, good. No, I'll talk to you later. Call me when you're done."

Roy climbed slowly down the ladder with a smile on his face.

《《——》》

Bennett McRee had led a long and assorted life, or so Roy had been told, until the man's various bad habits had placed him in Roy's territory. Though Bennett's gut had grown considerably in the three years since Roy first rented the man a room, he still had plenty of muscle from his days as a boxer.

Six months after the man had moved in, and two months after he had missed his first rent check, Roy had come to him with an offer:

59

Bennett helps Roy evict the undesirables and Roy lets Bennett stay free of charge.

The six-foot-two Bennett opened on the second knock and eyed Roy with a look of almost joy. "Got another?" Bennett asked, always pleased, Roy realized, to prove he could still take a guy down.

"Not quite. Can I come in?"

Roy stepped into Bennett's much cleaner apartment, mainly cluttered with weights and other remnants of the man's past. "I've got a proposal I thought you might be interested in. Good money, but this isn't legal, so if you say no, I'll be on my way."

But Roy knew Bennett, and knew the man would lean back and say, "Tell me about it."

"Got a guy I rented a room to a few weeks back. Rich one: CEO. Came here with his boy, and I just know he's running from someone. Probably doing some deals on the side and one went belly up, who knows? What I do know is he just freed up a million bucks for quick access but he won't be here for much longer."

"So what are you thinking?"

"Guy came here to hide, that much is certain, and he won't want others knowing where he is."

"Blackmail him then?"

"We can't blackmail him or he'll bolt. I have a better idea. He doesn't leave often, but when he does, I want you to get in that apartment and take his kid."

"Kidnapping?"

"Sure. Just hide the kid in the shed in the back of the lot in the trees. Haven't used the shed in years, no one would know about it, and he isn't going to go to the cops because then it might get out and alert people about him."

"We getting the full million?"

"Nah, too much. Leave a note asking for fifty thousand or so; it'll be some nice change for us but nothing to him. He'll pay it fast to get things over with. So, you willing to do this?"

"What are the odds of this coming back around to bite us in the ass?"

"Trust me on this. I don't plan on getting caught."

"Okay then, I'm in."

《《—》》

60

He gave it two days just to make sure the money had gone through and funds were available before he called Bennett and told him to head over. A moment arrived when Charles left, so Roy watched Bennett slip into the apartment and walk out with the unconscious boy in his arms.

Roy didn't mind doing it during the day when prying eyes might see Bennett with the kid. People in his part of the city knew how to look, and then look the other way.

He sat out on his second floor balcony with a cold beer, swatting away the mosquitoes, and watching as Charles's car pulled to a stop at around four in the afternoon. The man got out with two grocery bags in his arms, trudged up his stairs, fumbled with the bags to get his key out, and walked into his apartment. Roy leaned forward with his arms on the guardrails, smiling, waiting for it, and sure enough Charles rushed from the apartment, heading right where Roy knew he would head.

He saw Roy on the balcony before he reached the office door, and Roy had never seen a face so pale before. "I need to talk to you," he shouted up.

"Oh sure, be right down," Roy said.

He took his time moving down the stairs into the office, finishing off his beer as he went. The second he unlocked the office door Charles came bursting in. "My son is gone," he said.

Roy feigned concerned. "Shit, really? Door busted?"

"No, but it wouldn't need to unlock a..." he began, then faltered. "No, the door wasn't broken."

"Sorry to say, but the locks around here are piss poor. Don't have the funds to upgrade them. If you want I can call the cops."

"That's not...I need to find him as soon as possible. I was only gone an hour. It must've...what if it was someone in the complex, or someone nearby? Did you see anything?"

Roy held up his hands, tried to act as apologetic as he could. "Look, I make my money by staying out of people's business, okay? I'll have to tell you the same thing I tell all the others coming to me: go to the cops. I can't help you."

"I'll pay you," Charles said.

Roy hid his smile. "I appreciate it, but like I said—"

"I'm dead serious. Name the price and it's yours, but we need to do something now."

"Look, the second I get involved with people's business, when my tenants see that, I risk them turning against me here."

"A hundred thousand." Charles's eyes narrowed, anger blotting away the white from his face. "Please," he said.

Roy sighed, ran his fingers through the remains of his hair, mentally throwing Bennett beneath the wheels. "Okay, deal. Look, I didn't see your boy, but I did see a tenant of mine hanging around the back of the complex about a half hour ago near a shed I never use anymore. Don't know any reason why he'd be back there, and the guy has a bad history with kids. Lot of people here have problems with this guy."

"We need to get there right away."

Charles was already out the door, hurrying down the parking lot before Roy called out. "We'll take my car; it'll be faster."

Roy got in and started the engine. Charles jumped in the car a second later, urging him to hurry, and the fear in the man's eyes—the near hysteria—triggered a deep concern in Roy, but he ignored it. The man just wasn't used to life's horrors.

They sped through the complex and came to a screeching halt near the back lot, Charles already out of the car, hurrying across the grass towards the shack while Roy hurried as fast as he could behind him.

Before they reached the structure, Roy heard the child shrieking in fear and pain and wondered how well he had really known Bennett. "He wouldn't," Roy whispered and pulled out the loaded gun he'd brought only for show, intended to scare Bennett and impress Charles with a shot at the ceiling if it were needed.

The feeling washed over Roy, ten times as intense as whatever he had felt when standing beside the apartment wall. The air thick with it. Charles pulled open the door and hurried through, his scream driving Roy faster, until he ran into the shed and froze right inside the door, reality nowhere to be found in that small room.

Along the wall he saw Bennett's remains, the muscular chest torn open, head ripped to the side and hanging limply against his right shoulder, dead eyes bulging out and his mouth agape. The boy was held to a table in the center of the room by what looked like intestines, his face covered in blood, voice growing hoarse from his shrill cries.

The creature looming above him turned towards the two intruders. Its head was like a mound of flesh at the top of the chest, no eyes visible, and only a thin slit of skin that might've been a mouth. The thick arms that stretched from its sides looked more like solid bone than skin, and it had four almost human looking legs sprouted out at the base of the torso. Charles charged at it, his scream incoherent, an object Roy couldn't place in his outstretched hands.

The creature swung out a long arm lined with sharp protrusions that tore into Charles's chest and sent him crashing into the wall. Roy brought up his gun with a blank face and fired. The bullets tore wet holes through the thing's chest. Roy emptied an entire clip into it, and yet it lunged across the room toward him.

What looked like fleshy fingers reached out of holes at the end of the boney arms to grab hold of Roy and slam him into the wall. He pulled out his pocket knife and jabbed it upward into the thing's mid-section. As soon as the grip loosened Roy stabbed again, carved the blade through what looked to be the face, and the creature lurched away from him, leaving a trail of sludge in its wake.

The flesh holding the boy down sucked back into the creature's body as it collapsed to the floor and melted into the wood, leaving nothing but thick black liquid. Roy stared dumbly at the oozing mass while Charles hurried to his boy and grabbed him.

"We need to get out of here," Charles said.

Roy complied, eyeing Bennett's remains as he allowed himself to be led out the door and back into the real world.

《《—》》

"You saved him," Charles said, all three of them in his glyph-covered apartment. His son slept against the far wall. Charles had washed the blood clean to find no cuts on the boy. All of the blood had come from Bennett.

Charles broke the silence. "If you hadn't helped me find him in time they would've taken him. A hundred thousand isn't enough. You can have as much money as you want for what you did."

"What happened?" Roy asked from his seat on the floor along the wall, hands limp in his lap, blood still drying on his arms from where the creature had torn into him.

"A man I once respected sold me out, or my son, that is. When he died they came to collect, but even they had rules, I was told. My friend had partially broken them by offering my son as his own. They said they'd give me a year, and if I could stop them from getting my son in that time, he'd be free. They called it an amusing game. These symbols," he said, gestured towards the walls, "can keep them out for a little while, but eventually they lose their power, and can never protect that location again. I've spent the past year running everywhere I could, until I was finally led here to wait out the final few weeks. By tomorrow it'll be over and my son will be free."

"Glad...I could help," Roy said with a strained smile. "So, you said something about money," he added, feeling his sense of reality returning, his old habits shoving aside the insanity.

"Any amount, but I have to warn you, I don't think you understand what you've done. These...things I was dealing with won't be pleased that they didn't win. They can't touch me or my son anymore, that was the deal, but there was nothing said about *you*."

"What exactly can they do to me?"

"I'm not sure," Charles said, but his eyes told another story, and Roy had a feeling they could do plenty of awful things. He pulled himself up and tried to tell himself he didn't believe any of it, no matter what he'd seen.

"I need to get back," Roy said. "You know, think things through and all."

Charles rose along with Roy, opened the door for him. "I'll talk to you tomorrow and give you all the material I have. And I just want to thank you again for all the help you gave me." He reached out his hand for a shake. Roy took it without any enthusiasm. *This is what you get for doing people favors,* he thought to himself as the door closed behind him.

The sun sank into the horizon. Roy stepped into his dim apartment and looked around at the mess, at the darker hallway leading back into his bedroom. He squinted into the darkness; saw a tunnel stretching out into oblivion and the image of a tall, gangly form walking down it towards him, its hands rubbing along the walls, its breath sending a wave of hot air towards Roy.

A flip of a light switch showed only his hallway towards the bedroom. "You didn't just see that," he told himself, but he didn't honestly believe it.

About Philip Roberts

Philip lives in Nashua, New Hampshire and holds a degree in Creative Writing with a minor in Film from the University of Kansas. As a beginner in the publishing world, he's a member of both the Horror Writer's Association and the New England Horror Writer's Association, and has had numerous short stories published in a variety of publications, such as the *Beneath the Surface* anthology, *Midnight Echo*, and *The Absent Willow Review*. More information on his works can be found at www.philipmroberts.com.

INCIDENT ON AND OFF A MOUNTAIN ROAD

by Joe R. Lansdale

When Ellen came to the moonlit mountain curve, her thoughts, which had been adrift with her problems, grounded, and she was suddenly aware that she was driving much too fast. The sign said curve: 30 mph, and she was doing fifty.

She knew too that slamming on the brakes was the wrong move, so she optioned to keep her speed and fight the curve and make it, and she thought she could.

The moonlight was strong, so visibility was high, and she knew her Chevy was in good shape, easy to handle, and she was a good driver.

But as she negotiated the curve a blue Buick seemed to grow out of the ground in front of her. It was parked on the shoulder of the road, at the peak of the curve, its nose sticking out a foot too far, its rear end against the moon-wet, silver railing that separated the curve from a mountainous plunge.

Had she been going an appropriate speed, missing the Buick wouldn't have been a problem, but at her speed she was swinging too far right, directly in line with it, and was forced, after all, to use her brakes. When she did, the back wheels slid and the brakes groaned and the front of the Chevy hit the Buick, and there was a sound like an explosion and then for a dizzy instant she felt as if she were in the tumblers of a dryer.

Through the windshield came: Moonlight. Blackness. Moonlight.

One high bounce and a tight roll, and the Chevy came to rest upright with the engine dead, the right side flush against the railing. Another inch of jump or greater impact against the rail, and the Chevy would have gone over.

Ellen felt a sharp pain in her leg and reached down to discover that during the tumble she had banged it against something, probably the gear shift, and had ripped her stocking and her flesh. Blood was trickling into her shoe. Probing her leg cautiously with the tips of her fingers, she determined the wound wasn't bad and that all other body parts were operative.

She unfastened her seat belt, and as a matter of habit, located her purse and slipped its strap over her shoulder. She got out of the Chevy feeling wobbly, eased around front of it and saw the hood and bumper and roof were crumpled. A wisp of radiator steam hissed from beneath the wadded hood, rose into the moonlight and dissolved.

She turned her attentions to the Buick. Its tail end was now turned to her, and as she edged alongside it, she saw the front left side had been badly damaged. Fearful of what she might see, she glanced inside.

The moonlight shone through the rear windshield bright as a spotlight and revealed no one, but the back seat was slick with something dark and wet and there was plenty of it. A foul scent seeped out of a partially rolled down back window. It was a hot coppery smell that gnawed at her nostrils and ached her stomach.

God, someone had been hurt. Maybe thrown free of the car, or perhaps they had gotten out and crawled off. But when? She and the Chevy had been airborne for only a moment, and she had gotten out of the vehicle instants after it ceased to roll. Surely she would have seen someone get out of the Buick, and if they had been thrown free by the collision, wouldn't at least one of the Buick's doors be open? If it had whipped back and closed, it seemed unlikely that it would be locked, and all the doors of the Buick were locked, and all the glass was intact, and only on her side was it rolled down, and only a crack. Enough for the smell of the blood to escape, not enough for a person to slip through unless they were thin and flexible as a feather.

On the other side of the Buick, on the ground, between the back door and the railing, there were drag marks and a thick swath of blood, and another swath on the top of the railing; it glowed there in the moonlight as if it were molasses laced with radioactivity.

Ellen moved cautiously to the railing and peered over.

No one lay mangled and bleeding and oozing their guts. The ground was not as precarious there as she expected it. It was pebbly and sloped out gradually and there was a trail going down it. The trail twisted slightly and as it deepened the foliage grew denser on either side of it. Finally it curlicued its way into the dark thicket of a forest below, and from the forest, hot on the wind, came the strong turpentine tang of pines and something less fresh and not as easily identifiable.

Now she saw someone moving down there, floating up from the forest like an apparition; a white face split by silver—braces, perhaps. She could tell from the way this someone moved that it was a man. She watched as he climbed the trail and came within examination range. He seemed to be surveying her as carefully as she was surveying him.

Could this be the driver of the Buick?

As he came nearer Ellen discovered she could not identify the expression he wore. It was neither joy or anger or fear or exhaustion or pain. It was somehow all and none of these.

When he was ten feet away, still looking up, that same odd expression on his face, she could hear him breathing. He was breathing with exertion, but not to the extent she thought him tired or injured. It was the sound of someone who had been about busy work.

She yelled down, "Are you injured?"

He turned his head quizzically, like a dog trying to make sense of a command, and it occurred to Ellen that he might be knocked about in the head enough to be disoriented.

"I'm the one who ran into your car," she said. "Are you all right?"

His expression changed then, and it was most certainly identifiable this time. He was surprised and angry. He came up the trail quickly, took hold of the top railing, his fingers going into the blood there, and vaulted over and onto the gravel.

Ellen stepped back out of his way and watched him from a distance. The guy made her nervous. Even close up, he looked like some kind of spook.

He eyed her briefly, glanced at the Chevy, turned to look at the Buick.

"It was my fault," Ellen said.

He didn't reply, but returned his attention to her and continued to cock his head in that curious dog sort of way.

Ellen noticed that one of his shirt sleeves was stained with blood, and that there was blood on the knees of his pants, but he didn't act as if he were hurt in any way. He reached into his pants pocket and pulled out something and made a move with his wrist. Out flicked a lock-blade knife. The thin edge of it sucked up the moonlight and spat it out in a silver spray that fanned wide when he held it before him and jiggled it like a man working a stubborn key into a lock. He advanced toward her, and as he came, his lips split and pulled back at the corners, exposing, not braces, but metal-capped teeth that matched the sparkle of his blade.

It occurred to her that she could bolt for the Chevy, but in the same mental flash of lightning, it occurred to her she wouldn't make it.

Ellen threw herself over the railing, and as she leapt, she saw out of the corner of her eye, the knife slashing the place she had occupied, catching moonbeams and throwing them away. Then the blade was out of her view and she hit on her stomach and skidded onto the narrow trail, slid downward, feet first. The gravel and roots tore at the front of her dress and ripped through her nylons and gouged her flesh. She cried out in pain and her sliding gained speed. Lifting her chin, she saw that the man was climbing over the railing and coming after her at a stumbling run, the knife held before him like a wand.

Her sliding stopped, and she pushed off with her hands to make it start again, not knowing if this was the thing to do or not, since the trail inclined sharply on her right side, and should she skid only slightly in that direction, she could hurtle off into blackness. But somehow she kept slithering along the trail and even spun around a corner and stopped with her head facing downward, her purse practically in her teeth.

She got up then, without looking back, and began to run into the woods, the purse beating at her side. She moved as far away from the trail as she could, fighting limbs that conspired to hit her across the face or hold her, vines and bushes that tried to tie her feet or trip her.

Behind her, she could hear the man coming after her, breathing heavily now, not really winded, but hurrying. For the first time in months, she was grateful for Bruce and his survivalist insanity. His passion to be in shape and for her to be in shape with him was paying off. All that jogging had given her the lungs of an ox and strengthened her legs and ankles. A line from one of Bruce's survivalist books came to her: *Do the unexpected.*

She found a trail amongst the pines, and followed it, then, abruptly broke from it and went back into the thicket. It was harder going, but she assumed her pursuer would expect her to follow a trail.

The pines became so thick she got down on her hands and knees and began to crawl. It was easier to get through that way. After a moment, she stopped scuttling and eased her back against one of the pines and sat and listened. She felt reasonably well hidden, as the boughs of the pines grew low and drooped to the ground. She took several deep breaths, holding each for a long moment. Gradually, she began breathing normally. Above her, from the direction of the trail, she could hear the man running, coming nearer. She held her breath.

The running paused a couple of times, and she could imagine the man, his strange, pale face turning from side to side, as he tried to determine what had happened to her. The sound of running started again and the man moved on down the trail.

Ellen considered easing out and starting back up the trail, making her way to her car and driving off. Damaged as it was, she felt it would still run, but she was reluctant to leave her hiding place and step into the moonlight. Still, it seemed a better plan than waiting. If she didn't do something, the man could always go back topside himself and wait for her. The woods, covering acres and acres of land below and beyond, would take her days to get through, and without food and water and knowledge of the geography, she might never make it, could end up going in circles for days.

Bruce and his survivalist credos came back to her. She remembered something he had said to one of his self-defense classes, a bunch of rednecks hoping and praying for a commie take-over so they could show their stuff. He had told them: *Utilize what's at hand. Size up what you have with you and how it can be put to use.*

All right, she thought. *All right, Brucey, you sonofabitch. I'll see what's at hand.*

One thing she knew she had for sure was a little flashlight. It wasn't much, but it would serve for her to check out the contents of her purse. She located it easily, and without withdrawing it from her purse, turned it on and held the open purse close to her face to see what was inside. Before she actually found it, she thought of her nail file kit. Besides the little bottle of nail polish remover, there was an emery board and two metal files. The files were the ticket. They might serve as weapons; they weren't much, but they were something.

She also carried a very small pair of nail scissors, independent of the kit, the points of the scissors being less than a quarter inch. That wouldn't be worth much, but she took note of it and mentally catalogued it.

She found the nail kit, turned off the flash and removed one of the files and returned the rest of the kit to her purse. She held the file tightly, made a little jabbing motion with it. It seemed so light and thin and insignificant.

She had been absently carrying her purse on one shoulder, and now to make sure she didn't lose it, she placed the strap over her neck and slid her arm through.

Clenching the nail file, she moved on hands and knees beneath the pine boughs and poked her head out into the clearing of the trail. She glanced down it first, and there, not ten yards from her, looking up the trail, holding his knife by his side, was the man. The moonlight lay cold on his face and the shadows of the wind-blown boughs fell across him and wavered. It seemed as if she were leaning over a pool and staring down into the water and seeing him at the bottom of it, or perhaps his reflection on the face of the pool.

She realized instantly that he had gone down the trail a ways, became suspicious of her ability to disappear so quickly, and had turned to judge where she might have gone. And, as if in answer to the question, she poked her head into view.

They remained frozen for a moment, then the man took a step up the trail, and just as he began to run, Ellen went backwards into the pines on her hands and knees.

She had gone less than ten feet when she ran up against a thick limb that lay close to the ground and was preventing her passage. She got down on her belly and squirmed beneath it, and as she was pulling her head under, she saw Moon Face crawling into the thicket, making good time; time made better, when he lunged suddenly and covered half the space between them, the knife missing her by fractions.

Ellen jerked back and felt her feet falling away from her. She let go of the file and grabbed out for the limb and it bent way back and down with her weight. It lowered her enough for her feet to touch ground. Relieved, she realized she had fallen into a wash made by erosion, not off the edge of the mountain.

Above her, gathered in shadows and stray strands of moonlight that showed through the pine boughs, was the man. His metal-tipped teeth caught a moonbeam and twinkled. He placed a hand on the limb she held, as if to lower himself, and she let go of it.

The limb whispered away from her and hit him full in the face and knocked him back.

Ellen didn't bother to scrutinize the damage. Turning, she saw that the wash ended in a slope and that the slope was thick with trees growing out like great, feathered spears thrown into the side of the mountain.

She started down, letting the slant carry her, grasping limbs and tree trunks to slow her descent and keep her balance. She could hear the man climbing down and pursuing her, but she didn't bother to turn and look. Below she could see the incline was becoming steeper, and if she continued, it would be almost straight up and down with nothing but the trees for support, and to move from one to the other, she would have to drop, chimpanzee-like, from limb to limb. Not a pleasant thought.

Her only consolation was that the trees to her right, veering back up the mountain, were thick as cancer cells. She took off in that direction, going wide, and began plodding upwards again, trying to regain the concealment of the forest.

She chanced a look behind her before entering the pines, and saw that the man, who she had come to think of as Moon Face, was some distance away.

Weaving through a mass of trees, she integrated herself into the forest, and as she went the limbs began to grow closer to the ground and the trees became so thick they twisted together like pipe cleaners. She got down on her hands and knees and crawled between limbs and around tree trunks and tried to lose herself among them.

To follow her, Moon Face had to do the same thing, and at first she heard him behind her, but after a while, there were only the sounds she was making.

She paused and listened.

Nothing.

Glancing the way she had come, she saw the intertwining limbs she had crawled under mixed with penetrating moonbeams, heard the short bursts of her breath and the beating of her heart, but detected no evidence of Moon Face. She decided the head start she had, all the weaving she had done, the cover of the pines, had confused him, at least temporarily.

It occurred to her that if she had stopped to listen, he might have done the same, and she wondered if he could hear the pounding of her heart. She took a deep breath and held it and let it out slowly through her nose, did it again. She was breathing more normally now, and her heart, though still hammering furiously, felt as if it were back inside her chest where it belonged.

Easing her back against a tree trunk, she sat and listened, watching for that strange face, fearing it might abruptly burst through the limbs and brush, grinning its horrible teeth, or worse, that he might come up behind her, reach around the tree trunk with his knife and finish her in a bloody instant.

She checked and saw that she still had her purse. She opened it and got hold of the file kit by feel and removed the last file, determined to make better use of it than the first. She had no qualms about using it, knew she would, but what good would it do? The man was obviously stronger than she, and crazy as the pattern in a scratch quilt.

Once again, she thought of Bruce. What would he have done in this situation? He would certainly have been the man for the job. He would have relished it. Would probably have challenged old Moon Face to a one on one at the edge of the mountain, and even with a nail file, would have been confident that he could take him.

Ellen thought about how much she hated Bruce, and even now, shed of him, that hatred burned bright. How had she gotten mixed up with that dumb, macho bastard in the first place? He had seemed enticing at first. So powerful. Confident. Capable. The survivalist stuff had always seemed a little nutty, but at first no more nutty than an obsession with golf or a strong belief in astrology. Perhaps had she known how serious he was about it, she wouldn't have been attracted to him in the first place.

No. It wouldn't have mattered. She had been captivated by him, by his looks and build and power. She had nothing but her own libido and stupidity to blame. And worse yet, when things turned sour, she had stayed and let them sour even more. There had been good moments, but they were quickly eclipsed by Bruce's determination to be ready for the Big Day, as he referred to it. He knew it was coming, if he was somewhat vague on who was bringing it. But someone would start a war of some sort, a nuclear war, a war in the streets, and only the rugged individualist, well-armed and well-trained and strong of body and will, would survive beyond the initial attack. Those survivors would then carry out guerrilla warfare, hit and run operations, and eventually win back the country from...whoever. And if not win it back, at least have some kind of life free of dictatorship.

It was silly. It was every little boy's fantasy. Living by your wits with gun and knife. And owning a woman. She had been the woman. At first Bruce had been kind enough, treated her with respect. He was obviously on the male chauvinist side, but originally it had seemed harmless enough, kind of Old World charming. But when he moved them to the mountains, that charm had turned to domination, and the small crack in his mental state widened until it was a deep, dark gulf.

She was there to keep house and to warm his bed, and any opinions she had contrary to his own were stupid. He read survivalist books constantly and quoted passages to her and suggested she look the books over, be ready to stand tall against the oncoming aggressors.

By the time he had gone completely over the edge, living like a mountain man, ordering her about, his eyes roving from side to side, suspicious of her every move, expecting to hear on his shortwave at any moment World War Three had started, or that race riots were overrunning the USA, or that a shiny probe packed with extraterrestrial invaders brandishing ray guns had landed on the White House lawn, she was trapped in his cabin in the mountains, with him holding the keys to her Chevy and his jeep.

For a time she feared he would become paranoid enough to imagine she was one of the "bad guys" and put a .357 round through her chest. But now she was free of him, escaped from all that...only to be threatened by another man: a moon-faced, silver-toothed monster with a knife.

She returned once again to the question, what would Bruce do, outside of challenging Moon Face in hand-to-hand combat? Sneaking past him would be the best bet, making it back to the Chevy. To do that Bruce would have used guerrilla techniques. *Take advantage of what's at hand*, he always said.

Well, she had looked to see what was at hand, and that turned out to be a couple of fingernail files, one of them lost up the mountain.

Then maybe she wasn't thinking about this in the right way. She might not be able to outfight Moon Face, but perhaps she could outthink him. She had outthought Bruce, and he had considered himself a master of strategy and preparation.

She tried to put herself in Moon Face's head. What was he thinking? For the moment he saw her as his prey, a frightened animal on the run. He might be more cautious because of that trick with the limb, but he'd most likely chalk that one up to accident—which it was for the most part...but what if the prey turned on him?

There was a sudden cracking sound, and Ellen crawled a few feet in the direction of the noise, gently moved aside a limb. Some distance away, discerned faintly through a tangle of limbs, she saw light and detected movement, and knew it was Moon Face. The cracking sound must have been him stepping on a limb.

He was standing with his head bent, looking at the ground, flashing a little pocket flashlight, obviously examining the drag path she had made with her hands and knees when she entered into the pine thicket.

She watched as his shape and the light bobbed and twisted through the limbs and tree trunks, coming nearer. She wanted to run, but didn't know where.

All right, she thought. *All right. Take it easy. Think.*

She made a quick decision. Removed the scissors from her purse, took off her shoes and slipped off her pantyhose and put her shoes on again.

She quickly snipped three long strips of nylon from her damaged pantyhose and knotted them together, using the sailor knots Bruce had taught her. She cut more thin strips from the hose—all the while listening for Moon Face's approach—and used all but one of them to fasten her fingernail file, point out, securely to the tapered end of one of the small, flexible pine limbs, then she tied one end of the long nylon strip she had made around the limb, just below the file, and crawled backwards, pulling the limb with her, bending it deep. When she had it back as far as she could manage, she took a death grip on the nylon strip, and using it to keep the limb's position taut, crawled around the trunk of a small pine and curved the nylon strip about it and made a loop knot at the base of a sapling that crossed her knee-drag trail. She used her last strip of nylon to fasten to the loop of the knot, and carefully stretched the remaining length across the trail and tied it to another sapling. If it worked correctly, when he came crawling through the thicket, following her, his hands or knees would hit the strip, pull the loop free, and the limb would fly forward, the file stabbing him, in an eye if she were lucky.

Pausing to look through the boughs again, she saw that Moon Face was on his hands and knees, moving through the thick foliage toward her. Only moments were left.

She shoved pine needles over the strip and moved away on her belly, sliding under the cocked sapling, no longer concerned that she might make noise, in fact hoping noise would bring Moon Face quickly.

Following the upward slope of the hill, she crawled until the trees became thin again and she could stand. She cut two long strips of nylon from her hose with the scissors, and stretched them between two trees about ankle high.

That one would make him mad if it caught him, but the next one would be the corker.

She went up the path, used the rest of the nylon to tie between two saplings, then grabbed hold of a thin, short limb and yanked at it until it cracked, worked it free so there was a point made from the break. She snapped that over her knee to form a point at the opposite end. She made a quick mental measurement, jammed one end of the stick into the soft ground, leaving a point facing up.

At that moment came evidence her first snare had worked—a loud swishing sound as the limb popped forward and a cry of pain. This was followed by a howl as Moon Face crawled out of the thicket and onto the trail. He stood slowly, one hand to his face. He glared up at her, removed his hand. The file had struck him in the cheek; it was covered with blood. Moon Face pointed his blood-covered hand at her and let out an accusing shriek so horrible she retreated rapidly up the trail. Behind her, she could hear Moon Face running.

The trail curved upward and turned abruptly. She followed the curve a ways, looked back as Moon Face tripped over her first strip and hit the ground, came up madder, charged even more violently up the path. But the second strip got him and he fell forward, throwing his hands out. The spike in the trail hit him low in the throat.

She stood transfixed at the top of the trail as he did a pushup and came to one knee and put a hand to his throat. Even from a distance, and with only the moonlight to show it to her, she could see that the wound was dreadful.

Good.

Moon Face looked up, stabbed her with a look, started to rise. Ellen turned and ran. As she made the turns in the trail, the going improved and she theorized that she was rushing up the trail she had originally come down.

This hopeful notion was dispelled when the pines thinned and the trail dropped, then leveled off, then tapered into nothing. Before she could slow up, she discovered she was on a sort of peninsula that jutted out from the mountain and resembled an irregular-shaped diving board from which you could leap off into night-black eternity.

In place of the pines on the sides of the trail were numerous scarecrows on poles, and out on the very tip of the peninsula, somewhat dispelling the diving board image, was a shack made of sticks and mud and brambles.

After pausing to suck in some deep breaths, Ellen discovered on closer examination that it wasn't scarecrows bordering her path after all. It was people.

Dead people. She could smell them.

There were at least a dozen on either side, placed upright on poles, their feet touching the ground, their knees slightly bent. They were all fully clothed, and in various states of deterioration. Holes had been poked through the backs of their heads to correspond with the hollow sockets of their eyes, and the moonlight came through the holes and shined through the sockets, and Ellen noted, with a warm sort of horror, that one wore a white sun dress and...plastic shoes, and through its head she could see stars. On the corpse's finger was a wedding ring, and the finger had grown thin and withered and the ring was trapped there by knuckle bone alone.

The man next to her was fresher. He too was eyeless and holes had been drilled through the back of his skull, but he still wore glasses and was fleshy. There was a pen and pencil set in his coat pocket. He wore only one shoe.

There was a skeleton in overalls, a wilting cigar stuck between his teeth. A fresh-UPS man with his cap at a jaunty angle, the moon through his head, and a clipboard tied to his hand with string. His legs had been positioned in such a way it seemed as if he was walking. A housewife with a crumpled, nearly disintegrated grocery bag under her arm, the contents having long fallen through the worn, wet bottom to heap at her feet in a mass of colorless boxes and broken glass. A withered corpse in a ballerina's tutu and slippers, rotting grapefruits tied to her chest with cord to simulate breasts, her legs arranged in such a way she seemed in mid-dance, up on her toes, about to leap or whirl.

The real horror was the children. One pathetic little boy's corpse, still full of flesh and with only his drilled eyes to show death, had been arranged in such a way that a teddy bear drooped from the crook of his elbow. A toy metal tractor and a plastic truck were at his feet.

There was a little girl wearing a red rubber clown nose and a propeller beanie. A green plastic purse hung from her shoulder by a strap and a doll's legs had been taped to her palm with black electrician's tape. The doll hung upside down, holes drilled through its plastic head so that it matched its owner.

Things began to click. Ellen understood what Moon Face had been doing down here in the first place. He hadn't been in the Buick when she struck it. He was disposing of a body. He was a murderer who brought his victims here and set them up on either side of the pathway, parodying the way they were in life, cutting out their eyes and punching through the backs of their heads to let the world in.

Ellen realized numbly that time was slipping away, and Moon Face was coming, and she had to find the trail up to her car. But when she turned to run, she froze.

Thirty feet away, where the trail met the last of the pines, squatting dead center in it, arms on his knees, one hand loosely holding the knife, was Moon Face. He looked calm, almost happy, in spite of the fact a large swath of dried blood was on his cheek and the wound in his throat was making a faint whistling sound as air escaped it.

He appeared to be gloating, savoring the moment when he would set his knife to work on her eyes, the gray matter behind them, the bone of her skull.

A vision of her corpse propped up next to the child with the teddy bear, or perhaps the skeletal ballerina, came to mind; she could see herself hanging there, the light of the moon falling through her empty head, melting into the path.

Then she felt anger. It boiled inside her. She determined she was not going to allow Moon Face his prize easily. He'd earn it.

Another line from Bruce's books came to her.

Consider your alternatives.

She did, in a flash. And they were grim. She could try charging past Moon Face, or pretend to, then dart into the pines. But it seemed unlikely she could make the trees before he overtook her. She could try going over the side of the trail and climbing down, but it was much too steep there, and she'd fall immediately. She could make for the shack and try and find something she could fight with. The last idea struck her as the correct one, the one Bruce would have pursued. What was his quote? *If you can't effect an escape, fall back and fight with what's available to you.*

She hurried to the hut, glancing behind her from time to time to check on Moon Face. He hadn't moved. He was observing her calmly, as if he had all the time in the world.

When she was about to go through the doorless entryway, she looked back at him one last time. He was in the same spot, watching, the knife held limply against his leg. She knew he thought he had her right where he wanted her, and that's exactly what she wanted him to think. A surprise attack was the only chance she had. She just hoped she could find something to surprise him with.

She hastened inside and let out an involuntary rasp of breath.

The place stank, and for good reason. In the center of the little hut was a folding card table and some chairs, and seated in one of the chairs was a woman, the flesh rotting and dripping off her skull like candle wax, her eyes empty and holes in the back of her head. Her arm was resting on the table and her hand was clamped around an open bottle of whiskey. Beside her, also without eyes, suspended in a standing position by wires connected to the roof, was a man. He was a fresh kill. Big, dressed in khaki pants and shirt and work shoes. In one hand a doubled belt was taped, and wires were attached in such a way that his arm was drawn back as if ready to strike. Wires were secured to his lips and pulled tight behind his head so that he was smiling in a ghoulish way. Foil gum wrappers were fixed to his teeth, and the moonlight gleaming through the opening at the top of the hut fell on them and made them resemble Moon Face's metal-tipped choppers.

Ellen felt queasy, but fought the sensation down. She had more to worry about than corpses. She had to prevent herself from becoming one.

She gave the place a quick pan. To her left was a rust-framed rollaway bed with a thin, dirty mattress, and against the far wall, was a baby crib, and next to that a camper stove with a small frying pan on it.

She glanced quickly out the door of the hut and saw that Moon Face had moved onto the stretch of trail bordered by the bodies. He was walking very slowly, looking up now and then as if to appreciate the stars.

Her heart pumped another beat.

She moved about the hut, looking for a weapon.

The frying pan.

She grabbed it, and as she did, she saw what was in the crib. What belonged there. A baby. But dead. A few months old. Its skin thin as plastic and stretched tight over pathetic, little rib bones. Eyes gone, holes through its head. Burnt match stubs between blackened toes. It wore a diaper and the stink of feces wafted from it and into her nostrils. A rattle lay at the foot of the crib.

A horrible realization rushed through her. The baby had been alive when taken by this madman, and it had died here, starved and tortured. She gripped the frying pan with such intensity her hand cramped.

Her foot touched something.

She looked down. Large bones were heaped there—discarded mommies and daddies, for it now occurred to her that was who the corpses represented.

Something gleamed amongst the bones. A gold cigarette lighter.

Through the doorway of the hut she saw Moon Face was halfway down the trail. He had paused to nonchalantly adjust the UPS man's clipboard. The geek had made his own community here, his own family, people he could deal with—dead people—and it was obvious he intended for her to be part of his creation.

Ellen considered attacking straight-on with the frying pan when Moon Face came through the doorway, but so far he had proven strong enough to take a file in the cheek and a stick in the throat, and despite the severity of the latter wound, he had kept on coming. Chances were he was strong enough to handle her and her frying pan.

A back-up plan is necessary. Another one of Bruce's pronouncements. She recalled a college friend, Carol, who used to use her bikini panties to launch projectiles at a teddy bear propped on a chair. This graduated to an apple on the bear's head. Eventually, Ellen and her dorm sisters got into the act. Fresh panties with tight elastic and marbles for ammunition were ever ready in a box by the door; the bear and an apple were in constant position. In time, Ellen became the best shot of all. But that was ten years ago. Expertise was long gone, even the occasional shot now and then was no longer taken...still...

Ellen replaced the frying pan on the stove, hiked up her dress and pulled her bikini panties down and stepped out of them and picked up the lighter.

She put the lighter in the crotch of the panties and stuck her fingers into the leg loops to form a fork and took hold of the lighter through the panties and pulled it back, assured herself the elastic was strong enough to launch the projectile.

All right. That was a start.

She removed her purse, so Moon Face couldn't grab it and snare her, and tossed it aside. She grabbed the whiskey bottle from the corpse's hand and turned and smashed the bottom of it against the cook stove. Whiskey and glass flew. The result was a jagged weapon she could lunge with. She placed the broken bottle on the stove next to the frying pan.

Outside, Moon Face was strolling toward the hut, like a shy teenager about to call on his date.

There were only moments left. She glanced around the room, hoping insanely at the last second she would find some escape route, but there was none.

Sweat dripped from her forehead and ran into her eye and she blinked it out and half-drew back the panty sling with its golden projectile. She knew her makeshift weapon wasn't powerful enough to do much damage, but it might give her a moment of distraction, a chance to attack him with the bottle. If she went at him straight on with it, she felt certain he would disarm her and make short work of her, but if she could get him off guard...

She lowered her arms, kept her makeshift slingshot in front of her, ready to be cocked and shot.

Moon Face came through the door, ducking as he did, a sour sweat smell entering with him. His neck wound whistled at her like a teapot about to boil. She saw then that he was bigger than she first thought. Tall and broad-shouldered and strong.

He looked at her and there was that peculiar expression again. The moonlight from the hole in the roof hit his eyes and teeth, and it was as if that light was his source of energy. He filled his chest with air and seemed to stand a full two inches taller. He looked at the woman's corpse in the chair, the man's corpse supported on wires, glanced at the playpen.

He smiled at Ellen, squeaked more than spoke, "Bubba's home, Sissie."

I'm not Sissie yet, thought Ellen. *Not yet.*

Moon Face started to move around the card table and Ellen let out a bloodcurdling scream that caused him to bob his head high like a rabbit surprised by headlights. Ellen jerked up the panties and pulled them back and let loose the lighter. It shot out of the panties and fell to the center of the card table with a clunk.

Moon Face looked down at it.

Ellen was temporarily gripped with paralysis, then she stepped forward and kicked the card table as hard as she could. It went into Moon Face, hitting him waist high, startling, but not hurting him.

Now! thought Ellen, grabbing her weapons. *Now!*

She rushed him, the broken bottle in one hand, the frying pan in the other. She slashed out with the bottle and it struck him in the center of the face and he let out a scream and the glass fractured and a splash of blood burst from him and in that same instant Ellen saw that his nose was cut half in two and she felt a tremendous throb in her hand. The bottle had broken in her palm and cut her.

She ignored the pain and as Moon Face bellowed and lashed out with the knife, cutting the front of her dress but not her flesh, she brought the frying pan around and caught him on the elbow, and the knife went soaring across the room and behind the rollaway bed.

Moon Face froze, glanced in the direction the knife had taken. He seemed empty and confused without it.

Ellen swung the pan again. Moon Face caught her wrist and jerked her around and she lost the pan and was sent hurtling toward the bed, where she collapsed on the mattress. The bed slid down and smashed through the thin wall of sticks and a foot of the bed stuck out into blackness and the great drop below. The bed tottered slightly, and Ellen rolled off of it, directly into the legs of Moon Face. As his knees bent, and he reached for her, she rolled backwards and went under the bed and her hand came to rest on the knife. She grabbed it, rolled back toward Moon Face's feet, reached out quickly and brought the knife down on one of his shoes and drove it in as hard as she could.

A bellow from Moon Face. His foot leaped back and it took the knife with it. Moon Face screamed, "Sissie! You're hurting me!"

Moon Face reached down and pulled the knife out, and Ellen saw his foot come forward, and then he was grabbing the bed and effortlessly jerking it off of her and back, smashing it into the crib, causing the child to topple out of it and roll across the floor, the rattle clattering behind it. He grabbed Ellen by the back of her dress and jerked her up and spun her around to face him, clutched her throat in one hand and held the knife close to her face with the other, as if for inspection; the blade caught the moonlight and winked.

Beyond the knife, she saw his face, pathetic and pained and white. His breath, sharp as the knife, practically wilted her. His neck wound whistled softly. The remnants of his nose dangled wet and red against his upper lip and cheek and his teeth grinned a moonlit, metal good-bye.

It was all over, and she knew it, but then Bruce's words came back to her in a rush. *When it looks as if you're defeated, and there's nothing left, try anything.*

She twisted and jabbed out at his eyes with her fingers and caught him solid enough that he thrust her away and stumbled backwards. But only for an instant. He bolted forward, and Ellen stooped and grabbed the dead child by the ankle and struck Moon Face with it as if it were a club. Once in the face, once in the midsection. The rotting child burst into a spray of desiccated flesh and innards and she hurled the leg at Moon Face and then she was circling around the rollaway bed, trying to make the door. Moon Face, at the other end of the bed, saw this, and when she moved for the door, he lunged in that direction, causing her to jump back to the end of the bed. Smiling, he returned to his end, waited for her next attempt.

She lurched for the door again, and Moon Face deep-stepped that way, and when she jerked back, Moon Face jerked back too, but this time Ellen bent and grabbed the end of the bed and hurled herself against it. The bed hit Moon Face in the knees, and as he fell, the bed rolled over him and he let go of the knife and tried to put out his hands to stop the bed's momentum. The impetus of the rollaway carried him across the short length of the dirt floor and his head hit the far wall and the sticks cracked and hurtled out into blackness, and Moon Face followed and the bed followed him, then caught on the edge of the drop and the wheels buried up in the dirt and hung there.

Ellen had shoved so hard she fell face down, and when she looked up, she saw the bed was dangling, shaking, the mattress slipping loose, about to glide off into nothingness.

Moon Face's hands flicked into sight, clawing at the sides of the bed's frame. Ellen gasped. He was going to make it up. The bed's wheels were going to hold.

She pulled a knee under her, cocking herself, then sprang forward, thrusting both palms savagely against the bed. The wheels popped free and the rollaway shot out into the dark emptiness.

Ellen scooted forward on her knees and looked over the edge. There was blackness, a glimpse of the mattress falling free, and a pale object, like a whitewashed planet with a great vein of silver in it, jetting through the cold expanse of space. Then the mattress and the face were gone and there was just the darkness and a distant sound like a water balloon exploding.

Ellen sat back and took a breather. When she felt strong again and felt certain her heart wouldn't tear through her chest, she stood up and looked around the room. She thought a long time about what she saw.

She found her purse and panties, went out of the hut and up the trail, and after a few wrong turns, she found the proper trail that wound its way up the mountainside to where her car was parked. When she climbed over the railing, she was exhausted.

Everything was as it was. She wondered if anyone had seen the cars, if anyone had stopped, then decided it didn't matter. There was no one here now, and that's what was important.

She took the keys from her purse and tried the engine. It turned over. That was a relief.

She killed the engine, got out and went around and opened the trunk of the Chevy and looked down at Bruce's body. His face looked like one big bruise, his lips were as large as sausages. It made her happy to look at him.

A new energy came to her. She got him under the arms and pulled him out and managed him over to the rail and grabbed his legs and flipped him over the railing and onto the trail. She got one of his hands and started pulling him down the path, letting the momentum help her. She felt good. She felt strong. First Bruce had tried to dominate her, had threatened her, had thought she was weak because she was a woman, and one night, after slapping her, after raping her, while he slept a drunken sleep, she had pulled the blankets up tight around him and looped rope over and under the bed and used the knots he had taught her, and secured him.

Then she took a stick of stove wood and had beat him until she was so weak she fell to her knees. She hadn't meant to kill him, just punish him for slapping her around, but when she got started she couldn't stop until she was too worn out to go on, and when she was finished, she discovered he was dead.

That didn't disturb her much. The thing then was to get rid of the body somewhere, drive on back to the city and say he had abandoned her and not come back. It was weak, but all she had.

Until now.

After several stops for breath, a chance to lie on her back and look up at the stars, Ellen managed Bruce to the hut and got her arms under his and got him seated in one of the empty chairs. She straightened things up as best as she could. She put the larger pieces of the baby back in the crib. She picked Moon Face's knife up off the floor and looked at it and looked at Bruce, his eyes wide open, the moonlight from the roof striking them, showing them to be dull as scratched glass.

Bending over his face, she went to work on his eyes. When she finished with them, she pushed his head forward and used the blade like a drill. She worked until the holes satisfied her. Now if the police found the Buick up there and came down the trail to investigate, and found the trail leading here, saw what was in the shack, Bruce would fit in with the rest of Moon Face's victims. The police would probably conclude Moon Face, sleeping here with his "family," had put his bed too close to the cliff and it had broken through the thin wall and he had tumbled to his death.

She liked it.

She held Bruce's chin, lifted it, examined her work.

"You can be Uncle Brucey," she said, and gave Bruce a pat on the shoulder. "Thanks for all your advice and help, Uncle Brucey. It's what got me through."

She gave him another pat.

She found a shirt—possibly Moon Face's, possibly a victim's—on the opposite side of the shack, next to a little box of *Harlequin Romances*, and she used it to wipe the knife, pan, all she had touched, clean of her prints, then she went out of there, back up to her car.

About Joe R. Lansdale

Joe R. Lansdale is the multi-award winning author of thirty novels and over two hundred short stories, articles and essays. He has written screenplays, teleplays, comic book scripts, and occasionally teaches creative writing and screenplay writing at Stephen F. Austin State University. He has received The Edgar Award, The Grinzani Prize for Literature, seven Bram Stoker Awards, and many others.

His stories "Bubba Ho-Tep" and "Incident On and Off a Mountain Road" were both filmed. He is the founder of the martial arts system Shen Chuan, and has been in the International Martial Arts Hall of Fame four times.

He lives in East Texas with his wife, Karen.

CIGARETTES AND CICADAS

by David M. Buhajla

Steven Milsap reclined on his bed in the gloom of his bedroom while he smoked a cigarette and contemplated death. He watched the smoke from the end of his cigarette creep up to the ceiling to gather in a fog and disappear. He was all alone in his small Ozark Mountain house in northwest Arkansas. He listened to the cicadas and tree frogs chirping and croaking their mating songs.

"If only I had a chance to talk to you one more time," he muttered. "There was a lot that I wanted to say to you, Grandpa. I wanted to ask why you had always been such a mean bastard. You always was a sumbitch. Full of nothing but piss and vinegar to anyone who ever wanted to do anything nice for you."

Taking another drag on his cigarette, he hoped sleep would come. It was 2 AM. He was careful to blow the smoke out of the bedroom window, which was cracked open a couple of inches to let in the humid nighttime air.

The sounds of the deep Ozarks reached through the window. The cicadas called out in their loud buzzing conversations, dying down and then coming back in waves. The tree frogs groaned and croaked and the bustle of small animals scratched and scrambled in the underbrush. A solitary whippoorwill let forth its haunting call in the distance.

Steven finished his smoke, reached down to the floor, and crushed out the butt into a plastic ashtray that he had stolen from a local diner.

"Shit. I gotta get some sleep," he said.

Reclining back deeper into his pillow, he rubbed his eyes. He thought about how glad he was to be living in Arkansas again. That last couple of years in that little town in Northern Illinois had been a nightmare. Now, living alone in the middle of the mountains gave him the freedom from people he'd missed in those two years away.

Steven knew things were better here. He had good friends and nobody fucked with him. How could anyone fuck with him when every person around was pretty much as poor as the next? That was life in the Ozark Mountains. He was glad that he was a hillbilly again.

He couldn't turn his brain off. "Goddamnit. Shut up. Just shut up."

Groaning, he rubbed his forehead in an attempt to soothe himself. His eyes felt gritty, so he closed them and tried to think of nothing. The yard light bled through the windows and into his eyelids.

He reached up and tried to adjust the curtains, but they kept slipping open to let the light in. Frustrated, Steven let the fabric fall from between his fingers. They swayed for a moment and then settled back into place. A narrow beam of light from outside stabbed into the room and hit his face again. He lay back and threw his arm over his eyes, knowing that he couldn't get to sleep that way.

He cursed his insomnia. He had always had been a light sleeper, even when he was a little kid. And his father had always said that if a mosquito farted across the road, Steven would snap awake at the sound. Most of the time, his light sleeping had been an annoyance, but sometimes it served useful purposes as well. Nobody could sneak up on him when he was asleep, which had screwed up the idea of Santa Claus when he was a child.

Steven angrily realized that his mind had gone off on another tangent when he should have been trying to think of nothing. Pulling the blanket over his head, he left an air hole by his left shoulder so that he could breathe. He laid there for a few minutes, his mind racing, knowing that it was going to be a long night...knowing that he would probably lay there until the sun rose. He sighed at the futility.

More hours passed and he lay, feeling unhappy. After what seemed like an eternity, he finally began to drift off into a fitful doze.

Suddenly he awoke with a start. His blanket began to slide down off of his forehead, past his nose, and across his lips and chin. It reached his chest and dropped back down onto his body. Adrenaline pumped through him as he sat up and scrambled backwards. His back thumped against the wall and he raised his balled-up fists, ready to lash out. He got his feet under his body and he stood up. His foot slipped on his pillow and he almost lost his balance, but he recovered at the last instant and kicked the pillow onto the floor.

A figure loomed over his bed, hunched and looking into his eyes. Steven looked back and saw no features in the figure's face, because the figure had no face. It was a chunk of night cut out and made into a human silhouette.

Steven gasped as his balls drew up and a deep chill overtook his body. His breath came out in a mist. The face was only a couple of inches away from his own and he lashed out with his fist, aiming for the thing's head, but it leaned back and Steven's fist caught nothing but air.

The creature thrust out its own hand and grabbed him quicker than anything Steven had ever experienced. Cool fingers wrapped around his forearm like the small grass snakes he'd caught as a child. The fingers were gentle but firm. They didn't pull the skin from his arm or freeze him solid like Steven would have expected.

The ghostly entity spoke. "Steven. It's okay. It's just me." There was no sibilant hiss in its voice. No deep growl like an animal. No mad laughter.

It spoke with the voice of his dead grandfather.

"Who...what?" Steven spluttered.

A mental image of his grandfather's casket as it was lowered into the ground blasted through his mind. That had been three weeks ago.

The hand didn't move from his forearm. The figure stood over him, unmoving. Waiting. Steven tried to tear his arm free, but the grip was still firm, like he was stuck in cold cement.

And then panic set in.

Turning his body to the right, Steven swung out with his left arm and screamed. He tried to throw a punch, but his body refused to obey. His arm flew out limp and weak, the kind of slap that drunks threw with meaty arms at their friends the instant before they passed out.

Steven's arm crossed his field of vision as he punched out, blocking his view of the figure for an instant. In that split second of blindness, the grip on his arm disappeared. He blinked and realized that the apparition was gone, as if swinging his arm had somehow banished it from existence. Where had it gone?

Jumping from the bed, he expected the thing to appear behind him and wrap bitter fingers around his throat or drive a fingertip into his eye socket. He stepped toward the light switch by the door and flicked it on, his breath coming out in gasps.

"Son of a bitch. That didn't happen, did it? I was asleep, right? Now I'm awake." But Steven couldn't stop his heart from pounding. He could almost feel those fingers still gripping his arm. He lowered his eyes and lifted his arm to take a look. His skin was pink where the thing's hands had gripped him, as if from a mild sunburn where it had touched him. If it was a dream, it had been a seemingly real one.

A chill scampered across his shoulders and threw him into action. He needed to get the hell away from his house.

He had seen too many horror movies where stupid characters always stayed in places that posed a threat. They had to go investigate creepy noises and moans in dark rooms. When they heard a noise, they always shouted into the dark, asking if anyone was there. They just had to look out windows that had shadows gliding across them.

"No, I'm not gonna be that kind of douche-bag," he said into the empty room. "Time to jet."

But then he looked at his bedroom door and paused for a second. Was the apparition standing on the other side of the door, waiting for him to open it so it could drag him into a shadowy corner?

He threw open the door and jumped across the threshold with a yell. There was nothing but the short hallway leading into the living room.

Heart pounding, chest heaving, Steven hurried down the hall, past the closed door of the spare bedroom on his right and past the bathroom on the left. All he could hear was the smoker's wheeze of his breath, the patter of his bare feet on the floor tiles, and the rasp of his jean shorts. He glanced at the darkness of the bathroom as he hurried by, paranoid, the tiny voice in his mind telling him that the shadow man was waiting in the gloom, ready to come up behind him and tear both his t-shirt and the flesh of his back into ribbons that would flutter as he fell.

Emerging from the hallway and into the living room, Steven felt as if there were eyes on him. It was the same feeling that he got when someone stood close to him in line, or when the shadow of a flying vulture crossed his own when he was hiking in the far places in the mountains.

Shuddering, all he could think about as he crossed the kitchen was his car keys and his cell phone that rested on the table next to the front door.

And then a voice came from the hallway.

"Steven? You said you wanted to speak to me one more time. I can't find you. Where are you? I can't see."

Now there was no doubt whether it was real or not. Feeling a wet patch growing in the front of his pants, the only thing that he was conscious of was tearing open the front door, grabbing his keys and cell phone, and running outside as fast as he could. The heat and humidity of the Ozark Mountain air hit him like an iron bar. The cacophony of the cicadas and tree frogs assailed his ears, increasing his panic, almost as if they were mocking him; telling him that he wasn't going to make it.

Pain knifed into Steven's foot as he stepped on the first rock. Stumbling forward, he pinwheeled his arms to keep from falling onto his face and he lost his grip on his cell phone. It went tumbling away and he yelped as the next rock bit into the sole of his other foot. He kept his balance as he reached his beat up sedan.

He opened the car door and got behind the wheel. His hands shook as he started the ignition. A blast of heavy metal music burst forth from the speakers and Steven jumped high enough to bang his head on the ceiling. He saw stars as he bit his tongue from the impact. He tasted blood.

"Ah, God," he moaned.

He glanced back for a moment, just in time to see all of the lights in his house go out. A fresh blast of panic wracked his entire being.

Throwing the car into reverse, he started to back out of the driveway, heading for the gravel road at the end of it. He almost hit one of the pine trees that stood at the edges of the driveway. He stepped on the brake pedal a bit so he wouldn't rear end the trees because he didn't want to be stuck on the property with that freakish thing in his house.

Steven forced himself to take a deep breath and continue on down the driveway. He was only about ten feet from the road and his eyes narrowed in concentration as he stared into the rear view mirror. He winced at the pain from his sore tongue and bruised feet as he did so and he hit the gas again, harder this time. He turned the wheel and peeled out, kicking up dirt and gravel, leaving his house and the entity behind.

《《——》》

Steven lay on the hotel room bed in Fort Smith and stared at the textured bumps on the ceiling. He lit a cigarette and took a drag from it, watching the tendrils of smoke creep from the burning end.

After a couple of drags, he crushed his smoke out. He didn't want the rest of it. He took up his ashtray, his cigarettes, and his lighter and set them on the nightstand next to his bed. He watched television for a while, changing channels and looking at infomercials and crappy talk shows, but he couldn't concentrate on the images that flitted across the screen. They started to morph into a large amorphous blur.

Fifteen minutes later, his eyelids closed and he drifted off to sleep. At least there were no cicadas here. And no ghosts.

«« — »»

Snapping awake from a dark and dreamless sleep, Steven's body was covered in a cold sweat, as if he had just had a nightmare. Then he realized that he wasn't in his bedroom, he was in a motel. The only light was from the parking lot outside; the television was dark and silent.

And his blankets were being pulled down his face.

Body trembling, he tried to say something. Anything. But he was paralyzed and his tongue was numb in the dry, cracked cavern of his mouth. He kept trying to move, kept trying to speak. His mouth gaped open and closed like a suffocating fish as something stood over him and pulled the blankets from his face.

A voice spoke. "It took me a while, but I finally found you. All I had to do was learn to see. And when I did, I saw you running. Pointless."

The entity grabbed him by the arm and throat, lifting him off of the bed and holding him up in midair. The pain from the ice-cold grip of the shadow man was horrendous. Steven felt nothing but blind panic. Lifting his free arm, he tried to pry the fingers from his throat but it was like trying to pry apart a crack in a glacier.

Grunting from the pain in his neck and face, Steven kicked his legs forward into the thing's chest. His grunt turned into a high-pitched squeal as he stubbed the bare toes of both of his feet into the diamond-hard chest of the shadow man. In response, the entity raised Steven up, bringing him to the black plane of its non-face. Steven's breath turned into mist from the piercing cold that radiated from the thing's very being.

It studied him, head nodding up and down only once, before letting him go. Steven dropped onto the cheap hotel carpet next to the bed with a dull thud, falling on his backside, teeth slamming shut from the impact. He let out a sob of pain and fear in front of the thing that had followed him from his house.

And then the ghostly creature spoke again. "You weren't there," it said. "You should have been there."

"I don't know what you are talking about," Steven cried out around the coppery taste of blood.

"You know it's me, Steven."

Steven knew that it was true. He realized that he had known since fleeing his house. He knew his Grandfather's voice. He had known that evil bastard's voice since birth.

But his Grandfather was dead.

Trying to reason with the ghost to save himself, Steven babbled, "Where should I have been?"

"In the car with me, when I went into the darkness."

"Why?"

"Because you are the only one who would understand. Because you've wanted to go there yourself. I've seen you with the gun to your temple, with the cigarette burning circles into your flesh. I wanted the darkness, too. All I had to do was turn the steering wheel at the right time on the expressway to get what I wanted. I chose to die. I chose, and you can choose too, with my help."

Steven's mind whirled, awash with fright. Still, there was an undercurrent of understanding; the darkness really had been what he had wanted at one time. But not now. When faced with the actual probability of death, he found he didn't want it after all.

He hadn't even known until this moment: he wanted to live.

Standing up, Steven pretended like he needed to use the nightstand to brace himself. As he did, he grabbed the heavy brass lamp that sat on top of it, pivoted his body to the left, and swung the lamp up, aiming for the side of Grandfather's head. The power cord yanked free from the wall, the lampshade crumpled from the impact, and the bulb shattered as Grandfather's head was knocked back a fraction of an inch. The lamp bounced back. Grandfather just stood there, staring.

And then Steven knew he couldn't do any damage to this thing. It was like hitting a statue. He also knew that he couldn't get to the door with Grandfather in his way.

Undaunted, unfazed, the apparition asked, "You refuse me?"

"Yeah. I don't want to turn into a freak like you," Steven said as he threw the bulky lamp at the window of his hotel room. The window shattered, the lamp hit the sidewalk outside with a clatter, and glass showered the carpeting as he turned and sprinted to the window opening. He wanted to throw himself through it so he could make his escape across the parking lot. And so he jumped.

But he didn't make it. There was a split second when his body was in midair before Grandfather smacked him back down into the carpeting. Steven's face hit the floor, he saw stars, and agony exploded in his nose. The air blasted out of his lungs as his ribcage made full contact with the floor. He rolled onto his back as he spit glass from between cut lips, and he couldn't breathe or speak, but his mind raced. How could a ghost have a physical presence? Was everything he had ever been told about ghosts, all the stories…were they completely false?

The entity reached a shadow-shrouded hand up to its non-face and removed the black plate that Steven had thought was Grandfather's actual visage. The mask came off, revealing a pale corpse-face topped with a glistening red crown where the top of the head used to be. Grandfather's familiar brown eyes were milky. They wept droplets of darkness that turned into a flood and folded Steven up with the absolute gloom of unlight.

Screaming, Steven felt the unlight burn into the palm of his hand like a vicious, twisting knife digging into his skin to make a hole. He had never felt any pain like this before. Then he felt nothing as he fell into the darkness.

《《——》》

Opening his eyes to the sound of the morning news and the glow of the lights in his hotel room, Steven rolled over on broken glass and stood up. His entire body felt as if it was on fire and every movement brought pain. He swayed on his feet and stood there for a moment. His Grandfather was gone and the lights were back on. He could hear cicadas so he knew he was still alive.

He laughed aloud. It was a harsh smoker's laugh.

Bending at the waist, he checked himself over to see if he was still in one piece. Everything was there, even though his lip was cut, his toes and nose were broken, and his torso was one solid, angry bruise.

Which meant that everything that had happened had been real.

"Is it over?" he asked himself.

He raised his hand to rub the weariness from his eyes and he paused, looking at it.

A single droplet of darkness sat just under the skin of his palm. Small tendrils of ebony radiated from the center of it, pointing to each of his fingers. It seemed that Grandfather had left a little piece of himself, a little piece of that old piss and vinegar and darkness with his grandson. Flesh of his flesh and blood of his blood. Why? Maybe because Grandfather always had to have the last word. Even in death.

Steven moaned and felt dread—there really had been no choice at all.

And the droplet grew.

About David M. Buhajla

David M. Buhajla is a writer and poet living in Arkansas with his wife Marci and his daughter Maya. His work is available in *Counterexample Poetics, Sex and Murder, Danse Macabre, Rose and Thorn Journal, The Gloaming Magazine, Death Head Grin* and the "Winter Canons" anthology from *Midwest Literary Magazine*.

GERM WARFARE

by Eric J. Guignard

What do you mean, *why are you here*?

You came to me, I didn't go to you. You're the one who's sick here. It's not me, Jack, it's you. I guarantee you that much; signed, sealed, and delivered.

Yes, I know I may look sick, people tell me that all the time. But I'm going to give you another guarantee—this'll be two, in case you're keeping track: *I'm the healthiest person you'll ever meet.*

Don't judge me like the others. Appearances, as you know, can be quite misleading. There's so much more going on that you simply cannot see.

People say I'm too skinny; they call me bulimic or anorexic.

I'm not bulimic. Bulimia is when the sufferer binges on food and then purges it out. I simply don't eat.

Nor am I anorexic. Anorexia is the fear of gaining weight. That's just ridiculous. Who worries about such things when the real horrors of the world surround us at every moment?

Oh, and when I say *surround*, I mean *live within.*

It's the parasites, the microbes, the creatures that live inside us.

They're eating me alive. They're eating *all* of us alive. Did you know that the human body is host to over ten thousand species and strains of germs and mold and bacteria? *Sweet Jehovah*, can you imagine them, coating your lungs and trespassing on your very breath in order to procreate and create bastard offspring?

And worms, oh so many worms. There are pinworms, tapeworms, yeastworms, hookworms, whipworms, even humaworms. Have you heard of humaworms before? They spread in your intestines, living undetected for years, but growing strong, growing to incredible lengths, twenty feet, thirty feet, forty feet, and more. Their size is boundless if left unchecked. The human host dies before the humaworm does, that's for sure.

Then there are flagellates, the very harbingers of disease, self-reproductive and ravenous. They eat of your marrow and nerves, like filthy vampires. They form algae and attach to your blood cells, travelling the vascular highways of the body. Flagellates can even be passed through saliva or sweat. God forbid some sick crone ever sneezes on you.

Oh, don't get me started on protozoas...

But you know all this, don't you?

Of course you do, I'm sorry. I don't mean to be condescending; I just tend to ramble some times. Everyone knows these things that I'm saying. Everyone knows their body is a sloppy all-you-can eat buffet for germs and bugs. Like a calf being fattened for the slaughter, our bodies grow plump and rich. Our bodies are a garden of delight to parasites. Heck, not just a garden, but a universe. We know it and we accept it—we are after all, just carefree hosts to bacterial rapists.

They're eating us alive from birth, these things. They drink and feast and spread, bugs and parasites and other creatures which even scientists with their high-and-mighty microscopes can't see or begin to understand. Think about it! There are organisms living inside our body which defies the rationale of even the greatest of scientific minds.

That's a fact, Jack.

And the world is perfectly happy to continue to let these things feed off of them. *Laissez Faire* to the microcosm.

But not me, no.

That's why I don't eat. I'm not starving myself, I'm starving *them*.

Are you surprised at what I say? Did you ever consider how else to defeat these monsters that live within us?

Did you know that when the body starves, it will eat itself? Essentially, deep down inside, every one of us hides a personal cannibal. To survive, the body needs protein and sugars and all the other building blocks of life. That means that when it runs out of these things, it will turn inwards and start to digest those blocks that already preexist. The body digests its own muscles and fat first...but so too, does it the bugs, devoured finally by the body's response system.

That's how I'll get them. I'll starve and they'll starve, too. The difference is that I'm stronger than any single-celled organism. I'll live, and they'll die.

I have no doubt I will outlast the parasites. It's survival of the fittest. You see, the land the microbes have settled will grow desolate, barren. They will compete for the withering resources of my flesh and organs, until they perish, one-by-one.

Yes, it's true they may become more desperate. They will struggle to survive, as all life does. They may even adapt or…

Never mind. It's like I told you—I'm stronger than they are.

Do you see this? Already, their home inside me has dried and forced them outwards to the surface. See this lump here? No, this other one on my arm. Yes, the stitches are sloppy—I put them in myself, and it's not easy to do in my state. But you can't trust doctors to do that sort of work on you. They're filled with the bugs themselves—hell, they're mind-controlled by the bugs. They would recognize me as a free-thinker, as having escaped the pattern of host for the creatures and they can't allow that. I think you know what they'd do to me if they discovered my freedom…

Ugh, you distracted me. What was I saying? My head hurts, the mites are scavenging—I think they're in my brain.

Oh, I was talking about the lump, the one I had to stitch up. Well, I sliced it open the other day. It wasn't any accident—I knew exactly what was going on. The lump was swelling like a pregnant whore, and I knew the parasites were retreating from my innards. They were being forced out, so as not to be digested by my starving body, and they were huddling under the outermost layer of my dermis, their number growing with other germ refugees. The lump grew and I took a razor and sliced it open. It only confirmed my suspicions. What came out of that lump was yellow and speckled and filled with shrieks and pleas. I had rid them from myself—I had killed off the sycophants, the leeches, the murderers of my beautiful, beautiful body. I was victor!

From there, I opened up the lumps on my chest as well, and my thigh and neck and face. More of the parasites oozed out—that's how I knew I was getting rid of them. They're dying and I'm living.

You need to do it as well, you know. Before the bugs tip the scales in their favor—before it's too late.

But baby steps might be in order. Not everyone is as strong as me.

There's a bottle of Lysol on the table. I have cups, if you'd like. I didn't drink it straight the first time—I'm not crazy. I watered it down, fifty-fifty. I felt it burning inside me, the acid eating away the bacteria, the fire of purification.

It worked wonderfully—even the ad on the bottle says so. See for yourself. The label reads: *Kills germs*…

True, I had a lot of bleeding inside, but I'm pretty sure it was the blood of the bacteria. I vomited out all of their dead corpses. I told you I'm a winner, Jack. I'm a survivor—don't ever forget that.

Oh, another thing. Did you know your hair and fingers are the filthiest parts of the human body? Who would have known! I would have thought it was the rectum, that portal for filth to make its great exodus. But the hair and fingers…

That's why I shaved all my hair, head and body. Easy enough and only sensible.

The fingers were a little more difficult, though. I bore no misconceptions as to how life would be much more difficult without fingers, so I compromised. I cut off only the tips, right at the juncture of the first knuckle. This way I can still live a normal life, but the germs can't hide under the nails or the cracks of my cuticles.

Like I said, it's a war. You gotta make sacrifices to win. These vermin never tackled someone like me before.

Why are you looking at me like that? Has the horror set in? Have I opened your eyes? Do you realize now the nightmares that cover every inch of your skin, scouring, feasting, sexing, defecating, all over you, inside and out?

Oh, and be careful what you breathe. God have mercy on your soul, should you inhale the wrong kind of toxins or microbes. I wear a respirator at all times—I only breathe fresh, clean oxygen from this here tank. I suppose in my case, there isn't actually much of a choice anyway—I burned off the inner lining of my lungs by inhaling hydrochloric acid.

I might have gone a bit far that time, but we can only grow from experience.

Speaking of inhaling, did you know that dust is seventy-five percent shed human skin? You heard me right—that's what you could be breathing in every second of every day. The filthy, germ-coated skin of other slobs, just floating in the air, waiting to find a new home, a new human host, to infect. You don't have to worry about that in my home, though. I scrape and bleach my skin every morning.

But anyway, that's why you're in the cellar. Sorry, I do tend to ramble for awhile, but I wanted to answer your question. I had to explain myself so you'd understand.

I'm working so hard to be cleansed, killing these things. I can't have you come into my house, infecting my environment. Your germs are strong right now, they're potent. They've outgrown you and they're looking for a new home, a new host. I can hear them, excited, scrambling and ready to pounce on the unsuspecting passerby. Even now, your skin, your hair; it's all falling off you and spreading the disease, the creatures.

I don't care that you were only selling magazine subscriptions. You're infected like the others. The parasites don't make particulars regarding your occupation in life.

That's a fact, Jack.

But I can help, if you let me. I offer the light of salvation, the proverbial hope for your very survival.

If you cleanse yourself, I will let you out.

Oh the others? Yes, sorry you must be confined with them, but that can't be helped. I'm not going down there to touch them. Look at the mold and rot on their bodies. Filthy and putrid, really. They were infected, just like you. What am I supposed to do, quarantine everyone individually? That's just silly. I don't have those kinds of resources.

But you're different, I can tell. You're reasonable. Not like that one in the brown uniform over in the corner. He came to make a so-called *delivery*. A delivery of lice and infection was more like it. I offered him help, but he refused. Even spit at me. I closed the door and cleansed myself in a bleach bath. I heard him screaming a week later, but then it stopped.

That other one—that one by your foot who's wearing a tie—tricked me. He wanted to sell me a vacuum cleaner, so I let him in. Of course, I let him in—at least he was *trying* to help clean the world...or so he claimed. The next thing I knew, he had poured a pile of soot onto my floor as some kind of twisted way of making a sales pitch. Lord! Can you imagine? Needless to say, his was a hopeless cause.

But you...again, you're different. I can tell. I think you're ready to start, Jack.

What will you begin with...the Lysol or the razor?

About Eric J. Guignard

Eric J. Guignard is an award-winning author and editor living in southern California.

He writes fiction short stories in the genres of horror, speculative, and young adult. He also writes research and knowledge-base articles in genealogy, woodworking, and ecology. Eric has been published in numerous print and online media, recently including publications in: *A Very Short Story competition* (first place), *Coscom Entertainment, Hall Brothers, SNM Horror Magazine, Another Realm, Indie Gypsy*, and many others. He is editor of the acclaimed anthology, *Dark Tales of Lost Civilizations* (Dark Moon Books).

When not writing, Eric designs and builds custom furniture and is also an amateur entomologist.

Most importantly, he is married to his high school sweetheart, Jeannette, and father to an adventuresome toddler son, Julian James.

MOUTHPIECE

by Mike Goddard

Not that it should matter and I mention it merely in passing, but due to being caught-up in a freak industrial accident four summers ago, I've developed a second mouth directly below my first.

With both mouths now wedged into such close proximity, I've been forced to grow a figure-of-eight pencil-moustache which accentuates the second orifice; effectively highlighting it in inky stubble.

Unfortunately, I'd been at the manager's stag-do the night before the accident and, although being tee-total, I somehow tested positive for laudanum. Of course that meant I couldn't cash in on any large settlement; but I still sued for enough to pay off my mortgage.

Back when I only had one mouth, I'd taken to hanging out at the local garden centre, never realizing it would be where I'd meet a willing wife. But since commenting on Maria's obscenely chomp-able pumpkin at the centre's annual vegetable show, we'd become besotted with each other.

Sublime courting, a modest marriage, and a delightful son followed...then the unfortunate accident at the Leighman Brothers Power Plant.

At first we found my mutation fun; I was able to kiss Maria's lips and her neck both at once if I strained, and at the risk of heaping on the sexual gruesomeness, two tongues and four lips does wonders for foreplay. "It's divine," Maria would tell me, "like sitting on a rampant octopus."

But that affection only came behind closed doors, when the sun had gone down. In public, around other people, Maria was not as delighted with my deformity. She wanted me to stay hidden; sequestered. And she wasn't the only one who felt that way.

I've always campaigned for equality and inclusion—an end to discrimination on arbitrary grounds. In short, I was not about to hide my face…and this was always going to present challenges. One by one, these challenges robbed me of my freedom.

First to go was my much needed outlet at the garden centre. The manager had asked me to stop my browsing. I said that was quite insulting. He'd answered that was unintentional but unavoidable—that I was scaring his customers away. When I got home and explained what had happened to Maria, she didn't offer consolation—she just nodded in the weary manner she had affected as of late.

«‹‹——››»

Today is our anniversary and I suggest we take a trip to the zoo. Bravely, Maria agrees. Traipsing around the zoo, each supporting a dead arm of the rotting cadaver that had once been our love, I can't help but feel our time is running out. As if on standby, disaster strikes when we pass the sloth enclosure and one beast clocks me, then stares wide-eyed and transfixed.

This is a sensitive situation and I don't want to distress the poor creature. I try to maintain soft eye contact and emit petting noises while stealthily edging away. And then I realize this is the wrong tactic. With all the pent up sadness of lonesome captivity mixed with the terror of seeing my face, the sloth falls from its branch and begins wailing.

A small crowd gathers, and a concerned human voice wafts into my ear, "Sir, would you mind stepping away, your extra mouth's distressing Maria."

"Maria?" I say, looking at my wife, feeling perplexed. "No, this is Maria."

"She's the zoo sloth, sir. That's her name, Maria. The one you're currently traumatizing."

A deluge of voices begin hinting I should leave and I am reminded why I rejected corrective surgery on my mouth—not to petrify animals you understand; but to stir up the crowd of intolerance and to fight for my rights. Unfortunately, I can not make a stand now, owing to the overwrought sloth.

I place a hand over my lower mouth and gently squeeze my way through the crowd, who I hear buzzing their usual guttural amusement mingling with my wife's sad breaths. I can feel their caustic vanity burning into my warped and twisted, bastard body, as the plaintive boohoo-ing of that blubbering sloth adds melancholy to a soundtrack already smoldering with pathos.

I squeeze Maria's hand and she pulls it away—but follows me out of duty and we head towards the Zooper Zebra Café for an Americano with hazelnut syrup. Inevitably, Maria begins explaining why our couplet doesn't work again whilst making me the gift of real tears.

I want to take her seriously, honestly I do, but I'm starving and this cookie's so delicious. I hold her gaze and pout concern while surreptitiously draining the flavor with my other mouth.

"You're still eating, you jerk!"

"No I'm not; I'm paying a—" and we watch a large biscuit crumb dive from my extra food-hole and land inside her mocha.

"Super—having two mouths just isn't enough; you need to cultivate poor table manners to guarantee absolute negative attention."

"You're dumping me, at least you could allow—" a rigid claw landing on my shoulder interrupts me; it's attached to a stocky adolescent in an ill-fitting monkey costume.

"Oi," he says meanly.

"Oh, hello."

The Monkey falters, apparently losing his momentum. But then he puffs back up and says, "Don't try that amiable mesmerizing hokum in public; you're scaring people."

"I beg your pardon Monkey-Man," I say, rising out of my chair with outrage: a bit of disability indignation, just the prescription I need to alleviate some strife.

But The Monkey says, "Now why the gallivanting fuck might you be standing, you two-mouthed prick?"

"Listen, you Ape," I scream in stereo as I raise my fists, "my feelings are at stake!"

My final memory of the exchange is a worn-out looking Maria jumping out of her chair and left-hooking me unexpectedly in the jaw. Even my own wife wants to punch me.

I come to and a policeman has me pinioned against the bricks and is peering earnestly into my face; evidently I've become delirious and vomited against the wall...after generating some sort of sorry fracas.

"You're not a maniac, are you?"

"No sir," I inform him.

"Why did you attack that youth?"

"I didn't...maybe my wife did."

"Where's the meth?"

"Huh?"

"Where's the angel dust?"

"Are angels dusty?" I answer, flummoxed.

"Sir," he says gleefully while snapping on two sheer surgical gloves, "I'm going to have to run a finger through your mouth...both of them."

And so I spend a night in jail before charges are dropped for lack of evidence.

«« —»»

Fifteen bitter years have passed and Maria is long gone, taking our son with her. I am alone in the quiet village. I never intended to rub my family's face in my political decisions. I've just latched on to this opportunity presented by fate to challenge society's vanity which is good for my pride. And if that discrimination comes from my loved-ones, then I'll have to accept it.

I've created a website in the hope of meeting some friends:

The Mouthpiece for Tragic Merricks and Radium Girls, calling victims of industrial mutations for casual networking and friendly, approachable and non-judgmental banter—message me, Stephan Berm, editor and victim.

Below my name is a portrait photo, in which I wear a crushed-velvet chocolate bowtie on a cream shirt and two approachable smiles, which I ensured reached my eyes.

So far, not one single hit, and I wonder: am I the only freak?

And just as I find myself utterly alone with nothing but stubborn regret, I hear the computer chime with a reassuring message alert.

About Mike Goddard

Mike Goddard enjoys working with elderly people. When he can't be found reading or writing, Mike is usually experimenting with scrambled egg variations (brie, shiitake mushrooms and chili-oil being a recent success).

For pleasure he cleans his wonderful, 1989 red Ford named '*Noy Nah*,' which means custard-apple in Thai. Mike's favorite mysterious creature is the Madagascan *Aye Aye*—his favorite graphic novel is Sam Keith's *The Maxx*.

Mike has only one mouth.

FILMLAND

by Stewart Horn

I know; the name sounds a bit grand, and you're probably expecting a big shiny story about movie stars and stuff. But it's just the place I work.

Filmland used to just be a DVD rental shop, but there's no money in that any more, so Dave the owner flung out a few racks and put a wee café at the back, so it's managed to keep going for now.

As jobs go, it's all right. I do the backshift Tuesday through Sunday; I get to take home any DVD's that are still in the shop at closing time, and it's certainly not what you'd call demanding. Most days I get up fairly early, never much past noon, and I drink coffee and slob around, maybe watch a movie or go online for a bit. I call myself *Famous Monster* online.

Anyway, I start work at three-thirty. That's round about when the teachers come in for their fix of senseless violence; then there's another wee rush of office workers, always wanting the newest thing, then it tails off.

After Alison the day girl goes home at six, it's just me and my *regulars*. You'll have heard guys called babe magnets—well I'm a nerd magnet. If any of you ladies have a thing for kinda chubby guys with bad personal hygiene and underdeveloped social skills, come into my shop between seven and nine or so any weeknight...there's always a good selection. It's like that Islamic heaven with the seventy-two virgins, if Allah had a sense of humor.

My job is to talk to the guys so they think they have lives, serve them microwaved pizzas and cans of diet fizzy pish, and let them try to out-geek me on obscure movie trivia. Every so often one of them will rent a movie, but that's not really why they come in.

Anyway, this thing that happened—the thing I need to tell you about. It was a Tuesday. Tuesdays are always dead, so I usually dust the shelves and put all the covers back in the right places, 'cause the punters are crap at that, and sometimes I'll even put a movie on for the last couple of hours, instead of those trailer discs we're meant to show all day.

So it was quite late, after ten anyway, and this girl comes in— small, dark hair, smartly dressed, by herself. That's unusual by the way: guys quite often come in on their own, but girls are always either half a couple or one of a flock. I've thought before that someone could do a PhD on social and cultural norms based on gender behavior in video rental shops. I would do it myself but I'd have to go back to Uni and finish my degree first. And I'd probably rather be ripped apart by cannibals.

So anyway, I was watching an early Argento movie, one of his Giallos, when this lassie came in. I gave her my standard complimentary nod/smile combo from behind the counter and went back to watching the screen, but she came right up to the counter.

"Excuse me," she said, earning smile number two, my more-attentive-and-making-eye-contact version.

"Hi, what're you after?" I asked. She was smiling back, but one of my special powers is *trouble radar*, and something in her face right then was causing a big red blip on my screen.

"Do you have a telephone I could use? I'm very sorry to bother you, but it's rather urgent."

"Sorry, no. Even I'm not allowed to use the shop phone." I really was sorry—her smile was as thin and brittle as ice—I thought if it broke she might burst into tears, or possibly try to gouge my eyes out. "There's a pay phone just across the road there."

She looked over her shoulder at the dark street through the shop window then back at me. "This is something of an emergency. I can give you some money for the call." The smile was still there but wrong—the eyes were too wide or something, and the red blip on my radar was flashing faster than ever.

"Tell you what," I said when I couldn't stand it any longer. "You can use my mobile, if it's…" I fished it out of my jeans.

"Thank you," she said. She grabbed it like she was drowning and I'd thrown her a rope.

"So long as you're not phoning Australia or something—I've not got very much credit."

She ignored that, turned away and made a call, and I heard snippets of her conversation while still half-watching my movie. *On the screen a blonde woman in evening dress was being menaced by an invisible assailant in black leather gloves.*

"...me..."

"...video shop...on Glasgow Road..."

I glanced from the screen to the girl and noticed that her jacket was a bit ripped—one sleeve was coming off. It was disconcerting because she was otherwise so neat.

"...yes..."

"...mobile..."

The black-gloved killer had a hand on the woman's neck now, and a shiny knife flashed into shot. I suddenly didn't want to watch it any more and I fumbled for the remote.

"... saw him!"

"...okay...here."

She turned back and handed me the phone just as I managed to stop the movie.

"Thank you very much. I'll browse for a while."

"No bother." Aye right. I was bothered as fuck. I wanted this maniac out the shop and back to whatever soap opera she lived in, right now.

I even thought about calling Dave, the guy who owns the shop, but what would I say? "Oh, hi Dave, it's Charlie. There's a girl in the shop, she's browsing the racks, and I'm scared."

So I sat and bit my nails and waited for it to be closing time so I would have an excuse to make her leave. There were only about 14¼ minutes to go when the door opened again and this massive guy came in—I mean properly massive; he had to duck and turn sideways to get through the door.

This time I could have felt justified calling Dave and saying, "There's a fucking troll in the shop! What do I do?" The troll scanned the shop, taking in the girl, the racks, the counter and me cowering behind it.

I was certain there was trouble coming and I'd already decided that they were welcome to all the DVD's, the money in the till and our entire stock of Butterkist, but she just ran up to him and gave him a hug. If I'd been the guy throwing the rope, he was the life-raft—a pretty big one too, like a thirty-seater. There was a whispered conversation and the giant glanced over at me again.

A moment later he was walking towards me, and my trouble-radar screen exploded. It was like having a dinosaur bearing down on me, albeit one in a large nicely tailored suit.

"We appreciate your assistance," he said, his voice surprisingly soft. "However…" I think he paused here deliberately to let me worry about what he might say next. My best guess was *You've seen our faces so I'm afraid I'll have to kill you. Sorry.*

Instead, he said, "You have not seen us. We have not been in this shop or this area of the city at all. I cannot see a security camera. Is it hidden somewhere?"

"There isn't one," I said, before having time to think about what the fuck I was saying. I did have enough time call Dave a cheapskate bastard in my mind though.

"Good," he said. He laid a hand on the counter and I felt my eye drawn to it—he could have fit it round my head and probably squashed it like a rotten apple. "Forget us and you will never see us again. Tell me you understand."

"I understand."

He looked me up and down and I thought perhaps he hadn't quite made up his mind about me yet. He all but opened my mouth to examine my teeth. By now the girl had crept up behind him and was watching with interest. All her anxiety seemed to have vanished, lucky bitch.

Eventually he nodded and looked me in the eye. "Good," he said again, and turned to leave. The girl gave me a more relaxed and sympathetic smile than she'd managed earlier, the way you might smile at someone who's just survived a really bad car crash. Then she followed Gigantor out the front door.

I sat behind the counter for ages after they'd gone, staring at the glass door and the big windows on either side. Through the glass I could see across the street to the railway station and the other shops, all closed, nothing looking real in the street lights. There were no people, and only a couple of cars went past in however long I sat there in my little bubble of light. I knew I had to lock up and go home, but the darkness outside seemed to be staring back at me, daring me to get closer. After an age I felt my muscles begin to unknot themselves and only then realized how tense I had been. Even though, now that I tell it, at that point nothing had actually happened.

I took a deep breath, stood up and walked round the counter, taking the keys out of my pocket as I went. I walked towards the door, keys held in front of me like a talisman, but stopped again a couple of feet away. All I had to do was reach out, insert the key and turn it, and everything would be okay again, but I had this vision of a clawed hand bursting through the glass and grabbing my wrist if I got close enough to let it. I don't know how long I stood there, staring into that darkness, but finally I thrust the key in and turned it as quickly as I could. It stuck a little as it often did and I felt the panic rise before the lock clicked into place. At that moment somebody ran past the window, impossibly fast and inches from the glass, and I nearly shat my pants.

"Fuck!" I shouted, jumping backwards, and "Jesus fuck!" I breathed hard, swore again, and smiled at myself. He'd given me a hell of a fright, but just seeing another human being had broken the spell, brought me back to reality. I even imagined the jolly conversation we would have if I left the shop and saw him standing at the bus stop:

You won't believe how big a fright I got when you ran past the shop
Sorry, man, I thought there was a bus coming
No worries, I was just locking the door when you whizzed by me; nearly shit myself

I finished locking up and did my final check-around routine, all the time talking to myself, mainly telling myself what a diddy I was for getting so worked up over nothing. Even so, I was still tense when I left the shop. I looked around the dark and deserted street before locking the door again from the outside and pulling down the shutters.

I looked round some more as I started the short walk home, and I'm pretty sure I glanced over my shoulder a few times on the way. There are two little alleys I have to pass, and I'm always a bit wary of them, even though the crime rate in this part of town is almost zero. Tonight I kept my eyes firmly ahead as I passed them, but looked behind me again afterwards, just in case.

My apartment building has eight flats in it, two on each of the four floors. I live in a one bedroom flat on the second-to-top floor, and I have no idea who my neighbors are. It's a good setup; it suits my personality.

When I opened the door of the stairwell that night I thought there was a funny smell. I couldn't place it, though my first thought was that someone's dog had crapped in the apartment building. It was that kind of smell, but not exactly right. It got stronger as I went up the stairs, and I started to get more subtle notes in it, still with an essence of shit dominating though.

By the time I reached my floor it was strong enough to make me gag, with still no indication where it might be coming from. I was about to go into my flat and forget all about it when I heard a noise from the next floor up. It was a kind of heavy and ragged breathing. I guessed that my upstairs neighbor was too drunk to get into his flat and had passed out on the landing and most likely shit himself. That's happened before. I stood undecided for a moment, then headed upstairs to see if I could help.

"All right up there?" I called, starting to climb the last flight. There were noises from above: something like a pig grunting, something heavy moving or being moved, a slamming door, silence. I turned on the half-landing and looked up the last few steps. At first I just thought how red everything was—it looked like Jackson Pollock had done an installation in the stairwell but only remembered to bring red paint.

Despite the sick, sinking feeling in my gut, I walked up a few more steps, shoes sticking to the stairs, and I could see that the red stuff wasn't all liquid. There were *bits* scattered about, little gristly things like a butcher's discards. I stopped a couple of steps from the top and saw a bloody trail leading across the landing and vanishing underneath the door on my right. I stared at the door, made of simple paneled wood, so normal, familiar and innocent, apart from the stains.

Among the rest of the mess, the one object that caught my eye, the biggest, the most easily identifiable, and the one that has stuck in my brain like a cancer: *the hand*. It looked fake, something you might buy in a joke shop at Halloween, with its ripped flesh, protruding shards of splintered bone and unrealistic red stains. Mainly it didn't look real because it was *too big*.

I thought of the hand that had lain on the counter in my shop less than an hour before, attached to the unassailable man-mountain I had been so afraid of. I stared at the hand and everything else, my mind buckling under the weight of carnage, trying to make sense of it all, but I felt overloaded.

I'm not known for my quick decision-making, or quick anything for that matter, so I might have stood there all night if nothing else had happened, but then there was a noise from behind the door. I've no idea what the noise was—maybe I never knew or maybe the memory got lost among all the other stuff.

Whether it was the noise, the hand, or just the sight of the bloody door, I turned tail and ran like fuck. I ran as if every demon of hell was chasing me. I sprinted down the stairs, past my own door and onwards and downwards. I almost screamed when I heard a mighty crash from above—something like the sound a door makes when something big and scary charges through it and reduces it to kindling.

A moment later I was back out in the empty night, heading nowhere in particular except away from that building as fast as I could, not looking behind me even when I heard a howl—a fucking proper horror movie howl, the kind that's too clichéd to be scary on screen, but with a bowel-loosening effect in real life.

I didn't slow down when the inevitable stitch in my side kicked in, or when my legs started to ache, or when my lungs felt as though they were on fire, and definitely not when I heard something closing behind me. It was close enough that I could hear it breathe, hear its pads on the tarmac, hear a growl start to build in its throat.

I closed my eyes, still running, tripped over the pavement and sprawled on my belly, rolling and scraping and leaving a trail of skin and blood. The thing behind me had pounced at the same moment and it flew right over me, close enough for me to smell it, and feel the heat of it, and I heard it land heavily in front of me. I couldn't scream, or beg, or move, even breathing was hard work. Every part of me hurt, and I remember thinking *fuck it, just eat me then.*

I managed to lift my head and saw it for the first time as it slowed and turned to face me.

If I had expected a giant wolf, I wasn't that far off the mark. It was more like the shape of a hyena, but the size of a rhino, and absolutely black, apart from the eyes which were an anachronistic light blue. It didn't seem in such a hurry now that I'd given up running, and it raised its massive head and howled.

That sound, up close like that, was the most terrifying thing I've ever experienced—it felt like freezing hands suddenly clutching my kidneys, searing through centuries of civilization and speaking directly to the part of me that used to hide in the forest and dread the stench of the carnivore. As the beast padded towards me, I knew it was an anticlimax. I knew I was going to die, and expected that it would hurt— I only hoped it wouldn't take long and that the thing wouldn't howl again until I was properly dead and wouldn't hear it.

It was almost on me, blue eyes locked on mine, when suddenly it vanished, and there was a crunching noise from somewhere to my left.

I turned to look and saw it clumsily getting to its feet—the beast had somehow been thrown against the brick wall bordering the road.

I looked around to see what could have done it but there was nothing obvious, till a flash of something whizzed past me and slammed into the beast again. This time the creature didn't hit the wall but was thrown at least thirty feet down the street, rolling and grunting as it landed.

Then, miraculously, the girl from the shop was standing in front of me. She grabbed me by the jacket and lifted me to my feet like I was four years old. I'm quite chunky; she must have been stronger than she looked.

"Are you hurt?" she asked.

I couldn't answer, because I didn't know yet. I was busy adjusting my definition of *hurt*. My limbs were all still attached and when she let me go I didn't fall down—scraped and bleeding didn't count. Over her shoulder I saw the creature get up and start moving again. I made a noise and pointed. She looked behind her and back at me.

"Don't go away," she said. She accelerated like a rocket towards the staggering beast and hit it like a cannonball, driving it into another wall with a crunch that must have been some bones, probably a skull. I finally found my voice.

"I can't believe this," I said.

"Sorry about that," she said, beside me again. "He's not supposed to be here."

"He's not supposed be *anywhere*; he's not supposed to fucking *exist*," I said, still watching the now inert creature in case it got up again. She checked me over, lifting my arms to look underneath. For the second time that night I felt like a bull at market.

"You're fine," she announced. "You should go to the police now. If you didn't, it would seem suspicious." She looked me straight in the eye. "You still haven't seen us though, remember?"

"What is that thing I just didn't see? And who are you?"

113

She rolled her eyes. "Plebs are so nosey these days. I would just have let him eat you, if it wasn't for the paperwork. Now listen carefully; this is what you are going to say: You saw the mess in your building, panicked, and ran away. When you calmed down enough, you went to the police station to report it. Nothing else happened."

When she said it, it sounded true—I almost believed it. But then I asked, "What happened to the big guy? The guy from the shop."

"Nobody came into your shop tonight." She was smiling now. I was well out of my depth and gave in.

"Oh aye, I forgot."

Then she was gone, and so was the black thing that had tried to eat me. I fell back into my normal mode for a while: indecision and inaction. Then I went to the police.

I'm not sure what I told them, but they kept me in and asked me a lot of questions I couldn't answer. Days later, when they finally decided I was innocent, they sent me to a hotel until my flat was fit for use again—I don't know what they did with it but it was still a hell of a mess when I got back.

That was last week. Now I don't feel safe in Filmland when it gets dark and the street is quiet. Outside the glass door and big windows I imagine people...and *things*...hunting each other, with only that fragile film of glass keeping them from all us Normals. I get twitchy walking home and I never, ever turn my head and look behind me.

At home I don't sleep, but lie staring at the ceiling, knowing that anything, *anything* could be on the other side of those few inches of wood and plaster.

There are images that haunt me, both awake and asleep, and I keep thinking: if there is some kind of war going on, am I in it? Have I taken sides?

About Stewart Horn

Stewart Horn is a professional musician based in Glasgow, Scotland. He has had a passion for horror since childhood but has only recently started to share his own fiction with the world. He enjoys contrasting dark subject matter with the dryly humorous delivery typical of Glaswegians.

CLAWED SOD

by Christian A. Larsen

"Maxie, you're a good guy," said Mr. Barlow. "And I really don't want to fire you, but if you don't shape up and knock off the drinking, I'll throw you out on your ass, sure as shootin'."

"Yessir, Mr. Barlow," answered Maxie, tugging at the cuff on his sweat-soaked shirt. It was reflexive, meant to give him something to look at besides Mr. Barlow and something to think about besides his drunkenness, but the button popped off his sleeve, clattering on the floor in front of his boss's shoe. His life was falling apart. His shirt might as well, too.

"You don't have to deal with the families coming in here, complaining about the tire marks in the grass, or the weeds around the headstones," the boss continued. "Why, just this morning I found an empty case of beer by a new grave with crushed cans strewn all over the place..."

"That wasn't me, Mr. Barlow."

"No, but you didn't clean it up, either."

Maxie felt pretty bad for his drinking, and how it got Mr. Barlow in trouble with the visitors at the cemetery, but he wasn't a night watchman, and he couldn't set everything back to rights every morning before funerals started rolling down the single-lane blacktop at five-miles-an-hour. He had no intention of arguing, though. Maxie had enough to be sorry for.

"I apologize, Mr. Barlow. Really, I do."

"I know, Maxie," said Mr. Barlow, patting Maxie's shoulder. "If I can help you, you know, just let me know, but in the meantime, you need to do your job, or you'll be out of one, you got me?"

"Yessir, Mr. Barlow. You bet." He stood there, tracing the seams in the outdated office paneling with his eyes, waiting for Mr. Barlow to say something. A new layer of sweat started pearling on his forehead.

"That's it, Maxie. I'll see you later. Oh, and be sure to bring plenty of water with you on your Gator. It's gonna be a hot one today, isn't it? And humid."

"Looks that way, Mr. Barlow," answered Maxie, doing everything in his power to keep from running out of his boss's office. He felt like he was going to get swatted on his butt like a kid if he didn't hurry, but he didn't want to look like he was in a hurry. *Even drunks on their last luck have a little self-respect,* Maxie thought, *a very little*.

Mowing had been tops on his list, but after his talk with Mr. Barlow, he decided he should go and clean up the beer cans cluttering up Section J. It was the quickest way to show Mr. Barlow that he was paying attention.

He was careful to stay on the blacktop. Or what used to be blacktop. It was so paled with sunshine, pebbling and scaling, what remained was more a sickly white, like a leprosy patient made of asphalt. Occasionally, Maxie would try to patch it up, but it was a losing cause, and Mr. Barlow knew it, so Maxie never took any of the blame for its condition. Driving on the grass, though, that really riled up the boss, so Maxie drove his Gator as carefully as he could, like a child with a new coloring book, staying in the lines. His buzz was wearing off, though, and his nerves were as frayed as his cemetery overalls. It took forever to drive out to Section J.

The Gator lurched to a halt, jostling the tools and equipment (and bottles) in back. He could see why Mr. Barlow was pissed. It wasn't just a little garbage. Somebody had really tied one on last night, and no mistake. He could see it in his head just like one of those detectives on CSI. The guy (or girl, but he'd never seen a girl put away that many beers before) sat down against the back of the headstone, destroyed the case of beer, and hobbled off into the night. The grass was so dry that the guy's footprints were still pressed into the lawn. So was his ass-print.

Maxie started grabbing garbage and tossing it into a bag. As much as it was, at least there wasn't any damage. Vandals sometimes created days of work for him in a single, brainless second, but the only defacement Maxie found was a piece of paper stuck to the headstone with a wad of gum. It was a lined piece of notebook paper, folded in a square. He picked off the gum with a single, yellowed fingernail and unfolded his find with a genuine sense of anticipation.

Pete,

I miss you man. You were the only thing standing between me and hell. Can you believe Mom hasn't been out here since the funeral? A whole year since you've been gone. I hope you're a happy camper now, wherever you are.

Forever your bro,
Owen

Maxie felt like putting it back, but he'd catch hell for it from Mr. Barlow. Notes stuck to headstones with gum were a no-no, but he didn't want to just throw it away. Better to tuck it between the grass and the front of the headstone, and let nature take care of it.

He tossed the sack of trash into the back of the Gator and walked around the headstone, a nice big one, which didn't surprise him because parents tended to splurge on kids who died young. And this one did. Pete Sachs was nineteen when he died a year ago, but that wasn't what grabbed Maxie's heart and squeezed.

A dry, stiff-looking hand and arm were sticking up out of the grass. Four of its long fingernails were crusted with clay and grime; the fifth nail was missing. The filthy cuff of a cheap blue suit sleeve was half rolled down and filled with dirt.

His own hand was trembling as he reached for his hip flask, never taking his eyes off the bony hand sticking out of the ground. He could feel the walls over his arteries bulging with each quickened beat of his heart, and cold sweat collected like corpse dew on his forehead. He needed a drink almost as bad as he needed this to not be happening. He half-heartedly swallowed a shot, but it just made a blotch of nausea spread outward from his navel.

That kid's hand had somehow worked its way free of a casket and cement vault, not to mention about six-feet of earth. It wasn't a fresh burial—Pete Sachs had died a year ago, thereabouts—and no one else had seen the hand all that time, so it wasn't Maxie's fault. The kid had been buried. Completely.

So, Maxie wondered, *what's he doing above ground now, even if it's just the hand?*

117

He crept carefully forward, as if some sudden movement would make the hand dart back down into the grave like a garter snake. As he got closer, he slowed down even more, afraid now that the hand would grab him and drag him down into the grave with it, but it didn't move. It looked just the same, out of place but not supernatural by any means. Maxie nudged it with his boot, just to make sure he wasn't hallucinating, and the limb waved in the hot summer breeze, *mocking* him with its presence.

Stumbling backward, Maxie reached for the Gator, ready to ride hell bent for leather back toward the groundskeeper's shed, where he kept all his best liquor, but when he keyed the ignition he looked over his shoulder to see if the hand was somehow crawling after him, and it was gone, not a trace to be seen, except for a rabbit-hole sized rift in the sod. Maxie decided he still needed that drink, just to get through the morning.

On his way to the shed, he thought better of it, and decided to show Mr. Barlow what he found. When he pulled the Gator up to the office building, his boss was waiting at the door. Mr. Barlow could obviously hear the Gator coming down the road, and Maxie knew that his presence at the office at this hour would tip his boss that something was wrong.

"Mr. Barlow, Mr. Barlow," Maxie spat out, panting like a dog. "There's something you ought to see!"

"This had better be important. Can you drive me there?" asked Mr. Barlow, squinting at the sun. He didn't want to walk anywhere if he could help it.

Maxie swallowed hard. He really wanted a drink, but it would have to wait. When he was done with whatever was waiting for him back in Section J, he would drink as much as he could handle. For Maxie Miller, even on a bad day, that was quite a lot.

"What do you have to show me?" asked Mr. Barlow as they sped toward the back of the cemetery on Maxie's Gator.

Maxie was a drunk and a coward, but he wasn't a fool. Mr. Barlow would fire him on the spot if he tried to tell him. "You need to see it for yourself, sir."

Trying not to hurry too much, Maxie pressed the Gator as fast as he dared to go with Mr. Barlow on board. It wouldn't do to rut the grass, or even worse, pitch his boss off the side on a hard turn, but he wanted to get there so badly!

But when they pulled up to the headstone, the hand wasn't there, and Maxie could have kicked himself. Now he had to come up with something to explain why he'd dragged Mr. Barlow out to Section J in the blazing heat.

"Maxie?"

"Uh, yeah, Mr. Barlow, you see that hole in the grass there?"

"I forgot my glasses in the office, but I believe you."

"Well, it looks like we've got rabbits. Do you want me to lay down poison or traps?"

"Did you really need to bring me out here to ask me that, Maxie? I know you're a hard worker...when you're sober. You don't need to prove that to me. You use whatever you think will do the trick, I guess."

Maxie felt like an idiot. He drove Mr. Barlow back to the office almost as fast as he drove him out, his face burning up with embarrassment. The ride was as quiet heading back as it was heading out, but it was somehow more solemn, and Maxie could just feel Mr. Barlow judging him. Maybe it was more like 'evaluating', but it still made Maxie shrink into his shoes, and he felt a rush of relief when Mr. Barlow disappeared into the office building, allowing Maxie to double back to the Sachs kid's grave.

The Gator's tires were grinding a rut in the already crumbling road back out to Section J. Everything, "rabbit" hole and all, seemed as normal as could be. Maxie shifted the Gator into park and stepped onto the grass to take a closer look with a shovel in his hand. Maybe it was a rabbit hole, but he needed some insurance in case it wasn't.

But when he stepped next to the grave stone, the ground started to squirm, like the earth underneath was boiling, and slowly, inexorably, the hand periscoped back up, it's palm facing the trembling groundskeeper with the fingers curling over like a mop of hair. Maxie hadn't noticed before, but a grubby class ring sat askance on its third finger, the chipped blue stone shining dully in the midday sun like the eye of a corpse.

Maxie brought the flat end of the shovel's blade down on the hand like a hammer on a nail, biting his lip to focus on something, anything other than his terror. There was a horrible crunching sound and the hand went down, but not straight into the hole. It was flat against the ground now, its fingers bent in all sorts of impossible angles.

119

The hand did not withdraw, even when Maxie poked at it with the blade of the shovel. It looked like it was sunning its ghostly pale skin, now as hard as plastic after fermenting for a year in formaldehyde.

The engine was still running on the Gator, and Maxie wasted no time heading back to the shed where he could ply his nerves with his liquor stash. He may have even driven on the grass. Mr. Barlow could deal with him later. He kept replaying everything he'd seen that morning in his head, and by the time he pulled the Gator into the gravel lot and shut off the engine, he'd determined two things. First, there really was a hand, and second, it only seemed to pull its whack-a-mole maneuver when somebody was actually on the grave, or very close to it.

There was no air-conditioning in his shed, but it was very cool and dark, the perfect place to do a little drinking before he decided what should come next. Sitting with his back to his steel tool cabinet, Maxie finished off most of a bottle of Grey Goose as a memory came creeping back from his early childhood of his grandmother warning him not to hit his mother again:

"Hit your mother like 'at again, an' you'll regret it."

"Why, Grammy?" asked the young Maxie.

"'Cause your hand'll stick up out of your grave, an' everyone'll know whatcha did, that's why."

He didn't argue with her. If Grammy said it, it was the truth, at least as true as a four-year-old needed it to be. He imagined a maintenance worker bumping into a skeletal arm with his lawnmower, which seemed neither funny nor frightening to him at the time. He just wondered why he'd care if he was dead already. Now that he was grown-up and on the other end of the lawnmower, it was frightening. But it was becoming less so.

Maybe it was the alcohol, and then again, maybe it was the simple realization that the hand hadn't done anything to him, other than just be. It wasn't chasing after him. It wasn't trying to eat his brains. It didn't even seem to mind that he mashed it with a shovel. Heck, the hand treated him better than most of his so-called friends, and for his part, he felt a custodial concern for the Sachs' kid, to whom the hand belonged. He always thought of himself as the super for a growing community, even if it was a necropolis, and now was his chance to really help one of the tenants.

"What was it the note said?" whispered Maxie. "That his mom hadn't been out to visit the grave since the burial? Maxie, you smart devil, you just might be able to fix this thing!"

He waited until Mr. Barlow had left for the day and sneaked into the record room to look up the decedent's family contact info. There it was: *Ione Sachs. Mother.* He scribbled down her name and address, drove home to shower and change, and then went to find her. It didn't take long. Maxie had been a taxi driver in town before he lost his license the first time for a DUI, so he knew his way around. She lived in a bungalow on the edge of Brickton, and someone was home—the lights were still on, anyway.

Maxie felt like his tie was choking him. He pinched the knot away from his throat and rang the doorbell. Even with the sun down, it was still hot as ring baloney. It took forever before he heard footsteps, and they did not belong to a woman.

"Yeah?" asked the man who answered the door. "You sellin' sumpin' or want me to switch gods? Which is it?"

He was rough-looking, thick-limbed and dressed in a wife-beater and shorts, but it was his demeanor that raised Maxie's hackles. He was a rough-looking guy, too, but he wasn't a bully or a lout, even when he was tight.

"Mrs. Sachs home?"

A cloud of annoyance settled over the man's face, a face that had already looked annoyed enough. "There is no Mrs. Sachs. It's Mrs. Corcoran now. I'm Mr. Corcoran. Can I help you?"

"I'm from Brickton Cemetery. Name's Maxie Miller."

"You lookin' for money?"

"No, sir. I just need Mrs. Sachs—sorry, Mrs. Corcoran—to come to the office to sign some paperwork. Left over from the funeral last year. I know it's late, but there's state regulations and it could mean a small refund of some of the burial costs." It was a flimsy excuse, but as soon as Mr. Corcoran determined Maxie wasn't after his money, he didn't care what he had to say.

"Ione!" bellowed Mr. Corcoran. He pronounced it 'I own'.

She was a still a young woman, somewhere around forty, but with that rode-hard-and-put-away-wet look that Maxie supposed he had, too, from drinking and smoking. Her teeth were starting to go, too. Meth, maybe, or maybe just bad hygiene born of not caring anymore. It didn't take much convincing for Ione to climb in the car with Maxie, and he felt a little guilty at the deception, but if he could bring a little happiness back to the family, he'd try.

The ride to the cemetery was quiet, and she didn't ask many questions, and the ones she did ask didn't require answers that raised her suspicions. When she asked him why they weren't going to the office, though, she did sound a little worried, and that's when he came clean, at least as much as he could.

"Your son, not Peter, but the other one, Owen...he was here last night. Left quite a mess at his brother's grave. And a note. It said you hadn't been out here to see Peter's grave since he was buried."

"You can take the mess up with Owen," said Ione. "I'm not responsible for that kid anymore."

"No one's in any trouble, except maybe Peter."

"Huh?"

Maxie stepped out of the Chrysler, which was almost as wide as the road itself, and walked around to let Ione out of the passenger side. His buzz was almost completely faded. He felt good about himself, and not just because he was sober. He was doing a good deed that only he could do. He felt important for the first time since he graduated high school, and that was longer ago than he'd like to admit.

"Over here," he said, taking Ione by the hand. Despite her hard miles, she was still a pretty woman.

They stepped to the edge of the grave, but Ione was looking around so disinterestedly that she really didn't notice the ground start to move around the hole, like a mouth getting ready to spit. The hand thrust up with more purpose than Maxie had seen it do before, but instead of standing dumbly at attention, it clamped down hard on Mrs. Corcoran's ankle, wrapping its ruined fingers around her livid flesh and pulling.

That's when she started screaming.

Maxie grabbed onto her with both arms, afraid to get too close to the hand himself, but invested too deeply to let go. He had brought her to the brink. It was his fault.

"Don't let me go!" she shrieked, looking into Maxie's eyes with a desperation that only one's own mortality could bring out.

"Hang on, Mrs. Sa—I mean, Mrs. Corcoran!" Maxie ordered. He wondered why it was so important now that he get her name right. He looked around to see if there was anything he could use to help her, but his Gator was locked up, and his trunk was full of junk. Useless.

Besides, he'd have to let her go, and by the time he got back, she'd probably be gone.

When he looked back, he saw that she was shorter. Not shorter, but swallowed to the knees, like the graveyard was eating her. But it wasn't. The rest of the cemetery was as quiet as, well, a graveyard. It was Peter Sachs that was doing this, doing this to his own mother. Maxie realized he was sobbing. "Peter, don't do this!"

Ione slipped waist deep in the earth, and her death grip brought Maxie crashing to the ground. Her grip finally jarred loose, and Maxie wrapped his arms under her armpits, bringing him to the lip of the opening.

"I gotcha, Mrs. Corcoran!" But as soon as he'd said it, it became a lie. There were a few muffled screams under the earth, and it sounded to Maxie like she'd said, "Oh Peter, I'm sorry! So sorry!" before everything fell silent.

Maxie's mouth felt like cotton. He needed a drink worse than he'd ever needed a drink before, but not alcohol. He wanted water. There was a bottle in his front seat. He'd managed to uncap and dump some down his throat before he started gagging on his drymouth. He sat there, chugging the water with the dome light on and the car door dinging when a bicycle skidded up alongside the beat-up Chrysler.

"Hey, you okay?" asked the teenage boy. He had no business being here, but truth be told, neither did Maxie.

"No. You shouldn't be here."

"Yes, I should. I came to watch. My name's Owen Sachs, and that's my brother's grave."

"*You're* Owen Sachs?"

"What you just saw there? My mom, she had it coming. She'd been letting Corcoran do stuff to us for years. Corcoran finally killed Peter, but nobody could prove it. That was a year ago, and that's when he turned his sights on me. He's a monster, all the way. And she knew and she didn't do anything to stop him. She protected him instead of us."

He started to cry, pointing at the opening in the ground. "That was my mother. We were her boys. Her *babies*. What you just witnessed, mister? She deserved that. Every bit. Thanks for bringing her here. I'd been trying for a year. Peter and I had almost given up."

Maxie looked down at the claw marks that the mother left in the sod and sighed. "You're welcome."

123

About Christian A. Larsen

Christian Larsen writes short science-fiction, horror, and dark fantasy stories that have appeared in critically-acclaimed magazines and anthologies such as *Jersey Devil Press, Diagonal Proof,* and *Midnight Screaming.* His short story, "Bast," was published in *What Fears Become* (Imajin Books) and placed second in the 2011 Preditors & Editors™ readers poll for best short horror fiction. Mr. Larsen received his bachelor of science from the University of Illinois and studied secondary English education at National-Louis University. Follow him on Twitter @exlibrislarsen or visit exlibrislarsen.com.

SKELF

by John Forth

A mile or so from her grandmother's house, Sarah finally flagged down a ride. At least she would spare herself the worst of the rain. It came on without warning late in the afternoon, the heavy drops stuttering hard against the bonnet and windscreen, almost drowning out the casual chatter of the woman who had picked her up.

"Caught you by surprise, eh?" the driver said. "Nothing worse than being stuck out in the weather like this when you're not dressed for it. Doubt it'll last, though. Looks like it's just going to blow over. See the skies ahead?"

Sarah glanced through the glass at the melting world. The road had the consistency of damp mud, the trees on either side bent and weeping under the onslaught from above, but ahead the cement-shaded clouds broke to reveal a clear, if darkening, sky.

Each dip in the road left Sarah's stomach hanging somewhere behind, despite the woman's relatively relaxed speed. Every fresh corner revealed a new tangle of ugly branches, but before long, Sarah noticed the first of the wooden posts that marked the edge of her grandmother's property. If there had ever been a fence attached to those rotted stumps it was long gone, but at irregular intervals forgotten tangles of yellow police tape fluttered in the wind.

As they crested a fresh rise, the car stereo emitted a grunt of static, a fragment of voice, then died again. "Almost had it then," the woman said with the glee of an amateur butterfly catcher, flailing at the signal only for it to flutter out of reach again. "Must be coming back to civilization. I guess you like living out here, though."

"It's just over this next hill," Sarah said, straining forward against her seatbelt. They were almost beneath the cloudless patch of sky now, and the rain was beginning to ease off. Through the streaks on the glass, she could just make out the muddy turn-off which led to her grandmother's house. As the woman rolled her vehicle to a halt, the stereo barked out a few seconds of a news broadcast. Having to control the shaking in her hands, Sarah fumbled with the seatbelt release.

"I can take you up to the front door," the woman said, looking through the driver's side window at the ragged, overgrown path. "I don't mind."

Sarah, free of her restraint, shook her head. "It's okay, thank you. Believe me, if you went down there you'd never make it back." The mud; she meant the mud, of course. Sarah reached for the door handle, keen to be away before the radio found its voice entirely. "You've been too kind."

Outside, the rain had abated, but constant streams still poured from the branches above. The strong scent of damp wood and vegetation was almost overwhelming, the air so much fresher than the sweat-tinged halls of the institute. As the red tail-lights of the car disappeared behind a shimmering curtain of rain, Sarah turned to the cave of branches and leaves that hung over the path, and stepped across the boundary onto her grandmother's territory.

All around, the woodland sighed as it allowed itself to drip dry. What little light made it through the clouds failed to penetrate the densely locked fingers of the canopy. The path was a minefield of puddles waiting to slop their icy water over and into her stolen trainers. Sarah walked carefully over ground which bubbled and crackled beneath her feet. Once she almost stumbled off the path and into a black gap between the trees and she had the sense that her surroundings were trying to trick her. There were many paths through these woods— her grandmother had shown her just a handful—and some led to places where it wasn't safe to wander alone. The last time Sarah was here, fleeing blindly away from the house, she'd almost tumbled onto one of those shifting paths. From time to time over the past nine years she wished that she had.

Was the house built on one of the strange clearings which dotted the woods? Spotting its tainted white walls through gaps in the foliage, she couldn't help but wonder. There certainly didn't appear to be any sign that the broad space in which the house sat had been cleared by man, no tell-tale trunk stumps or irregularly cut-back branches. If anything, the woods gave the impression that they had grown around the house, scared to come any closer. The structure slumped at the centre of its domain like a massive albino toad with white columns in place of arms, a half-dozen windows instead of eyes.

126

She'd worried that maybe someone had bought the house during her absence, but one look told her that it had lain neglected all these years. Around the porch, overgrown grass snaked and writhed; scabs of brickwork were visible where the plaster had cracked and fallen away. The front door lay open, the interior of the hall stained by the elements. The wind through the open house leant a voice to the structure, though Sarah couldn't tell if it were calling to her, or warning her away.

Pulling her oversized sweatshirt tight around her twig of a body, Sarah walked up the cracked and leaning steps to the porch. Inside, the sounds of the woodland were muted but still they groaned, as if the trees were leaning forward to see what might happen next. The hallway was as she remembered it—floral wallpaper, sideboards sturdy enough to survive a nuclear blast nonetheless creaking beneath a weight of incongruous crockery and ornaments—but the color had been drained by the elements.

Whoever had been through the house last—the police, forensics, an estate agent doomed to have the property on his books forever—had left all of the doors open, and as she passed through, Sarah caught glimpses of the various rooms. In a small parlor, two high-backed chairs faced each other eternally; only cobwebs hung from the hooks in the cupboard. In the living room, she saw the grand wood and leather chair in which her grandmother used to sit. With her white moss of hair and thick wool blankets, the old woman sometimes appeared to be a part of the chair, the lines of her face as defined as those on the grain of the wood. Many times Sarah would sit on the rug in front of her grandmother, listening to croaked stories of the wood and the marsh and the things—things with names Sarah could barely pronounce then or now—she claimed to have seen when she was a child.

Sarah had been rapt, but her mother was less impressed. "Don't listen to your grandmother's tales," she'd told Sarah. "The things she thinks she remembers, well, she's an old woman. There are her memories, then there are stories she heard, things she read, things that happened to other people. Sometimes she gets confused."

Reaching the stairs to the second floor, Sarah started to ascend. There must have been a window open up there somewhere, permitting a draft to ruffle her straw hair. Drifts of dead leaves lay against the skirting of the upper landing, and the banister had rotted away to the point of collapse.

The door to Sarah's bedroom, last on the left, stood ajar and from the noise which came through, she fancied that it may well have opened straight on to the woods. But no, the room beyond was much as she remembered it: the heavy bed, crouched against one wall, ready to pounce; the dresser, triptych mirror displaying the room in dust-softened outline.

And the doll's house, with its front wide and welcoming, was just as Sarah had left it.

According to Sarah's grandmother, the doll's house had been built by Sarah's great-grandfather out of wood taken from the surrounding trees. It may once have been intended as a replica of its parent home, but the likeness was crude and time had altered it. It sat on an ottoman stool in the far corner of the room beneath a tear in the grey wallpaper which revealed the faded blue sky and yellow globe sun of the previous occupant's choice. Water pattered into the sodden carpet from a leak in the ceiling, just missing a stack of books and annuals slumped against the wall.

Lying on the cover of the topmost hardback, like a black scratch against the jolly color illustration of two girls laughing by a forest stream, was Skelf.

«««——»»»

She had found Skelf when she was a child, on one of the rare occasions her grandmother had managed to drag herself from the chair in the living room and out into the woods. Following the old woman along paths that seemingly only she could see was hard work for Sarah's small legs, and she had trouble concentrating on what her elder was saying. It was something about 'cages' and 'binding circles,' things that made no sense to Sarah.

When they reached the edge of one clearing, Sarah made to run forward and rest on the hollow trunk of a toppled tree, but the old woman had thrown out a large hand and clawed her back. "We don't go there," she said, brittle voice as full of fright as it was with anger. "We never go there. Rest at the edge, then we'll follow the path around and back." And with that she slumped against the nearest tree and closed her eyes, breath coming in long, wheezing gasps.

With nothing else to do, Sarah rooted around the bed of leaves and stone, upturning rocks to disturb the beetles and worms which sheltered beneath. Exposed to sunlight, they would scurry and squirm across the ground, always away from the clearing. Once, she picked up a single worm and threw it towards the empty patch of ground where it writhed briefly before lying still. She was watching for further movement when, right on the edge of the clearing, she saw Skelf.

Of course, he wasn't Skelf then. He was little more than a crooked finger of wood, topped with a single, knotted ball, clusters of woodland mush clinging to his splintered body. She had later named him Skelf after the Scottish word her grandmother used to describe the tiny green needles which jutted from his 'body,' threatening the soft skin of Sarah's tiny fingers. To this day, Sarah didn't know why, out of all the other broken twigs scattered on the ground, she chose to pick up Skelf. Nor did she know why she decided to take him back to the house.

Perhaps it was the shock of the abrupt cough her grandmother emitted, as she pushed herself away from the tree, which startled Sarah into stuffing the little shaft of wood into her pocket and leaping back from the edge of the clearing. Perhaps something else was at work. Whatever the cause, she took Skelf back to the house, and he had been there on that last night at the centre of the tiny drama that young Sarah played out within the walls of her doll's house.

As she had done that afternoon in the clearing, Sarah lifted Skelf from where he lay and held him up in front of her face, careful to avoid splinters. He had bit her that day, leaving tiny needles of wood under the skin of her small finger. Why she hadn't thrown him away then, Sarah didn't know. Instead, Skelf had become just another of her toys, living in the painted wood garden of her doll's house.

Was it something in one of her books that made her dress him the way she had? She remembered how exciting she found stories of highwaymen, and assumed that was why she'd clothed Skelf's body with a swatch of black fabric, a tiny, poorly-stitched brimmed hat on the knuckle of wood that served as his head.

The face was another matter. Sarah had no recollection of gouging eyeless sockets into the wood, nor was she responsible for the ragged diagonal mouth which almost divided Skelf's 'head' in two. She could only assume that the features had been there all the time, and wondered—as she had as a child—if Skelf had once been part of a larger figure, perhaps something left abandoned amongst the roots until only a fragment remained.

《《——》》

Holding Skelf securely in a tight fist, Sarah negotiated the slim pillar of water still pouring from the ceiling and stood before the doll's house. The remnants of her last game, the one she had been playing that final afternoon, lay where she had left them. The four other dolls were less crude than Skelf, but still basic, not much more than colored wooden columns topped with globular, grinning faces. There was a mother, a grandmother, a girl, and a boy. All of them lay on their sides in different rooms. If there had ever been a father to go with the set, he was long gone.

Kneeling down in front of the bare open rooms of the miniature house, Sarah regarded the toppled figures. Then, one by one, she stood them up, arranging them as best she could in their old positions. She felt like a scientist, attempting to recreate the exact conditions of an experiment.

Sarah almost laughed. That wasn't too far from the truth. Time and time again she had been told that her actions had held no bearing on what happened to her mother and the others, but she'd never believed. What had the doctor said? "To get better, you have to accept that you were not responsible." Well, she'd come to the house to find out once and for all what really had happened, whatever the consequences.

Holding him between her thumb and forefinger, she raised Skelf to the doll's house and tapped his head against the soft wood of its outer wall. Voice no more than a rasped whisper, she said: "Let me in, let me in."

The four occupants of the house remained silent and inert.

Reaching forward, Sarah curled her arm around the back of the house so that Skelf's face leered in through one of the back windows. The brim of his hat folded against the plastic, covering one pit of an eye. "Let me in," Sarah said again. "Let me in."

Had the wind outside picked up, or was something else pushing through the trees?

Sarah tried to ignore the sounds and concentrate on finishing her game. Her hand was trembling too much, though, and she was forced to grip Skelf tighter. As she moved the little effigy back to the side of the house, near the kitchen door, she became aware of a static smell in the air, sharp and penetrating.

A beam of amber light shone through the open window, casting shadow leaves onto the far wall before travelling across the room and flickering out. Surely the house was too deep in the woods for any car headlights to reach. She had an urge to rush to the window before the source of the illumination disappeared, but she held back because that wasn't what she had done before, and it would break the spell to do so now. Face fixed in determination, she pushed Skelf against the doll house door. "Let me in," she said. "Let me in."

Something slammed downstairs. A door caught by the wind, or a piece of furniture thrown aside?

Immobile, Sarah listened carefully as the old house breathed in and out. Irregular, heavy creaks came from below, the tentative footsteps of something that hadn't walked for a long while.

She glanced at Skelf, now standing in the dollhouse living room, so tall that she had to hold him at an angle to prevent his head from brushing the ceiling. The shaking in Sarah's hand had traveled the length of her arm and was now sweeping through her body. She longed to let Skelf go, to let him roll from her hand and fall to the ground, but the muscles of her hand were rigor-tight. If she gripped hard enough, would he splinter and fall apart? Sarah hoped so, but somehow she doubted it.

In the real house, there was another crash from the ground floor. In the dollhouse, unbidden and untouched, one of the child-dolls toppled over onto its face. Sarah stared at it, certain now that the doctors had been wrong all along: everything had been her fault.

The mother doll spun on its base before falling against the wall. Sarah jolted the hand holding Skelf back, fingers free. The figure of wood and cloth stood where she had left him, at an angle that should have caused him to fall. If she were stronger, Sarah might have lashed out, cast Skelf away from the dollhouse and onto the soft marsh of the carpet, but she could not move. All she could do was wait.

She could hear Skelf breathing, a dry, brittle noise which reminded her of the wind through a hollow log. And then he disappeared from the dollhouse.

In her grandmother's house, the stairs complained as a great weight was pressed down on them. A rustling, like fingers through foliage, accompanied the footsteps as they climbed, steadier all the time. The steps softened as they reached the landing carpet, creeping ever closer. Sarah imagined—or was it a memory—how Skelf would fill the doorway, how his body would creak and groan as he ducked to enter the room.

That was enough to galvanize her into action. Sarah threw herself backwards, twisting towards the door to the hall. She caught the briefest glimpse of the thing that filled the narrow passage before she ran back into her bedroom and slammed the door. Sarah pushed her weight against the door but it felt insubstantial; weak.

At any moment, she expected the giant Skelf to smash through, reducing both the door and her bones to splinters. She waited for the impact, trying to remember how she'd escaped before, but nothing came. Behind the door, she could hear the scratching of fingers along the wall, scrabbling for purchase to wrench the door away. Then there was silence, and Sarah braced herself.

And then a series of gentle taps sounded on the other side of the door. A voice followed, dry as a summer day, the words passed through vocal cords formed from strands of grass and taut reeds. "Let me in," it said. "Let me in."

About John Forth

John Forth's short fiction has appeared in *Midnight Street, The Journal of the British Fantasy Society, Estronomicon* and the *Monster Book for Girls*. Although a Scotsman by birth, he has lived in Brighton, England for the last five years. He can be stalked with impunity at www.twitter.com/johnforth, and his occasional ramblings on all things horror can be found at www.johnrforth.wordpress.com.

HOMECOMING

by Scott Nicholson

The wind cut through the valley like a frozen razor. Black clouds raced from the west, shrouding the setting sun. Leaves skittered over the brown grass. The air smelled of electricity and rust and dried chestnut and things long dead.

No ghosts flickered among the sagging fence posts outside, no spirits swept over the hay-strewn barnyard. Only earthly shadows moved in the twilight, nothing but swaying trees and night birds and loose gates. Charlie Roniger turned from the dark glass of the window.

"It's gonna come a storm," he said, drawing the dusty curtains. His wife, Sara, sat in her ragged easy chair and said nothing. She looked deeply into the flames crackling in the fireplace. Her wrinkled hands were folded over the quilt in her lap, hands that had once snapped green beans and wrung out wet sheets and caressed the soft down on a baby's head.

Charlie studied her face. It was fallen, as if the framework behind it was busted up like an old hatbox. He never thought she'd end up broken. Not the way she'd always been able to show her feelings, to hold the family together, to love the only two men in her life.

She was too much like that old spring up on the hill, just kept on slow and steady until you came to expect it to run on forever. Then when it dried up, you got mad, even though you had no promise that it would keep running. Even when you knew you had no real right to it. It was a blessing, and blessings weren't made to last. Otherwise, the bad things that God sent along wouldn't get their proper due.

Charlie reached into the front pocket of his denim overalls and pulled out a plug of tobacco. He twisted off a chaw with his three good teeth. His gums mashed the tobacco until it was moist and pliable. Then, with his tongue, he pushed the wad into the hollow of his jaw.

He walked to the door, unconsciously checking the lock. On a peg beside his overcoat hung the baseball glove he'd given Johnny for his

133

tenth birthday. The leather had shrunk and cracked from all the years Johnny had lobbed dewy walnuts on the tin roof of the barn, pretending he was catching fly balls off Yankee bats. Johnny had been a southpaw. He'd gotten that from Sara's side of the family.

Charlie wished he'd had more time to play catch with his son. But the fields always needed his plow, the hay had to be pressed into yellow squares, the hogs squealed for slop, the corn cried for water. The forest gave its trees but demanded in trade hours of stretched muscles and stinging sweat. Even the soil begged for his flesh, whispering to him to lie down and rot and feed the new roots.

So time went away, the sun rose and fell like a rib cage drawing in deep breaths. And chores and meals and church on Sundays stole the years. Charlie wondered if all you were left with at the end was the memory of all the things you should have said but never could. Things like "I love you."

He touched the glove that was as rough and parched as his own skin. He always thought it would be the other way around, with him fading out slow and gaspy and full of pain, while Johnny stood over the bed and tried to get up the nerve to hug him. And Charlie thought he might have been able to say it then, when they were both scared and had nothing to lose. Back when death looked like a one-way road.

Charlie stooped, his spine popping as he reached into the firebox and grabbed a couple of oak logs with his arthritic fingers. He carried the wood into the living room and tossed them onto the fire, sending a shower of sparks up the chimney. The reflection of the fire danced in his wife's glassy eyes, red-orange pinpricks on bald onyx. She didn't blink.

"Fire feels good, don't it, honey?" he said gently, squirting a stream of brown juice into the flames. The liquid hissed and evaporated as he waited for an answer, knowing it wouldn't come. Language had left her alone, even if the dead folks hadn't.

Outside, the wind picked up. The old two-story house creaked and leaned against the coming gale. A few loose shingles flapped, and the upstairs windows rattled. Blasts of cold air swirled under the front door and the first raindrops spattered the porch.

He gingerly led Sara up the squeaky stairs to bed and tucked her under the thick blankets. Charlie checked the weather once more, but all he could see was black and his own reflection. He tossed on a back log, spit out his chaw, and locked the door. He went upstairs to wait for them.

He fell asleep with his arm around Sara, nuzzling into the hard edges of her bones. The howling wind came into his dreams and turned into a familiar moan. He awoke in a sweat and blinked into the blackness around him. Faint blue-white shapes hovered above the bed. He reached for his wife, but felt only the cool sheets in the little hollow of the bed where she should have been.

She was with them, dancing and waving her frail arms, as she had every night since Johnny had been buried. The translucent wisps flowed over her, caressing her skin and weaving around her worn flannel nightgown. She floated two feet off the ground, embraced by the spirits. They were all locked together in a hoe-down of resurrection.

As Charlie's eyes adjusted, he could make out the feathery shapes taking form. It was the regulars, the happy hour crowd of the dead set. The ghosts filled the room like joyful clouds. They cavorted like they had time to kill and forever to do it in.

Familiar faces coalesced among the mists. There was Doris, the school teacher, who had passed on in the winter of '73, now as withered as a forgotten houseplant. Freddie, Charlie's old fishing buddy, was moaning and hooting like an eviscerated owl. He had drowned several years ago and his skin was stretched and pale like a bleached water balloon. Freddie had lost his hat, and Charlie noticed for the first time how large his ears were.

Colonel Hadley was hovering like a shroud on a coat hanger, wearing his military dress blues even though his ramrod days were over. The town gossip held that Fanny Coffey had run off with a traveling Bible salesman, but she couldn't have made it far on those amputated legs. The Bible salesman had answered a newfound calling to be a sex murderer, an about-face career change that caught Fanny by surprise. Consumptive old Pete Henries fumbled at his chest, aimlessly searching for another of the cigarettes that had nailed his coffin lid shut. The Waters bunch looked on, father and mother and child, still as ashen as they had been on the morning they were found in their garage with the Buick engine running.

Rhetta Mae Harper was among them, Rhetta Mae who had tried to seduce Charlie when Sara had been so knotted up with pregnancy that she couldn't bear her husband's touch. Sara's womb had taken his seed in late middle age, and the fetus that would be Johnny kept her in constant discomfort. Charlie had tasted Rhetta Mae's temptation and had nearly swallowed, but in the end his love for Sara kept him true. Rhetta Mae had been shot during some drunken, jealous frenzy, her voluptuous figure shredded by number eight buckshot pellets. Charlie found her charms much easier to resist now.

He kicked off the blankets and rolled out of the old cast-iron bed, the mattress springs and his bones creaking in harmony. The cold pine floorboards chilled his feet as he walked over to his wife. The ghosts crowded Charlie's face, but he brushed them aside like cobwebs. He put his hand on Sara's arm. She tried feebly to fight him off. She wanted to play with her see-through friends.

"Johnny isn't here," Charlie said to Sara. "They won't take you to Johnny."

She tried to answer but could only gurgle like an infant. She was finding ecstasy in those icy arms.

"Now get the hell outta here, you bunch of deadbeats," Charlie shouted at the ghosts, trembling with chill and outrage. For some reason he didn't understand, they always obeyed him, as if they hadn't a will of their own and took their masters where they found them.

The ghosts turned to him, blank faces drooping, like children who had been scolded for taking baby chicks out of a nest. They gently lowered Sara and she stood on the wobbly sticks of her legs. The figures flitted into shadows and disappeared.

The storm had blown over now and a sliver of moonlight spilled across the bedroom. Charlie laid his wife down and tugged the blankets over her. He got in beside her and watched the corners of the room. Johnny's photograph was on the dresser, the portrait grinning in the weak moonlight. Smooth skin and a proud shy smile, those eyes that Sara said were so much like his father's. *Damn shame about that boy*, he thought, as his rage faded like the ghosts had. Sorrow rose from a shallow grave in his heart to take its place.

They said Johnny had slipped down at the sawmill, his flannel sleeve yanked by the hungry blade that didn't discriminate between limbs of poplar, jack pine, or flesh. The lumber company sent a check and paid for his funeral. It rained the day they lowered Johnny's purple casket into the ground. Rivulets of red streaked the clay as the gravediggers shoveled. Charlie thought it was funny how they threw in that coffin and all that dirt, and the hole still wasn't full. He and Sara watched the rain drill down into the man-sized puddle long after the minister had fled for the shelter of his powder-blue Cadillac.

The ghosts had paid their first visit that night. Sara's mind, already splintered by grief, took a final wrong turn down the dirt road of madness. Charlie had been disbelieving at first, but now the midnight stops were another part of the day, as fixed in the rhythm of his life as milking the cows and gathering the eggs. Just another hardship to be endured.

Charlie turned his eyes from the photograph and reached for the tobacco. Since he was awake, he might as well have a chaw. He rested his wiry neck back on the pillow and worked the sticky sweet leaf with his gums. Something rustled by the dresser.

"You're a little late, the show's over," Charlie said. The noise continued.

Charlie raised his head and saw a faint apparition trying to form by the closet. *Damned if it ain't a new one,* he thought. Threads of milky air spun themselves into a human shape. Charlie blinked and looked at the photograph.

"Can't be," he muttered. Then he realized it was the one he'd been waiting for, night after long night. "Johnny? Is that you, boy?"

A voice like December answered, "Yeah, Dad."

Charlie sat up in bed, his heart pounding. He glanced sideways at his wife. Her eyes were closed, and the blankets rose and fell with her even breathing.

"How's it going, son?"

"Not too bad. I've been a little confused here lately."

"Didn't I tell you to keep an eye out for that damned sawblade? Just look what you've gone and done to yourself."

Johnny materialized more fully and stepped forward into the moonlight. Flesh hung in ropes from his ruined cheeks. His nose was missing, and chunks of his hair had been torn from his savaged scalp. His Adam's apple bobbed uncontrollably, dangling by a tendon from the gash in his neck.

Charlie gulped, feeling the tobacco sting his throat. "You're looking real good, son."

"How's Mom?"

"She's fine," Charlie said. "We better let her sleep, though. Her spring's dried up."

Johnny nodded as if that made sense. The Adam's apple quivered and made a wet sound.

"They took your pitching arm, son. That was supposed to win you a college scholarship."

Johnny contemplated his missing left hand as if he could still see it. "It happened so fast, Dad. Hurt for a second, like when you get rope burns or something, but then it was over. Seems like only yesterday, but seems like it never happened, too. Lots of things are funny that way anymore."

Charlie looked into Johnny's eyes that were deep as graves. He suddenly remembered teaching his son how to tie a slip-knot on a fishing line. They had stood in the shade of a sycamore, where the branches were highest, so the hooks wouldn't snag. Johnny's stubby fingers had fumbled with the line as his face clenched in determination, but now the fingers of his remaining hand were ragged and moldy, with dirt packed under the nails.

Charlie felt the blankets slip from his shoulders, and a coldness flooded his chest, as if his heart had frozen. "You feel like talking about it, son?"

"Well, I'm supposed to be looking for something. I thought I ought to come here," Johnny said, the bone of his head slowly swiveling.

"Home is where you go when you got trouble," Charlie said. "I told you I'd always be here to help you."

"Dad, it ain't the hurt, 'cause I don't feel nothing. But I'm lost, like. Can't seem to find my way."

Charlie gummed his chaw quickly and nervously before answering. "You know you'd be welcome here, but I don't think that's right. There's others that are your kind now."

"I reckon so," Johnny said softly, looking at and through his own torso as if finally understanding. Then his hollow voice lifted. "You remember when those Corcoran boys were picking on me, and you stared down their whole damned brood? Walked right up on their front porch, standing on them old boards ready to fight 'em one at a time or all at once. That sure took the steam out of their britches."

"Nobody messes with my boy." Charlie looked into the shadows that passed for Johnny's eyes.

"Say, Dad, whatever happened to Darlene?"

Charlie didn't want Johnny to rest any less easily than he already did. He couldn't say that Darlene had married Jack Corcoran when

Johnny was barely six weeks in the ground, before the grass even had time to take root over his grave. Fond memories might give the dead comfort, for all Charlie knew. So he lied.

"She pined and pined, boy. Broke her poor little heart. But eventually she got on with her life, the way a body does. That would have made one fine wedding, you and her."

"I only wanted to make her happy. And you, too, Dad. I guess I'll never get the chance now."

The dark maw in the center of Johnny's face gaped like an endless wet cave.

"We all got our own row to hoe, Johnny. I taught you that we take care of our own. But I also told you that you gotta make hard choices along the way. And it looks like this is one path that you better walk alone."

Johnny shuffled his shredded feet. "Yeah, I reckon so. But I ain't scared. I guess it's what ought to be."

Charlie felt a stirring in the blankets beside him.

"Them other ones been here lookin' for you. Been here ever damn night, bugging hell out of your mom," Charlie said quickly.

Sara sat up, her eyes moist with sleep. She gasped as she saw the scraps of her son. Charlie put a hand on her shoulder to keep her from getting out of bed.

A thin strand of drool ran down her chin as she tried to speak. "Juhhhnn..."

Johnny drifted forward. "Mom?"

Charlie pressed Sara's head down onto her pillow. "You'd best be getting on, son. No need to stir up trouble here."

Johnny moved closer, though not one of his limbs moved. He was beside the bed now, and Charlie felt the stale cold draft of his son's deathwind. Johnny reached out with a hand that was the color of a trout belly.

Sara squirmed under Charlie's arm, but Charlie pinned her and pulled the quilt over her face. When he looked back at Johnny, the vacant expression had been replaced by a look that Charlie had seen one other time. A possum had crawled under the henhouse wire, and Charlie went after it with a pitchfork when the animal refused to give up its newfound territory. Charlie must have jabbed the possum fifty or sixty times, with it hissing and snarling every breath right up until it finally died.

Charlie wondered what kind of pitchfork you used on a ghost.

The mottled hand came closer, and Charlie clenched his teeth. "Ain't proper for a grown man to be making his mother cry."

Johnny paused for a moment, and his eyes looked like they were filled with muddy water.

"That's right," Charlie said. "Your spring's drying up. You got other rivers to run to, now."

Sara kicked Charlie's leg, but he wasn't about to turn her loose.

Johnny reached out and touched Charlie's cheek. His son's fingers were like icicles. The hand trailed along the line of Charlie's stubble, as if remembering the scratchiness he'd felt against his infant skin. It was the first time they had touched in nearly twenty years.

"I'd best go with them. Seems only right," Johnny whispered in his lost voice. Affection and a strange pride fluttered in Charlie's chest. This was his only son standing before him. Did it matter that his decaying guts were straining against the cotton of his burial shirt? As a father, it was his duty to teach his son one more of life's harsh little lessons.

"A man's gotta do what a man's gotta do." Charlie pointed to the far corner of the room. "They went that-a-ways."

Johnny turned his mutilated face, a face that only a mother could love. Then he looked back. He leaned over Charlie and spread his arms wide. The raw meat of his throat jogged as he spoke. "I love you, Dad."

Without thinking, Charlie reached up, his hands passing through the moist silk of Johnny's flesh. But how could you hug a dried-up spring? How could you hug a memory?

Charlie loved the son who had walked this earth. The small boy who had sat between Charlie's legs on the tractor, pretending to steer while making engine noises with his mouth. The son he had taken to see the Royals play, who had built an awkward birdhouse in eighth-grade shop for his mother, who had slept in the hayloft in the summer because he liked the smell. The son who had buried his old hound himself because he didn't want anyone to see him cry. Johnny did those things, not this blasphemy hovering over him.

Johnny had been the flesh of Charlie's flesh, but this thing was beyond flesh. Resting in peace was a comfort for the living, not the dead.

He almost said the words anyway. But he found he'd rather take his regrets to the grave. Second chances be damned.

"It's good to see you, son." Like hell.

"Tell Mom that I miss her." Johnny's maw opened and closed raggedly. Sara was sobbing under the blankets, her fragile bones trembling.

"I will. You take care, now." Like he was sending Johnny off to summer Bible camp.

Johnny shimmered and faded, the dutiful son to the last. His stump of a left arm raised as if to wave good-bye. The essence that had been Charlie's only son fluttered and vanished just as the first rays of dawn broke through the room. The ghosts wouldn't be back. They had what they had been looking for.

Charlie relaxed and pulled the blankets off his wife's face. She turned her back to him, her gray hair matted against the pillowcase. He touched her shoulder but she shrugged him away. Something rattled in her chest.

He rose from the bed and dressed, working the tightness out of his stringy muscles. He rubbed his hands together to drive away the lingering chill of his son's touch. His heart felt like a charred ember in the ash of a dead fire. His eyes burned, but they had always been miserly when it came to making tears.

He knew you couldn't expect it to keep running forever. When the spring dries up, you had to remember that you had no promise that it would keep on. The water's for everybody or even nobody at all. You had no real right to it in the first place.

Charlie stopped by the front door and put on his overcoat and heavy work gloves. Firewood was waiting outside, frosty and unsplit. He took his ax and his loving memories out under the morning sun so he could hold them to the light.

About Scott Nicholson

Scott Nicholson is the bestselling author of 15 novels, 80 short stories, six screenplays, four comic series, and four children's books. His most popular thrillers are *Liquid Fear*, *The Red Church*, *Drummer Boy*, *Disintegration*, and *The Skull Ring*.

His Web site is www.hauntedcomputer.com.

EVE OF ALL HALLOWS

by Brian G. Murray

The bus meanders through the parish of St John, then onwards to St Mary on the island of Jersey. Before I know it, forty minutes have passed, my mind screams at me, and I jerk up. As usual, I nearly miss my stop.

Quickly, I reach forward and press the bell to stop the bus. The driver pulls over and stops the vehicle sharply, causing the wheels to judder. Luckily I remain seated else I would have been thrown forward.

I get up, try to avoid eye contact with the annoyed driver, and wait for the door to open. It doesn't. I turn and look across at the driver. I smile, but my grin quickly fades.

The driver, wearing a frown, is an old man with wrinkly skin, resembling weathered leather and looks like a third generation inbred local – you know, he has that goofy look. His bald head is covered in sparse tufts of wiry white hair and large, flaky patches of dried skin that snows onto the shoulders of his company jacket. He has a large bulbous nose, mapped with blue veins, thick, stout dark hairs and pores filled with black gunk. The unmistakable musky smell of the elderly clings to him, mixing with the odor of stale sweat. He smiles and his dark eyes glint with mischief as he looks me up and down.

"Did you know that these here parts were once ruled by pagans who worshipped the *Night of the Walking Dead?*" the driver begins with a sly grin, revealing yellow brown stumps, formerly teeth. Luckily, I can not smell his awful breath. "The night's festivities celebrated the end of the 'lighter half' of the year and the beginning of the 'darker half.' Back then, costumes were worn, but it was spirits and not children who would dress up."

"I would like to get off the bus please," I request politely, trying to pay no heed to his babble.

The driver ignores me and continues his ramble. "Them pagans would leave offerings or 'treats' for marauding spirits and build

143

massive campfires. They believed f they did not leave offerings, the spirits would haunt them during the 'dark half' of the year, bringing misery, bad luck and even death. So you be careful, young man."

Might as well play the old codger's game, I think with a sigh. "Why should I be careful?" I ask aloud.

The driver holds my stare for a long moment, then begins to laugh as he presses a button that opens the door. "Tonight be the Eve of All Hallows as it was once called," he wheezes. "See you again."

Confused, I alight and wait on the road for the bus to pull away. In my mind, I can still hear the old man's cackling laughter as he drives off. I watch the lights on the bus slowly fade as it disappears down the road, then I turn and look at the rest of my journey home, which I will complete on foot. Only then does it strike me...

I remember what the date is, and the old man's words start to make sense.

I'm not the superstitious type nor easily fooled, but I do believe there's some truth behind many myths and the old driver's ramble sparks a distant memory. Today is the Eve of All Hallows, as the old man had said, but during the creation of Christian holy days, it became the night before All Saints' Day. Many people had remembered the original name, but over time it changed, gaining a more sinister version, one that invokes thoughts of witches, ghosts and ghouls. It is also a night that, for some reason, always seems darker, foggier, colder and scarier than most other nights. Tonight, parents will dress their little darlings up as ghosts, witches, goblins or even skeletons then let them go out 'trick-or-treating.'

I am a thirty-something well-educated man, but you know what, just thinking of the word —Halloween—makes my bladder momentarily threaten to weaken. Here alone on a country road after dark, it seems ominous indeed.

"Stupid," I mutter to myself as I delve into my leather satchel and pull out my metal flashlight. A torch seems just what I need to make the night less threatening. St Mary is in the northwest of Jersey and has farmland crisscrossed with narrow, twisty roads. Well, lanes is probably a more accurate description, most lacking street lights.

See what a sensible adult I am? I even carry a torch. With a smug grin, I press the 'on' button and a cone of light streaks from the end. With that reassurance, I check the road, looking left and right, then cross over and head down a narrow lane.

As I step onto the lane, a gust of wind blows into my face, peppering me with dried leaves and coarse grit. I'm forced to cringe and turn my head away. I continue on, each step an effort. After a long moment, the squall dies down and the air turns still, unnervingly so. Nothing moves. I pause, look down the lane and raise my torchlight.

Suddenly, I involuntarily shiver as the icy finger of fear runs down my spine. I hear a whoosh mixed with a cackling rustle. I lift my torchlight higher and gasp. It looks like a rolling transparent wave is flowing towards me, causing most branches to sway and the few remaining leaves stuck to them to flap like small, rigid flags.

The invisible force moves closer and the branches all point towards me, as though I'm a target. Closer and closer it gets until the gust of wind washes over me. The sudden blast of air forces me back a step and I have to lean into the wind. Then, once more, as quickly as it started, the wind dies. And just like that...utter stillness.

I take a deep juddering breath. "Halloween," I whisper softly. "You're letting it get to you."

I am afraid because there are no sounds. No animals are crawling or running, and no birds are flying or squawking or chirping in the trees. Nothing is moving. I look up at the sky. An oppressive blackness that blots out the hoary moonlight and twinkling stars seems to press down on me, forcing me to cower slightly.

"Oh, get real, you child," I hiss at myself, then with a smile start to sing a children's rhyme. "Ghosties and ghoulies and four-legged beasties and things that go bump in the night..."

Slowly shaking my head, I stride confidently down the lane with the light from my torch leading the way. For extra security, I wave the bright beam from left to right to avoid any sudden, unforeseen surprises.

The lane I'm walking along is wide enough for only one car to pass, and has a gentle hump. The gradient is getting steeper on the far side, where it also eases to the left. On each side are fields, some plowed, others left fallow, while tall banks, topped with thorny shrubs and trees covered in parasitic, climbing ivy that glistens in the moonlight, hem in the narrow road. The trees' canopy reaches up and hangs over like lovers holding hands with fingers interlaced, so even during the day the lane feels gloomy, permanently in shadow. On a night like this, they make it look like a horror movie.

In my local pub, I have heard many stories about these lanes, including two vicious unsolved ritualistic murders, sightings of ghosts and dismembered body parts being found but never identified. I push those dark thoughts from my mind and dismiss them as urban legends.

And then something starts tugging at my subconscious. Halfway down the lane at the crest of the hump, just before it starts to bend to the left, I slow my pace. My mind starts to race and a kaleidoscope of thoughts tumble over each other in a maddening, garbled muddle.

I remember a deeply buried fact. During the Eve of All Hallows, the pagans believed spirits roamed the lands, possess corpses and, with their rotting costumes, become the undead. Not only that, unlike the children who dress up today and consume masses amounts of candy, the pagan spirits gorged on flesh...fresh, salty human flesh.

Oh, why did I have to remember that piece of information now! I take a shuddering deep breath.

The air turns frighteningly still and a mist starts to fill my torchlight. As I walk, the mist billows as though someone is blowing cigarette smoke directly into the beam. The brightness begins to fade and the mist swallows its intensity and shortens the cone of light's length.

At that moment, the artificial light flickers.

My eyes widen. "No. No. No!" I plead aloud.

The electrical sputtering continues. My flashing beam reflects against the ever thickening fog, creating a claustrophobic cocoon of white that closes in with every blink.

The periods of darkness grow longer and longer. Then...

Ping!

The touch bulb dies. Blackness swamps me with a permanence that feels palpable like the devil is crushing me in his massive fist.

At the same moment, another gust of wind blasts down the lane, funneled by the interlocking trees. The invisible flow of air rustles the branches and leaves around me and lifts debris high into the air. Soon, dry, fallen leaves are snatched by the intensifying wind and slap me this way and that. My clothes are whipped back and flail behind me, seeming to urge—no, demand—that I flee. I lean into the wind and bow my head. Above me the gust carves through the trees' canopy, whistling tunelessly. Every fiber in my body wants to scarper, but I'm nearly home, and anyway, what is there to be afraid of...after all, this is Jersey.

Just then, I hear something...a deep, guttural growl.

Did I? I'm sure I heard something...didn't I? I cannot be sure because my nerves are already pulled taut and the blustery wind hinders my hearing. The mournful whistling increases in volume, getting louder and louder, building to a deafening crescendo that hurts my ears. I pray for the wind to stop and...

Miraculously, as though I commanded it, the squall stops.

The suddenness of the wind dying surprises me. I stagger forward, barely stopping myself from falling over. Frowning, I look to my left then right. Nothing. I turn around and stare back towards the main road. Again, nothing, just a backdrop of pure thick, inky darkness.

Crack!

A noise erupts from my left and, in the blackness with my senses heightened, it sounds thunderous, causing me to jump. Was that a dry twig snapping or...something else, something just as brittle, like...like a bone?

I pray for my eyesight to pierce the dark and I shake my torch, silently begging it to work. My prayers go unanswered. I swallow, but my mouth is dry and a large, gelatinous lump remains lodged in my arid throat. For a long moment, I stare into the blackness. Nothing.

I slowly turn my head away from the sound and glare to my left. At the edge of the field stands an old disused granite barn that has been left to rot. It's one of those creepy buildings with a sagging roof, missing many terracotta tiles, but still light does not penetrate inside. Even on the sunniest day, the interior remains utterly black, its shadows appearing almost tangible, keeping dark secrets hidden from prying eyes. Tonight, with my mind playing tricks on me, the building seems so much closer, so much bigger and its secrets feel so much more menacing and ominous. Rape, torture, murder or mutilations; what heinous crimes have been committed in there?

I turn back to face home and step forward. My black oxford shoe heel clicks loudly on the tarmac. I pause and listen.

Nothing. I sigh with relief.

I take another step but my polished shoe squelches into something thick and gooey. After a belief moment, the ripe stench of rotting horse dung pollutes my nostrils. I hop around like a demented rabbit, trying to get the manure off my shoe by wiping it on the road.

Rustle!

Standing on one foot, I freeze.

The bushes next to me start to shake. I think something is in the shrubs next to me. I can not be certain. There's no wind blowing so that means...something is out there...

I quickly forget about the horse dung covering my shoe but nearly lose my footing as I step down and slide through the thick excrement. I silently curse then look to my left. Just darkness. My breathing shortens and my heart begins to pound in my chest. My imagination begins to take over. Are there shapes moving?

Without warning, a throaty howl reverberates around me, tainting the night air, reaching a shrilling climax and then silence once more swamps me, like a heavy, sodden woolen cloak, weighing me down.

I set off towards home, my gait quick. The lane begins to gently fall away from me, one shoe clicking on the tarmac, the other squelching. I've walked along this lane so many times in the past, but tonight it seems so alien, like it is somewhere completely different. I actually feel lost.

A drop in temperature sharpens the air and inhaling becomes painful. I tremble from the cold and the icy air pricks my skin. I can just imagine my breath misting around me, thickening in the still, frigid air. My heart is thumping inside my chest and my blood is roaring in my ears, sounding like a stormy sea crashing onto a shingle beach. My rising panic turns my breaths into gasping, high pitched squeals.

I quicken my pace, now jogging.

Suddenly I slam into the right-hand bank, having forgotten to ease round to the left with the turning of the lane. My legs, arms and torso strike the sodden, moss covered muddy bank, and sharp thorn-covered branches slash at my face, neck and shoulders. Almost instantly blood oozes from many small lacerations. I quickly lurch back then yelp as barbed thorns tug and tear at my skin and clothes.

Something clatters on the road next to me, causing me to jump. My senses quickly return and I can only groan when I hear my torch roll away, skittering along the tarmac. I curse myself for dropping it. It may have been dead, but it could still have been useful as a weapon.

Just then I hear footsteps pound along the lane. I can not tell if there is only one person, or more than one. I break into a run.

Blindly, I start to sprint down the lane but, in my haste, I forget how steep the slope becomes. Soon, I am battling my own feet, trying not to lose my footing as the leather soles of my shoes skate and slither along the tarmac. Then my legs slide out from underneath me and I dive forward.

I land heavily, my hands and face slamming against the cold tarmac. My momentum causes me to skid down the gradient and the coarse surface scrapes away my skin as grit grinds into fresh cuts and grazes. I tumble over and over before coming to an ungainly stop on my back, panting heavily.

I can still hear the footsteps behind me, and now they are getting faster; closing in.

I try to sit up but my body protests at the sudden movement. I persist, daring my body to defy me. I manage to struggle to my feet but feel giddy and sway badly. I feel pain so overwhelming that tears begin to well up and sting my eyes.

Silence. Where did my pursuer go?

Then...I hear breathing. Wheezing breaths rhythmically inhaling then exhaling, slowly and steadily, in then out, in then out.

I turn to run but something is wrong with my left leg; what did I do to it? It hurts so badly and I am unable to make it function. I reach down to touch my calf and I realize that not only are my trousers torn but I can feel a bone protruding, pressing against the fabric. I cannot run; I am trapped.

"Don't move," he tells me.

I recognize the voice. A breeze picks up and the clouds momentarily break. A streak of hoary light illuminates the lane.

It's the bus driver. And I can see a gun glistening in the silvery moonlight.

"I loved them pagans, and do you want to know why?"

"I think my leg is broken," I hiss between clenched teeth.

The old man ignores that and starts talking. "They knew. How does the saying go again? Ah yes, they knew which side their bread was buttered on. They honored and worshipped my kind, giving us wonderful treats and paying homage by lighting great fires. Unlike you 'civilized people' dressing up and sending your little brats out trick-or-treating, disrespecting us. So now I turn the tables and disrespect you by dressing up like you humans."

The old man begins to laugh, a scratchy, cackling sound full of malevolence. After taking a wheezing deep breath, he continues, "I need to change my costume. I've had my current costume too long. This one is starting to smell and decay."

149

Large, icy-cold leathery hands point the gun at me.

"And, in order for me to get a new costume," the old man adds, "I need a corpse."

I watch his finger slowly tighten on the trigger as the clouds smother the moonlight.

About Brian G. Murray

Brian G Murray was born and educated in London, where he fell into the rat-race trap and became an accountant. Although this pays the bills, like all aspiring authors, his ultimate ambition is to escape the hum-drum of the routine. In the long term, he hopes to write full time and put his creative talents to better use. His genre of choice is fantasy, but he enjoys testing his writing prowess by delving farther into a darker side.

His book *Siege Warriors* is a collection of twelve stories released and available through Kerlak Publishing. He has had other short stories published and a catalogue of manuscripts that he hopes will see the light of day in the not so distant future.

He now lives in Jersey (in the English Channel), with his family and a large collection of comics.

You can keep up to date with his writing endeavors at www.briangmurray.com.

THE LOST SHEEP

by Jason Reynolds

Wendell covered his mouth while he coughed and used his free hand to rub a clear spot in the foggy window. The snowflakes were whirling even harder, shrouding the backyard and highland pasture. Gray clouds topped Bald Mountain like clumps of unwashed wool. Earlier that morning, he'd laid out quilts and weighted the corners with rocks in hopes of saving the vegetables. He hated the notion of having to start the garden over. The quilts were now covered in snow.

He warmed his hands over the kitchen stove—the smell of eggs and ramps still wafting up from the grease-caked skillet—and pondered the whereabouts of his sheep. They were probably still on the Bald, and if it was flurrying here in the hollow, it was surely a white-out on the high ridges.

"Reckon I better go find them," he said, lifting his voice so Gracie could hear. She was in the front room by the fireplace.

"Stop your fretting," she said. "You finished the dishes?"

He glanced at the dirty plates in the sink and coughed again.

"Let the sheep be, Wendell," she said after a while. "It's April already. Cain't be much of a snow, and you shouldn't be out in the cold with that cough."

"I'm fine, and I don't like the look of the sky," he said. "The sheep are nearly naked up there."

They'd just sheared the flock a few days ago, and Gracie had been so busy carding that morning—combing the wool back and forth into rolls thick enough to spin—she hadn't seen how gloomy the clouds had gotten since breakfast.

"If it's that bad," she said, "they'll come down of their own accord, like always."

Not one had returned, though, and Wendell wondered if the queer weather had them confused. The flock was used to rushing back to the barn when snow fell in late October or early November. But they'd just been let loose for spring grazing. A big, late-season snow like this might've confounded what little sense the poor creatures had.

"Sheep's a jittery animal," he said, speaking over the brushing and rubbing.

"You're a jittery animal," she said. "After you finish those dishes, come in here and give me a hand."

Wendell didn't bother to tell her he was leaving; there wasn't time for arguing. He grabbed his coat from the peg and headed down the back-porch steps, screen door flapping in the wind. He trudged up past the barn and through the pasture, watching flakes collect on the newly-greened grass and shrubs. It seemed a waste to have made it this far into spring, only to kill off the life that'd sprouted. He wondered what the Good Lord was thinking. *Guess He don't mind starting His garden over,* Wendell mused as he stifled another pesky cough, *but I do mind.*

As he climbed the trail through the woods, the wind picked up; the snow thickened, and he fretted over having forgotten his gloves. If Gracie hadn't been so fussy, he thought, I wouldn't have been in such a danged rush. For the last few months—ever since the boys, Harold and Daniel, had gone off to fight the Kaiser in the war to end all wars— Wendell had noticed a real pushy, pestering streak in Gracie, like it was her job to oversee all the chores now that they were the only able bodies around.

But Wendell had decided to let her be. It was just her way of handling the worry. He figured his mama had done likewise while he was off fighting the Injuns in South Dakota, but he could bear it until Harold and Daniel came home.

Hopefully the Great War would end soon. It was 1918; they'd been gone for many months. He missed his boys and hoped they'd both come home in one piece—healthy and ready to get on with their lives. He prayed they'd return clear-headed, not racked with the kind of nervous spells and nightmares that still haunted him from his stint in war.

He heard a spattering of *baahs* and *meehs* that brought him back to thinking about what he was supposed to be doing. The sounds seemed to come from the mountaintop. Scurrying in that direction, he followed the narrow trail as it bent sharply around a rocky outcropping. There was more noise, closer this time, and then a low thumping sound. He couldn't tell if it was from the wind bearing down on the trees or hooves clomping in the snow.

Suddenly the sheep rushed around the bend, and Wendell lunged to get out of the way, losing his footing on the icy wayside, and tumbling down the mountain.

《《——》》

When he looked up, everything Wendell put his eyes on was blurry and doubled, and the back of his head throbbed. A thin covering of snow slid from his backside when he rolled over and realized he was beside a chestnut tree. His fingertips were so numb he couldn't feel the grooves of the bark, so he coiled his pale-purple hands into a ball and blew in some heat. Sitting up and gazing down the foggy mountainside, he patted the back of his achy head. Thank the Lord for the tree, he told himself. If he hadn't rolled into the chestnut, no telling how far down the steep ridge he would've gone.

Wendell climbed to his feet, and as his vision began to clear, realized he wasn't but ten yards or so below the trail. He trudged back up to the path, which, though shrouded with fresh snowflakes, was still dotted with tracks from the sheep. *Probably back at the barn by now*, he thought, studying the flow of the tiny hoof prints around his feet. Leaning against the jutting shelf of rocks, he caught his breath and wondered how long he'd been out.

The sky was still pure gray, and the forest was shadowless, giving no clue as to the time. Rubbing the tender spot on his head, Wendell chuckled. *Bum-rushed by my own flock. Gracie will get a kick out that.* He pictured her with her fists on her hips, shaking her head: *Told you they'd come back. You just didn't want to do them dishes.*

A gust of wind raked the trees overhead and dumped snow on Wendell, and then, as the breeze and his rattling teeth settled, he heard a faint *baah* and *meeh* drifting down from the mountaintop.

Wendell shuffled around the rocky bend and gazed up the trail—which ascended the steep, snowy grade like a worn stairwell—and wondered if what he saw lying at the trail's edge was actually there. It looked like a ram's head placed upright in a pool of dark, crystallized blood. It was almost as if the thing were staring at him. He wondered for a moment if it was a rock, but, as he focused, the details sharpened, and there was no doubt.

A ram's severed head. The rest of the body was gone. He wandered up and crouched beside it, taking the ear-flap between his pale fingers

153

and checking the under-bit and topnotch cuts he used to mark his flock. It was his ram—black eyes gazing at nothing in particular. *What got you?* Wendell thought, running his numb fingers across the scratches in the coiled, frosty horns.

Then, off to the side of the trail, he noticed thin, dark-red splashes, which led to a bigger splotch several yards away. Beyond that he could see a thick trail of icy blood that disappeared into the gray trees. Running along in between were vague tracks, but here—where there were no rocks to provide cover—the wind and snow had made them difficult to identify.

Nevertheless, images of what could've happened flashed into Wendell's head: snowflakes salting tawny fur, cloudy breaths pouring from between glistening fangs, claws like unsheathed knives—the panther swiping the ram's throat and the head flying off, flinging blood as it tumbled onto the trail. He imagined the ram's body collapsing like a felled tree, and then the big cat clamping the front flank between its fangs and dragging the headless corpse away. That must have been what terrified his flock and sent them barreling around the bend, knocking Wendell down as they fled.

Couldn't be a panther, though, he reminded himself, rubbing the sore spot on the back of his head. Growing up, he'd heard countless stories about mountain lions. But his pa claimed to have killed the last one in Concord County decades ago. Wendell had heard of sightings and livestock attacks since then, but he didn't give the stories much credence. They were tall tales—the kind folks told their children by the fire to put a good scare in them. But what, besides a panther, could do this?

Bobcats lacked the strength and size to kill a ram in such a brutal manner. No doubt a black bear could, but he'd never heard of a bear going after livestock. They mostly fed on leaves and bugs, and it was unlikely one would square off with an ornery ram, unless it was a mama protecting her cubs. Maybe Pa didn't kill the last panther after all. Regardless of the cause, they'd have to get a new ram now. *There goes the wool money*, he grumbled.

Baah. Meeh.

The faint sounds came from up the trail, making him realize that one of his flock hadn't made it home after all. *Stupid animal*, he thought. *Panicked and ran the wrong damn way.*

Wendell wanted to go after the lost sheep, of course, but what if the thing—be it a panther, a desperate mama bear, or the biggest bobcat he could imagine—was still skulking through the foggy trees, waiting to pounce? He looked down the trail and considered heading home, but he just couldn't stomach the idea of leaving one of his sheep behind. If only he'd brought his rifle, but he'd been in such a hurry earlier he'd forgotten it. Just like his gloves.

Bet whatever did this is hiding the carcass of that ram. After all, only the head was left behind. He blew into his hands. *The killer animal is probably in a cave somewhere, so it won't come after me yet. I got time.*

Wendell hoofed it up the steep ascent, grabbing limbs and saplings whenever he needed leverage. He'd lost the stamina he'd once had—back when he could still beat his boys to the Bald—and soon a breathless, woozy spell took hold. He stopped and waited for it to pass, the thin, chilly air burning his nose. The snow was ankle-deep, shrouding the mountain ash and azaleas along the trail. Broadleaf trees had given way to firs and spruces and stubby beech trees, limbs sheathed in clumps of frozen fog.

He looked down the ridge. On a clear day, he could've seen his farmhouse, but today, the clouds blocked out everything beyond the stunted growth around him. He recalled standing at the kitchen window earlier and gazing up at the cloudy spot where he now stood. He pictured Gracie standing there now, watching and shaking her head.

She's going to be sore at me, he thought. *But I was right about the sheep.*

I was right.

Wind blasted a long stream of snow across his backside, and as he pulled his coat tight and waited for the wind to calm, he heard the lone, lost sheep call out again.

Poor critter's up on the Bald, he figured, picturing it trembling among the shrubs or scrambling along one of the trails which looped around the mountaintop like a hastily coiled rope. So Wendell followed the trail to where it started to level out, and then heard another round of *baahs* and *meehs*.

But this time it sounded like it was coming from down the mountain.

Thank the Lord, he thought. *Poor thing's finally heading home.*

155

Up ahead the trail forked around a moss-spotted boulder crowned with snow. A left turn would take him up to the Bald, a right hair-pinned back down the ridge towards home. Taking the right-hand trail, Wendell picked up the pace, and, before long, the trail curled around a clump of firs. When he rounded the bend and gazed ahead, his belly sank, arms dropping to his side like ice-laden branches.

Before him was an open, tree-less stretch, blanketed in snow, rhododendron hedges zigzagging here and there.

The Bald.

Now how'd you manage that? he wondered, glancing back. *You took a right back there. Maybe the fog and snow had somehow confused me.*

With no trees for protection, the wind in the Bald was even colder, so he laced his quivering hands together and blew in as much heat as he could before shoving them back into his pockets.

The sheep called out again, but this time, the cry sounded like it came from the Bald—not down the mountain like he'd thought before. How could it change direction so quickly?

He shuffled along beside a hedge of rhododendrons—the plump bushes looking like ghosts in ragged sheets—and, in the blurry distance, thought he saw a man, sitting beside the trail—balled up tight, as if to keep himself warm.

"Hey there, feller," Wendell yelled, waving.

The man didn't seem to hear or see Wendell. *Is that even a man?* he wondered, narrowing his eyes on the fuzzy shape. *Or is it a rock or something?* The heavy snow swirled, so it was hard to be sure

"Hey over there! Hey, I'm talkin' to you!"

The man still didn't move. Wendell started to yell again when he heard someone say, "I'd leave that one be."

He spun around and saw somebody standing beside the rhododendrons. The wind died down, and he could make out black pants and a long coat. The man looked old—face leathery and dark like an Indian's. He wore a tall hat, crumpled on one side like a dinted can, and wiry strands of white hair fell over his shoulders.

"Pardon?" Wendell asked.

"That one by the trail," the old man said, his voice dry and slow. "I'd leave him be. I tried to help him earlier, but he's beside himself and doesn't want to be bothered."

"Why's that?"

"He can't find his stock," the old man said, each dawdling word leaving his lips with a cold puff.

"I lost one of mine, too," Wendell said, hearing his own teeth chatter. "This damn weather. Surprised there ain't more folks up here hunting their livestock." Wendell turned to the man by the trail. "Maybe he's seen my sheep."

"I don't think so. He hasn't seen anything he can speak of."

Wendell looked at the old man. "You seen a sheep?"

The old man shook his head. A white gust bore down on them. "Built a shelter and a fire over there," he said, pitching his voice over the wind and casting a gnarled finger toward the middle of the bald. "You can wait out the storm there."

The old man then ducked between two rhododendrons. Wendell shuffled over and angled his head between the bushes. The old man's black coat was fading into the distance. Wendell glanced at the man by the trail. He wanted to talk to him—see if he'd seen his sheep. But if the old man's account was correct, it probably was best to wait.

The old man was about to disappear into the snowy shrubs, so Wendell slipped between the rhododendrons and followed him. Shelter and a fire sounded like the best thing right then. The old man curved back and forth through the narrow maze. The farther they went into the heart of the Bald, the higher the snow piled, coming up over Wendell's boots, clumping in thick layers on the leaves, falling on his shoulders and head whenever they scooted through the path's tighter passages.

He couldn't remember ever being so cold, so frozen he hardly felt it. The numbness bothered him; he feared what it might be hiding. If he came home all frostbit, Gracie would be sorer at him than she probably already was. If he lost some toes or a foot over this, what kind of man would he be then? He tried not to pay it any mind and focused on the trail instead.

Soon they entered a clearing, circled by rhododendrons. Surely Wendell had been here before, but the swirling wind and heaps of snow made the patch unfamiliar. The old man took him to a little lean-to hut he'd erected with spruce limbs and covered with thick-needled fir branches. The ground beneath was clear, and a small fire smoked inside.

Wendell was impressed—amazed actually—at the stranger's craft, given the conditions. The old man sat beside a pile of wood and needles. He laid a couple of sticks—old, weathered ones which looked like chicken bones—across the little fire. He sprinkled some needles and blew. The needles sparked and smoked, throwing off a pleasant, orange glow. Wendell sat across from him and warmed his hands over the persistent little flames.

"Thanks for sharing your shelter. Name's Wendell. What do they call you?"

"They don't anymore," the stranger said, flames reflecting in his pupils. The glare made Wendell uneasy. Then the old man drew his lips into a little smile. "Call me Smith."

Comforted by the smile, Wendell said, "Well, Smith, sure glad you found me and brung me here. Don't know what that one by the trail is thinking."

"He's not," the old man said, eying the fire again.

The fir thatching held the heat, and Wendell actually began to feel cozy after a while. He stretched out, scooted close to the fire, and propped his head on his elbow. "Just need to warm up before I get back to tracking my sheep. Cain't believe this weather. Never seen it snow like this in April. Not even on the Bald."

The old man laid more wood and needles on the fire and blew. The flickering light seemed to have a hold over him.

"How'd you come to be up here?" Wendell asked.

"I'm always up here."

"Never seen you. Where you from?"

"That way," the old man said, tilting his head eastward.

"Carolina, huh? I got some kin over there. Not on the reservation, of course." If the old man was from Carolina, Wendell figured he had to be an Indian, given how dark his skin was. "Anyhow," he continued, flexing his hand over the flames, "ain't seen my Carolina kin in years."

Wendell's body was thawing; he could feel his hands and feet again, but also the throb in the back of his skull. He rubbed it.

"What'd you do to your head?" the old man asked.

"Wouldn't believe me if I told you."

The old man lifted his eyebrows, as if to say, *Try me.*

"Got bum-rushed by my own flock. Damn critters knocked me off the trail, and I rolled into a tree."

"What spooked them?"

"Not sure. Whatever it was, it killed my ram." An image snagged Wendell's tongue for a second: steamy breaths and fangs, claws and the ram's black eyes. "Took its head," he continued, awkwardly, "clean off."

"Mountain lion?" Smith asked, glancing up.

Wendell shrugged. "I was out cold, and, when I come to, the damned thing was gone. My pa said he killed the last panther around here years ago. You ever seen one?"

"Not directly, no," Smith said. "How would you know for sure? In the woods, they could be as close to you as I am now and you'd never know...Sneaky creatures."

"Reckon so," replied Wendell. "Never seen one myself. Heard all kinds of stories about them, though." Wendell started to feel drowsy. "Know what time it's getting to be?"

Smith shook his head.

"The wife's going to have my hide if I don't get home soon."

The old man said nothing. Apparently Smith preferred silence, just like Gracie did sometimes. On more than one occasion, she'd asked Wendell to stop prattling on all the time. But Gracie didn't understand: talking was how he hushed and calmed his head.

He still had nightmares about fighting the Injuns in South Dakota; sometimes, he had wide-awake flashes—frozen-faced men and the stiff, bullet-riddled bodies of women and children stretched out in the snow. Wendell hadn't been there when it'd happened—hadn't been party to the shooting spree—but he was part of the detachment that went back to Wounded Knee to dig the graves. He helped carve a long trench into the icy ground and toss in the bodies. Over twenty years had passed, but time had done little to wear down the memories.

He could never find the comfort in silence that Gracie did. She could spin wool for hours without a peep as if the purr of the wheel were all the conversation she needed. Talking put Wendell out of his own head for a little while—talking about anything and everything, except for his time in the Army.

So Wendell listened to the wind—how it pitched a fit, then hushed, only to get riled up again. His eyelids drooped, and he widened them, trying to stay pert. From across the fire, Smith's dark skin looked so frail and papery a strong gust might peel it off.

"You got a story or something?" Wendell asked, fighting off a yawn.

The old man gazed at him.

"To pass the time, I mean. Something, you know, with deer and rabbits."

The old man gave him a confused squint, as crumpled as his hat.

A yawn welled up and stretched Wendell's lips until his jaw quivered. "You look like an Injun is all."

Wendell couldn't fight it any longer. He curled his arm up like a pillow and rested his head. "Guess I'll nap a spell before...heading out."

«« — »»

When Wendell awoke, the fire was just ash and a few thin curls of smoke. The old man was gone. Wendell called for him, but there was no reply, so he crawled out of the hut. The snow had let up considerably, but the sky was still pure gray.

He finally spotted Smith beside a row of rhododendrons and walked over. Through a gap in the hedge, Smith was pointing to the valleys on the other side of Bald Mountain. The sky was cloudless, and the ridges stretched out like frozen waves, each one a lighter shade of blue.

The land looked somehow purer than Wendell remembered, like it had when his pa had first brought him here—like he'd imagined it'd looked to his boys Harold and Daniel the first time he'd brought them here. It made him think of South Dakota—a few days before the massacre—when he'd looked out across a purple, grumbling sky and endless grassy plain and felt no bigger than a grain of sand next to the whole of God's creation.

"Looks like, like..." Wendell muttered and then stopped. It wasn't something he could put into words.

The old man grinned.

Wendell glanced over his shoulder. Towards home, the sky was still gray. "Should be clearing up on this side soon. Need to be getting back. Y'aint seen or heard my sheep have you?"

Smith wagged his head. He pointed down into the valleys. "You should go down there and see your kin."

"Told you," Wendell said, pointing over his shoulder, "I come from the other side of the mountain. I don't even know my kin down that side no more."

The old man drew his lips into an odd little smile that unnerved Wendell a little.

Faint *baahs* and *meehs* came from the cloudy side of the Bald, and Wendell bolted in the direction of the sound. He darted through the rhododendrons, following the faint remnants of the footsteps they'd made earlier, until he was back at the trail, catching his breath.

A little, gray-spotted ewe skittered his way, *baahing* and *meehing*. He'd never been so happy to see an animal. He could finally head home, lost sheep in tow. Then he heard Smith ask, "Where're you going?"

Wendell turned. Smith was between the rhododendrons.

"I'm taking my sheep and heading home."

"That sheep doesn't belong to you."

"What?" Wendell asked, practically spitting the word. He was fed up with weird weather and odd-acting animals and strange people. He just wanted to go home.

"Look here," he said, scooping up the ewe by the belly, "this is my mark."

He grabbed its ear to show Smith the under-bit and topnotch cuts, but, when he got the ear between his fingers, he saw that the ewe hadn't been marked.

"It belongs to no man," Smith said. When he stepped onto the trail, the ewe bucked and wiggled out of Wendell's arms. It scampered away, disappearing into the cloudy trees.

"Deer and Rabbit get caught in a flash flood," Smith said as he approached Wendell. "They grab the limbs of a sycamore tree before the stream carries them away. The water keeps rising, and Deer loses his grip and is carried off by the angry waters. But Rabbit holds on. His grip is strong. The water keeps rising. Soon Toad comes along, jumping from branch to branch against the current. Rabbit asks him, 'Did you see Deer back there?' And Toad says, 'Yes, he made it to higher ground.' 'What's the trick to making it there?' Rabbit asks, and Toad says, 'The trick is being strong enough to let go.'"

Wendell nodded anxiously but was still thinking, *What kind of man don't mark his sheep?*

When Smith placed his hand on Wendell's shoulder, he smacked it away, as if it were a wasp. Smith stepped back and tilted his head. Something about the old man's voice and eyes and leathery skin suddenly terrified Wendell.

He took off down the trail, running until he was clear of the Bald and barreling through the woods again. He was going back to the big boulder—to the place where the path forked—except this time, he was going the other way, the right way.

He didn't even care about the sheep anymore. He just wanted to see Gracie—wanted to be by the fireplace, watching the spinning wheel and her ruddy cheeks as she wound the yarn. This image kept his legs churning through the dark woods—past all the crooked beech branches grabbing for him—kept him steady over all the slick patches where he nearly lost his footing—all the way back to the big, moss-speckled boulder.

He leaned against the cold rock for a spell. It felt like the most solid thing on earth. Get going, ordered a voice in the back of his achy head, so he staggered to the fork and hunched, studying the diverging trails.

Right one takes you down the mountain. Left one goes back to the Bald.

Are you sure this time?

Has to be. I just came down the left one.

He darted right of the bolder and ran until the trail bent around a familiar clump of firs, and Wendell's stomach sank. He caught himself before toppling to the ground and staggered past the rhododendrons where Smith still stood. "Nothing belongs to nobody."

Wendell refused to look at him. He kept hobbling down the trail until his feet gave out, and he toppled into the snow. He dragged himself to the side of the trail and sat down.

When a gust whipped sheets of snow across his body, he stretched the coat over his head. He wrapped his arms around his shins, pulled his thighs to his chest, and buried his face in the dark gap between his legs and his shirt. The breaths warmed the hollow spot enough to keep his teeth from chattering.

He couldn't feel his hands, though. It was as if they were no more a part of him than the rocks and trees. He cursed himself for leaving his gloves. Should've listened to Gracie. Should've washed those dishes.

And then suddenly he knew.

He turned and saw Smith standing on the trail a few feet away.

"Is this another one of my spells?" Wendell asked.

Smith shook his head.

"Did the mountain lion get me?"

"No," Smith said. "It was the flu. The Spanish flu. You were already sick. That's why you fell down on the mountain. Haven't coughed in a while, have you? Son, you never got up from that fall."

162

"What will happen to Gracie? My boys?"

"This Spanish flu is a plague—whole world's eat up with it. Millions are going to die—more than in the war to end all wars. But one of your kin will survive to take care of the sheep."

"Which one?"

"You'll know soon enough."

"When?"

"When you get up and head to the other side of the mountain." Smith said, each word forming a tiny cloud of steam. "Then, you'll see."

Suddenly Wendell changed his mind. "Nah, this is just another one of my spells," he decided. None of this could be true. Otherwise... "It'll pass. And then I can head home."

"We're going to keep on doing this over and over, Wendell, until you let go, stand up, and head to where you need to be. It's up to you."

It'll pass, Wendell assured himself, staying in denial. He continued to sit, balled up tight, burying his head in the space between his knees and his chest. At least in this little gap—warmed by his own breaths—he could picture the spokes of Gracie's spinning wheel, ceaselessly purring in the orange flicker of the fireplace. Clumps of wool becoming long strands of fine yarn to be knitted into sweaters for Harold and Daniel when they returned from the war over in Europe.

Soon he heard a voice rise up over the wind. "Hey there, feller."

Wendell lifted his head slightly and shifted his eyes down the trail. In the blurry distance, he thought he saw somebody standing near the rhododendrons, waving at him. Wendell couldn't quite make out his face in the swirling snow, but his hands were bare. Apparently, he'd forgotten his gloves, too.

"Hey over there! Hey, I'm talkin' to you!" the man yelled.

The familiar voice tore through Wendell like claws.

About Jason Reynolds

A native of East Tennessee, Jason Reynolds now lives in the mountains of North Carolina with his wife, Jennifer, and their two beloved dogs, Charlie and Bowie. He is currently teaching English Composition at South College in Asheville. In his free time, he's usually hard at work on fiction pieces which blend the regional and dark fantasy genres in order to explore ecological and philosophical themes. His work has appeared in speculative fiction magazines such as *ResAliens* and *Indigo Rising* as well as the forthcoming *Midnight Diner* anthology.

He can be contacted at: mrgalapagos@hotmail.com or through his blog at: http://uroboros73.wordpress.com.

SKELETONS IN THE CLOSET

by Cheryl Kaye Tardif

Many families have secrets. Shameful events formed from deception, humiliation or guilt. Some have buried their secrets where no one will ever find them. Some have spun a web of lies so convincing that even they start to believe them. Others hold onto their shame and wrap themselves in it, like a protective fur coat. Every family has "skeletons in the closet," and I was about to unearth mine.

On this auspicious spring evening, I had parked my car in front of the behemoth grand manor that had been the family home for four generations. The house sat regally atop Hallowed Hill, just four miles north of the city. It was constructed from dull gray brick and small windows. Overall, a cold, dreary welcome. Even the thunderous skies that boiled overhead seemed to be warning me away. I turned deaf ears to it. Maybe I should've listened.

I used the key Grammy had given me and the front door squealed in rebellion. I entered the family home with a sense of excitement that wouldn't last long.

"Some doors are never meant to be opened."

I wish I had listened to Grammy's wise words, but the self-assured adult I had become shrugged off the advice. Funny how we think we know better than those who have lived far longer and seen much more.

After a quick tour of the lower floor, I was satisfied to see that everything was in its place, exactly as I remembered it. Pausing at the bottom of the stairs, I sighed. My eyes were drawn to the upper landing. For a minute I thought I saw someone crouched near the rails.

"Hello?" My voice echoed through cavernous walls. "Is anyone here?"

No reply.

Laughing at my paranoia, I headed upstairs and followed the hall to the room at the end. Grammy's room. I reached out and a visible spark

165

flew from the shiny metal knob to my fingertips. I jumped back, startled and slightly breathless.

"Jesus!" I covered my mouth with one hand.

"Don't take the Lord's name in vain, Emma." I could hear Grammy's voice so clearly in my mind it was like she was standing right behind me.

My eyes darted guiltily down the hall. There was no one around, no one to hear my slip. But one could never be too careful.

"Sorry," I said, feeling like a child again.

I looked at the antique keys on the tarnished silver key ring in my hand. Grammy had given me the keys at the hospital. She'd told me to go check out my inheritance. Told me to stay out of her bedroom closet. Just like she had so many years ago when I had visited her in the house at the top of Hallowed Hill. A house that I had once sworn was haunted.

"Emma..."

I jumped, certain I'd heard the deep voice of my grandfather, the one I recalled from my youth. His voice made me think of lollipops and pony rides. That's how I remembered him. How I *wanted* to remember him.

Grampy had been a war hero. When I was about six, he'd sat me on his knee and told me how he'd rescued his buddies in Vietnam after their chopper was shot down by enemy troops. Grampy had flown in, dangling on a line suspended over the heads of the Vietcong, all the while dodging bullets and machine gun spray.

Whenever I thought of Grampy, I pictured him hanging in the air.

Suspended.

When he'd returned home, he wasn't the same man. That's what Grammy always told my mother. He started drinking and fighting with other war vets in bars. He'd also broken bones and bloodied noses of those who were against the war. Grammy said he always walked headfirst into a fight, with his big mouth flapping and his fists up and ready.

I'd never seen that part of him. Only the aftermath.

Too many times, my mother had gone out in the middle of the night to pick him up, half-carrying him inside. I woke up on these nights, troubled by Grampy's loud slurring and my mother's chastising anger. When I saw Grampy the next morning, he always smiled at me and called me his "Punkin." He'd take me out back where I'd watch him polish and repair one of his old cars, while I handed him the tools. We were both covered in grease by the time he was done.

Grampy was my hero.

Until he disappeared a week before Christmas. I was eighteen. He left my poor Grammy heartbroken, my mother without a father and me without my favorite person in the whole world. That's when I started resenting him. I couldn't help it.

"Emma..."

There was a cool draft in the hall and I blamed it for my imagination running wild. The house was empty. Except for me.

Wasn't it?

I turned the knob and stepped into my grandmother's room.

The master bedroom appeared to be never-ending, a series of three rooms connected by wide archways and stone pillars. This room was a mystery to me as I'd never been allowed inside whenever I'd visited. It had been Grammy's private sanctuary. Still was.

"Grammy?" I whispered. I almost expected her to answer.

I entered and flipped on the light. A warm golden glow shone down on me as I stepped into the floral sitting room, which held a mahogany bookshelf, a flower-patterned sofa and matching high-back chair with ornately carved arms and padded rests. There were tables of all sizes and heights, stained in shades of warm oak and many adorned with crystal bowls and vases. Grammy had once told me that Grampy had brought back much of the wood furniture and crystal from places like Italy, Germany and England.

I passed through the archway at the opposite end and entered Grammy's bedroom. A canopy bed sat regally on a raised platform in the middle of the room. The ceiling in this section was about fifteen feet high, with elaborate crown molding and inset ceiling tiles from Italy. A pathway covered in thick, lush carpets completely framed the floor around the bed.

I followed the carpet path, admiring numerous pieces of furniture and artwork that I suspected were originals and valuable, but it was the bed that really intrigued me. Larger than any other I'd ever seen, it seemed fit for a king.

Or a queen.

Elegantly draped fabrics in gold and crimson tones hung from carved posts and swayed from one top corner to the next. Embroidered bedding in matching tones covered the bed, and I stared at it, wondering what it must be like to sleep in such luxury.

I resisted the urge to throw myself onto the bed. It wasn't easy.

The scent of perfume lingered in the air. Chanel No. 5. Grammy's favorite. Every Christmas since the late 1930s, Grampy would buy her a new bottle.

Grammy's warning in the hospital came back to me.

"Stay out of my closet, Emma."

I glanced at the closet door. It was plain and uninteresting, no etching, no fancy design, just solid wood, iron hinges and a lever handle instead of a doorknob. I shrugged, wondering why Grammy had been so adamant about me not going in her closet. What was the big deal?

"Maybe that's where she's hiding her stash of medicinal marijuana," I muttered, though I doubted she'd ever tried the stuff.

I let my fingers drift over the surface of the furniture as I strolled around the room. I left a clean trail in the dust on the surface of everything I touched.

The colonial oak dresser at the far end of the room displayed various family photographs. I picked up a photo of Grammy and my mother, when she was a teenager. They both looked happy and carefree. I put it back, my attention drawn to a baby picture. Me, when I was two. I was a chubby baby, with squinty eyes, sausage links for arms and legs and three chins. Scowling, I set the photo down on the dresser, backwards. The other photographs revealed family members I couldn't identify. There wasn't one picture of Grampy.

I looked at the closet door again. Was it open a crack?

I approached it, telling myself I'd make sure it was closed, just as Grammy wanted. When I'd seen her in the hospital, she told me she'd made arrangements for someone to pack up all her personal belongings, including whatever was in the closet.

"When that's done," she'd said, "you can do whatever you want with the room. With the whole house. It's yours."

I reached for the handle and opened the door.

The design of Grammy's bedroom closet was early walk-in style. Extra wide, extra deep and very dark. I reached for the light switch and flicked it on. The light bulb flickered and hissed. Then it died.

I was thrown into partial darkness, the light from the bedroom casting a pale slice about halfway inside. The far end of the closet was submerged in shadows.

I sniffed and scowled. A musty smell lingered in the air.

"You could use some Febreeze in here, Grammy."

I took in the colorful clothing that lined one wall of the closet. Grammy had her own flamboyant style. Wearing flowing jackets, caftans, silks from China and India, all in bright colors and patterns, she liked to stand out in a crowd.

On a shelf above the clothing were six mannequin heads with various colored wigs, from blond to auburn. They were remnants of Grammy's battle with cancer—one she'd beaten with finesse.

I fingered the shoulder length blond wig. It reminded me of my mother, whom I hadn't seen in a while. She'd taken off on an around-the-world tour. She sometimes sent me postcards from one exotic place or another.

"Why did you leave me here all alone, Mom?" I asked the mannequin head. "Why did you make me responsible for Grammy?"

I resented my mother. But I loved her too. Sometimes when I thought of her, I missed her so badly I wanted to curl up and cry my heart out.

I took a few steps into the shadows. Somewhere over here was the old trunk that Grammy was adamant about moving to her new home. Another step into the dark brought me up against the trunk. I wondered how heavy it was.

Before I changed my mind, I yanked on the corner of the trunk and was surprised to find it moved quite easily. Sliding my hands around it, I discovered handles on both sides. The trunk was too wide for me to carry, so I dragged it across the floor until it caught on a floorboard. I heard a soft cracking sound and gave another sharp pull.

The trunk slid into the light.

There was a large keyhole on the front. Was it locked?

I pushed the lid. It didn't budge. I tried all the keys on the key ring. Nothing.

Peering over one shoulder, I examined the room.

Where would Grammy hide the key?

Her dresser beckoned me. There were three drawers down each side and two cupboard doors in the middle. I opened each drawer and felt around underneath Grammy's clothes. It was a bit uncomfortable searching through her undergarments, especially when I came up empty. I opened the doors. Two shelves of sweaters. Nothing else.

I was about to walk away, when I noticed a small groove on the strip of wood that ran above the cupboard shelf, just under the dresser top. I hooked my fingers in the groove and tugged. A hidden drawer slid out.

And there it was. The key.

"I just know you're the right one," I murmured.

Walking back to the trunk, I pushed the key in the lock and turned it. There was a quiet click. The lid popped open a quarter of an inch.

"Okay, Grammy," I said, exhaling. "Let's see what you've got in here that's so important."

Papers. The trunk was filled with all kinds of papers. Envelopes, some old and some unused. Stacks of letters bound by elastic bands. A pile of photographs and a small box, which when opened revealed postcards.

Probably from my mother.

A black leather folder caught my eye. My name was on it.

"Looks like I've got some reading to do."

I grabbed the folder. As an afterthought, I took a stack of letters and the box. Placing these on the bed, I decided I'd spend the night reading.

Okay, I was snooping. But she was my grandmother after all.

An uncomfortable feeling swept over me. I was invading my grandmother's privacy. Logically, I knew I should put everything back and forget about it. But something illogical urged me on.

I plumped up the pillows on Grammy's bed, turned on the lamp and settled into the softness of duvets and feathers. I placed the box in my lap, opened it and splayed out a handful of postcards. Photos of familiar and unfamiliar worldwide landmarks greeted me. Paris, Italy, Germany, Spain...the destinations were varied.

"Definitely from my Mom." I gritted my teeth. "So let's see what she had to say to you, Grammy."

I turned over a postcard. It was blank. Frowning, I turned over another. Blank too. I flipped over the pile in my hands and fanned them. Not a word or signature on any of them.

It didn't make sense.

I dropped the cards back in the box and reached for the letters. Removing the elastic band, I examined the top envelope. It was addressed to Marilyn Ingram, my grandmother. The sender was R.V.P.H., with an address about five miles out of the city. A charity perhaps?

I opened the letter, dated in December of the previous year.

Dear Mrs. Ingram, the letter stated. *I hope this Christmas season finds you well. With regards to the resident, she has been showing signs of severe emotional distress, just as we predicted. This seems to be the most stressful time of year for her, and so we'd advise against your monthly visit. However, if you do decide to come by, please be aware that we've had to adjust her medication so she may not be fully alert or even aware of your visit. Also, please note that she still insists that she's traveling through Europe and is unaware of her actual surroundings. At this time, we cannot recommend her release.*

I stared at the letter. "What the hell?"

The word *resident* jumped out at me. And the word *medication*.

"*She still insists that she's traveling through Europe,*" I read aloud.

Oh. My. God. My mother was insane.

I ripped another letter from the stack. The date was January 15, 2010.

Dear Mrs. Ingram, the resident is still unaware of her situation and she insists she's visiting Scotland. The staff feels confident that she will regain both her memory and her sanity. She did appear less confused after your last visit. We look forward to seeing you again.

I swallowed hard and tasted bile. Blinking back tears, I stared at the envelope. *R.V.P.H.* was some kind of Psychiatric Hospital.

I flipped through the envelopes, reading the postmarks. They dated back to March of 2005.

With my heart pounding, I strode to the trunk and removed the other letters. Again, I checked the postmarks. These dated back to 2001, the year Grampy had disappeared. Was there a connection?

Something sparkled on the floor of the closet.

Thinking Grammy had dropped a piece of jewelry, I entered and crouched low, my hand grazing the rough wood floor. "Ouch!"

A splinter stuck me on my palm. I plucked it out and sucked at the wound. Then I caught sight of the sparkle again. Something had fallen into a hole in the floorboard, a hole I'd created when I'd dragged the trunk across the floor.

I tried prying the board with my fingers, but I wasn't strong enough.

"Hammer," I muttered. I'd seen one earlier, under the bathroom sink.

Returning from the bathroom with hammer in hand, I used the clawed end to pry up the loose corner of the board. The overpowering scent of mothballs made my eyes water. Coughing, I wiped my eyes and continued working on the board. A few minutes of prying resulted in success, but before I could lift it, I heard a door slam downstairs.

"Emma?"

It was Grammy.

A surge of red hot heat flared through my cheeks.

What was I doing? Not only had I disobeyed Grammy's request to not open the closet, I'd read her personal letters, ones that weren't meant for my eyes, and now I was ripping up her floor.

Guilt rebelled against resentment.

How could Grammy keep this from me? How could she hide what my mother was? A nutcase in some psycho hospital. What right did Grammy have to keep that from me? Footsteps sounded on the stairs.

Shit! I had to put the trunk back. And the letters.

With my heart racing, I tossed the letters in the trunk, along with the box of postcards. I dragged the trunk into the closet.

"Emma? Are you in here?"

Wiping a dusty hand against my brow, I emerged from the closet, only to be confronted by my grandmother. Her snow white hair was pinned into a bun, accentuating her gaunt appearance. Wire-rimmed glasses had slid halfway down her matriarchal nose and she pushed them up with a boney finger. She puckered her lips, reprimanding me wordlessly from a distance.

In her hand was the black leather folder I'd left on the bed.

"You shouldn't be poking around in someone else's belongings," she said, resting heavily against her cane. She frowned. "You scratched the floor."

I didn't know what to say. Two fresh gouge marks marred the hardwood floor, disappearing into the closet.

"We need to talk, Emma." She held up the folder. "Did you peek?"

I shook my head and held my stance as she squinted at me and tried to determine if I was lying.

"Let's make a pot of tea," Grammy said in a tired voice.

In her world, a pot of tea was the solution for everything.

I followed her down the stairs, pausing with her as she caught her breath every so often. A million questions swarmed through my brain, and I wanted to bat them away. I knew that once I'd opened Pandora's Box and asked those questions there would be no turning back. No more living in denial.

Grammy puttered around the kitchen, filling a tarnished kettle with water and setting it on the gas stove. She set two tea cups and saucers on the small table in the corner, then gathered a silver serving tray with cream, sugar and two spoons.

She waved me over as the kettle whistled. "Have a seat, dear."

I sat down across from her.

She placed the folder on the table, centering it between us like a barrier. Then she ignored it and went about preparing the tea. "You still like yours weak?"

"Yes, Grammy."

She poured my tea and waited her usual three minutes before pouring her own. I silently added a dose of cream and a spoon of sugar to my cup. I needed all the fortitude I could get.

"Did you snoop through anything else in my trunk?" she asked.

"I didn't snoop—" I caught myself in the lie. "Okay, sorry, I did. I found the letters and the postcards."

Grammy blinked a few times and turned away. When she spoke, her voice was strained. "Did you read them?"

"Yes." I took a sip of the tea. It scalded my tongue.

"So you know…"

"That my mother is a nutcase?"

Grammy's head shot up. "Don't say that."

"I *know*, Grammy. I know that my mother isn't traveling around the world, living her easy breezy carefree lifestyle. She's locked up in some hospital because she's crazy. With a capital *C*."

"Emma!" A tear rolled down Grammy's cheek.

"You don't have to pretend anymore. I can handle it."

"Can you?"

"I'm not a child. I can handle the truth."

Grammy leaned forward and placed a frail hand on the folder. "If it's truth you want, it's all in here. But I have to warn you, you won't like what you find." She hitched in a breath and wiped her eyes. "It's not what you think, Emma."

"Nothing's what I think anymore, is it?"

Grammy slumped in the chair, her shoulders deflating. "No, it isn't."

"What I don't get is why you waited so long to tell me."

"They told me to wait. Until you started asking questions."

"Who told you?"

"The doctors."

I allowed this to sink in. My mother's doctors knew she had a child, but thought it better to wait to let me in on the big secret until I started wondering what the heck was going on. Nice doctors.

I reached for the folder and for a moment I wasn't sure Grammy would release it. But she did. Begrudgingly.

"After you've read that," Grammy said, "I know you'll have questions. I can stay here—"

"No." When I realized how ungrateful that sounded, I softened my voice. "I'm sorry, Grammy. I'm really tired. I'll read it in the morning and call you right after."

"Are you sure, dear?"

I nodded, part of me wondering whether I was making a mistake in letting her go before I'd learned the whole truth. *And nothing but the truth, so help me God.*

When we were finished with our tea, I escorted Grammy to the door.

"Make sure you call me tomorrow morning," she said, "as soon as you read it."

"I will. I promise."

I watched her walk down the sidewalk to the awaiting taxi. Once the taillights faded, I closed the front door and rested my back against it. Exhaustion had set in. I felt it in my bones and even my teeth. My body ached to curl up on a soft mattress and sleep. But my mind was all chatter.

What's the scoop on my mother? How crazy is she? What will I find in that folder? Don't I want to look now? Why wait until morning? Go on, read it now.

I grabbed my head with both hands. "Shut up!"

I returned to the kitchen and approached the table. The folder lay there so innocently. Papers and words. That's all it was.

And truth.

"If it's truth you want, it's all in here," Grammy had said.

"I want the truth," I said to the empty room.

I sat down. I inched my fingers toward the folder. When I touched it, it seemed hot.

You're imagining things.

Though I'd told Grammy I'd read the documents in the morning, there was no way I could wait that long. I had to read them now. I had to know.

I opened the folder, drew out the first page and read it. Then I read the next sheet. And the next. With each page, my confusion grew. Terror set in.

Oh my God.

I read every page twice, pinching myself occasionally to make sure I wasn't dreaming. This was real. This was the truth.

I stood up, my legs trembling. Even my hands shook. Leaving the folder open on the table, I wandered into the den. I needed something stronger than tea and I knew where Grammy kept the good stuff. Her bourbon collection was the talk of the town.

Two glasses later, I felt calmer. I brought a third glass into the kitchen and stared at the file, willing it to burst into flames. I considered destroying it, but I suspected there were other copies.

I picked up the final page and read it once more, allowing every word to sink in. I was desperate to remember my mother's face. That last day. The day when tragedy had struck...

A glimmer of a memory surfaced and I hissed in a breath. My mother had gone out late that night to bring Grampy home after one of his late night binges at the local bar. When they'd returned, they'd woken the entire house. I remembered the loud voices and vicious words. They scared me.

I massaged my forehead, struggling to recall what had happened next.

I'd gotten out of bed and was heading down the upper hallway when I heard my Grampy roar. It was the one sound that made everyone nervous.

Though I was eighteen years old at the time, fear reduced me to a quivering child. I crept to the landing and peeked over the rail. Grampy and my mother were fighting, pushing each other. He was trying to leave the house again and my mother wouldn't let him. He smacked her hard against the face. I sucked in a shocked breath. My hero was beating on my mother.

My mother hit him back. A few feet away, Grammy cowered against the wall, trembling with fear. "Stop it, Walter! Leave her alone. She's just trying to help you."

"I don't need her help," Grampy roared, his fists lashing out at my mother.

Terrified, I sobbed on the landing above them. My head felt like someone had taken a jackhammer to it. Panic robbed me of breath and my vision grew blurry.

Now as I recalled this fateful night, my head started to hammer.

The scene in my mind switched. I saw Grampy. Lying on the floor. Soaked in blood. Unmoving.

Dead.

"Oh, Jesus," I whispered. "It can't be true."

The vision grew more defined and I saw my grandfather's pocket watch. It lay next to him, also covered in blood.

The vision faded and I stared up at the landing, picturing a scared teen, her face between the rails, watching the violence below.

I plodded up the stairs.

Entering Grammy's bedroom, I went to the closet and yanked the trunk along the floor, anger surging within me. Again, the trunk caught on the loose floorboard and it cracked and lifted.

The glimmer drew me closer.

Crawling on my knees, I waved at the cloying scent of mothballs and ripped up the remainder of the board. I tossed it aside. The space beneath was large, and it wasn't empty. My grandfather's pocket watch rested on top of a four foot wide blanketed shroud. The shroud, about six feet in length, was surrounded by mothballs.

I picked up the watch and stared at the shroud.

Grampy hadn't left my grandmother for another woman. He hadn't left Grammy at all.

"Grammy, what did you do?"

"I did what I had to, Emma."

I turned.

Grammy stood in the doorway, tears pouring down her cheeks. "I couldn't leave you tonight. I knew you'd never wait until morning to read the reports."

"I'm starting to remember."

"I figured you would one day."

I flicked a look at the shroud beneath the floorboards. I knew what it was. *Who* it was. With gentle moves, I peeled back the blanket, carefully pulling it away from the skeletons that rested within its cocoon.

Grampy and my mother. She was wrapped lovingly in his arms.

They looked peaceful.

"He killed my mother," I sobbed.

"I tried to stop him," Grammy said, hobbling over to me.

I reached for her, hugging her tightly. "I know. But he was drunk. He didn't know what he was doing. She was dead before she hit the floor at the bottom of the stairs."

"I thought you'd die too," Grammy said, gulping in breaths of strained air.

"I didn't mean it."

"I know, dear." She stroked my hair. "It was an accident."

Grasping her hand, I led her to the bed and we sat down as the past washed over us, all of its terror and guilt finally setting us free.

I reached in my pocket and pulled out the last page from the folder.

"When I found the letters and the postcards, I thought I'd figured things out," I told her.

"I did what I had to do to keep you safe. I didn't want you taken from me too." Grammy took a deep breath. "I wrote the letters that were supposed to be from your mother because the doctors thought it best. At least until you started remembering."

"But it took so long."

"I know. Sometimes I thought you'd never remember. Then I could take this to my grave. All of it."

"Grampy pushed my mother down the stairs."

My heart was heavy with the burden of truth.

"I didn't even know you were awake," Grammy said quietly. "I saw you charge at him when he reached the top."

"And I pushed him down the stairs," I said, shaking my head slowly.

"You were upset that he'd hurt your mother. It was an accident, dear."

I gazed into her eyes. "You hid their bodies. Lied about where they were. To everyone. Even my doctors."

Grammy looked away. "I'm not proud of that. I wanted to tell your doctors the truth. In the end, I didn't have to. You refused to speak to anyone. Refused to eat." She took my hands and kissed them. "I had no choice, Emma. To keep you safe—to help you—I had to lie to them and hide the truth. I didn't realize the damage I'd done until it was too late."

I watched her, knowing that in her heart she thought she'd made the best decision. I knew that her choice was dependent on two factors. She feared what would happen to me if my guilt were to be known and she was deathly afraid of being alone.

I thought back to earlier in the week. I hadn't gone to see Grammy in the hospital, like my deluded mind had led me to believe. She'd come to check me out and bring me home. *I* was the patient. Every paper in the folder had *my* name on it, not my mother's. I'd been a resident of River Valley Psychiatric Hospital for the past nine years.

Everything shifted into place, like the magical brick wall from Harry Potter. Like a hazy fog being lifted from my eyes. What was once a fantasy world was now a reality far different than I could ever imagine.

"I'll make arrangements to have them buried," Grammy said, interrupting my thoughts. "Private arrangements. No one besides us needs to know what happened. I'll take care of everything."

I nodded. As I watched her make a phone call, I thought of how good Grammy was at taking care of things. She'd looked after me for nine years.

Now it was time for me to take care of her.

"I love you, Grammy."

"I love you too, dear."

Yes, many families have "skeletons in the closet," and on this day I learned that mine was one of them. Literally.

About Cheryl Kaye Tardif

Cheryl Kaye Tardif is an international bestselling Canadian suspense author of various published novels, including *Whale Song*, which *New York Times* bestselling author Luanne Rice calls "a compelling story of love and family and the mysteries of the human heart...a beautiful, haunting novel."

Besides her novelette *Remote Control*, an anthology titled *Skeletons in the Closet & Other Creepy Stories,* and novels *Children of the Fog, Divine Justice, Whale Song, The River* and *Divine Intervention,* Cheryl penned *Lancelot's Lady* under the pseudonym Cherish D'Angelo.

Booklist raves: "Tardif, already a big hit in Canada...a name to reckon with south of the border."

BLEEDER

by Paul Edwards

The deeper I go into myself the more I realize that I am my own enemy.
— Floriano Martins

Closing the bathroom door, Carey unfolds her brother Zach's letter and re-reads it. She found it this morning, on the mat in front of the door to Jude's apartment. She has no idea how Zach had found her, or when he had dropped it through, but he had made it clear to her that he missed her, and that he thought about her all the time.

Raking a hand through her hair, she closes her eyes for a moment. Deep inside her chest her heart pounds like a distant drum. She thinks about Jude; about how lifeless and vacant he has become. When she presses her ear to his chest, why can't she hear his heart anymore?

She stuffs the letter into her pocket just as the bathroom door squeaks open. Jude scuffles in, long hair hanging in greasy ribbons around his shoulders, his expression empty, lost, pale. Heavy-lidded eyes shine at her, then he moves toward the mirror on the bathroom wall.

Carey thinks about how different he is from her brother Zach, and stares at her hands as Jude glares into his own sallow face. Then he gives a derisive snort, snatches open the mirror and reaches for something.

Moments later he's standing over her, proffering her his pearl handled razorblade. His face is stoic, blank: it gives nothing away. Nodding, she rolls up the sleeve to her shirt and takes the razor. The flesh on her arm is criss-crossed with scars. She closes her eyes, whispers something, a black prayer perhaps, and then cuts herself.

180

For a moment there's nothing. Then a droplet of blood surfaces and Jude turns away in disgust. And that's when Carey knows they are going to the house.

«« —»»

The house on Blackhart Hill watches over the other tenements in the street like a hooded sentinel. No one has lived there since the seventies. The windows are boarded up, most of the roof tiles are missing, and enormous cracks snake the walls.

Jude knows a way in: round the back of the property, behind a tangle of wild nettles and creepers, is a shattered window. Hesitantly Carey follows, dropping down on to the rickety floor of a basement. Everything is black; her nostrils flare with the scents of rot and damp, dust and decay.

"Jude?" she calls.

He grabs her arm. "This way," he breathes, leading her through the darkness. Slowly, very slowly, her eyes discern vague shapes in the cloying shadows: a wooden chest, barrels, coils of thick rope, stripped copper wire. She sees an old rocking chair, a framed picture covered in a patina of dust, the metal skeleton of a bed.

Carefully, Jude wrenches open a door, which reveals a narrower, smaller chamber. The half-moon glows faintly through a dust veiled window, high up in a crumbling wall. Cobwebs swathe the corners; pieces of broken tile lie scattered across the floor. Carey's eyes alight on something at the back of the room, and as she steps forward she realizes she is staring into her own petrified reflection.

"I wanted to show you this place," Jude whispers, splaying his hands on the mirror's cobwebbed pane. "I've been here before. Quite a few times now." Sucking in a breath, he tries his very best to smile. "Never on a full moon, though."

She edges around an overturned armchair. "W-what do you mean?"

"They only come on a full moon."

Carey narrows her eyes. "They?"

Shoulders sagging, Jude's eyes drift from their brittle white reflections to glare at her. "Them," he says. "The wraiths."

The first time she'd stared into his eyes was in the squalor of The Cellar Bar in the city centre. "You're one of us," he'd told her, peeling back the sleeve of her jacket to reveal the self-afflicted scars on her arm. "I knew it as soon as I saw you." He'd licked his lips; smiled a

181

vague, broken smile. Staring into his eyes, she'd discerned a darkness more intense than any she'd ever seen before.

"Let's get out of here," Carey whispers, turning, snapping out of her reverie.

Jude steps away from the mirror. "We'll come back, yeah?" he says. He looks frightened and disorientated; on the verge of panic. "I...don't want to step over alone."

She nods once. "Next full moon," she says. "I promise, Jude; promise I'll be ready."

That broken smile flashes across his face, and in that terrible room she knows that her fate is sealed. And so they leave the house, and without even discussing it, both wind up back at Jude's. Tonight he's withdrawn; too tired to even speak.

Jude is squatting in the corner of his bed-sit, pitch black eyes staring into space, mouth open, stagnant. There's no furniture in the room; he's thrown everything away. The bathroom's equally as bare. Silent, Carey drifts toward the mirrored cabinet and for a moment doesn't even recognize herself: her eyes are black-ringed, her hair lank, her skin too thin and pale, almost translucent. She presses a finger to her face, pulls back the skin from her right eye.

Bloodless.

She snatches open the cabinet. The shelves are empty, except for the pearl handled razorblade on the middle shelf. She picks it up, turns it over in her hands, stares at it. Then, perching on the lip of the bathtub, she applies the razor to her flesh.

Don't think, she tells herself; *don't feel. Disassociate yourself from everything.* As the wound opens up, she waits for the blood to come.

It doesn't.

Moments later she's back in the main room standing over Jude. His expression is unchanged—the blank, vacant stare of a mannequin. "Jude," she says, shaking him. "Jude, look."

She shows him her arm.

As his narrow eyes clear and blink and focus upon her raw, damaged flesh, he frowns and tilts his head slowly to one side. "I'm like you," she whispers, tracing the cut with her fingers. "I don't bleed."

That faint, broken smile passes briefly across his face, and he reaches for her with trembling hands. Together they wait for the right moment, the right night.

«« —»»»

The full moon rises like a death's-head.

Without a sound, they leave Jude's apartment and step out on to the silent, moonlit street. Jude reaches for Carey; grips her hand. As they cross the road, Carey hears a car door slam. She glances over her shoulder and sees a person silhouetted against the bone-white moon. For a moment she thinks he looks a lot like... No, she thinks, shaking her head, it can't be.

He steps forward, a streetlamp shattering his face with light.

It is.

Jude's grip tightens around her hand. "Come on," he urges, pulling her toward the house, away from the street, the figure. "We have to go."

Suddenly Zach breaks into a run, leather coat flapping around him. "Carey!" he shouts, and she stops and turns; stares into his wide, blue, desperate eyes. "I-I saw you the other day," he gasps, breathing hard, face greased with sweat, hands splayed out on his knees. "I-I followed you here. That's how I found out where you lived. Mum and Dad and me...we miss you, Carey." His voice cracks at her name.

Jude mutters, swears, and Zach looks at him. "I'm Carey's brother," he says, straightening, extending a hand.

"Carey hasn't got a brother," Jude spits, spinning violently away. Faltering, hesitant, Zach looks helplessly at Carey, but Jude is already pulling her toward the house, toward her destiny.

"Carey!" Zach cries. "Please...just listen to me."

The house looms over them, drenched in shadow and streetlight. She leaves her brother helpless and alone on the dark street, rejecting his pleading; following Jude because he is her destiny.

As soon as Carey drops down on to the basement floor, she searches and gropes with her hands. She stumbles a couple of times, but Jude grabs her and steadies her and leads her to the door at the back of the room. Slowly, it creaks open to reveal the mirror and the window framing the bright full moon. Jude shuffles, zombie-like, through the chamber, eyes like jagged slivers of flint.

"What now?" Carey asks, voice quivering, and for a moment she fears he senses it; he hears that quiver too.

Before he can speak, the mirror ripples and shimmers and Carey steps back, hands clasped to her face. Their reflections are alive; stepping up to the glass, they spill through the frame and crawl out into

183

the room on all fours. Then they straighten, faces like cracked sheets of ice, and unlike their human counterparts their skin is grey and their open eyes and mouths are empty and black and choked full of dust.

Carey squats on the rubbish-strewn floor. A shadow falls upon her, and as she peeks through her fingers she sees her reflection loom inexorably over her.

Show us, they say in slow, stuttering voices, *you're ready.*

Carey drops her hands, nods, and rises. Then, silent, expressionless, the reflections stoop to gather up pieces of shattered glass.

Tentatively, Jude takes a shard from the palm of his reflection's outstretched hand. Then, biting his lip, he presses it to his arm and cuts. The flesh opens: bloodless. Empty.

Carey takes the sliver of glass from her own reflection's hand. Presses it for a moment against her flesh.

We miss you, Carey.

Carey chokes back a sob. Bites the inside of her mouth.

Her reflection stares into her. *Cut.*

And Carey cuts.

For a moment there's a line, a stripe; then comes the blood, trickling in a rivulet down the inside of her arm, and her reflection laughs bitterly.

Face creased, Jude's eyes flash with something—hurt? Anger? Betrayal? She doesn't know; can't read him any more.

With a godless stare, Jude's reflection grips his upper lip and, as if pulling back the hood of a coat, wrenches his face clean off. Carefully the thing scrunches up the flesh and presses it into its mouth. It tears away Jude's clothes, proceeds to strip the rest of the flesh, unwinding it, revealing the nothingness beneath. Then, once it has devoured the rest of him, it turns back toward the mirror.

Carey shrieks. Whirling, shaking, she flees from the room and her own dead-eyed reflection, racing for the window at the back of the basement, leaping now, hands scrabbling, grabbing, levering herself up. Then she's up on her feet and sprinting from the house and she doesn't even realize she's screaming until she runs straight into Zach, who grabs her by the shoulders and steadies her and holds her against him as she shrieks and sobs into his scuffed leather coat. "It's okay," he shouts, "It's okay, Carey! You're safe! You're with me now, safe..."

He drags her away from the house. Just as they are approaching the car, she throws one last look over her shoulder and sees a piece of rotting wood come away from one of the ground floor windows. There, framed between the remaining slats, is her doppelgänger—staring out at her with screaming eyes. With a grey hand pressed against the glass it mouths something; four words: *A matter of time.*

With a loud, choked sob, Carey turns away from the house, away from that thing and allows herself to be guided into the sanctuary of her brother's waiting car.

«« —»»

The thing watches Carey collapse into the car. Watches as the car speeds off into the night. Then it comes away from the window and perches upon a broken chair in the corner of the room.

With gray hands scrunched together in its lap, it waits.

She'll be back, it thinks, *assuredly.*

Her kind always come back.

About Paul Edwards

Paul Edwards has had around forty publications in a wide range of magazines, anthologies and web-zines. He's had two honorable mentions in the *Year's Best Fantasy and Horror*, and one of his stories, 'A Place the Night Can't Touch,' was made into a short film by students at The Surrey Institute of Art and Design. A collection of his stories, 'Now That I've Lost You,' has been accepted by *Screaming Dreams*, and he's currently hard at work on a second, 'Black Mirrors.'

You can find out more about Paul here:

http://www.pauledwards76.blogspot.com/

THE NIGHT VISITOR

by Joe McKinney

For more than thirty years now, I've had to live with night terrors. That sounds silly, I know. After all, I'm a grown man, fifty-seven years old. A retired San Antonio police detective. You'd think I'd be above something that's only supposed to bother children. But apparently not. I get them, and I get them bad.

It goes something like this: I'll bolt upright in bed, my eyes wide open. I look crazed, but I'm asleep. Sometimes I scream. Sometimes I can't. My heart pounds in my ears. Confused, unable to move, I panic, because I know there's something in the dark there with me. But even with that knowledge, I can't make myself move.

Thankfully, my wife's a light sleeper.

Frightened as my terrors make her, she shakes me. That's always enough to wake me. I come to, out of breath, still half-convinced the walls are closing in on me, and find myself sitting up, damp sheets knotted around my legs.

"The dream again?" Margaret says.

I nod. And while she goes to get me a cup of water, I hang my head. Defeated doesn't quite describe how these terrors make me feel, but it comes close. I feel old, fatigued beyond anything that rest can alleviate. Sitting there in the bed, waiting for Margaret to come back with my glass of water, I hate myself for what feels like weakness. But that doesn't stop the terrors from coming.

Two or three nights a week I go through this.

Margaret and I have been to doctors and we've tried their snake oil. Nothing helps.

In fact, things have gotten worse.

«‹‹—››»

In April, 1981, I was working in the San Antonio Police Department's Crime Scene Unit. Back then, nobody outside of police circles had ever heard of CSI. They didn't make TV shows about us because we weren't interesting. We did our thing and tried to stay out of the way, like janitors. The closers, the real detectives, they were the glory boys.

But everybody gets their fifteen minutes of fame, and back in 1981, I got mine. I was taking pictures of a busted lock on somebody's tool shed when Juan Felan, who was the sergeant in charge of my unit, called me back to headquarters. It was two o'clock in the afternoon. I was supposed to get off at three. I'd been doing a pretty good job recently; I figured maybe he'd send me home early. Sergeants did that for their troops back then.

Instead, he told me he was driving me out to Brady, Texas, three hours west of San Antonio, to investigate a murder. I had to admit I was intrigued. Getting called out to the sticks to help other jurisdictions wasn't unusual. We had mutual aid agreements with most of the agencies from the Texas Coast to the northern limits of the Hill Country. But every time I'd been called out before that, it had always been as an afterthought, always as a support player for the heavy hitters. If I was hearing him right, Sarge was going to let me be the lead on this one.

But Sarge was smiling, and that always made me suspicious. "Is there something you're not telling me?" I said.

"No," he said. "Honest. DPS asked for us. They said they needed a fully staffed forensics unit. All their guys are down in the Valley on some kind of drug sweep. That makes us the closest team available."

I frowned at him. Now I had it figured out. Sarge was a good guy, but he was one of those supervisors who always went looking for ways to prove his unit had a purpose, which made him look good, but usually just meant more work for guys like me.

I said, "They asked or you volunteered?"

"Whatever. Look, I want to make a big splash with this one."

I shook my head. "Sarge..."

"There's a shallow grave," he said.

That stopped me. "What now?"

He just smiled.

«« — »»

We rode up in his truck, all of our gear in the back. On the way, he told me what he knew.

Earlier that morning, shortly before dawn, a State Trooper named Bo Farris had been eating breakfast in a little cafe in downtown Brady. In staggers this babbling, wild-haired farmer named John Welfare. Despite his last name, he owned a farm north of town, where he grew lima beans and peaches and kept a few horses. He'd never been in any trouble. But that morning he was covered in dirt and lurching about like a loon, muttering something about impaling a woman on a fence post and burying her in a shallow grave on his property.

"That's it?" I asked.

"That's what Trooper Farris told me on the phone."

"And exactly what am I supposed to do?"

"We'll do what we always do, Phil. They need us to process it so they can close the door on this guy. We're going to be the ones to make that happen."

"Sounds like the door's pretty much closed already," I said. "I mean, the trooper got a *res gestae* confession, right? Even a bunch of rednecks should be able to get a conviction on that."

"Phil, please. This is important."

I shrugged. "Yeah, well, as long as you're paying the overtime," I said.

《《——》》

We got lost twice, but eventually we pulled onto a dirt road that wound back through a tunnel of mossy oak trees to a little rundown farm waist-deep in Johnson grass. Trooper Farris' Dodge Diplomat waited in a little clearing to one side of the house, and on the far side of that, a white Chevy van with the Channel 5 News logo on the side.

I whistled.

"Damn," Sarge said. "What's the news doing here?"

"I don't know. Looks like they got here without getting lost, though."

He glared at me. "Shut up."

We got out. It was getting to be late afternoon and crickets jumped in the tall grass. I looked around. A brown, bored horse watched me from a nearby pasture. A breeze caused me to shiver unexpectedly. I could smell a storm coming.

"I think we better hurry," I said.

Sarge nodded. "Yeah. There's Farris."

The Texas Highway Patrol fosters this reputation that their troopers are big and bad and beyond reproach. They bill themselves as the preeminent law enforcement body in Texas. But in reality, most of the troopers you meet are rednecks in shiny uniforms. They're good guys, most of them, and good cops, nearly all of them, but they're still rednecks.

And redneck pretty much summed up my first impression of Bo Farris. He was tall, real tall in fact, slender, a Marine Corps anchor peeking out from under the sleeve of his right arm. A regular civilian might have seen a rugged good 'ole boy who had things well in hand. But I was a cop, and I recognized that harried look in his eye. I knew he was glad to see us.

Then I saw a flash of red hair over by the news van and I knew why.

"Howdy," Farris said. He tipped his cowboy hat at Sarge and extended his hand. "You Sergeant Juan Felan?"

"I am," Sarge said. Sarge pointed at me. "This is Detective Carroll."

"I'm the one who does all the work," I said. "Call me Phil."

Farris smiled and we shook hands. "Bo," he said.

Farris looked back at the news van. He pushed his cowboy hat up on his forehead and huffed.

"Maureen giving you trouble?" I asked.

He gave me a blank look.

"The redhead," I said. "Maureen O'Connell."

"Oh," he said. "Yeah, she's, uh...well, she's a determined lady."

"She's a bitch," I said. "How long has she been here?"

He chuckled. "Yes sir, sounds like we're on the same page. She's been here about two hours. Keeps asking why I'm not doing anything but standing here. Between you and me I'm running out of excuses."

I grimaced. I could only imagine what his afternoon had been like. Maureen O'Connell used to date one of our Homicide detectives. This guy, his name was Jesse, was a real smooth talker, great in the interview room. Great with suspects. He could talk to anybody. More importantly, he could make *them* talk. He was a good looking guy and he was single and he had a thing for newscasters.

Turns out, he was also dating one of the reporters from the local Spanish station at the same time he was going out with Maureen. The two reporters were at a murder scene when they confronted each about it and got into a nasty fight. A fiery Irish redhead and an equally fiery Spanish lady—it was a fight to remember. And of course Maureen had had it in for cops ever since.

"She's a firecracker," I agreed.

"I'll talk to her," said Sarge.

Farris looked relieved. "I'd appreciate that."

"Looks like we're going to get some rain here before too long," Sarge said, pointing off to the west where a dark line of clouds was forming. "Why don't you two get started?"

He left to go talk to Maureen O'Connell.

"That was pretty decent of him," Farris said.

"He just wants to see himself on TV. Where's the grave?"

He led the way down a narrow path through the tall grass. We crossed a dried up creek bed, went through some scrub brush, and entered a small clearing surrounded by hackberry bushes. I saw a jagged piece of wood sticking up through a patch of ground that had recently been turned over.

He pushed the brim of his cowboy hat up his forehead. "That's it," he said. "You have any idea how long this is gonna take?"

"Hard to say. You ever watched an archeological dig on TV?"

"A what?"

I frowned. "This could take a while."

First thing I did was photograph the scene. Next I stuck probes in the ground and measured the decomposition gases coming up through the soil. That gave me a picture of the body's orientation and helped me gauge how much ground I was gonna have to dig up. After that, I drove stakes in the ground at the corners of the plot and used string to set up a search grid.

I took more photographs.

By that time a crowd had gathered. Sarge and Trooper Farris stood to one side, Maureen O'Connell and her camera crew stood by opposite them.

I started to dig, slowly peeling back layers of dirt.

About six inches down, I found the body.

In the Texas heat, bodies can turn bad pretty fast. I saw a murder victim once that had been floating in a creek for two days. The body was bloated and blackened. Turtles and carp had gotten at the face and eaten away everything below the nose. What was left of the hair and scalp slid off the skull in a greasy ooze when the body was extracted.

Even the veteran cops were gagging from the smell. My job was to get in close and search for evidence, but even from six inches away I couldn't tell the victim's sex or race.

I figured this one wasn't going to be anywhere near that bad. It had been in the ground less than twelve hours. Rigor mortis would have set in, leaving the body stiff as furniture, but nothing too much beyond that. It shouldn't have started to rot, or smell, puff up the way bodies will do.

But I could smell it even before I cleared away all the dirt.

I caught movement out of the corner of my eye and saw Maureen O'Connell and her camera crew backing away, lips curled in revulsion.

I frowned to myself, then looked back at Farris. "I thought you said this happened this morning."

He nodded. "Yeah, just before dawn."

"That's when he killed her, or that's when he reported it to you?"

His eyes narrowed, like he hadn't considered that question before. "Both," Farris said. A pause. "I reckon."

I shot Sarge a worried glance. He swallowed and squinted at the body.

Still frowning, I knelt over the grave and went back to work, brushing away the dirt. The body didn't look right. When somebody dies, when their body sits out for a while, exposed to the Texas weather, the eyes start to film over. The skin turns waxy and a little yellow. The low parts, where gravity pools the blood, turn a dirty looking purple. Arms and legs stiffen from rigor mortis.

But none of that had happened with the body upon which I was working. I could tell it was a woman I was looking at, but she was ghastly.

Her clothes were nothing but soiled rags. Where there should have been white, smoky-colored eyes, there were black gummy pits. The body was almost skeletal, the skin of the arms and legs cracked like old dried leather. Her hands were blackened and gnarled, the fingers spindly as oak twigs. Her face was almost unrecognizable, malformed and diseased. The expression, with those black, vacant holes where the eyes should have been, was malignant. I can think of no other word to describe it.

As I stared into that repulsive face, the split and cracked lips started to twitch. I felt a hitch in my throat. I gasped for air, but before I could

191

breathe, the woman's mouth fell open and a centipede writhed its way through the lips and tumbled down her chin.

"Oh God," I said, battling the nausea welling up inside me.

I heard one of Maureen O'Connell's camera crew throw up.

Something buzzed in my ear. I looked up, and noticed flies murmuring in the air around me. I waved them away, but they were insistent, landing on the woman's face and testing the borders of the eye pits.

Maggots caused a ripple in the decayed cheek. I snapped a couple of photos and then gingerly touched the woman's lips. Her mouth sagged open slightly, enough that I could see a jagged line of cracked and blackened teeth that looked as though they had been sharpened. There were wide gaps between them, and they were different sizes and pointed at odd angles. But they were like fangs. I took my hand away and rocked back on my heels.

Flies buzzed in front of my face.

I heard Maureen gag and I looked up. She was staring at the body, a look of disgust and horrified curiosity on her face.

A rain drop hit the dirt beside me. I realized then that I'd been so overcome by the grave stench beneath me that I hadn't noticed the gathering storm above me. I looked up through the trees and saw a black, roiling sky rolling in. The Texas Hill Country doesn't get gentle rain the way other places do. It gets long stretches of hot and dry punctuated by apocalyptic rain storms. I could see black clouds rolling over rocky hillsides, lightning snaking its way through ominous darkness. We were going to get a belly washer.

Thunder shook the air as though in answer to my thoughts. Already the wind was tossing the trees about, and the raindrops stung my cheeks.

I stood up. "We're gonna need to cover the scene," I said.

"What are you going to do?" Maureen said.

She was looking at Sarge, and he answered her. "We'll cover it up as best we can. It's getting dark anyway. I have a tarpaulin and a frame tent we'll put over the scene here. That should keep it dry for the night. We'll pick up where we left off in the morning."

We went back to the truck to get the supplies. Sarge climbed into the bed and handed the tarp down to me, followed by a hammer and some tent spikes. "You saw that woman's face," he said.

"Yeah."

"What do you think?"

"I think it's time to turn this over to the locals. I don't want any part of this."

"We can't do that, Phil. We got obligations."

Suddenly I felt resentful. What business did he have talking about obligations when it was down there in the grave digging around the lady with the pointy teeth?

But the anger cleared the next instant. Sarge meant well. He was one of those men who went through life not really knowing the hardship they cause for others. He was blissfully ignorant of that.

I could have argued with him about it.

But I didn't.

For all his eagerness to please the higher ups, and for all his vanity, Sarge was basically a good man trying to do a good job. He cared about people, even if his decisions sometimes raised a few eyebrows.

You can't really argue with a man whose heart is in the right place.

"I don't think we're getting the full story," I said, trying to turn the conversation back to his original question.

"Yeah," he said. "You and me both."

«« —»»

Later, after the scene was as safe as we could make it, Trooper Farris asked if we wanted join him in his patrol car. The storm was upon us by then, lightning snaking across the black sky, rain moving across the open fields in wind-driven, silvered sheets. The bored horse that had been staring at us when we first arrived was now snorting loudly, obviously scared. I felt for it, but I had no idea how to help it. I knew nothing of horses.

"Wait a minute," Maureen O'Connell said. She was holding a clear plastic poncho over her head, and she was nearly shouting to be heard over the rain. "Why can't we go inside the farmhouse?"

"It's still a possible crime scene, ma'am," said Sarge. "Nobody goes in until it's been searched and cleared."

"Where are we supposed to go, then?"

Sarge shrugged. "You can head back to San Antonio or you can sleep in your van."

She glared at him, but Sarge didn't back down. I had to hand that to him, he didn't back down.

Finally, Maureen motioned to her people and they went back to their van.

Farris watched her go, then turned to Sarge, "You guys think we're gonna do any more work tonight?"

"We're done for the night," he said. "Tomorrow morning I figure we can finish up and then go for breakfast."

Farris nodded. "Well, if we're officially off-duty...I got some beer in the trunk, if you guys are interested?"

I glanced at Sarge and caught his smile.

"Yeah," I said. "I could go for a few beers."

«« — »»

Sometime during the night, a flash of lightning woke me. I was drunk. My eyelids felt like they were made of concrete. I was sprawled across the back seat, and when I rolled over, a wave of beer cans clattered to the floorboard.

Groaning, I sat up.

Sarge was sleeping in the passenger seat, his raincoat over him like a blanket. Farris had his face pressed up against the driver's side window. He was snoring softly.

More beer cans fell to the floor and Sarge grunted, but didn't wake.

The storm had picked up outside. The wind was really slamming the trees, throwing them about with howling gusts so strong they even rocked the car.

Another flash of lightning lit up the night.

I leaned forward, my forehead almost touching the window, squinting out at the dark.

Someone was walking around out there.

I strained to see into the darkness and the rain, but it was no use. The house was a looming shadow off to my right and the trees around it danced crazily in the wind. It was hard to think straight with all the beer I'd drank. My mouth tasted horrible and my neck hurt from sleeping on it wrong. Briefly, I wondered what the horse I'd seen earlier was doing.

And then the lightning came again and I saw Maureen O'Connell walking toward our car. No, that's not right. Staggering is a better description of how she was walking. She had one hand up over her face, shielding it from the slashing wind and rain, and she was struggling to keep her feet.

Great, I thought. She was on her way to shoot video of the cops passed out on a pile of beer cans. *Great.*

I put my head down on the seat. For a moment I considered trying to hide the beer cars, but drunk as I was I could tell there were too many of them for that. Besides, my head was spinning, and I was sinking down into unconsciousness.

I belched and closed my eyes.

Slipping back into oblivion, I wondered what was taking her so long to knock on the window.

«« — »»

The storm was gone by morning. I woke with sunlight on my face, my skin hot. From the front seat, Sarge groaned like a wounded animal. Farris grunted, sniffled, then sat up straight.

"What, huh?" he said.

I patted him on the shoulder. "At ease, Marine."

He sagged down into his seat, remembering where he was, and mopped a hand over his face. "Oh God," he groaned.

"Yeah, you and me both," I said.

I burped, and felt an acid burn climb up my esophagus. I had to pause for a second, unsure if the burn was going to lead to me puking my guts out. Finally, my stomach settled and the burn subsided.

"Okay," I said. "Who's ready to go look at a dead body?"

We climbed out of the car.

While I was stretching, trying to work out the kinks I'd developed from sleeping in the car, I saw Maureen O'Connell's mutilated body in the grass a short distance away.

"Whoa!" Sarge yelled. "Hey Phil!"

"Yeah, I see it," I said.

I walked over to the body. She was on her back, one knee bent, her legs spread open. Her skirt was hitched up to her waist, revealing pantyhose over a surprisingly plain pair of white panties. But it wasn't the panties I noticed.

I was looking at the hole where her neck had been. From the base of her chin to the top of her sternum, her neck was just gone. Her face was pale from lividity, flecked with blood. For a moment I got lost in the emptiness of her gaze.

I thought, *Maybe a mountain lion. Maybe a wild hog. They have both out here.*

195

Either way, it was going to be hard to explain how a woman died so close to two police officers.

It was hard to do, but I forced myself to look away. The dead have a way of drawing you in. I scanned the tall grass for tracks around the body, but there were none. None that I could see anyway.

I turned back to Maureen's body. Back to her face. Back to her open eyes.

I couldn't help it.

"What the hell's going on?" Farris said from behind me.

"We need to lock this area down," Sarge told him. "Do you have anyone else who can help us?"

"County might be able to send us somebody."

"Call them, then. Christ, I can't believe this. Right under our noses. This is bad, very bad."

"Looks like a mountain lion got at her," Farris said. "If it was a mountain lion, hell, she could'a been attacked right next to us and we'd have never heard nothing."

"That's not what I mean," Sarge said.

"Huh?"

I shook my head. Farris might not have known what Sarge was getting at, but I sure did. Here was the SAPD's biggest critic, brutally slain just a few feet from one of their detectives and a supervisor. When the news got a hold of this, they were going to crucify us.

I rocked back on my heels and thought for a moment.

From where I squatted in the tall grass, I had a view under Maureen's news van to a small patch of ground on the other side.

Something caught the light of the morning sun.

I got up and walked over toward Maureen's van.

"Phil!" Sarge said sharply. "Hey Phil, where you going?"

I didn't answer him. I made my around the back of Maureen's van and saw one of her cameramen flat on his back, neck ripped open. I didn't see the other one, at least at first. He was behind a hackberry bush, on his side, one arm draped over his forehead like he was trying to shield his eyes from the sun. Only the morning sun hadn't reached that part of the yard yet. It was still dark from the overhanging trees and a curtain of Spanish moss.

I stepped around so I could see his face and the gaping wound. His face was ghostly pale, dark in places with dirt. Bits of grass were

196

caught in his black hair. His mouth hung open in a perfectly formed O, as though he were still surprised by what he'd seen in his last moments.

Only then did I notice the total lack of blood in the grass. With the wounds I was seeing, the scene should have been ankle-deep in it. But aside from a few spattered drops here and there, nothing.

I started back to Maureen's body.

Sarge and Farris met me as they were coming around the back of the news van.

"Looking for blood," I said to them, and kept walking.

"What?" Sarge said. He watched me walk back to Maureen's body. "Where the hell are you going?"

I stood over Maureen's body and looked around.

No blood. Why hadn't I noticed that before?

I put my hands in my pockets. There was a chill in the air left over from the storm the night before. By midday, as the Texas sun beat down on the grass, this place would be hot and damp as a sauna. But for now, I shivered.

I looked over to the horse pasture. The horse was gone. I figured it would have enough sense to get out of the rain, but I didn't see any signs of where it had got off to. The fence to his enclosure was still intact, the gate closed.

The main house was quiet too, nothing there.

Finally, I went over to check the crime scene that had brought us to John Welfare's farm. The tarp had been nailed down with tent spikes, but now it was thrown off the shallow grave like a carelessly tossed bed sheet. Uneven ruts in the mud extended out of the grave, like the body had been dragged from it. I found the fence post a short distance away.

At the time, I remember telling myself the rain had washed the blood off the business end of that fence post. I told myself that the ruts in the mud were marks of a mountain lion dragging a carcass away. There was a reason Maureen and her camera crew had been, for lack of a better word, exsanguinated.

An animal had done all this, of course.

A mountain lion. Maybe a feral hog, but probably a mountain lion.

And when the body in the shallow grave disappeared, we figured the dead woman with the jagged teeth had been dragged away by scavengers, more animals. We were in the country, after all.

It was the only thing that made any sense.

And that is what we reported, with Farris our witness to back up our account. We took the heat from the press, and barely hung on to our jobs. The ensuing months were stressful until new stories pushed Maureen O'Connell's death out of the headlines and life went on.

«« ——»»

For everyone else, the nightmare faded from memory. But I still get night terrors. In my dreams, I wake up on the backseat of that patrol car and I sit up, and I see Maureen staggering onward against the wind and the rain. Only in the dream her face isn't lost in blur. I can see it clearly.

And I recognize the delirious panic and fear in her eyes. In the dream, I don't fall back to sleep amid a clatter of beer cans. In the dream, my gaze wanders across the empty field, and I can see the dead woman with the jagged, pointy teeth pulling herself from the shallow grave, clawing her way free of the tarp and through the mud.

It's only a dream, of course. But in that moment before my wife wakes me, and I'm paralyzed with fear, I can hear something wet clawing and slapping its way from the hallway into our room.

And in recent months, the dream lingers long enough for me to see the thing raise its head and open its mouth, exposing a jagged line of sharpened teeth.

About Joe McKinney

Joe McKinney is the San Antonio-based author of several horror, crime and science fiction novels. His longer works include the four part *Dead World* series, which includes *Dead City, Apocalypse of the Dead, Flesh Eaters* and *Mutated*. His other books include *Quarantined, Dodging Bullets, The Red Empire, The Predatory Kind, Dead Set: A Zombie Anthology* and *The Forsaken*. His short fiction has been collected in *The Red Empire and Other Stories* and *Dating in the Dead World and Other Stories*.

In his day job, Joe McKinney is a sergeant with the San Antonio Police Department, where he currently works as a patrol supervisor. Before promoting to sergeant, Joe worked as a homicide detective and as a disaster mitigation specialist. Many of his stories, regardless of genre, feature a strong police procedural element based on his fifteen years of law enforcement experience.

A regular guest at regional writing conventions, Joe currently lives and works in a small town north of San Antonio with his wife and children.

This story, "The Night Visitor," was written by Joe exclusively for this book, *A Feast of Frights from The Horror Zine.*

ALWAYS SAY TREAT

by Christopher Nadeau

It will be dark soon and the children will return.

Rick draws the curtains and locks the doors and turns off all the lights. Perhaps this year they'll overlook his house and move on to someone else to torment. Surely they've grown bored with him by now. How many times can they return and experience the same joy?

But who can understand what they call entertainment?

He still remembers the days before the children started coming with fondness, but the images are becoming more difficult to summon. The world as remembered is a fading fairytale. The children have seen to that.

Rick gasps as the sound of his ringing doorbell punches a hole through the silence in the house. He tip-toes to the front door and peers through the peephole, relaxing once he knows who is standing out there. He opens the door and raises an eyebrow at the man standing in his doorway wearing a nervous facial expression.

"What do you want, Earl?" Rick says.

Earl's eyes dance around in his head as he leans forward and opens his nearly toothless mouth. "Thought I'd hang out with you tonight." He affects a chuckle that sounds dry and forced.

Rick shakes his head. "You know better."

Earl blinks and looks him up and down. "Come on, Rick. They're gonna be coming soon."

Rick suppresses the disgust he feels upon hearing Earl's whiney tone of voice and again shakes his head. "They don't like it when people double up. Remember Mrs. Medevoy?"

Earl looks away and sighs. "She had a houseful of people, though."

Rick stares blankly at the older man and fights the urge to reach out and strangle him with his bare hands. Earl knows full well what the rules are yet here he is trying to elicit sympathy. Rick finds it impossible to feel sorry for anybody who's in the same situation as him, no matter how pathetic he acts. With a small amount of guilt, Rick finds himself hoping the children will knock on Earl's door tonight.

"Go home, man," he says. "Keep low to the floor and for Christ's sake, turn off all your lights."

He watches Earl hang his head and shuffle-walk away back to his house. Rick lingers only long enough to make sure the older man has ascended his porch before closing his own door and locking it once again.

Rick takes a deep, shaky breath and leans against the front door a moment longer, wondering if he did the right thing. The world is not what it once was but does that mean he has an excuse to stop being compassionate? Sighing, he pushes himself off the door and heads into the kitchen to make a cup of coffee; the last thing he needs is to fall asleep before the trick or treating is over.

He walks past the refrigerator and tries without success to avoid looking at the photographs on the door. But the photo of Rachel stares back at him as if in accusation and he finds himself unable to move from the spot.

"I tried," he says. "I did try."

Her picture doesn't respond but he hears something in his head, the sound of her final screams on the front porch as Rick stood on the other side of the front door, leaning against it in case the children came for him next. Every part of him screamed to open that door, to throw it open and run out there with some kind of blunt object and start swinging like a samurai. His legs and arms wouldn't respond.

He remembers standing there with his legs shaking until something struck the door so hard it actually sent him reeling back into the hallway. Then, slowly, he approached the door and forced himself to unlock and open it. She wasn't there. All that was left was her red slicker; except...Rachel wore a clear rain slicker.

"Oh, God," Rick moaned. "Oh, God, Oh, Jesus."

The high-pitched giggling of children filled the air, causing him to whirl around until he faced them. He tried not to look. People always said don't look at them directly but he couldn't help himself. He had to know what these things were and why nobody seemed to be able to stop them.

They stopped giggling as soon as he stopped looking away. He couldn't quite make them out in the dark since they were backlit by the floodlight from Earl's house, but they seemed to be small and in constant motion, shuffling from foot to foot and leaning forward and then back.

"It's not as much fun when they want to die," one of their number said in a hoarse whisper.

What was it talking about? Rachel didn't...no, he wouldn't even allow himself to entertain that perverse notion. These things liked to screw with peoples' minds but they'd chosen the wrong SOB this time.

Rick swallowed audibly and forced himself to speak. "Where is her...where's her body?" He felt his lower lip quiver and sucked it back inside his mouth.

This caused great amusement among the children whose giggling resumed. "Don't you worry about that, Ricky. We gave it a *niiiicccce* home."

Rick felt his body tense and his adrenalin pumping so hard his vision became blurry but his sense of smell was heightened. He wanted to run across the porch and slam into them like an angry linebacker and rip them to shreds but somehow he knew he would never get to within more than a few inches of them. That was why the police and everyone else pretended they didn't exist. Those who had tried to get rid of them paid the price.

"Someday we'll give you a nice home too, Ricky," one of them said. "Someday."

"Shut up!" Rick yelled. "Why are you doing this?"

One of them stepped forward and cocked its head. "It's Halloween, silly."

The clock ticks down the minutes slowly, as if it too is reluctant to deal with whatever events will transpire later tonight. Rick peers through the curtain covering his picture window and takes note of the position of the sun. Soon it will have disappeared completely.

Rick wonders what the people in the other houses in his neighborhood are doing tonight. For that matter, he wonders about the rest of the world. Have the children paid visits to people in other cities or are they unique to this place? He can't remember the last time he saw an actual child in the streets. Maybe they all turned into...those things.

He still remembers the days when all those religious groups started protesting Halloween, claiming it was becoming too mainstream and that it was replacing Christmas. They weren't wrong. Any trip through the stores from September on revealed an enormous amount of Halloween paraphernalia which often lingered after the so-called holiday had ended. That seemed to be when everything started getting weird, at least around here.

Trick or Treat took on a whole new connotation.

The rules weren't so clearly defined in those days. Rachel never seemed to understand them and she paid for it. How many times had Rick told her to always say "Treat?" Only fools and the suicidal said "Trick." Only fools...

Rick jumps and spills half of his coffee at the sudden intrusion of his loudly ringing telephone. Cursing his jumpiness, he sets the mug on the nearest end table and walks over to the answer the call. He is shocked to hear the voice on the other end.

"I'm tired, Rick."

Rick scrunches up his face and looks at the phone receiver as if it's a foreign, diseased object. "Earl?"

A heavy sigh comes through the phone. "Tired of being scared. I'm done with it, I mean, I think I am...Yeah, I am."

Rick shakes his head. Why is Earl calling him about this now, *tonight?* Can't he wait until tomorrow when the sun is back up and everyone is pretending there's no such things as evil creatures?

"Listen, Earl," Rick begins, "I don't really have time for..."

"If they come to my door I'm going to say 'Trick,'" Earl says in a breathless, panicked rush of words.

Rick shushes him. "Are you insane? Don't say that out loud!"

"I don't care anymore, Rick." Earl sounds calmer now, more resigned to his chosen fate.

Rick sits down on the nearest couch and stares at the floor. "What made you decide to do this?"

"You did."

Rick goes numb; the room seems to withdraw from him into a tiny, indistinguishable point. He thinks he might faint but somehow he remains conscious. He'd been Earl's last stab at hope, a cry for help that went unheeded in the face of Rick's selfishness and bitterness.

"Earl, I didn't mean..."

"Gotta go, Rick. Thanks for listening."

As the call ends with a click, the irony of that last statement isn't lost on him. He's always wondered if Rachel decided to say "Trick" that day or if she made a mistake. Was she ready to go? Was life with him so horrible? Rick wipes the tears from his eyes and heads into the kitchen to get some paper towel so he can clean up the coffee spill.

He's on his knees scrubbing the stained carpet when he hears them for the first time tonight:

> *Trick or treat, trick or treat, trick or treat we say!*
> *If you don't have treats for us, we'll never go away!*

Rick freezes in mid-scrub. So soon? He figured at least another hour before they showed up. Oh, God. They sound really close. Are they near his house? Dropping the paper towel, he slowly gets to his feet and heads for the picture window, pausing to turn off the living room light as he goes. He peers around the curtain into utter darkness. Even Earl's floodlight is turned off and Rick allows himself the brief hope that his neighbor has come to his senses and changed his mind about what he's going to say if the children come to his door.

"Riiiickkkkyyyyyy!"

"No," Rick whispers. "No, not yet. Please, no."

"We've missed you, Ricky!"

Rick shakes his head over and over, unable to stop saying, "No." He wants to back away from the window but is frozen to the spot, staring into the inky blackness that now seems to contain a host of small, hunched over figures.

"Come on out, Ricky," one of them taunts. "Come on out for tricks or treats."

Choose somebody else, his mind screams. *It's not my turn! It's not my...*

One of them giggles. "Don't worry, Ricky. We didn't come for you yet."

Rick stumbles forward, ramming his nose into the wall. He cries out and resumes his surveillance from the window. Where are they headed? Whoever they find, he sincerely hopes they say "Treat" and provide an acceptable offering.

> *Trick or treat, trick or treat, trick or treat we say!*
> *If you don't have treats for us, we'll never go away!*

Rick isn't sure he knows what an acceptable offering is because it seems to change by the year and sometimes even by the moment.

The children stop giggling and chanting, meaning they've chosen someone.

"Please make it quick," a familiar voice says.

A child giggles. "Oh, Earl. It's never quick."

Not again, Rick thinks.

Earl's screams are blood-curdling, worse than anything he's heard before. There's betrayal in that scream combined with grief and regret and a fear that goes beyond human understanding. Rick hops from foot to foot, his own lack of action making him want to vomit. Not again. Not Earl, too. What do they want from us?

He runs to the door and throws it open, screaming, *"What do you want from us?"* Earl's screams fill his ears and Rick breaks into a wild run across his front lawn and into the middle of the street, calling for the children to stop, to leave Earl alone, to go away back to hell where they belong. It takes him a moment to realize Earl has stopped screaming.

"All done," one of the children says.

"All done," another echoes.

"One by one," a third adds.

And that's when he understands what's happening, what's going to keep on happening. "Why?" he says weakly.

One of them cocks its head and looks at him from the shadows. "It's Halloween, silly."

They're never going to stop coming. Not until everybody has caved in and let them do whatever they want. Well, not him, not ever. They can keep coming until the sun burns out for good and he will never give them the satisfaction.

"See you again next year, Ricky," one of them sings.

He watches them go, shuffling down the street and around the corner, no doubt headed for another street to terrorize. He stands there in the darkness between his house and Earl's and breaks down into a fit of sobbing that forces him to his knees.

Because, despite what he tells himself, deep down he knows the day will come when he won't want to "Treat."

About Christopher Nadeau

Christopher Nadeau is the author of the novel *Dreamers at Infinity's Core* available through COM Publishing's Sword & Science imprint and Amazon as well as the short story, "Rosa, Rosa Come out of Your Room" in the horror anthology, *Saturday Evening Ghost*.

He was recently interviewed on Suspense Radio as part of its up and coming authors program and has collaborated on a "machinima" film with UK animator Celestial Elf called *The Gift*, which can be viewed on YouTube. He has also written and published over a hundred print and online articles ranging in subject matter from local politics to pop culture and New Age cults, the latter providing inspiration for a novel currently in the works.

Christopher lives and works in Southeastern Michigan and is an active member of the Great Lakes Association of Horror Writers.

THE AUDIT

by Susie Moloney

Poor Janet lay in bed listening to the alarm, trying to ignore it and knowing it would never, ever go away. In the first few blinks of waking up she had nudged at Les, curled up on his side beside her. When he slept on his side, he didn't snore as badly. She nudged him and felt his body roll with the force of it, but otherwise, gave no other response. She was about to speak *Les get up time for work* when she remembered that Les wasn't working these days and then the day ahead washed over her and her stomach tightened and any thoughts of sleeping in or not getting up were lost in churning waves of stomach acid and tightened shoulders.

I'm being audited.

The alarm kept up its tinny shriek, a cross between bells and a rattling aluminum door. It sounded just like one of those wind-up alarm clocks of the sort that she remembered in her parent's room from when she was a kid, but it wasn't. It was a plug in. The wind-up clocks wound down eventually, and after a minute of the ringing, you could go back to sleep. If you could stand a minute. In January you could; when the floor was cold and the car had to run a full fifteen minutes before you could drive it without stalling, and if the coffee had to be made and if you forgot to make your lunch for work before going to bed, you could stand it. Probably you could stand two minutes of ringing if it meant not putting your bare feet on to the cold January floor. The plug in alarm didn't run down. It rang until the little button was pushed. It was Les' mom's old alarm clock. She gave it to them when Jan complained about Les not getting up for work. The clock was procured like magic, practically out of a hat. Les's work record embarrassed his mom. They fought about it all the time. When he wasn't working, they avoided his mom's place.

Les-than-a-man. That was what Jan's mom called him.

It was all the way across the room. To shut it off, you had to get out of bed. You couldn't even crawl to the end of the bed and reach out to the dresser and shut it off. He'd done that too many times. They started to put it on the chair in the corner. Something about the chair made it sound louder too. *It's the acoustics*, Les-than-a-man had said, grinning. *Makes the chair vibrate with it.*

Janet didn't know if that was true, but it did seem louder.

"Shut off the fucking alarm," Les mumbled from under the blanket. Jan was already half-way out of bed by then, so she didn't say anything back. The bedroom was freezing. They all but shut the heat off at night *save a little dough*, Les said. Les-than-a-man.

It was 5:30. She had five hours to get her shit together before her meeting with the government accountant. She was being audited.

I'm being audited. Jan thought it to herself as she pushed in the little button on the back of Les's mom's alarm clock in hopes that the words would lose some of their power, the power they had held over her for the last two weeks, but in spite of the two weeks that she had to get used to the idea, it all still made her stomach tight and sore and her head ache.

I'm just a dumb waitress, she thought. *I'm a big nobody. What do they care what I have?* She'd said this and more to everyone who would listen for the last two weeks, until Les-than-a-man told her to can it. She scuffled a foot under the end of the bed fishing for her slippers and found one and put it on. She got down on all fours to find the other one. Les had pulled it off her in a stupid gesture (it was supposed to be romantic or something but it had just been *stoopid*) last night when he wanted to have sex. She told him she wasn't in the mood, but he said *I'll make you in the mood* and then what was she supposed to do? But her slipper had gone flying.

He always did the wrong thing at the wrong time. Like mornings, when he slept instead of going to work.

The house was cold enough that she wrapped her robe around her middle tight and hugged her arms to her middle. She slipped out of the bedroom and closed the door behind her. The first thing she did was turn the heat up. No way was she doing bullshit paper work in a cold house. Then she made coffee. Strong.

It was still dark out when she went down into the basement and started hauling boxes of receipts upstairs. She brought the first two up and even just the sight of them, with their box tops folded in on each

208

other in a pinwheel felt so overwhelming that she decided to start with just the two of them and then work her way up to the other box, still in the basement, and then the assorted bags and folders with the other papers in them.

The boxes were from the liquor store, from when they moved. One was a Captain Morgan's Rum box and the other a Canadian Club. Scratched out with black marker was the notation "kitchen" in her handwriting. Written under that was "tax shit," in Les's handwriting. *Ha ha*, she thought, *Les-than-a-man*. That's what it was, though. Shit.

The coffee maker gurgled as though there wasn't a care in the world that couldn't be taken care of by Maxwell House in the Morning, but it filled the kitchen with such a warm and homey smell, that Janet thought she might cry. It reminded her—the dark, the coffee smell, the tight stomach—of when she was in school. Her dad would get up and make coffee *come on girls* and then call her and her sister to breakfast. Her mom worked a night shift at a bakery and she slept while the three of them ate and mumbled quietly at the table before school and work. Jan hadn't done well in school, mornings before she went filled her with a familiar, comfortable sort of dread, based more on the tedium of the long day ahead than any real fear. It wasn't she was worried about failing a test, or a grade or getting a bad mark on a paper. She didn't do well, and wasn't expected to by either her parents or teachers. Sometimes it just worked that way. She left after tenth grade, not exactly with her parent's blessings, but with a basic understanding that neither she nor school were doing each other any favors. She went right to work at a diner on Rail Road, making $3.25 an hour. She'd been a waitress ever since. And she was a damn good one. She even liked it. Her parents had her sister to be proud of. Betty had gone all the way through school and then, in a move that was incomprehensible to Jan, went on to more school. She was a medical secretary now, and worked at one of the hospitals in the city. She was married with two kids. Her husband was a mechanic. He made good money too.

But no tips, was their joke together. Not very funny, considering it was the tips that got her into this mess.

I could just kill Terri Pringle.

Janet had been waitressing for ten years. Never once had she claimed any tips. Not once. Ten years, ten tax reports filed, not once had anyone said fuck all about tips. Then she was talking to a new waitress, Terri Pringle, who said, in passing one day, that you had to claim your tips on your income tax.

"They'll come after you if you don't," she'd said. Terri worked part-time. She was a student at the community college and she had said the whole thing with such confidence that it shook Janet up.

Tentatively she had said to Terri, "I've never claimed my tips." She'd tried to say it with as much mustered confidence as the younger, student-y Terri, but hadn't managed as well.

"My dad's an accountant," she said. "They'll come after you for that." Then the shift had changed and everybody went home. Terri didn't even work there long.

Jan had asked around after that. She asked the other waitresses and they would sigh and the debate would start, but most of them said they never claimed their tips. One girl said they automatically assume tips on top of your wages. "Ten per cent," she said. "Look over your last year's return. Where it says: undeclared income?' Look there. They'll have added ten per cent."

They hadn't. Her mother and dad said not to worry about it. "You get it done at the H and R Block, don't you?" She did.

"They do it for you there." But her mom had looked a little frowny over the whole thing. *You don't want to do anything to get into trouble,* she'd said later, when they were alone.

Don't be such a putz, Les-than-a-man said. "Declaring your tips would be like when we borrow ten bucks from my mom and then declaring it as income." He laughed at the very thought and then watched TV. He reminded her, though, when they were going to the H and R Block to get their taxes done. *Don't be a putz,* he'd said, and he shook his finger at her and raised his eyebrows in a perfect imitation of his mother when she said to him, *you get a job now, you hear? don't be a bum like your father.*

In the end, she declared her tips. Or at least, a rough estimate of them. The H and R man had raised his eyebrows, too, and Jan had trouble deciding whether that was because she was claiming them, or because the number was so low, or too high. Her face had reddened and she felt like she'd been caught in a lie, but of course she had no real way of knowing if she was lying or not because Terri Pringle—*I could kill Terri Pringle*—hadn't even mentioned declaring tips until nearly October. Jan had guessed based on what she made from around November-mid when she decided inside her head to play it right to the end of the year. She thought she was safe in her guess because people tipped more around the holidays, and she counted them.

She poured coffee into her bunny mug and got down on her hands and knees on the floor in front of the first box. She cracked it open, not knowing even what year she was about to see, let alone whether or not it would be her stuff or his. Les had a business on the side sometimes, fixing bikes. His stuff was mixed in with hers, but he only claimed the money he made working extra for his buddy Tom, who had a bike shop, because Tom declared it.

The box was filled to the top with little pieces of paper. A musty smell came from the box, like old books at a garage sale. A couple of little pieces fluttered up and settled back down, like fall leaves when you swipe by them on your bike on the way to school. Thinking about school set her off again. She wanted a Tums, but she'd eaten the last of them the night before.

Gee-zus.

Her and Les were both savers of paper. Paper had some kind of authoritarian hold over her feral self. Paper made her feel more feral than human, or certainly sub-human in some way. Especially white paper. Around very white paper with lines and numbers or words on it, she felt stained and dusty and smudgy. The lines, even and black or blue, the careful tally of numbers in a row, the dots matching up with each other, they seemed like representatives of some kind of legal authority. She also felt this way about soldiers and policemen, doctors and dentists; pieces of paper felt like they could boss her, regardless of what was written on them. Could as easy be a receipt from the drugstore for Tampax as a subpoena, didn't matter. Colored paper wasn't so bad. She kept the pizza flyers and the two-for-one deals that came from the carpet cleaning people, and ads offering her fifteen per cent off her next oil change, with a sort of grown-up sigh, and filed them in a pile on the table beside the front door. Anything that came in a white envelope (especially a white envelope with a little window on the front) went reverently over to the desk in the corner, where she paid bills. She even kept the newsletters sent by her member of parliament, just in case. You never knew. Someone might ask. Something.

You never knew.

She didn't claim much on her income tax. She claimed panty hose and her uniforms, of course. And shoes, but they were the special (ugly) orthopedic shoes that she had to wear because of her bunions—an occupational hazard of working on your feet for ten years. In a few years she imagined she would have to have some sort of an operation on varicose veins. Annie had it done last year after she nearly couldn't walk for the pain. The operation fixed her up pretty good, she said, but by the end of the year—*when Terri Pringle left never to return—I could kill Terri Pringle*—new ones were troubling her.

She claimed gas mileage whenever she had to work extra at a catering job that her mother sometimes got her through the bakery. Mostly Bridge Lady teas and things, but once a Sweet Sixteen party. That had been quite a bash. Not only had it been catered, but the whole place had been professionally decorated by one of those balloon joints. They turned the No. 16 Legion Hall into a pink cloud, with a real balloon waterfall in the corner. Not just streamers, either, but yards and yards of pink fabric had been draped over walls and tables and the whole thing had been just beautiful, although a little hard on the eyes after an hour or so. Most of the teenagers took off after the presents were opened, but that was okay because the mothers and aunts and old ladies had stayed for hours, wanting only more tea and the waitresses weren't too taxed on their feet and were paid for the whole day. Her mom and the others had made tiny little cakes -- twelve kinds -- the sort that were just a bite and sickly sweet after the first couple, but lovely to look at. Just perfect. They were tipped as a group and shared after those events. She wondered if the others had claimed the tips on their income tax.

Janet started going through the receipts, one by one, noticing that while her whole body felt sick and tired, and shaky, it was only her hands where it showed.

«««—»»»

Sometime over the next two hours, Les woke up and ambled into the kitchen and poured himself a cup of coffee. Janet, engrossed in 1996 fuel receipts didn't even look up. In fact, didn't realize he was up at all until he kicked and scattered a pile of health-relateds (Les's filling, but paid for by her, ergo *her* health-related receipt, plus two massages and a visit to the chiropractor, all from 1998) receipts when he opened the fridge door to get the milk. They went flying towards the free-standing cabinet where she kept her baking stuff and Tupperware.

"*Don't,*" she shrieked, shocking them both. She bent over double from her position, sitting on the floor surrounding by boxes and pieces of paper (almost of them white), and fished out two receipts that had slipped under the cabinet. "This took me *hours*," she said.

"Sor-*reee*," he said, and muttered something about someone being a little cranky under his breath. He settled in on the living room sofa, out of Janet's line of vision, but she heard him open the paper.

She felt mildly guilty for snapping at him when he'd just woken up—Les was not a morning person—and so called to him in the living room, "How come you're up so early?"

He grunted. She waited for his answer, and realized the grunt was going to be all she got, and so bent back over her receipts, searching for something, anything, over the last six years that would save her ass.

«« —»»

"Dear Mrs. Lancaster," the letter had started. Right away, reading it, before she even opened the envelope in fact, she knew it was bad news. The long, thin, pristine white envelope was addressed to her and her alone, the erroneous "Mrs." making it somehow worse. The corner was stamped with a government of Canada logo and no return address. Under the logo was "Department of Revenue," and her stomach had tightened.

She had come home after her shift smelling like French fries and mud pie and wanting nothing more in the whole wide world (ever again) than to take her shoes off and sit on the couch. Les's truck hadn't been in the drive and that had given her a little lift. The house would be empty and quiet. She didn't even wonder where he was, didn't give it a thought (although hoping in the same breath that he was out looking for work and knowing that it was more likely he was playing pool at the Legion or else was at his mother's cadging twenty bucks). She grabbed the mail not even looking at it and threw it on the table. The letter from the government skittered out, sliding across the Formica with its weight.

"Dear Mrs. Lancaster," it began. "A review of your 2000 tax remittance noted that you filed $362.96 in income under 'other source.'

"Your explanation of the additional income was for gratuities received through your employment at the Happy Diner where you are listed as 'serving personnel.' A sequential review of tax information filed for the years 1996-1999 indicated that while during those years you were also employed by the Happy Diner as serving personnel, no gratuities were claimed for those years.

"You are therefore required to appear at your nearest tax office on or before February 13, 2001 with records indicating this discrepancy in an independent audit. Please call the number at the bottom of this page to make an appointment with your auditor, no later than ten days after the receipt of this letter."

It was signed by a secretary for a director at Revenue Canada (Auditor's Department!) whose name was Mr. Peter Norris. Peter Norris. She'd never heard of him, never would meet him, but she had a vague feeling from then on that he had her file on his desk ready to be stamped, "Guilty," the implications of which could only be dreamed about, in a nightmare fashion.

She'd left the letter lying around for a couple of days, never once forgetting about it for even a moment. That had been a Friday. Saturday night her and Les had gone out for a couple of beers with their friends Gord and Paula and Janet had drank more than a couple of beers, uncharacteristically, pissing Les off because it meant he had to drive them home and he'd had a warning four years earlier for drinking and driving. "They'll cut my ass off, I get caught," he'd said, petulantly, more than a little in his cups himself. She'd laughed at that. "They won't *cut your ass off.* They'll take away your license," she'd said, matter-of-factly. "Cut your ass off. What does that even mean?" She could get snarky like this only when she was a little drunk.

"Same thing," Les said. She fell asleep in the car and *even then,* didn't stop thinking about the audit.

She finally told Les about it that Sunday, when he was trying to watch football and nursing a hangover with a beer. "Get yourself a lawyer," was what he said.

She told her mom and dad that same day, walking over to their place right around supper time, needing just a little comfort food and maybe a bit of advice. What she thought she really wanted was to hear her dad tell her it was all right and then to tell her to bring her stuff over to him and he would take care of it. Maybe call her Princess, like when she was little.

"Just get your things together and explain to the government that you didn't know you had to declare your tips and that you're very sorry and you won't do it again," her mother told her. She made beef casserole with shell noodles. It tasted like grade five and homework, because of how she felt.

"You never should have declared them in the first place," her dad said, from his chair in the living room, where he was watching the game and switching over to Matlock between quarters.

On the following Monday, Abby at work said, "You get yourself a good accountant and let them do the work."

She got herself Ramona Jacobson, who *tsk-tsk-ed* and *oh my-ed* everything, called her *Lancaster* and charged by the hour and talked really fast. The woman wore those half-glasses that old people wore, even though she didn't look more than ten years older than Janet, and sometimes she peered at her over them as though Janet were some sort of alien creature worth a second study.

Ramona Jacobson scared her almost as much as the audit, but at least she was on her side.

«« — »»

The phone rang at eight-thirty, just about knocking Janet out of her slippers. Her eyes were stinging from being open so long and her fingers were black and coated with ink. It rang twice before she realized Les wasn't going to pick it up and she got up off the floor, very careful not to disturb any of the fifteen piles of varying years and subject matter (unfortunately in no particular order) that were distributed around the floor in the kitchen.

Les was still reading the paper. He shifted without looking at her, his bulk moving slowly over the vinyl seats of the sofa, so that air escaped from one of them making a hissing sound, like a fart.

She grabbed the phone on the fourth ring.

"Hello?" she said, like a question.

"Lancaster, I just wanted to remind you to bring all the co-malgamated T-7s. And while I got you, don't forget the super-annuated close forms. Even the ones for your spouse." Ramona Jacobson spoke *very* fast on the phone, breathing it all into Janet's ear like sitting too close to a speaker for too long.

"Huh?" she said. "Bring the what?"

"That's right. And the T-6s, too. From the Legion work. Gotta go. If you need anything, I'm in a meeting for the next hour and then you can get me on my cell. You have that number?"

"I don't know."

"It's—" and then at the speed of light she rattled off what seemed to be an account number at the world's largest bank.

"Um thanks," Janet said.

"You can get me on it until 11. *Shit!* I have your Geswins! Well, that's all right. What time's the appointment?"

"Um—"

"1:30, right. Hmmm. Forgot about that. Anyway, I'll meet you there. If you need me, you can still get me after the hour. Gotta go, I'm late, good luck!" And she hung up.

Janet hung on to the phone, desperation creeping over her face more quickly as she realized that Ramona Jacobson had hung up before she had a chance to ask what co-malgamites were. And the super-annuated thing? Had she said that? Malgamites, or something. What was that? Something else too. She hung up before Jan had a chance to ask....

What everything is.

She hung up and stared at the phone as if it was going to ring again. It didn't.

"Who was that?" Les said from the couch.

"The accountant," she said, bewildered.

"Oh yeah, when's that thing?" He turned a page of the newspaper with such slowness, such snapping of newsprint, such rolling of fat that she wanted to turn and scratch him to pieces as though making him bleed and scream would somehow release the rising pulse of terror inside her.

"1:30," she said. The only thing she knew.

"Well, you're in for it. Shouldn't have claimed them in the first place," he said, then he chuckled. And he folded the paper over, smoothing the pages down against the coffee table. Jan went back into the kitchen, glancing up at the clock. It was 8:35. She had three hours left before she had to get in the shower and get dressed and down to the auditor.

《《—》》

There was a fourth box in the kitchen when she re-entered. It was perched on the edge of the vinyl chair that was covered with brown flowers, a cast off from her mom's place. Their old kitchen suite. The kitchen chairs of her youth. If you got close enough they smelled like her sister and mashed potatoes.

On the side of the box was written, "Taxes 1997." She thought she had been through all the 1997's. Her heart sank, and yet lifted at the same time, as though in this new box might be the answer, the legendary, mythical piece of paper that would lead to the path that could keep her out of prison. The Holy Trail.

Ignoring the rest of the receipts in the box she'd last opened ("Tax crap 98 or 96"), she went right to the new box and pulled open the flaps. Little pieces of paper fluttered up. She grabbed one closest to the top.

"Windlemiers," it said at the top. She frowned. Windlemiers? She shook her head. There were a series of code numbers at the top. Then a lonely figure. "$267.95." Two more figures followed, the only two she could puzzle out. The itemized taxes: Provincial and federal. *Okay that's good.* Janet nodded encouragingly to herself. *Taxes, right, good; that was what she was looking for, right?* Under the taxes was the total and then another series of codes. A figure that might have been the date seemed absent. She puzzled over the first series of codes, in case that was it, and then the one at the bottom. Nothing seemed remotely date-related. She tried to think of what on earth might cost $267.95 all at once and could come up with nothing but a car repair. They rarely had $267.95 (or even just $267.00) all at once to pay something. Not after pay day, anyway.

She nodded to herself. Car repair. That would be good. She could say it was car repair to get to a Legion job. There was no date. Her heart pumped a little harder with the lie. (Not that it was *necessarily* a lie, it could be true, how did she know? *How on earth* was she supposed to *know?*)

She dropped it with haphazard abandon in the vicinity of the pile supposedly of "car repair." The year no longer seemed to matter. She could hear the clock ticking in her belly.

《《—》》

The phone rang again about twenty minutes later and it was for Les. Jan had just cut her finger, a paper cut, and it stung. She stuck it in her mouth and sucked, the pain exquisite and small. Through that, she heard him mumbling into the phone, listening with only half an ear (he wasn't currently cheating as far as she knew, and he wasn't actively seeking employment and so it would only be some bum friend or other and therefore was not very interesting. Then he called from the living room.

"Hey Lancaster!" he called (he had taken to calling her that when she told him about the accountant calling her that; he thought it was funny). "Call-waiting for you." She stumbled into the living room, her eyes unable to see great distances after all their small work.

She looked at him questioningly. He shrugged.

"But get off, cause I have Beaner on the other line." A bum friend.

She took the phone and the man on the other end was talking before it even got to her ear.

"—confirming your 1:30 pm appointment. You understand that you're expected." Her mind snapped awkwardly on the moment and gave her all her reference material out of panic.

"Yes, I understand. I will be there. I am meeting my accountant," she said, hoping the last bit came out with some authority.

"Good, good," he said, and then paused with horrible time-stealing importance and affability. "So many people just try to avoid the inevitable by not showing up, you understand. It's not that I believe you won't be here—I'm not saying anything at all about you personally, it's just that many people try to avoid the inevitable," he said. It seemed to Jan that he had just spoken in a loop, saying every word with such deliberation that the time it took excluded the others and so he repeated them, endlessly.

"Yes," she said, because she couldn't think of anything else.

"And you'll be sure to bring your liabostities?" he asked.

"Yes?" she said firmly, having no idea what he was talking about. *The accountant will take care of it,* she heard her father's voice in her head. And Abby's. And her mother's. Even Les might have said something like that right after sex. Maybe.

"Good, good," he said again, his voice on a loop. She nodded into the phone, eyes glazed over, looking towards the sunburst clock over the dresser they kept in the living room to keep their CDs in. There were sweaters in the bottom drawers. "Yes," she repeated, because he seemed to need something more.

"Good, good, then," he said. It was almost 9:30. "At 1:30 PM, then," he finally finished, as though it were an affair or something pleasant. His voice was *affable,* something she'd only read about and that filled her with suspicion. He hung up and she handed the phone back to Les.

"Thanks for taking so long," he said, sarcastically. She went back into the kitchen.

218

Three more boxes were in the kitchen when she came in.

One was beside the stove, and written in big, bold black letters, all capitals was, "Existentials, 1999." The other two were half-hidden under the table, but she saw them, even as they tried to wiggle closer under. The box she had been working on was only just started, but she tore into the new one with a fierce sort of will. The kitchen was littered with paper, her comings and goings had scattered some of the neat stacks until they were literally piles. *You get piles from sitting on cold cement in your pajamas,* she thought wildly; her mother used to threaten that.

Ripping open the new box she stared blankly at a receipt that appeared to have no dollar figure. The date was 1999, though, as the box had promised. For this, she was eternally grateful. *June 16, 1999. Thank you, Jesus, I am absolved of sin in the blood of the receipt. Thank Jesus.*

Jesu anumi ablo...

What would Jesus do?

"Jesus wouldn't have claimed them in the first place," Les said from the door. "I'm Picking up Beaner and we're getting that starter for the pick up," he said vaguely. "I might stop over at mom's after," he said. She didn't look up. He picked his way around the piles of paper and said nothing about them.

Good bye. Maybe she only thought it.

《《──》》

Ramona Jacobson called back at ten. "Don't forget the willimusteers and the mono-magnisiums. Also the Pat-Rilancers; they're with the S-2 forms. *Okay?* Gotta run. You know you didn't bring them to the last meeting and that was your choice, Lancaster. Oh! For god's sake, jiggle things around and make sure there's at least a thousand bucks in your mainstream, eh? Get me on the cell, 873dog95-24eat at sam's30." And she hung up.

Janet cut her finger, a paper cut, on the pad of note paper by the phone. She sucked at it.

There were six more boxes, all unopened when she walked back into the kitchen. She stared at them with a baleful, exhausted sort of defiance. They were marked only randomly, some had the routine, black felt marker scrawled across, others didn't. They were marked,

"Hornets, 98." "Case Histories, 1996." And worse, "Receipts and Recipes for Disaster, 1998."

In one she found a bird's nest.

Her grade ten orienteering report.

A bill of sale for a car she'd never owned.

A copy of the *Desiderata* on pink paper, decorated with filigrees on the edges.

A receipt for fourteen pairs of panty hose (taupe) in size 7.

"Go placidly among the noise and haste—" she recited, remembered from a vague and unmemorable adolescence.

«« — »»

Sometime after four that day, Les and Beaner walked into the house and heard the phone ringing. They'd picked up the starter for the truck and then dropped by Les's mom's place. She'd given him twenty bucks after a hard ride. *You get a job, Lester. Get a haircut, Lester. You're living in sin, Lester.*

He and Beaner had laughed at this at the Kegger on Main, Les a little less hardier than Beaner, whose mother was dead and in her grave fifteen years.

"You gotta tape that, Mom, put it on a loop so I can play it back later, like a motivational thing, you know," Les had said to his mom. They'd repeated this bon mot up until their fourth beer when they got into sports with more of a vengeance.

"Janet," Les screamed when he walked in. The phone rang. "Let the machine get it," he said to Beaner. "Old lady's not home. Must be working," he said to Beaner.

"Wanna beer?"

"Does the Pope shit in the woods?" Beaner answered. This struck Les as hilarious.

In the living room the machine picked up the phone. A woman's voice screamed fast, into it. "Lancaster! Lancaster! Lancaster!" The boys ignored it.

Beaner followed Les into the kitchen. The fridge was blocked by an enormous pile of paper, literally blocked. Everywhere in the room was paper. It reached as high as the counter.

"What the *hell?*" Beaner gasped.

Les tried to get the fridge door open and couldn't. He looked around at the mess, a mess he sure-as-shit wasn't cleaning up.

"She had some tax thing. Guess she didn't get it cleaned up. She'll do it later," he said, but his mouth was dry. It was more paper than he'd ever seen, ever. He brought a hand up to shield his eyes, the sunlight, filtering in the west window was shining off the endless white, nearly blinding him. "Fuck," he said, equally vaguely, utterly unsure as to what to do. The paper presented a problem.

"Holy *shit*!" Beaner said. "What the hell is that?"

Les looked at his buddy and then followed his gaze to a spot on the floor where the mountain dipped nearly to linoleum. Pinky-brown flesh showed against the blinding white. A slender wrist and hand.

Without a word, Les stepped one giant step around the mound nearest the fridge and crouched, piles of paper reaching right to his crotch, a necessary lunge that pulled his groin muscle.

He picked up the hand, gingerly, like he might a mouse. "Cold," he said, but not without feeling. "Better call someone," he added, his voice cracking. Beaner didn't move.

There were tiny scratches all over the arm, little nicks in otherwise, white, smooth flesh.

"What are those marks?" Beaner said.

"Looks like paper cuts," Les said, nodding. One summer Les had worked at a heating and ventilating company in the city. Mostly he had stuffed pink insulation into walls and then covered them up. He stuck his hand through the mounds of paper, along the route of the arm that he'd just felt, curious.

The body itself was warm.

"Body's warm," he said. He looked over his shoulder at Beaner's pale, sick face.

"Paper's a good insulator," he said.

About Susie Moloney

Susie Moloney was born and raised in Winnipeg, Canada. It's fitting then that her very first novel was about a very Canadian *phenomenon*, a snowstorm that wouldn't quit. Published in 1995 by Key Porter Books, *Bastion Falls* made Susie's first mark in the world of fiction.

Two years later, her break out novel *A Dry Spell* was published all over the world, translated into multiple languages, and included a movie option with Cruise-Wagner Pictures, Tom Cruise's production company.

The Dwelling followed with critical acclaim and became a best seller. Her newest novel, *The Thirteen*, is released by Random House in Canada and HarperCollins in the United States.

This story, "The Audit," was written by Susie exclusively for The Horror Zine.

MIDNIGHT PASSAGE

by M. C. Shelby

Lightning raced across the night sky, illuminating the dark silhouette of the man walking steady through the soft rain towards the Texaco station. Some traveler stranded at this god-awful time of night and weather, no doubt his car broken down and his family stuck inside it.

Jon glanced up at the cheap white clock that hung above the rain-dewed double doors. The hands indicated the time to be 12:45 AM, but he knew it ran a bit slow. He absently stuffed the twenty he had lifted from the register into his pocket and closed the cash drawer. Lightning cracked again, followed close by a rattling clap of thunder that shook the window panes. Jon saw that the man had almost reached the far edge of the parking lot. The rain might be soft now, but Jon suspected it was going to start pouring hard any minute. The last thing he wanted on a night like this was some stranded, derivative soul.

Jon settled back on his stool, sighed, and leaned over to grab his bottle of Cherry Coca-Cola. At least he had some coffee brewed. Midnight travelers always wanted coffee. As slow as nights were, that usually meant some pretty old coffee for the poor bastards. Tonight's guest was in luck in that respect, at least, since Jon had set the pot less than an hour ago. He had just grabbed the phone book with the Coke bottle held dangling between his teeth and was flipping the pages to find the number for Rick's Towing, just to be prepared, when he heard the punctuated low voice.

"How much for a coffee?"

"Huh?" Jon's head jolted up. The Coke bottle drifted into free-fall before bouncing across the floor and erupting into a fountain of creamy foam that shot across the tile.

"Shit!" He reached down and scooped up the spewing container in mid-spin, felt the stickiness of the soda spill over his fingers. It was the man he had seen walking, of that he was sure, but how had he gotten inside so fast? Hell, he already had a cup of coffee in his hand. Why hadn't the door chime gone off? He threw the Coke bottle into the trash and wiped his hand against his jeans. He had a bare moment to glance outside to check his sanity, where he saw nothing in the darkness, before he was beckoned by the man again.

"How much for a coffee?" the voice, slick as oil, asked again.

Jon shot a furtive glance at the clock. 12:45. Dead batteries.

"Oh. Uh, sorry. Didn't hear you come in," Jon said, still trying to wipe the tacky feel of the soda from his hand. He adjusted his Orioles tee shirt and swept one hand back through oily brown hair. "Ninety-five cents."

A hand, glittering with diamond rings, counted out four bright coins that looked as if they might have been minted yesterday. Jon collected the change, which felt warm against his palm. He rang the transaction through, and as he started to hand the difference back he mustered up a concerned voice before politely inquiring, "So, your car break down?"

The man waved off the change.

"Don't own a car. Death contraptions the way I figure it. You never know when you might get caught in some accident. Ever seen some of those people that get tangled up in those wrecks?" The man removed his hat, and there was something wrong with that image, but Jon couldn't place his finger on it. The hat reminded Jon of those old hats they used to wear in gangster movies, a fedora. Underneath, the man's hair was jet black and short-cropped. He had a static smile that didn't seem natural to his face. Rather it was a face that might be more accustomed to the yelling countenance of a drill sergeant.

"Of course," the man continued, "you don't have to be in a car to actually be involved in an automobile accident. Sometimes people just get hit." The man leaned ever so slightly over the counter towards Jon, as if he might be about to share a story, or a secret. "You ever seen someone hit by a car?"

A shiver ran down Jon's spine. He had never felt so uncomfortable around someone, and he glanced towards the door. "No, I ain't never seen nothin' like that." Lightning flashed outside and the lights flickered before returning to a steady burn. Jon coughed. "Pretty rough night to be out on foot isn't it?"

The man shrugged out of his trench coat and folded it over the arm holding the hat, and one diamond encrusted hand brushed back through his own dark hair in a fair imitation of Jon. He wore a black shirt and pants, and a silver belt buckle that also looked like it was embedded with diamonds. "Well, I've been through worse than this, let me tell you. Sometimes you just have to face your fate, take what God throws at you and spit it right back at him. You know—"

The man stopped and glanced over as the door chime rang, a look bordering on annoyance crossing his face. When he saw the little rounded man standing there shaking rain from his shoulders, the previously unwavering smile slid completely off his face.

"WhooEEE! Quite the night out there. Nothing like a good storm to revitalize the earth," the new arrival said. He flashed them a good-humored, warm smile. He pulled off a pair of fogged spectacles and rubbed them against one sleeve. "Good to be in out of it, though."

The man plopped his eyeglasses back on his nose, smiled once more, and walked over towards the coffee maker. The dark haired man rapped his knuckles across the counter, snapping Jon's attention back to him.

"Well, Jon," the dark man said, "I believe I'll just go over to one of those tables there and enjoy my coffee for awhile, if that's all right by you."

Jon nodded. "Sure."

"By the way, my name is Prziel. It's been a pleasure meeting you." The smile was back in place and he tipped the hat back on his head. He walked off towards the tables lined against the windows, his boots clicking solid across the floor.

Prziel? Jon wondered. What kind of name was that? Must be French or something. And foreigners had strange ways. He didn't know what one would be doing out here in BFE, but it might explain why he was out walking in the rain. Jon had heard of people who walked from one side of the country to the other for charity or causes. This man didn't strike him as the charitable sort, but maybe it was for some other reason. Or maybe he was just weird.

Jon would just be happy when he was gone. He noted without surprise that Prziel's boots were black as well. Maybe he thought he was the second coming of Johnny Cash. Jon smirked at his own humor. Something else occurred to him as he was preparing to focus on the newest arrival. Jon didn't wear a name badge. There was little point in a small town. He looked back as Prziel was taking his seat. "Hey, uh, Preezil? How'd you know my name?"

Prziel's smile increased minutely, and he pointed a long white finger to an area just behind Jon's right shoulder. Jon cocked his head to look. Behind him on the wall hung a corkboard with various items pinned to it—liquor license, phone numbers, the previous night's winning lottery numbers.

But most of the space was filled with pictures: Ray, the store owner, with last season's trophy buck, Susan and her two boys at Ned's fifth birthday party, and regular customers with their small town accomplishments and celebrations. Not only was Ray's the only gas convenience store for the town, but it was a place people liked to come. Ray welcomed them all. Each picture was labeled and dated with a black marker. Tucked down low in the left hand corner was a picture of Jon standing with a giant flathead catfish that came close to rivaling him in size. Even holding it up to head high level, its tail nearly brushed the ground. It read "Jon Michael: Big Game Hunter, 7/12/05." He couldn't imagine that anyone would have paid that kind of attention to the board, but it did satisfy the question. Maybe he had one of those photographic memories or the like.

"How much for a coffee, young man?"

Jon's eyes turned to his newest customer. He was a frazzled looking old man, perhaps sixty or so Jon guessed, and was cloistered inside a beat-up raincoat. He was balding, and what little hair he had left was plastered around his head from the rain. He held his coffee just under his chin, as if to warm his face. His eyes were bright and alert, however, and he smiled genially.

"Ninety-five cents."

"WhooEEE!" the little man let out again, apparently taking delight in this expression as he dug one hand into a pocket. "I can remember when it was a nickel a cup. Times have changed, I suppose. Let me see here, I know I have one in here someplace. My name is Dahaviel, but you can call me David. Or Dave. Did I catch your name right? Jon, wasn't it? Ah, there it is."

Dahaviel pulled out a damp dollar and laid it on the counter.

"Yeah, Jon," Jon confirmed, taking the dollar. Didn't they say trouble came in threes? What weird name was coming through the door next? It was times like this he wished the store wasn't located right off the highway.

"Quite the pleasure to meet your acquaintance, Jon," Dahaviel said. "Hope you don't mind if I rest myself a little over by one of your tables."

"Go right ahead," Jon nodded, returning a nickel to him. "I didn't see you pull in. Are you walking too?"

Dahaviel winked. "Nope. Flew in on the wings of angels. Ha! You believe that?"

"Not quite," Jon said, returning the man's smile.

"And you'd be right! Angels don't have wings. All those pictures just drive me silly. Like an angel would need wings to get around." Dahaviel rolled his eyes and took a sip of coffee. "You do believe in angels, though, don't you?"

Jon didn't want to hurt the old man's feelings, but he didn't want to get drawn into a religious debate either. He could see this conversation continuing no matter how he answered, so he kept it simple. "Not really."

"It's okay to believe in some things, lad," Dahaviel said, a bit more serious now. "Otherwise this world will just swallow you up whole. You just have to watch out for those artist types. Poets and painters. They like to gild the lily, so to speak. But that doesn't mean the underlying truth isn't still there."

"Maybe so," Jon said, hoping that would end it.

"I'll be over there at the table drinking my coffee, if you want to talk," Dahaviel said, tilting his head. He wrinkled his nose as he looked. "Don't think I'll sit next to that tall fellow, though. He doesn't look so pleasant."

Jon nodded and tried to keep his expression neutral. Looked like he was stuck with Mr. Creepy and Born Again tonight. He better make some coffee if these two were going to stick around. He circled the counter and reached towards the coffeepot, picking it up and preparing to dump what was left.

"Oh, and Jon," Dahaviel said, "you should really put back that twenty you pocketed. Internal theft is one of the most crippling things there is for a business."

"What?" Jon nearly let the coffeepot drop from his hand. A quick juggle brought it back under control, but he could tell he would have a blister on at least one finger. He stuck the finger in his mouth and stared at Dahaviel. The little man just winked at him and continued on his way to a table.

227

Jon stood for a few seconds, watching him sit and scoot into one of the table benches. How had he known? He must have been outside and watched him do it. Had Ray caught on to his thieving and sent these two to spy on him? Jon hastened himself into nervous action, prepping a new coffee filter and starting a new pot. He returned to his stool behind the register and sat, trying hard not to look at Dahaviel. He found he couldn't do that, and his eyes crept to look at him. But the little man wasn't watching him, he just stared into his coffee cup and every now and again took a sip. And Prziel's gaze seemed to be riveted on the building storm outside, as if at any moment some monster would come rolling out of the flashing darkness. He was smiling.

Jon forced his attention away from the pair. He didn't like thinking about them. Then he realized he was fingering the twenty in his pocket. Had Prziel really read his name off the corkboard? And all that talk about car wrecks and accidents. Something was very strange here, something that made Jon distinctly uncomfortable. He pulled the twenty out of his pocket. Sure, he had lifted some cash every now and then, but not very often. Only when he needed it. He just voided out a sale or two to help balance things out. But not too often, or Ray might get suspicious. Jon didn't think he paid much attention to the bookkeeping anyway, but best not to press one's luck.

Still, it wasn't right, was it? And okay, sometimes he snacked on the food during the late hours, like that Cherry Coke, but he always paid it all back when his paycheck hit, didn't he?

He held the twenty, peering at its woven texture. He had once heard that money was some of the dirtiest stuff you could handle, because it was handled by everyone and it just soaked all that germy crap right in when people didn't wash their hands and such. You might wash your hands when you're finished in the restroom (although practical observation at the station had proven to him how few people did even that), but who washed their hands after handling money? He hit the *No Sale* key—K-ching!—and placed the bill back in the tray. He glanced at Dahaviel, and thought he saw the barest of smiles on the old man's lips.

Jon sighed and leaned back on his stool. The minutes passed slowly. Nearly an hour went by when out on the highway he saw a pair of headlights approaching. Finally, someone with real transportation. Maybe one of these could hitch a ride if the car actually stopped. As he watched the headlights grow closer through the driving rain, it finally struck him what had been wrong with Prziel earlier when he had taken off his hat. He hadn't been wet.

The car wheeled into the parking lot, hardly losing speed and almost fishtailing into the gas pumps, and Jon felt his heart skip a beat as it slid to a halt at the front door. He could see there were at least two people in the car, but only the passenger side door opened to let someone out. The man passed in front of the dripping headlights and stepped inside the store, heading straight for Jon. Jon was having trouble making out this new man's features, they were all blurred. He barely recognized that a gun was pointed at him. Everything was happening so fast. He was still trying to make out the man's face, when he realized the man had some sheer type of hosiery pulled over his head.

"Hand over all the cash now, gas boy," the featureless face said. The words came out a quivering tumble, nervous and scared.

"What?" Jon said. His brain was having trouble processing this all. The gun looked huge, as if it might swallow him whole.

"Open the fucking register, before I blow your fucking head off!"

"Dahev...Dave?" Jon looked hopefully over at the tables, but Dahaviel just looked at him with a certain sadness, and Prziel was looking at his watch as if nothing were happening at all.

The gunman turned his head, feet dancing, looking at the tables and then around the store. "Who the fuck you talkin' to?"

Jon opened his mouth, but nothing came out. The gunman danced from one foot to the other, still looking around. Jon pressed the No Sale key once more—*K-ching!* The man jumped and fire exploded from the gun's muzzle.

For an instant Jon thought the cash drawer had caught him in the gut. But the pressure was too great for that, sending his body flying backwards to strike the corkboard. He couldn't control his legs, and felt his body sliding along the wall to the floor. Something dark and heavy fell over him, pushing him further down. He heard the familiar door chime like a distant church bell, the sound of tires spinning on wet pavement, and gravel pecking at the window glass.

Jon tried to pull himself up, but found he didn't have enough strength. His hand, which had reflexively reached for his stomach, felt warm and wet. *Shot. I've been shot.*

For a second he thought he couldn't see, but then realized it was the corkboard. It had fallen on top of him. He pushed it off and propped it to one side. He let out a low moan and tilted his head back against the wall.

"That's a nasty wound you have there. Gut shot. Those are the worst. Slow death. Not likely to be anyone through here soon to help you, either."

Jon opened his eyes. It was Prziel.

"How would you know?" Jon groaned again as he tried to pull himself to a sitting position. He needed to call an ambulance, somebody to come help him, but his legs still wouldn't cooperate.

"Oh, I just have a knack for things like that. Call it intuition. Just like I know the phone lines went down with that lightning strike not too long ago."

"Who are you?"

Prziel took in a little breath and squatted beside him. "I want to show you something, Jon." He grabbed the corkboard and positioned it so Jon could see it. "What do you see on your little board of fame here?"

Jon looked at the corkboard. It seemed no different than it had before. He shrugged. "I need help. You have to get me help."

"This is important, Jon. Look hard."

Jon focused on the corkboard once more. It seemed the same...except for one picture. His picture. Instead of standing beside a humongous flathead, it was the broken and bloodied body of a little boy that swung from his fist. The caption below now read "Jon Michael: Child Killer, 6/13/2003."

"No."

"I was there when you ran over that little boy, Jon. Got away with murder there, didn't you?" Prziel said, his lips close to Jon's ear as if they might be sharing an intimate secret.

"No. Didn't...didn't mean to..."

"Of course you didn't. Best of intentions. Hell, I'd guess if you hadn't been drinking, why, you probably would have missed him. But you didn't even touch the brakes, Jon. That's really neither here nor there, though. As awful as that was, how did it really separate you from the rest of the greasy monkey turd human screw-ups that bloat this planet? But when you allowed someone else to take the blame, and you skated free, I must say I was highly impressed. That caught my attention. I thought to myself, 'Now that's my kind of guy. There's somebody I can develop and turn into a real soldier.' I'm here to take you home, Jon."

Prziel was kneeling beside him now. He dipped one finger into Jon's wound. Jon screamed but Prziel ignored his pain and licked the blood from his finger. "I can shorten your pain, Jon."

"No. You...you're...evil."

"That's a matter of perspective."

"Don't believe him, Jon. He's not as smart as he would like to think." Dahaviel's voice floated around him, but Jon couldn't see him.

"Not for a second, Dahaviel. This one is ours." Prziel looked down at Jon. "No then to a quick death?" Jon only stared back, pain and fear arcing through his body. Prziel smiled. "Very well."

Jon lay there, Prziel crouched and watched, and it seemed as if time might be stretching out into eternity. And then he heard the clock chime. It only chimed once, and Jon knew that couldn't be right, it had to be way past one o'clock. He saw the expectant smile on Prziel's face fall for the second time. Jon's eyes glanced around, but all he could see was the top edges of the cash wrap. How much time had passed? Too much, Jon was certain. Time enough for atonement? Or would he just be one of those hypocrites who repented all their sins on the deathbed, just in case? Was true repentance even possible at this point?

He had tried so hard to forget the boy, whose name had been David, but the event still came into his dreams. What the boy had been doing out so late, he didn't know. He shouldn't have been out, that's what he always told himself. Where had his stupid parents been? Didn't really matter. Dead was dead.

No matter how drunk he had been, he had never been able to forget the *feel* of the boy's body catching the fender, or the image of his bloodied body flying up over the windshield and back into the street. He had been too terrified of all the possibilities facing him to admit his guilt—the family disgrace, the social stigma from town and friends, his entire future voided. Jail. What future would he have had after that?

And so he had managed to cast that bad fate on someone else. Donnie Cope, a high school buddy, was now paying the sentence for all those woes. Even if he could forget the boy, there was still the thought of Donnie, serving his time one county over, to remind him. Donnie, who had felt so guilty before the trial he tried to kill himself with an overdose. Donnie, who had been so drunk that night he didn't know any different. He had been in a blackout, and it was easy to incriminate

231

him. After all, it had been his car. Donnie cried at the trial and said how sorry he was.

And that had all been for what? Now look at the future he had saved for himself. A pathetic college drop-out working a gas station in his old backwater home town. He had never been steady at anything since that accident.

"Hello? Is there anyone here?" A woman's voice drifted tentatively through the air. "I need a gallon of milk."

Milk? Who needed milk at this hour in this weather? Once he would have wondered at the strange trips people made in the middle of the night for things that could wait. Now it was sweet music.

"Help..." Jon managed. He could see a weave of blonde hair on the other side of the register.

"Hello? Hello? Oh Lord."

The woman was standing over him now, and Jon smiled. Dahaviel had been right after all. Some people would say their whole lives led up to singular points in their careers and whatnot, but Jon realized that the only singular point to be reached was where he was at now. People called it death; some said it was an end, others a beginning. And what you left behind could be just as important as what you took with you. It might even be the same thing.

"Hold on, hold on. I'll call an ambulance," the woman was saying, her hands flying around the counter and fluttering nervously as she searched for the phone.

"Phones...out. Come here...please."

The woman paused, then came and knelt beside him. He had recognized her at once, for she was in his dreams too. But instead of standing there with tears streaming down her face condemning Donnie with her anguish as she had in that courtroom years ago, it was him she spoke to. The sorrow, he thought, had never really left her face. She had moved on, but the pain lingered.

"For...give me." His face felt warm and wet now, and he realized he was crying.

"What? Jon, what?" She bent closer. He knew she had felt ill against him, too, these many years, because he had been in the car too. He couldn't blame her, but she had to know the full truth.

"Wasn't...Donnie...killed...David. Me. Forgive me...so...sorry." Jon looked into her eyes and would not let go, but he could say no more. Only try and desperately convey what he meant, what he needed, through that connection of windows into each other's souls. He owed her that. Owed Donnie that.

She seemed far away now, and he focused harder. He saw the cloud of anger twist her face when understanding dawned, and thought he felt her clench him tighter in that anger, but it was gone then and tears welled out of her eyes. Her head dropped, the blonde hair falling about her face so he couldn't see her eyes any longer, and he felt himself slipping further away. He didn't know how long her head hung down like that, there was no sense of time and every moment was an eternity. When her eyes raised up, she reached out and touched his forehead. "I forgive you."

Jon heard Dahaviel call his name, and he let go of the world.

About M. C. Shelby

Born in Missouri, M. C. Shelby developed a love for dark fantasy and horror almost since the time he could read. In 1988 he won first place in the Central Missouri State University journalism competition for editorial writing. He graduated from CMSU with a B. S. in the Administration of Criminal Justice with a minor in psychology. He enjoys billiards, RPGs like *World of Darkness*, and an occasional foray with an Xbox when he isn't writing. He is working on several writing projects both large and small, and this is his first professionally published work. He currently resides near Nashville, Tennessee.

THE FAVORITES

by Chris Castle

The lights went out one by one, *pop-pop-pop*. The teenagers in the class yelped a little and then followed it with the first ripple of laughter. Then, inevitably, came the busy, excited chatter amongst themselves.

"Quiet down," the teacher said and they immediately subsided. They feared him and the knowledge of that burnt like a beacon inside his heart. It had lasted him twenty-seven years and the feeling had yet to weaken in the slightest. Sometimes the fear was all that made him get out of bed in the mornings. The power he held, that surge, made others weak but it made him grow stronger. It was, to a fifty-five-year-old man, the closest he knew to breathing the same air as God.

"This must be the ghost haunting us," he said slowly, the classroom in darkness, a few faces outlined by the low hum of mobile phones. They looked up, wanting to question him but not quite having the strength to actually do it. Instead they kept peering at him, one part scared, and another curious.

He loved seeing their young faces looking back at him; the desire for answers was offset by the anxiety that only he could create. He felt a low burr of energy run over his skin as he slowly cleared his throat.

"Yes, this school is haunted," he went on, keeping his voice intentionally low, making them lean forward and strain to follow each word. "I thought that was common knowledge."

He shrugged and looked through the doorway briefly, as if the rest of the story was written on the corridor walls. He heard the other teachers scrambling, looking for torches to alter the darkness. They feared him and loathed him just as the students did, and he enjoyed that knowledge. They did not trust him, but not one of them would stand in his doorway and ask what it was he was doing.

"Yes, yes, it's quite common knowledge in the local area. A ghost presides in these halls, sometimes causing power outages like what we have right now, and fooling with the school equipment. It's written in the town library as a course of public record, I believe." He felt the next twinge of joy run through his body; he used unfamiliar words to confuse them, and then lies to keep them suspended inside his story. It was against the rules and inappropriate, of course, but all the best things were, he found.

"The story is familiar to your parents, if you'd ask them." He knew they would do no such thing. Teenagers communicate as much with their parents as he did with the ghost in question. He allowed a thin smile to run over his mouth; it was so tight and unfamiliar, he thought the children would mistake it for a grimace. He pulled himself off his seat and away from the desk.

"The ghost in question was a former student, of course. One that misbehaved terribly throughout his time at the school. Whatever rule was established, that student sought to break it in double-quick time." He slowly walked down the aisle that separated the two sets of desks. Some looked up to follow him and others looked away, pretending to be distracted, but no less rapt. The young listened to those they feared.

"He was, in short, a monster." He reached the back of the classroom and stood in the dark for a long, perfect moment. He let his mouth open slightly and quickly bit into the air, almost tasting it. The anxiety in the room was almost tangible now.

"But this monster was to have quite a comeuppance, I'm afraid. Yes, young monsters always do, in real life." He began to walk back up the aisle and let his hands trail a little loosely, catching the nape of a neck or brushing an arm. Every one of the students he touched jolted and made the atmosphere even more charged.

Halfway down, he stopped. The two students sitting next to him now, to his left and to his right, were his Favorites. He had these in each class and he favored them above the rest. He enjoyed the hurt it created in the others, enjoyed it as much as the pride and beaming he found in those he singled out. *Yes,* he almost said out loud, *a teacher must always have his Favorites.*

"The monster-student went on in his way, causing his merry hell, much to the joy of the classmates and the frustration of the teachers in question. But then, on one day, a simple day, he no longer showed up at the school. At first poor attendance and absenteeism were offered up, as they always were with such troublemakers, but then the absence went on longer, the reasons not forthcoming. It was as if the student vanished," he told them, popping his hands open in a flourish; his

235

Favorites winced and he walked on, hiding the smile that was almost threatening to burst wide open now.

Troublemakers often do have their comeuppances, he thought, almost idly. Over the years, he had seen to that. Not at the time, of course, not while the miscreants in question were still sloping through the school gates, but after. A year after, two; enough time for them to drift, to fail, to become vulnerable enough to accept a seeming harmless invitation, a ride and a retreat from the cold and the bitterness of everyday life. Yes, there had been trouble makers in the school over the years, but each had learnt their lessons, whether inside the school or out in the vast sprawl of the real, cruel world.

"The trouble maker was never found of course, but there were stories of his disappearances, tales too sordid, too unpleasant to bring up now. But suffice to say, there can be no rumors without a kernel of truth, and no suspicion without a drop of possibility."

He walked on and felt an unfamiliar sting on his fingertip as he made his way to his desk. He snapped his hand up and looked down to the child in question. For a second the boy, Davies, seemed darker than the others, shrouded deeper than the others, almost not looking like the boy at all. Then, in the next instant, the familiar image of a nervous boy snapped back into place. But the cool feeling on his fingertips lingered.

"Well..." he said, temporarily thrown off. He cleared his throat and reached his desk. The coolness of his fingertips seemed to crawl higher inside him and he flexed his arm. "The boy was never found, but they say his spirit returned here soon after...whatever happened to him."

He tried to smile as he turned but what he saw in-front of him took his breath away. Each of them, sitting at their desks, were shrouded in the same darkness; every one of them something other than a child, something darker. Their eyes appeared hollow, their hair dry and course, as if made from straw.

"He was...he was," he tried to continue, peering into the image before him, the way rubber-neckers did at car-crashers, trying to see that little extra piece of horror. Their hands were all bone, their fingers little more than burnt coat hanger wires. But still gripping their pencils and their books, even in the darkness. Was that what horrified him more? The fact they were still...in attendance?

"They say he haunts the corridors, causing mischief from time to time," he went on weakly. He was supposed to be the one to create fear in others, not to feel it himself. He blinked and pulled the glasses from the bridge of his nose. He blinked again, deeply and looked up, seeing the horror show receding. Faces were returning, skin was slipping back over wire bones. He drew a breath and found his voice. He continued, trying to dispel the foolishness.

There was only one thing that was stopping him; even though the teenagers had mostly reverted to their real, present form, each of them clung onto the hollowed, sunken black eyes.

"They say...they say he never left the school. That his presence is retained in the walls, the very bricks of the building." His voice was growing weak, even though he was drawing stronger, thicker breaths.

For a moment he looked to the door, but found it had slipped almost shut. He listened for the voices of the other teachers but couldn't hear them. The commotion of a few minutes ago seemed to have disappeared entirely. Where there was once a sort of good natured chaos, he was now only aware of the utter silence of the place. And more than that; a stillness he had never felt before, not in all his years.

"They say he was buried in the foundations of the school," he said, aware now that his voice was barely more than a whisper. Was he really saying that out loud? The story was becoming too involved now, growing too close to the truth of the things he had done over the years. He wrung his hands, trying to burn himself back to reality; he was practically confessing in front of his students!

He tried to shake his head clear, but found himself too weak to move, too weak to stop himself. He was faintly aware of crossing a boundary and being unable to stop himself, the acceleration too powerful, the drag too consuming.

"The boy was trapped, trapped in the walls, that's what they said." He felt dizzy now, and found himself clawing for the support of the desk. The desk was his shield, his protection from the monsters, the unruly mobs. If he could just settle his hands on the desk, feel the cool sting of the wood, then he would regain his footing and recover. But the desk itself seemed to morph into something else, something the consistency of butter and he slipped away from it. There was a sensation of being pushed and he stumbled forward, falling almost neatly into the spare chair kept at the front of the room.

The naughty chair. It was the chair he had forced children to sit in over the years, removed and isolated from their friends and shamed. A chair that he had grown to love for the loathing it inspired. A chair he had sought out and ordered, so much like the one he kept in the cellar of his own house, meant for when those poor strays followed him home, looking for solace and a friendly smile. The chair had become a sort of throne upon which he sat in the darkness...after it had all happened, feeling exultant and something like a king. Now, he found himself in the same place.

He had wanted distance, but the room had conspired to force him even closer to the class. He willed himself to look up and once again the monsters had stripped away any pretense it had once held; gone were the children, their true monster forms on display.

Back were the wired hands, the hollowed sockets running deeper now; the straw hair sat at angles covering the face, leaving other, rotting spaces open and gaping. Mouths opened, the teeth stumps or dirty jewels in the mouth. Some had tongues, while others had clumps of dark pink flesh in their place. All of them looking at him, all of them expectant and hungry. And finally a voice came, one long and hollow chord, asking him for more, wanting to hear the next confession, the next story, the next truth. All of them hungry to consume the dirty truth of his heart. All of them flicking tongues and stumps and phlegm, hungry to hear each sordid act laid bare.

He continued to talk, now unaware of whatever it was he was saying. He had no sense of time in the darkness; no real understanding of what it was that was happening to him. All he knew was he was sitting in the victims' chair and he was telling a gallery of terrible, undead things, all the secrets that were packed deep within his soul.

At first he spluttered, muttered, tumbled over words, and licked dry lips. But then the bone wire fingers reached out to him. They held his hand and almost caressed him. They nurtured him and stroked the stories out of him.

Then the grip tightened and they grew impatient. When they reached his darkest secrets they had no patience at all. The wiry thumbs reached higher, jamming fingers into his throat, pulling back the fat flaps of his lips. They loosened his teeth and scratched at his tongue.

When they grew more restless still, they tired of forcing the words from his throat and grew greedy; they plunged deeper into him, their reach sinking up to their dirty elbows and they rooted around for the blackest, oiliest things they could find. They plundered him with greed and desire and when they were done, their arms were blood black and their straw hair was damp with sweat. They each took their turn and each savored their secret until they were all sated and their bodies full.

He slipped out of the chair and slid onto the floor. His insides were outside, he thought idly. His mind was torn and his flesh was laying over him like some rain-soaked mackintosh. The tangled mush of his mouth could no longer speak, but it did not matter anymore. He slumped into the darkness, feeling his own wetness all around him; once he lifted his hands, seeing torn stumps where his fingers should have been, making out the harsh pattern of the teeth-marks.

He tried to stroke the cheeks of his Favorites just one more time, but they moved out of his reach. Instead, the straw bodies shifted back into their seats, their work done and not one of them even thought to look down at the dying man. He watched them from the floor as they re-positioned themselves in their seats and angled their backs neatly against the desks. In a final, perfect act, they gripped their pencils tight in their hands, their lessons learned and hungry for the next.

The lights came on and the other teachers opened the door to the classroom and found Mr. Newman dead on the floor. Later, it would be confirmed he had suffered a massive heart attack and would have been dead before he hit the floor. Not many tears were shed, and in truth, jokes in the staff room abounded as much as in the classroom.

There was just one note that struck the people involved as eerie; the collective amnesia of the students in the classroom. There were factors; the darkness for one, the shock for another.

But the blanket of non-recognition when they tried to coax anything out of them left the other teachers feeling unnerved. It wasn't that the teenagers' eyes changed exactly, but it was almost as if something else, something brighter, burned behind them. The teachers who were questioning them decided to stop the talk then and there and let them go back to their friends. It just seemed safer that way.

About Chris Castle

Chris Castle is English but works in Greece as a teacher. His writings have been accepted over one hundred and fifty times in the last two years, ranging from sci-fi to horror to straight drama. He has also been published in several end-of-year anthologies.

Chris is currently beginning work on his fourth book. His influences include Stephen King, Ray Carver and P.T. Anderson. He is also working on a poetry collection.

IMPRESSIVE INSTANTS

by David A. Hernandez

Grayson shoveled a copious spoonful of piping hot peach cobbler into his mouth; his third serving of the afternoon. His belly oozed and conformed to the edge of the Formica tabletop.

He feasted alone, the table shiny and slick from globs of peach syrup and grease, some of which had become hardened, encrusting the laminate surface like amber. As he grazed, oblivious to the disgusted stares of his neighbors on either side in their own booths, he read the newspaper.

The newspaper screamed of terrible things. In India, over a hundred people died in a landslide while pilgrims visited a mountaintop temple. In California, a well-respected health guru was found hanging in her bathroom, in a supposed suicide, but the odd thing was that while forensics presumed she had only been dead a few hours, her body was desiccated and withered as though she'd been there for months.

More alarming was the front-page story of a man in Canada who slaughtered a passenger on a Greyhound, while he was sleeping. The suspect—viewed by other passengers upon hearing the man's blood-curdling scream—was said to have stabbed the deceased in a vicious succession of stabs with a hunting knife, and then decapitated the man and partook of the man's flesh.

Grayson, mouth full of sweetness, didn't even flinch at all the horror in the world as he swallowed, a thick sliver of fleshy peach sliding down his throat and into his stretched stomach. It would take more than a freakish, murdering, flesh-eating Canadian to make him lose his lunch.

He loved food. It was everything that was good about the world now. But it was not always this way. He wasn't always fat.

Once he had relished a life as a metropolitan chameleon, shape-shifting his way around the city. He had felt adaptable and fully aware of himself in his myriad roles as a proud member of the gay

240

community, hardworking and loyal employee, resilient party-goer, and most of all, Eric's lover.

But today? Today he was twenty-eight years old and that world he had once been so passionate about now seemed like someone else's life in a parallel universe.

Most of all, he missed his partner, and he felt a self-loathing because somehow Eric found him wanting, and had simply walked away. The self-loathing created a hole inside. Grayson knew he could go back to some semblance of his old life...all he had to do was embrace it.

Instead, it was the demon that he embraced nowadays; a voracious craving for food to fill that hole inside. Midnight was the worst, because then came the witching hour of his demon's *need*.

He remembered the first time he heard the demon's call. It was the night Eric ended their two-year relationship over dinner at their favorite Mexican restaurant.

"I think we should break up," Eric had said, taking a sip of his margarita.

"I'm sorry?" Grayson had responded, bewildered.

"We're from two different worlds, Gray. I'm going one way, you're headed another."

"And when did you come to this conclusion?"

"Don't act surprised," Eric said, a smug grin on his dark, handsome face. "I'm not interested in something serious. I thought that was clear when we met."

"It's been two years, Eric. Isn't it kind of late to reestablish the basis of our relationship?"

"As far as I'm concerned, we don't have one."

"But I love you," Grayson had said, reaching across the table to meet Eric's hand resting flat on the table. "Doesn't that mean something?"

Eric slipped his hand away from Grayson's and wrapped his fingers around his margarita glass, bringing it to his lips. He took a long drink and then, setting the glass down, leaned forward and said to Grayson with unwavering resolve, "But I'm not in love with you."

The demon howled and the eating began; at first a slow dance, a romantic interlude that eventually evolved into a passionate tryst bordering on frenzy; dangerous and sharp as the ends of steak knives slicing into thick, juicy cutlets.

This was a sensation he'd never felt with Eric or the others. This was a sensation of being corporeal, of being full. It was umbilical. It was substantiation at the end of a fork.

«« — »»

Grayson made his journey up the long flight of stairs that led up to his top floor apartment. Sixty pounds ago it hadn't seemed so stringent a trek, but as he reached the second of three floors, he realized it was taking its toll on his ankles.

A man in a plain black suit stood knocking at Grayson's door.

"Are you looking for me?" Grayson wheezed, steadying himself on the wrought iron banister.

The man in the black suit turned around, a sincere smile on his sun-baked face. His eyes were stunning cobalt and his chestnut hair was clipped and combed with nary a strand out of place. His features were smooth, unlined; teeming with a youthful exuberance, though Grayson was certain the man had to be in his late thirties or early forties.

"Name's Caplan and I think I'm the guy who can help you," the man said holding up a small unimpressive blue cooler with the words *Impressive Instants* pasted on its side in large bold, gaudy purple letters, a shade darker than his necktie.

"So you're selling something. I'm not interested," Grayson said as he tried to push past the man.

"Quick to the point, ain't ya. I like that. Well," said Caplan, dabbing his lips with a handkerchief, "how do you know you're not interested if you don't even know what it is? What if I told you I can help change your life?"

He paused, licked his lips again, and placed his load on the floor of the hallway. He flipped open the top of the purple cooler, and an icy steam billowed off the top like a deepfreeze. The handsome stranger gestured with his slender, manicured hands and claimed a curvaceous, oval-shaped bottle from the cooler. The bottle gleamed, made of sultry obsidian, with a long swan neck. Caplan held the bottle up in front of Grayson's face.

"Now," Caplan said, "don't you want to know more about this?"

The bottle had a small label placed at its midsection with the words *Impressive Instants* written in a much finer, intricate script than the cheap sticker on the side of the cooler.

"Beautiful, ain't it?"

"What is it?" Grayson asked marveling the bottle's suggestive shape. Something about it mesmerized him, and he abruptly asked, "Why don't you come inside?"

"Thought you'd never ask," Caplan said, picked up the cooler, and followed Grayson inside the tiny apartment. Sitting on the malformed couch, held the bottle up once again as though he understood the effect it had on his prospective client.

Fragrance wafted into the open air. There was pungency about the aroma, the scent of wilted peony shrubs and wine grapes.

"What's in it?" Grayson asked, sniffing the odd aroma that emerged from the mouth of the bottle.

"Oh, only the best stuff, of course. Perfect for a guy like you."

A guy like me.

"Most of our clients are overweight and want a simpler way to get trim. *Impressive Instants* provides that."

"So, an easy fix?"

"Exactly! That's exactly what it is. One case will change how you look at yourself forever."

Caplan poured a little of the liquid into a small tumbler. Grayson examined the fluid swirling in the tiny glass, noticing varying shades of purple and tiny seeds floating at the top in a frothy cloud. The inside of his mouth dried up as a cracked desert floor, his face puckering as he brought the rim of the glass to his mouth.

"It has bite, I tell ya, but trust me, it's worth it," Caplan said, a wink in his steely eyes.

The liquid funneled down Grayson's throat in a bitter sizzle, settling and cooling in his belly. His mind raced with disturbing thoughts. He imagined the tiny seed particles bursting in his stomach acids and birthing an alien entity that would come to command his body.

But instead, nothing happened. Nothing at all.

"There, see, not so bad, eh?"

"No," Grayson said smacking his lips and feigning a smile. "But what does it do?"

Caplan grinned and said, "It will stop your demon."

Grayson was stunned. *How did he know?*

"So," Caplan said searching Grayson's face. "Should I set you up with your first order?"

And after Caplan left and Grayson realized he was stuck with twenty bottles of hype, he tried not to think about the selling of his soul to mass market miracles, but the bottle of *Impressive Instants* stuck out in his mind like a monolith. His stomach groaned as he went to the kitchen table and he cradled one of the bottles in his hand, his fingers tracing rhythmically over its shiny black surface.

He was hungry again.

It'd been only an hour and a half since his last meal, but already the twinge of appetite was stabbing into his chest, the demon grinding its teeth. This time, for the first time, he did not cater to the demanding animal that was his appetite. He denied it and instead of devouring something sweet, he popped open the top of the obsidian bottle, massaged its abdomen like a genie's lamp, and poured another helping of the purple fluid down the hatch.

《《——》》

"So you say you've seen Grayson?" Eric Vega asked as he sat at his desk one rainy, Tuesday afternoon, sifting through various files, his mind distracted from the anxious voice of Benjamin Palmer on the other end of the phone.

"We'd been seeing him all the time a while back. We had all been hanging out again since he started getting his life back into order. Even *you'd* be proud of him. He looks amazing, nice and thin. But then a couple of weeks ago, he disappeared on us again. He doesn't email, text, call. Nothing. I've even called his work. They told me he's been let go because he stopped showing up. I'm wondering if I should call the police."

"Have you gone by his place?" Eric inquired emptily into the phone, the obliviousness showing in his tone.

"Of course. Jorge and I went over to his apartment, but his neighbors claim no one has come in or out of his apartment in weeks. They assume he's on vacation."

"I honestly don't know what you'd like me to do about it."

"You were his lover, Eric. You messed him up royally."

"Don't you go there, Benji. Don't blame me for Grayson's problems."

"Look, I'm not asking for you to pull a rabbit out of your hat, but you could try some sensitivity and pull your head out of your ass and check on him. You owe him that. And don't call me Benji. I always hated you for that."

Surprised, Eric finally looked up from his papers. "Fine, I'll check on Gray if it will get you off the phone."

"Thank you."

"Welcome."

"Asshole."

Dial tone.

At the end of the day, Eric finally dialed Grayson's landline number. There was no answer. He tried once more and it just rang and rang. Thinking he'd done enough, he prepared to head out before the storm coming in got any worse.

But as he set about to leave his office, he noticed his keys. They still contained a spare key to Grayson's apartment. What would it hurt to drop by the apartment? Besides, he figured he'd like to see for himself if Grayson really had gotten his life back on track, and his weight down.

He drove to the east end and headed up the stairs to Grayson's door. "Gray," Eric called out. "Are you in? It's Eric."

No answer. Eric let himself inside with his key. "I don't mean to barge in unannounced, but I just wanted to see if you're okay."

The apartment was dark, damp, and cold as a cave. He had to hold his nose as he maneuvered, because a foul stench saturated the dank air like a locker-room filled with sweaty socks and rotten fruit. He stumbled in the dark, crushing paper and what sounded like aluminum under his feet as he felt around for a light. He managed to grope his way into the kitchen and flipped the switch.

Yellow fluorescence lit up the room in a disorienting half-life. The living room area remained partially masked in shadow, while the kitchen blazed. He had to take several turns and glances to gauge the extent to which the mess he found himself standing in had spread. Under the dining room table, which was now pitched over on its side so that it nestled against the wall like a tent, was a single patch of floor, while the rest remained overgrown with cellophane wrappers and aluminum cans strewn violently; brown stains from soft drinks flowered into the fibers of the carpet like bloodstains.

The kitchen was no better, with piles of dishes thick with old, moldy food. The basin was rancid with oily water, and a number of glass tumblers were aligned in an odd harmony, a bizarre domino effect, and each one's mouth was broken, a parade of rows of jagged teeth.

Continuing on, his foot hit against something hard, sending it rolling into a nearby corner. He searched the ground for the culprit and saw, cradled in a nest of candy bar wrappers and egg cartons, a single black bottle. It was the most beautiful bottle he'd ever seen. He knelt down slowly, never minding the sting in his lower back, and scooped up the shimmering bottle. He looked it over carefully. It was a perfect oval with a slender neck. He turned it over and read the label etched elegantly: *Impressive Instants*.

The cap was twisted off. He pressed his nose to the opening and quickly threw the bottle down to the ground, wincing at the stench that flew up his nose like plumes of smoke from a burning building. It mixed with the foul incense of the apartment, turning his stomach. He hunched over, retching, fighting to keep his stomach down, but everywhere he looked was another filthy display.

He stiffened suddenly and stood upright as he heard something shuffling about within the apartment. It came from the direction of the bedroom.

His stomach settled and Eric stepped gingerly over the clutter to enter the hallway. Nervous, he wiped his sweating palms against his new, tailored khakis, but it made no difference. The perspiring persisted.

He braved the darkened door of the bedroom, pushed it open and entered.

The aroma of filth hit him, a swift jab that jolted his senses and caused him to shrink back from the slit of the doorway he divided. He could see straightaway that Grayson's bed was standing on end up against the window like a barricade.

A small shaft of light stole through the top of mangled Venetian blinds, glazing the room in dim, wraith-like phosphorescence. It was enough for him to make out vague shapes but too dark to see clearly what the shapes were.

Standing awkwardly, not quite in but not quite out of the bedroom, one hand to his nose, the other sliding against the wall, Eric felt around, reaching for a light switch he knew was there. But the shambling sound of movement within the room caught him off guard and he reined in his hand as though his fingertips had met fire, and the light remained off.

Something was close. He sensed it at his ankles, a shapeless mass lightly brushing against his leg, its presence prevented from touching him only by the thin cloth between him and the unknown.

"Grayson?"

The thing in the room slid across the floor in the dark, the shadowy outline of a form shifting and pushing itself upright against a far wall.

"Gray, is that you, babe?"

"Babe?" a voice rasped and gurgled, like a pot of coffee bubbling over. "I didn't know we were back to the pet name stage."

"Gray, are you okay, you sound...terrible."

"All things considered," the voice grated.

"Gray, let me find a light."

"No! Leave it off. You won't like seeing me in my...condition."

"Are you fat again or something? I don't care about that. Look...Benjamin, he and Jorge have been trying to reach you. We're worried about you."

"We're? How thoughtful of you to insert yourself into the equation."

"That's not fair. I do care about you, I just...we've been through this. Now stop the attitude and let me help you." Eric stepped forward, but the stink only got heavier further in. "Jesus...what is that smell?"

"The smell grows on you. I don't even notice it anymore."

"Smells...rancid."

"Oh, yes. An unholy scourge, I assure you."

The huddled mass continued to move up the wall, becoming more upright. It shuffled its feet uncontrollably and its bones seemed to crack like wet heels on linoleum. In the vague light, Eric caught the sight of a pair of eyes staring at him, eyes he knew despite the disorientation, were Grayson's.

"Stop playing games," Eric said. "I don't like it."

"You can leave now; your conscience is clear. You can tell Benjamin and Jorge that I can't come out to play anymore."

Eric stepped forward. "Gray, come on, come with me. Let's get you—"

"No! Stay back. I-I don't know if I can contain myself. Stay back."

"Contain? Contain what?"

"The eating."

"Gray, I told you....if you're fat again, I don't care. There are places that can help you with that sort of thing."

"No," Grayson said and it sounded like something between a laugh and a snarl. The shape that was Grayson ambled forward, propping himself up with what looked like a crutch. "I don't think that's possible now."

Eric felt drops of sweat crawling down his neck, moistening his stiff collar. His vision wavered as Grayson passed through the shaft of light from the blinds, a hunched figure that appeared to be wearing a sheet or trench coat; he couldn't be sure.

"Grayson," Eric muttered, feeling for the doorknob. "I'm going to go get help."

"*You're not listening to me!*" Grayson roared as though he were chewing on a mouthful of broken glass and enforced his anger by hobbling forward, covering more distance than Eric found comfortable. "The formula... Caplan, he called them '*changes*'."

"Caplan? Who is Caplan?"

"I called him over days ago for another order. A trick of course, but I needed to see him, to find out what was happening to me."

"What, Gray? What is happening to you? For christsakes, let me turn on a light."

"No light. *Changes...*" Grayson hissed. "He promised I'd change. He was not mistaken."

Grayson shrugged off the trench coat that had covered his body. Even in the very faint light bleeding weakly through the window blinds, Eric could see the thin outline of Grayson and raised his hand to his mouth, choking back a sudden compulsion to scream.

Eric found the light switch.

Suddenly the room was bathed in brightness, and Eric could see.

Eric's eyes watered and he shuddered as though stricken with a stab of pain. It clamped his focus into place, unyielding, and his hands enclosed into a fist, his manicured nails biting his palms. It was no bad dream he could simply pinch himself awake from; this thing that was supposed to be Grayson was very real, shambling toward him on stiff legs, the definition of calves and thighs indiscernible from creaking stalks.

This shriveled, sallow *creature* slouching in front of Eric was a virulent husk of a man, naked and enveloped in a lacerated field of scourged flesh. The creature's eyes stared wide and unblinking, lidless and manic. Dried blood wormed into the folds of curdled wrinkles under the bloodless orbs. The skin contoured to Grayson's face like a decomposing head bound tight in plastic wrap; spade-edged cheekbones forced their way through the caving mounds.

Eric could see what looked like bite marks amidst patches of dried wounds running up and down his forearms. The nipples on Grayson's chest were gaping bullet holes and the pectorals hung low like deflating balloons.

The sparse patches of unmarred flesh shone to near transparency in the faint lamination and as Eric's eyes traveled down the atrocity of his former lover's body, a spray of vomit erupted from between his lips and hit the floor.

He closed his eyes, gasping and wheezing, unable to rid the sight of Grayson's groin, nearly as sexless as a Ken doll; the genitalia savaged with only the bloated scrotum crudely encased by bandages stained black with blood, hanging like a rotted gourd between his thighs.

Grayson began coughing bile into the air. "Something happened...a mutation...caused my cells to cannibalize themselves!" he cried. "And now it is not just eating my cells, but every organ is feeding on itself."

Eric realized that Grayson looked as though he might topple over. The creature leaned forward, gasping, air lodged in his throat. Eric's arms thrust out instinctively to thwart the creature's perilous advance, but the wet touch of naked skin cracking audibly against the palms of his hands loosened a squeal he'd been resisting since he was sick in the kitchen.

Grayson's parchment-like fingers crawled up Eric's cheeks, clutching for balance, the membranous skin between the fingers tearing and splaying his hands like bloody fans. Eric fumbled backwards, lost his footing and went down to the dark carpet as Grayson's strange assemblage of flesh ridden limbs collapsed on top of him.

The creature scurried up the length of Eric's legs, a wiry-framed cockroach bracing him fast at the hips. Eric could feel the blunt edge of knee caps and thigh bones pressing against his lower torso, the human wishbone seizing him with impossible strength even as he struggled to escape. Grayson's back arched and he pressed his hands against Eric's chest.

Eric fought against Grayson, but his hands met a greasy inversion that had once been Grayson's corpulent belly. He could feel the thin walls of bone where the ribs crowned and he became convinced that one good thrust would tear clean through the middle of Grayson's back. He made a fist and prepared to attack but suddenly Grayson's arms weakened under their own depleting musculature. The creature keened softly as he nuzzled his head against Eric's chest like some kind of animal determined to make its burrow in the space between the man's ribcage.

How many years had it been since they'd lain just like this? Tumbling over one another, each one resisting the other in a frantic game in which Eric had always proved the stronger, pressing Grayson onto his back with a sly grin carved on his face.

Only now Eric was on the bottom staring up, and this wasn't one of the lurid encounters he'd experienced many times over. He made an attempt to push away Grayson's head, expecting to tangle his fingers in his ex's thick curls, but instead met the cold, clammy curvature of a creature's bald skin. The front of his shirt grew warm as Grayson pressed against him, soaked in darkness he feared was actually blood. Grayson whimpered against Eric, weak hands moving around Eric's waist and sliding, thin, spidery fingers along the small of his back.

"Remember...when you would hold me like this?" Grayson said, his voice a weak shadow of what it had been. "You're so warm. Caplan wasn't nearly as warm as you are now."

Eric's back tensed under the touch of Grayson's fingers slipping under Eric's shirt and drumming along the sharp V of his chiseled torso. He wanted to get out of the bedroom; out of the house. He had already left Gray once, why on earth did he come back?

"Let me up, Gray," Eric whined in fear, twisting slightly in an attempt to wriggle free.

"Not until I tell you about what I've done," Grayson said, pushing his mouth to Eric's shirt and taking a long, deep, sniff. "He's part of what you smell..."

"Who? Who do I smell?" Eric still struggled against Grayson's restraints. "Let me go."

Grayson laughed, his body rising into a rigid arc. Eric took advantage of the moment and pushed Grayson away, crawling up onto his feet and skirting along the wall. The smell hit him again like a diesel truck, shoving him against the bedroom door and accidently closing it. Eric was confronted with Grayson, who for all his frailty, was somehow beside him again.

"He did this horrible thing to me." Grayson snarled. "Me and who knows how many others."

"Grayson, we have to go, we have to get you to a hospital. For God's sakes, let's get out of here."

Grayson didn't seem to hear him.

"We can get you help," Eric urged desperately, pulling at the bedroom door. It was stuck, why was it stuck? "You're still alive. They can fix whatever's wrong."

Grayson took a step forward and Eric saw something fall from his leg and hit the floor with a very distinct flop.

"Jesus Christ," Eric gagged, cupping his mouth, resisting the urge to vomit again, eyes wide and stinging, but unable to look away from what lay on the floor. A piece of what was once Grayson had fallen off his thigh like a six-ounce steak.

Eric couldn't believe what he was seeing. "You're rotting all the way through! Oh my god, you're coming apart!"

"No doctor can help me now." Grayson said, slamming a hand against the wall, wiry, purple veins showing through cracked, translucent skin. "There is only the demon."

"That's not true," Eric gagged. "I can get you help. Let me go. Please! I'll come back for you, I promise."

But Grayson pushed Eric, sliding him along the wall, away from the door. The creature was blocking the way out, now in-between Eric and the door.

"You've always promised. Always promises. You never delivered on any promises, ever." Grayson's feet oozed blood as he staggered forward. Eric looked over the creature's shoulder and spied the corner of the bedroom. There was a bizarre altar of a dozen or more *Impressive Instants* bottles encircling a mangled, bloody lump on the floor. A man's corpse lay amid a collection of shredded clothes with a pair of silver cutting shears protruding from the figure's back. A mauve-colored necktie was looped through the shears' handles.

"All my years watching sci-fi monster flicks...Now I've become one."

"Grayson," Eric whispered, his voice lost in a dark corner of his throat. "Please let me out of the room."

Ignoring that, Grayson continued, "I just wanted to be perfect, the way you wanted me to be."

"Get back," Eric said, trying to slide around the monster towards the door. But Grayson was still blocking any escape as he was moving even closer, the light catching something fierce in the glassy sheen of his bloodless pupils.

In desperation, Eric lunged past Grayson and reached the doorknob. He pulled it, but it wouldn't open, just like before. How had it locked?

He screamed, "This isn't my fault! I won't let you blame me for this!"

The creature's voice cut like ice picks. "You never took responsibility for anything."

Eric's eyes dodged from Grayson to the window, to the mass surrounded by shiny black bottles. He saw the silver shears, so close. If he could only be quick enough to grab them and fend Grayson off long enough to get out of the apartment, but Grayson was inching closer, a flesh-eating virus on two legs.

Eric could feel his bladder start to loosen. He tried to move towards the window, but somehow Grayson was quicker, clutching Eric at the shoulders and leaning into the man's trembling face. Eric whimpered as though all his childhood nightmares were personified and amassed in front of him. He wet himself at the musky scent of Grayson's breath, redolent of mausoleums. Death was here, standing with an open, yearning mouth.

"But the one thing I discovered early on is that the hunger suppressants don't work. In fact, my hunger's grown beyond myself. I'm so hungry, Eric."

"Please! Gray, please!"

But the savage mouth closed in around him.

«« — »»

After several minutes, Eric's body ceased grunting, the last few flickers in his dying nerves kicking and fading like a dying candle. Grayson arranged pieces of him, gnawed and gnashed around his altar of black bottles of *Impressive Instants*. He caressed their necks, a filmy coating of the fluid sticky and gummed along the bottles' mouths. He then touched the remains of the two people who had hurt him.

The demon churned inside of him, ferocious and strong. It was in his cells now, feeding, forever feeding. Maybe it was never *Impressive Instants* at all. Maybe it had always been him and his demon, feeding on one another.

He took the shears from Caplan's remains and set them to work on his own flesh, snipping a short, plump tendril of his inner thigh. It came away easily, like a fleshy slice of an orange.

It'll never fill me up, the demon thought to himself as he gulped on the oily slice of his own flesh, grinding it between his teeth as he'd done many times in the past weeks, before setting about to remove a second, tender chunk out of his forearm.

About David H. Hernandez

David Alan Hernandez is a native-born Texan currently working on his bachelor's degree in creative writing/education. His work can be found published in various online horror and fantasy ezines including *The Harrow, Sonar4, Flashes in The Dark, The New Flesh, Sex and Murder, Microhorror* and the college literary journal, *The Rio Review*.

In addition to a number of other projects, he is currently keeping a blog at www.truthiscreation.blogspot.com showcasing a dark fantasy web novel, *Dividing Canaan: The Journals of Canaan Quintanilla*.

HUSKS AND FORMLESS RUINS

by Tom Piccirilli

Dedicated to Jack Ketchum

Pace was having a painfully intense *How the fuck did I get here* moment. He checked the rearview again, shaking his head, trying not to sigh.

In the backseat were the dwarf porno actress, the guy with the wire wrapped around his nuts—wearing gray sweatpants stuffed with sponges to soak up his blood—and the cute chick Pace had just met in the bookshop, named Sara.

Beside him in the passenger seat sat the Hexenhaus woman, muttering spells of damnation and making odd gestures on occasion. Like she was throwing magic powder in the air, as if the light of a flaming cross was in her eyes. She'd flinch and snap down to the dashboard and then jerk back against the headrest, having a mini-seizure in place every so often. Pace stared ahead at the twin beams of his headlights chopping the darkness and realized he still didn't know how the hell he'd gotten into this situation.

Boredom is the mother of some serious fuckin' stupidity.

The night had something to do with meeting Sara at the local mega-bookstore, crossing paths with her over in the paranormal/new age section. She was quietly giggling as he walked by. He was feeling listless and weary, as usual, heading to grab himself a double mocha latte with skim milk in the café.

She glanced up and spoke to him like they'd been comfortable lovers for years. Like this was an infrequent outing while the mother-in-law was watching the kids, and they'd be back home in a couple of hours, lying in bed making each other laugh before turning out the light, and rolling quickly toward one another beneath the blankets.

It got him low in the guts and nearly made him moan. He'd been waiting his whole life for a pretty girl to talk to him like that.

"You believe what this guy says here?" she asked, moving closer to him, entering right up into his personal space and thinking nothing of it. She stood there, tilting against the shelves, about three inches from him but looking down at the book. Holding it open so he could read it too if he wanted. "He writes that the only way to serenity is through extreme bodily sacrifice."

Pace thought, *Okay now, her eyesight must be bad. She's lost a contact or something. She's really talking to her boyfriend, but the guy's moved off, in some other aisle someplace, but we must be dressed alike. I'll answer her and she'll gawp and back away with that stunned, slightly terrorized look, and she'll go scampering for the beau. Tell him that some guy was bugging her in the paranormal section, and then I'll have some bastard trying to throw down on me.*

"What's the definition of 'extreme bodily sacrifice?'" Pace asked, waiting to see what would happen.

But she didn't run. Just leaned in even nearer until he could see the flecks of gold deep in her brown eyes. She pressed her fingernail to a line on the page, moving it so he could follow along. "Self-mutilation. Flagellation, impalement, chopping off your naughty bits, pouring boiling oil over yourself."

"I've never been much for serenity anyway," Pace said. "Christ, the price of happiness sounds a little too high."

"I think so too."

"They must've mis-shelved the book. It doesn't seem very paranormal-ish or new age-y."

"There's lots of other stuff about astral projection, karma, telepathy, curses, divine healing, guardian spirits, flying ointment, ghost dances, and soul renewal in here. But in this chapter, the writer gets kind of carried away."

Pace reached out to touch the book, and ran the back of his knuckles lightly over her hand, reveling in its softness and warmth. When you got down to it, he really didn't need much in this world. "There an author photo? He holding a whip with only two fingers on his right hand?"

"No photo. You think he's bashful because of all the third degree burns on his face? How he took his nose off with a potato peeler?"

"If he's serene, he wouldn't be embarrassed, would he? If he is, then his theories are no good anyway."

255

"I agree," she said but kept hold of the book, clutching it to her belly. She turned her full attention on Pace and gave him a steady once-over, openly checking him out. Pursing her lips now, not overly impressed but not appalled either. "This is a present for a friend of mine. She's having a party tonight. It's only a couple miles away, off Route 231. You want to come?"

"Sure," he said.

Bored all right, but always a little curious about this kind of thing, a chance to witness new people in their element. A sharp chick, an unfamiliar group of folks, a different kind of action, whatever it might be. Willing to check out the scene but not expecting much. A couple of free beers, some goofyass conversation, maybe a little necking with this girl. He figured that was all he could hope for, and it was enough.

"I'm Sara," she told him, and took his hand, firmly, first shaking it and then sort of rubbing it, holding it tightly. She was strong and maybe a bit too forceful, but he'd wait and see. "No H. You got a nice car?"

"Yes," he said.

"Really?"

"Yeah."

A '69 Mustang, cherry red Boss 429, with 375 horsepower and 450 lb-ft. A street racer, bigger and heavier than previous models, and with an increased height came a jump in horsepower. Improved handling. Muscle.

"Great," Sara said, giving him the studious look once more. "I'll leave my piece of shit Civic at the Jester Burger next door. It's open twenty-four hours and I'll park out front under the lights. Pick me up there."

Giving him a delicate order. Authoritative but sort of sweet, almost like they were into something together now. There was a subtle implication that they were already a duo, a team. He held back that strange, irritating neediness welling in his chest as she did a semi-strut up to the cash register and paid for the paranormal/new age book about butchering your own flesh to find inner peace.

He picked her up over at the Jester Burger. He enjoyed the expression on her face when she got in and realized how much of the horsepower you could feel thrumming through your body. The potential power in the car, ready to be unleashed. It was a temptation he had to fight all the time. He'd scrapped a '65 GTO and a '71 Chevy

256

Nova 350 V8 in the past few years, wiping out in a couple of fairly spectacular crashes. Knowing he was lucky to still be alive, but uncertain why he should care.

Sara made small talk but he could tell she was thinking of other things, maybe how her friends would react to him. She gave him precise directions to her friend's place.

"I know it," he told her.

He'd passed the house on Route 231 about a thousand times back in his racing days, tearing down the narrow lanes and ripping through red lights. Shaking the cops when he could, and spending a few weeks in the local lockup when he couldn't.

The house was sitting there on the corner, down the block from the only gas station for five miles in any direction. It's where he'd juice up and do whatever small fine-tuning to the engine that still needed to be done before a race. He'd stare at the house while he was at the pumps, doing a final check-through. A white saltbox with an old-fashioned iron weathervane up top, a small yard full of pink flamingos and wildflowers.

They drew up to the house and she ushered him in. The minute he stepped off the welcome mat she slid away and said she'd be right back. Pace stood there looking around at everybody and realized, *Ohboy, no beer.* Not even any pretzels, no potato chips, no mixed drinks. Just a blurring of loud voices trying to drown each other out.

They were all into some kind of new age thing of one sort or another. A couple of dudes in the corner wearing yellow robes and talking about reincarnation, how it was better to be a dog than a flea. A speed freak jittering all around the room talking about Aztec gods, eviscerated cows, and alien abductions. A pair of resounding creation myths being debated in the kitchen. A graying hippie on a window seat lecturing a group of college kids on the five levels of purgation and ascendency to paradise. The six paths of enlightenment. The fourteen centers of the perfect orgasm.

The girls giggling, the guys looking like they wanted to take notes.

Pace kept wandering around the small house, everybody ignoring him. He liked the feeling it gave him, that he could simply move in nearby, hear somebody really going off on how to achieve communication with god-like entities, and then move off. Hear some other cats explaining how the Catholic church has the bones of Jesus sealed in a glass tube under the Vatican.

He couldn't help himself and burst out laughing a couple times, but nobody seemed to mind. He kept circling the place, moving in, then drawing away from these people. So different in complexity of their doctrines but pretty much the same in their naive, near-hysterical exuberance of belief.

But Christ—the Hexenhaus woman was different.

She wasn't lecturing or converting or preaching. She sat in a tiny, shadowy alcove looking beautiful and fragile, murmuring eloquently under her breath. Talking to herself about how they tortured witches in Germany three hundred years ago, with the *bootikens* that crushed feet, and the stonings, and burnings, and the *strappado*, where they'd tie people with their arms behind their backs and then drop them from high bars to break their shoulders. Pace stepped closer and turned his ear to her as her voice faded to a whisper. She said the jails where they performed these atrocities were called *Hexenhauses*.

He very much believed her. As she spoke she made luscious winces and frowns that could either be pain or lust. A flood of emotion pinched her features, like she was being mauled from the inside out. It was frightening and provocative and set his back teeth on edge. He felt strange and kind of pervie to be aroused by the sight of it.

She wore a plain cotton dress with a knotted golden rope around her waist, and well-worn sandals. Like she'd stepped here from the Grecian shores. Baby's Breath in her wild dark hair, and bee-stung lips that made him grimace every time her tongue flailed and licked them. She may have been the most beautiful woman Pace had ever seen, except for the fact that she was obviously insane.

A drop of sweat curved along her cheek and touched the corner of her mouth, and he thought, *There it is, there, all it takes is some instant like that to seal your fate.* His pulse started hammering so hard that his wrists hurt. He stared at her long and hard, wondering if he'd always be attracted to deranged girls. It seemed to be the case. What was it that drove him to this?

Sara ambled over, holding a bottle of beer. A knowing grin tugged her mouth askew. "Here, you look thirsty."

"Well, you did say party."

"I misspoke, I'm afraid. I should've said function. Or gathering."

"That might've been more accurate." Pace drained half the bottle in one pull, then gestured with his chin at the various groups of folks pontificating on man, god, and the devil. "They don't seem to be having much fun, most of them. You do this a lot? Attend these kinds of functions?"

"I just sort of stumbled into it." She rubbed the back of her hand against his, the way he'd done it to her earlier. He realized she knew this action had some kind of control over him. His shoulders tightened. It was the simple things that made his breath hitch in his chest. "You dig her, don't you?" she asked.

"What?"

Sara got in close again, nearly nose to nose with him, and pointed to the Hexenhaus woman. "Don't be embarrassed. Every guy swoons for her. Beautiful, always crying. Weak, in need of a protector. Probably crazy. Men like to try to save her."

"Is that why she does it?" he asked. "Acts that way, alone in the corner? So guys can fall in love with her?"

"No, it's who she is now."

There was a lot of history in Sara's tone. Anger, familiarity, alliance, and maybe even a touch of jealousy. Pace perused the rest of the group, everybody doing their own thing but at essential odds with one another. All leaders and no followers. The distracting growls of fierce arguments, stemming from the best way to find clarity and love. No fisticuffs yet, but Pace could imagine it happening. A couple of these guys throwing down on which crystals made the best conduits to beings beyond the veil. The Buddhist throwing down on the penitent.

"Who's party is this, by the way?" he asked.

She again indicated to the Hexenhaus woman, wrapping an arm around his waist, as if knowing he was being drawn away and didn't want to let him to go yet. "Hers."

"What's her name?"

"She doesn't have one anymore."

Pace frowned at that and finished his beer. "What do you mean?"

With a sad but anxious expression, Sara got even closer until he thought she was going to kiss him. He set himself and leaned in expectantly, but she only searched his eyes. It really threw him off, having somebody watching him like this, inspecting him, digging down beneath his surface for no reason he could see. "She was in a car accident a couple of years ago. Since then, she's gotten deeper into *this*. The way she is now."

"Schizophrenic?"

"Disassociated. She smacked her head pretty good, but she was only held overnight in the hospital. It's not like she was dead on the table for two minutes or went into a month-long coma. They put a bandage on her and she was released."

The Hexenhaus woman disregarded them completely. She continued talking to herself, having what sounded like an interesting discourse. Two or three different people inside her all having a thoughtful discussion on witchcraft and persecution. For a few seconds she went into a mini-convulsion and Pace started for her, but Sara held him back.

"Leave her. Mostly she's like this, but occasionally she has moments of lucidity. She'll phone up everyone in the area who's a spiritual seeker. The folks dabbling in the occult, throwing themselves into theology, studying mythology, ways to get closer to the supernatural."

"How does she get along? Who takes care of her?"

"I do." Sara gave him the once-over again, like maybe she had spotted something more to him now, in places he didn't notice himself. She asked, "Can you give me another ride?"

"Home?"

"No, out to the meadows. The other side of town, you know?"

"Yeah. But why?"

"I'm not really sure." Conflicted about even asking him, but deciding what the hell. She nuzzled his neck, like getting him horny would be the answer. "Earlier she was crying that she wanted to go out there."

"To the meadows in the middle of the night?"

"Yes."

"That *is* pretty disassociated."

"It's where her accident happened. There's a tree out in a field that she ran into. She believes it has some kind of occult power. She wants to go see it again. Who knows? Dance around it maybe. She used to love dancing. I think it has something to do with the autumn solstice."

"That was two weeks ago," Pace said. "On September twenty-third."

The fact impressed her enough to lead him into the kitchen and give him another beer. "Now how do you know that?"

"I know lots of trivial shit," he admitted.

"There's more than a few people here tonight who'd say it wasn't so trivial."

"Yeah, but would they be right?"

She grinned at him, studying him while he drank the bottle down fast. "You don't take this seriously do you?"

"Take what?"

"All these people's ideologies."

"I don't see any real convictions at all, just a bunch of folks with some fun ideas."

"You sound cynical."

"Do I? Anyway, that all explains why she wants to go, but why do you want to go out there?"

"Like I said, she's a friend of mine. Or used to be. I try to look out for her."

All of this conversation, but Sara hadn't mentioned the Hexenhaus woman's name even once. How close a friend could she be?

"Okay," he said. "Whenever you're ready."

"A few others want to go as well."

"To see a tree?"

"We're sort of a coven," Sara told him. Her lips were on his ear now, teeth nibbling, like she decided this was the way to keep him from running. She must've scared off a lot of guys in the past.

Pace said, "I thought you needed thirteen members for a coven."

"We're a small coven."

"I guess so."

"And even though I bought the book for her, another friend has already started reading and using it. He'll be along too."

"What do you mean that he's using the book?"

"Practicing mutilation."

Now this was starting to turn into a pretty funky night. "How do you practice mutilation? You either mutilate something or you don't."

"You're right. He's doing something to himself with wire, I'm not sure what. I think he's trying to castrate himself."

"Christ!"

Sara dropped her chin and shook her head. "Yeah, he's spiritually a little lost right now."

"That's one way to put it!"

"Anyway, he's bleeding, but not too badly. You mind taking us?"

He thought about it, wondering if the guy's blood was going to get on the 'Stang's seats, if he was really going to saw off his balls right there in back of the car.

And if the Hexenhaus woman would snap out of her torpor and look him in the eye.

"No," Pace told her, and that seemed to be how this jaunt got started.

On the back roads on the far side of town, heading through the fields and the rising hills with empty swathes and stretches of highway where he used to race back in his teens, he watched the road and imagined how the road must be watching him.

"Hey," the guy squeezing his own nuts off with the barbed wire said, "you think maybe you got a rag in the trunk you can give me?" His voice was thick and intense with agony, but there was a crazed giggle hidden in there too. "That last bump we went over jostled me pretty good. I'm starting to bleed even more and the sponges aren't soaking it all up. I don't want to stain your interior."

"You sure you don't want to go to a hospital?"

"This is the only way to purity and serenity."

"Okay, man." Pace pulled over, opened the trunk, and found a rag he used to clean off the dipsticks with. The guy stuffed it down into his drawers. Pace got in behind the wheel again and stomped the gas, watching the headlights tear across the weeds heaving in the wind.

"You seen any of my films?" the dwarf porno starlet named Belle asked. She stood about two and a half feet high and wore a shiny leather outfit with chains dangling in front of her chest, a long leather coat that dragged behind her like a wedding train. She had a tattoo of two snakes eating each other wrapped around her neck and a tiny rose on her face just under her ear. Short dyed black hair and a very sexy mouth. She was kind of freaking him out a bit. Every time he looked at her, for a second he only saw a little girl playing dress up.

"No," Pace said.

"You sure?"

"I'd remember."

"You better believe you would."

"You think you could lend me some tapes of your movies?"

"Tapes? Honey, don't you have a DVD player, or blu-ray?"

"No," he told her.

"I don't think I have any tapes." She smiled, turned her head so the flower under her ear caught some moonlight breaching the clouds. "Got you interested, eh?"

"I'm curious about a lot of things."

"Good boy."

"You work with other dwarves too? Or you specialize with the big guys?"

"All kinds, man. Get yourself a DVD player and see for yourself."

"I'm gonna have to now."

The Hexenhaus woman flailed awake from her stupor and glanced at him. The cotton dress had lifted to reveal the jut of her bare knees. Some of the Baby's Breath in her hair had dropped free and sprinkled across the dash. That tongue came out again and licked the bee-stung lips. Her black, insane radiance brushed up against him like a natural force, a storm about to break.

She asked, "Do you love me already?"

"No," Pace said, but it sounded like a lie. She reached over and touched his knee gently, and then her grip tightened until it hurt. He had to forcibly remove her hand, and when he looked in her face he saw she was mumbling to herself again, eyes rolled back in her head.

The guy with the wire in the bad place said to the porno actress, "Tell him about that scene you did with Dave Hardup that one time, Belle." The weird giggle in his voice was on the verge of delirium.

"He had a twelve inch crank with a big bend in it that—"

Sara cut in. "Let's leave that story for another night, okay, Belle? We're on a sort of mission here." She reached over the passenger seat and toyed with the Hexenhaus woman's hair, which appeared to quiet her a bit.

"You're right, it's best to keep our priorities straight. Besides, I don't want to distract him while he's driving. It's easy to get lost around here."

Pace tapped the gas a little more, feeling the throb of the engine work into his belly, his rib cage, his throat.

The Hexenhaus woman had quieted down, but she was also trembling. Her eyes refocused and Pace saw a sharp intelligence there, as well as great sorrow. "We approach the commencement and endowment of values," she said. "The genesis of creed, canon, and law. The embracing place of the possessed."

Sara leaned forward and touched Pace on the shoulder. "She means her accident. Another guy was driving her and hit a slick part of the road one rainy night. They went into a spin and off the road."

Pace fought down the icy sting at the base of his spine. Sara had left out that little detail before. "What happened to the guy driving?"

"He died."

"Let's hope history doesn't repeat itself."

"Yes, let's."

"Ow," the wire guy said. "Fuck, this hurts!"

The 'Stang hugged the curves well as Pace banked easily along the road, knowing that the Hexenhaus woman would alert him when they got to the tree in one of these shadow-laden fields.

It didn't take long. Her hand snaked out to clutch his knee again.

Around the next bend, standing off about a hundred yards in the meadow, he saw the silhouette of a gnarled oak rising in the moonlight. He could picture just how the crash had happened.

The driver taking this turn a little too fast in the rain, jerking the wheel as he overcompensated, and the tires slipping and hydroplaning. Carrying them off the side of the road, the driver trying to hit the brake but the car bouncing too badly for him to recover and hit the pedal. Sluicing in the mud and attempting to brace himself against the wheel as the Hexenhaus woman screamed in his ear and the tree loomed wider than death.

"That's the tree," he said.

"Yes," Sara told him. "How'd you know?"

He slowed and pulled off down the embankment. His headlights picked up the tree and he noticed the scarring on the bark. The other guy, he'd been driving a muscle car as well. Pace could tell by the kind of scraping the grille had left.

He'd seen a lot of trees mangled like this. A few of them he'd done himself, taking it to 110 mph on the streets, closing his eyes, and trying to ease around the curves blind. He didn't think he had a suicide wish, but maybe he wasn't the best judge.

He parked the 'Stang and left the lights burning against the trunk of the oak. The wind lifted the Hexenhaus woman's dress and twirled her hem wickedly around her legs. Belle and Sara helped the wire guy out of the back of the car and kind of carried him over to the tree. He kneeled before the scarred markings and looked up at Pace.

"I'm giving up my future generations." He wasn't giggling anymore, and the thick sweat glittered on his face.

Pace said, "Man, couldn't you just have gotten a vasectomy?"

"No," he said.

"Why not?"

"That's not irrevocable!"

"I'm not too sure about that," Pace said, because he wasn't. He'd heard the procedure was reversible, but he thought about doctors going in there and clipping tubes and stopping the potential flow of your children, and then starting it back up again. It made him shudder.

"It's not a sacrifice unless you give it up forever," Belle said, smiling with all those teeth. The black snakes around her neck looked like they were crawling in the dim light. Slithering, chewing.

"What?"

"If you can get it back, then it's not a sacrifice. It's like the Catholics giving up, what, chocolate, for Lent. Like it's a big concession. Then after their forty days are up, they eat twelve pounds of Easter rabbits. Splurging, making themselves sick on it. You think that holds much sway with God?"

"I don't know."

"You think that's what He's got in mind when He's talking sacrifice? Abraham had to drag his kid to a rock and yank his head back and expose his throat and stick the knife right to it. He was supposed to give up his son. For eternity. None of this Lent shit. None of this, hey, Abe, it's only for a little while, you can see your kid again in a few weeks. No. Sacrifice is forever."

Pace stared at the little dwarfy broad and wondered exactly how she could handle a twelve inch crank with a big bend in it. He had to get a DVD player soon.

"This wire doesn't seem to be working," the really stupid wire guy said, groaning, beginning to whimper. His sweatpants were soaked in blood now.

Sara crouched beside him and started pulling out the dripping sponges and rags. "You need to make it tighter, leave it on longer," she told him.

"But I need to perform the ritual tonight!" Pointing to the Hexenhaus woman. "So she has demanded!"

"Then you'll have to yank on the ends and...ah...saw into yourself."

"Oh God!"

Belle told him, "If you need me, I'll help."

Pace thought, *I need a satellite dish. If I had Guatemalan soccer coming in or all the HBO stations, I might not climb the walls so much. In fact, I might be quite comfortable staying in.*

The beautiful Hexenhaus woman dropped to all fours and went into a furious fit in the meadow. Pace wondered what he should do, how he could help her, how he could make everything all right for the both of them.

Sara said, "Don't touch her!" but Pace had no intention of doing so anyway. That jamming a spoon in their mouths so they didn't swallow their tongues was the worst thing you could do. Wrestling with them, forcing their mouths open, sticking shit in there that they might choke on. You let hem ride it out until they were finished. It was, in a fashion, a very pure act.

Although she kept writhing in the grass, the Hexenhaus woman's right arm snapped straight out, finger pointed at Pace. "You!"

"Me?"

"Tainted!"

"Me?"

"Carnal! Profane!"

Pace thought, *Ohboy, dirty talk.*

The Hexenhaus woman quieted, her violent movements slowing, until she stopped, and merely lay on the ground, the side of her lovely face glowing in the headlights. She spoke in a voice that was as ancient as the desert, full of sandstorm and destroyed temples. "You are all husks and formless ruins, collapsing at the bottom of the well of time."

Pace thought, *She's got something there. That's exactly how I feel.*

The wire guy reached into his pants and started tugging on the barbed wire wrapped around his testicles, grunting from the exertion. He made one tremendous effort and let out a shriek. "I can't do it! Oh lord, I'm not strong enough! Forgive me!"

"Holy goddamn," Pace said.

With a giggle, Sara stepped over. Pace didn't see much to be laughing about, and watched her approach. She had her arm pressed to her side, but he saw something gleaming in her hand.

"What've you got there?"

She held it out to him like she expected him to take it, but she was still too far away. A burnished ceremonial knife, the edge bright and lustrous. "This is an *athame*. A witch's blade."

"That right? And what are you going to do with it?"

Moving in on him again, slinky, with real skill, holding the knife low the way you were supposed to do. None of this yank it back over your shoulder and stabbing down, but loose and jabbing towards the soft meat of the belly, where it wouldn't get stuck in the ribs. She let out a laugh that was meant to be sexual and disarming, as she acted like she wanted to slip into his arms, make love to him right here in the grass, the blade weaving, twisting forward.

Pace's hand flashed out and caught her wrist. "That's a little too much extreme bodily sacrifice for my taste," he said, grinning. Sara struggled, and her smile turned to a leer, but she still seemed to be having a pretty good time.

"So what was the idea?" he asked. "You leave me here under the tree?"

"Yes."

"Dead in this spot. Like her boyfriend?"

"He died in the crash and look what it did for her."

Pace glanced over. "It's made her looney."

"It's given her power! She's a vessel for forces out in the darkness, beyond the eternal void. She can see into the future and the forgotten, archaic past."

"Yeah? And what good does it do her?"

"That's doesn't matter! It's an honor to be a crucible for the gods!" Saying it all like she wasn't quite sure if she even really believed it, but had decided to give it a shot because she had nothing else to put her faith in.

He knew the feeling. He thought about where he was and what he was doing, and how he'd gotten here. He was starting to feel a little abused. Sacrificed to a frickin' tree by the pretty girl who'd tapped him in a bookstore because he'd wanted a double mocha latte with skim milk.

Pace yanked the blade from her and backhanded her across the cheek. A little too softly. She wrenched forward and tried to get the knife again, and Pace grabbed her by the hair, drew her head back, and socked her in the jaw. It was enough to make her drop on her ass. He didn't feel particularly proud or ashamed for punching out a girl he'd wanted to make, but he was glad to be alive. Odd, that.

Belle reached into her jacket and started to come out with what looked like a .38 filling her hand. The front sight got hung up in her pocket as she tugged on the pistol. Pace didn't know what to do. He could dive behind the 'Stang or make a run to hide behind the tree. Or maybe he could charm her with some talk, ask about her movies again, invite her over for some pizza. There were times when he thought that something like that would be more than enough to keep people from coming totally unglued.

The Hexenhaus woman said, "By my hand only shall the basins be emptied," and Belle fumbled the pistol and shot herself in the foot.

She screamed but not as loudly as Pace would've thought. It looked like her two biggest toes were gone, and she stood there wide-eyed in shock. The .38 dropped from her fingers and she lurched sideways, bracing herself against the wire guy's shoulder, where he kneeled on the ground bleeding out.

"Help me!" he whined. "Get me to a hospital!"

"I gave you your chance," Pace told him.

Belle said. "I sacrificed my foot. I didn't even mean to. Please, drop us off at an emergency room."

Pace angled his chin up the embankment, pointing further into the hills. "You head a mile, mile and a half in that direction and you'll find a service station. We used to race these back roads and gas up there. Of course, that was a long time ago. It might have closed up by now."

"You're leaving us to die?"

"You'll probably make it, but it's going to hurt like hell. Think how purified you'll feel when you get there."

"You cruel son of a bitch," Belle snarled.

Pace thought about grabbing up the gun and just making a clean sweep of things, but he figured it was more fun this way. "You were going to let her cut my throat, weren't you?"

"Yes," Belle admitted, trying to do something sexy with her mouth again, but the pain prevented her from pulling it off. "We're sorry."

"You're getting what you deserve."

The wire guy was really leaking now. "Oh God, I'm bleeding to death!"

"You feeling serene yet?"

"Oh God!"

Pace helped the stupid shit up and Belle took hold of the wire guy's thigh and together they lurched a few steps in the wrong direction. Pace pointed again. "Over there, about a mile or so."

He reached down and yanked Sara to her feet. She didn't look angry or hurt or even upset, all kinds of expressions creeping across her features and canceling each other out. He handed the knife back to her, wondering if she'd make another go of it. "You never should have bought that book."

"I know," she said.

"You might consider not going to anymore of these functions."

"I have nowhere else to go," she said, and started to sob. She held her arms out like a scared child and he hugged her tightly, aware of where the blade was, waiting for her to try again. She didn't. After a minute she slipped from him and started off after the other two coven members limping and leaking in the dark.

The beautiful and insane Hexenhaus woman said, "A demon inhabits this form. It will feed on your heart and your being. When you die, there will be nothing at all left to bear up to God."

"Okay," Pace said.

The Hexenhaus woman kissed him, and her demonic tongue was alive and twitching and stabbing his mouth. He pulled her closer and she moaned and wept, like someone lost alone in everlasting shadows. She tensed in his arms and let out a heinous laugh. "You are no mere husk. You are filled with endless hell and enduring hate."

"Sure," he told her and viciously pulled her onto him in the black meadow. When you got down to it, he didn't really need much in this world.

About Tom Piccirilli

Tom Piccirilli is the author of more than twenty novels including *Shadow Season, The Cold Spot, The Coldest Mile*, and *A Choir of Ill Children*. He's won two International Thriller Awards and four Bram Stoker Awards, as well as having been nominated for the Edgar, the World Fantasy Award, the Macavity, and Le Grand Prix de l'Imaginaire. Learn more at his blog: www.thecoldspot.blogspot.com

MASKS

by Taylor Grant

Jonathan dabbed at the blood on his neck and licked his crimson-stained fingertips, savoring the sharp, coppery taste.

"What the hell's taking so long?" Margaret yelled from outside the bathroom door. "I'm going to be late for my spinning class."

Startled from his reverie, Jonathan noticed his reflection in the mirror and recoiled at the face staring back. He'd never smiled like that in his life; it was more of a grimace.

"Hurry up, goddamn it," Margaret said, pounding on the door.

Jonathan's fists tightened. He forced himself to take a deep breath before opening the door. "Sorry, honey," he said, "I nicked myself shaving."

Margaret brushed past him, shoved him out the door, and slammed it so hard his scrotum tightened.

With a familiar sigh, he continued his morning routine.

«« —»»

Later, while crouched over his computer at work, Jonathan couldn't shake the disturbing reflection he'd seen in the bathroom mirror—and that horrible gash of a smile.

It's just work-related stress, he thought. *God, please let it be that.*

He couldn't take another year like the last—and he sure as hell couldn't afford the therapy, although it seemed clear he needed another session with Dr. Hatchman. He warmly recalled his former therapist's signature western wear, bushy white beard, and perpetually rosy cheeks. He looked like Santa Claus moonlighting as a country-western star.

Jonathan chuckled at the mental image, gradually returning to the job at hand. He attempted to analyze a spreadsheet of projected revenue figures for the next fiscal year, but found it impossible to focus. He glanced down and noticed his fingers tapping at the keyboard as if they belonged to someone else. The spreadsheet minimized on his screen and was replaced by a Web browser. Moments later, a parade of violent, sexual obscenities marched across his screen.

He felt the twisted grimace of a smile invading his lips once again. He sat immobile at his desk, both repulsed and intrigued by the imagery on the computer. It was like driving past a particularly gruesome car wreck, not wanting to look—yet unable to tear his eyes away.

And then he noticed his hands. *Jesus Christ, my skin looks like....*

"Mr. Bailey?" a soft voice beckoned.

Startled, Jonathan quickly minimized the images on his computer screen.

A petite brunette with perfect teeth to match her perfect smile peeked inside his office. "Mr. Bailey, your three o'clock is here."

"Thank you..." Jonathan's voice wasn't his. It was deeper. Colder. He cleared his throat and tried again. "Thank you, Jenny. Tell them I'll be just a moment."

She gave him a curious look. "Are you okay?"

"Fine," he lied. "I'm fine."

She raised her shoulders in that little shrug he hated and closed the door with a click.

"Whore," he heard himself mutter, feeling surprised at the venom of his tone.

He turned his hands palms up, then down, studying every inch. They appeared normal again. It's just work-related stress, he told himself for the second time that day.

«« — »»

He'd chewed two of his fingernails down to bloody nubs by seven o'clock that evening. He swore if he had to create one more Power Point presentation he was going to rip the skin from his bones. In an uncharacteristically bold move, he ignored a handful of last-minute email threads and left early.

Jonathan drove home, thinking about the bizarre events of the day with an increasing sense of unease. He longed for a session with Dr. Hatchman. Unfortunately, he'd already used up the allotment of counseling sessions his pathetic HMO covered. If he wanted to reenter therapy, he'd have to pay out of pocket—and he simply couldn't afford that. He and Margaret were hemorrhaging money due to her obsession with home renovation, and he didn't have the balls to stop her.

He forced a deep breath; he was probably over-dramatizing. End of the year was notoriously crazy and he was simply overworked. Hell, a weekend by the pool with a few dry martinis, and he'd feel like a new man.

Actually, I feel better already, he thought.

Suddenly, two teenage boys in a gray Impala cut him off. Jonathan instinctively jerked the wheel to the right and nearly lost control of his Taurus but was able to straighten out. The pimple-faced driver laughed at him and pressed his middle finger to the window.

Jonathan's fingers coiled around the steering wheel like tiny, hungry pythons as he slammed onto the accelerator. He raced up alongside the Impala, honking his horn viciously. As the boy glanced over, Jonathan was surprised to see the boy react in fright and swerve away.

It only heightened Jonathan's bloodlust; he veered toward the Impala even more aggressively. The pizza-faced driver panicked— weaving into the far lane.

But there was no far lane.

Jonathan caught a glimpse of the boys' faces frozen in silent screams as their car sailed off the road to be engulfed by the blackness below. The canyon was so deep that Jonathan didn't hear the impact.

He glanced up at the rearview mirror as he drove away, searching for any witnesses. He was relieved to see that the only visible headlights were tiny pinpricks—at least a mile in the distance. Whoever they were, they were too far off to have seen anything, much less identify his car.

He exited the road at the next turnoff and took a dizzying maze of side streets to get home. As he drove through a desolate warehouse district, he caught a glimpse of his frightful reflection in the rear view mirror—and nearly lost control of his car. The Taurus spun wildly as he careened over a hill. He slammed on the brakes, flung open the door and tumbled out onto the oil-stained asphalt.

Oh, God...Oh, Jesus...Oh, God, he thought, scrambling to his feet. His features had been horrifying, as if they were stretched over some monstrous *thing* beneath his skin. Is that what the boy had seen—why he'd looked so terrified?

He walked aimlessly along some long-forgotten railroad tracks as the realization of what he'd done—the enormity of it all—began to sink in. He might have *killed* two young kids.

Wait, he thought. Temporary insanity. Yes—that would be his plea if he got caught. It made perfect sense. He'd already been through a nervous breakdown the previous year. Dr. Hatchman was a character witness; perhaps he could confirm that Jonathan had a pattern of psychosis. Would it be a far stretch to say that he'd never fully recovered? He played out every scenario he could think of.

He wandered silent streets until he'd formed what he thought was a reasonably convincing narrative. When he finally returned to his car, it took him an additional twenty minutes to find the courage to climb inside.

He avoided looking into the rearview mirror as he drove home.

《《——》》

Jonathan watched the evening news and scoured the morning paper for several days. He discovered the brief news item while eating breakfast. It was a missing person's story, with requisite quotes from worried family members and a reward offered for any information. As it turned out, fourteen-year-old Andy Creeter and seventeen-year-old Rusty Creeter—pizza-face himself—were brothers. The police considered it a runaway case due to the boys' past histories and juvenile records.

A conspiratorial grin crossed Jonathan's lips. There were no bodies, suspicions of foul play, motives to uncover, or any living witnesses. If there were such a thing as a perfect crime, this came pretty damned close.

He studied the news story for so long that his corn flakes fused into a single membrane floating aimlessly in his bowl. For a moment, he worried that Margaret might have noticed his preoccupation with the story—but she was far too busy renovating the kitchen.

While she savagely attacked some drywall with a chisel and hammer, he made his move toward the sink and dumped his bowl of mush into the disposal. He was about to leave for work when he heard Margaret mumble "Have a good day," with a distinct lack of interest.

He started to offer his automated response, "You, too," but was cut off by her vicious hammering. It seemed as if the only thing that interested Margaret these days was tearing things apart.

Within a few days, he'd put the whole dreary Creeter affair behind him. A voice inside his head offered constant reassurance; told him that everything would be just fine.

The voice wasn't his.

《《——》》

At work, others began to notice changes in Jonathan.

The Tuesday morning executive meeting began as a typical corporate affair, with Don Henry, the company CEO pontificating about quarterly milestones and meeting stockholders' expectations. Don's formidable business acumen was second only to his quick-tempered nature. He had a reputation for verbally assaulting anyone who questioned his authority.

Jonathan sat in a cold sweat, fighting an overwhelming urge to leap across the table and rip the son of a bitch's tongue from his mouth. Adding to his discomfort was a strange and extraordinarily painful throbbing sensation in his lower back.

Eventually, Don called him out. "Is there a problem, Bailey?"

Jonathan dug his fingernails into his wrist to keep from laughing at the silver-haired man. When Don asked him again, Jonathan burst into such a howl of laughter that spittle flew from his mouth.

The veins pulsed in Don's neck. "What the hell's so funny?"

"You," Jonathan heard himself say. "If you think anyone in this room gives a rat's ass about meeting stockholders' expectations, then you're an even bigger corporate stooge than I thought."

Silence choked the room. All eyes bounced between Jonathan and Don Henry. No one knew how to react. No one dared make a sound. After an unbearably long moment, Don collected his charts. "See me in my office," he said and left the room.

Jonathan snapped up his papers and started after Don, feeling the entire room staring into his back. As he reached the door, he turned to Peter McIntyre, a particularly sycophantic Director of Marketing, and *snarled* at him.

Peter turned white.

Jonathan could still hear nervous laughter from the conference room as he reached Don Henry's palatial corner office. He didn't bother to knock.

Don stood before a large bay window, staring out at a spectacular panorama of the city. His voice was solemn. "Have a seat."

Jonathan plopped into one of the designer guest chairs and winced from an electric jolt to his tailbone. Don circled like a pin-striped predator sizing up its prey. "You've seen the African masks on the wall behind my desk?"

Jonathan grunted; everyone in the office knew of Don's collection of crude wooden masks and his oft-told tales of traveling through the Dark Continent. Each mask represented a different human expression: joy, sadness, lust, anger...the entire spectrum.

Don gave Jonathan a furtive glance as he stepped behind his massive oak desk. "Ancient tribesmen believed that by wearing one, you could draw power from the expression it represented." He removed an angry mask from the wall, appeared to silently address it, and then peered at Jonathan through the eye slits. "You have a mask, Bailey. And it's cracking. I can see it happening...hell, everyone can see it. Things have never been quite right since your...'episode' last year."

Jonathan thought: *Oh, but it's your mask that's cracking, Don. I can see the fearful little creature behind the puffed-up façade.*

He leaned forward, matching Don's steely gaze; he was still surprised by his own audacity. "What's your point?"

"My point," Don said with a nervous tic in his eye, "is that I don't want you anywhere near me or this office when you finally crack apart."

Jonathan rose to face Don. "You talk a lot about me and my mask, old boy, but what about yours?"

"Excuse me?"

"You're a frightened little man," Jonathan heard himself say, "hiding behind your self-important position like a child hides behind his mother's knees." He took several steps forward, moving around the desk toward Don.

Don took an involuntary step back.

Jonathan grinned, but there was no warmth there. "You know that beneath this pretense of boss and subordinate, we're no different than wild beasts back in the jungle."

Don's face was turning ashen. "What the hell are you talking about?"

Jonathan took another step forward, tightening his fists. "I'm talking about the truth behind our masks."

Suddenly, Don's knees buckled and he stumbled back into his custom-made leather chair, gasping for breath. Jonathan loomed over him, well aware of Don's history of heart trouble, including two heart attacks and triple bypass surgery. He leaned in and bared his teeth for effect. "Because once you lose your perceived advantage, you know I'll eat you alive."

"Get out!" Don wheezed, clutching at his left arm. "You're fired!" His face was covered with sweat, twitching wildly. He tried to reach for his phone, but Jonathan stood in his way.

"You were right, Don. My mask *has* cracked. Wanna see behind it?"

Don looked into Jonathan's eyes and gaped in horror.

When Jonathan stepped out of Don's office a few moments later, he smoothed the sweaty, tousled hair back from his brow and adjusted his tie. He sauntered toward Don's assistant's desk, where Meg, a stony-faced woman glanced up.

"You might want to check on your boss," Jonathan said casually. "He's not looking so hot." And then he strolled off toward his office.

He took his time packing his personal belongings into a box. There were several professional keepsakes, a withered office plant, and a framed photo of him and Margaret with obligatory smiles. He carried the box into the hallway just outside his office and dumped everything into a nearby recycling bin.

He continued toward the building's main entrance and noticed a crowd of coworkers. The double doors at the end of the corridor were open, and the light of an ambulance beyond it pulsed like an artery, bathing the lobby with the color of blood.

As Jonathan reached the crowded room, coworkers began to whisper like schoolchildren. Jonathan glanced outside as two paramedics carried a stretcher with Don Henry on it toward the ambulance. He locked eyes with Don, who was alive, but seemed unable to speak. Don's face was frozen into a mask of terror, the result of what appeared to be a massive stroke.

Meg stood near Jonathan, her eyes dark with worry. "What the hell happened in there?"

Jonathan didn't answer. He just watched Don being loaded into the ambulance and tried his best not to grin.

As he drove to his physician's office a few hours later, Jonathan tried to convince himself that he was still in complete control. But the truth was that he'd been unable to suppress his wild ravings in Don's office. It was as if he were watching from outside himself, helpless against his baser instincts.

A sharp jolt in his lower back made him speed even faster.

«««——»»»

"Very unusual..." Dr. Stanton mumbled as he studied Jonathan's x-rays.

Jonathan shuffled across the antiseptic room, rubbing his back. His eyes followed Dr. Stanton's finger as he pointed at a bizarre growth toward the bottom of Jonathan's spinal column.

He was almost afraid to ask, "What is it? A tumor?"

Stanton leaned in for a closer look at the x-ray. "Too early to say. If it wasn't so ridiculous, I'd swear your coccyx is growing."

"What's the hell's a coccyx?"

"Your tailbone," Stanton said, clearly as puzzled as Jonathan.

An hour later, Jonathan limped out of the doctor's office. Stanton gave him a prescription for some heavy-duty painkillers and told him to make an appointment with a specialist.

«««——»»»

Every facet of Jonathan's life was spiraling out of control: his career, his marriage, his mind—and now his own body. Desperate for pain relief, he raced to the nearest pharmacy to fill his prescription.

It was early evening when he reached the quiet streets and perfectly groomed lawns of his neighborhood. The medication had kicked in rather nicely, turning his sharp pains into dull aches.

As Jonathan drove through the streets of the planned community, past the familiar imported trees, man-made ponds, and uniformly designed homes, he felt strange, like an outsider in his own life. What had once felt comfortable and safe now seemed oppressive; a prison of cookie-cutter suburban conformity.

He felt a renewed pain in his coccyx area, and recalled something he'd learned as a boy in science class. The tailbone—according to some evolutionists—was a leftover from man's early origins. He imagined himself growing a tail and regressing into some form of primordial beast. Turning into...*oh shut up, you idiot.*

He reached his home, a nondescript box in an endless row of tract housing. As he pulled into the driveway, he caught sight of Margaret walking past a tall casement window facing the street. She was going to bed and wore a short plaid nightshirt; her long, sinewy legs looked remarkably sexy. Jonathan imagined them wrapped around his waist as he thrust into her like a frenzied animal. Despite the medication, he felt a rise in his pants. It was a pleasant surprise.

By the time he reached the master bedroom, Margaret was feigning sleep. It was a familiar routine: he'd climb into bed and lightly kiss her cheek, her neck, and gradually move down to her shoulder. On rare occasions, she would stir, which was the green light for sex. Otherwise, she'd lie as stiff as rigor mortis.

As Jonathan reached her shoulder, it was obvious that this was going to be another *Night of the Living Dead*. He was disappointed, but not surprised. They hadn't had sex in nearly a year. After undressing, he lay down next to her and stared at the white, spackled ceiling. His thoughts drifted to Don Henry's words.

Your mask is cracking...

Is it? Jonathan wondered. And if it was, what was underneath? He suspected it was something terrible.

He mused about the people in his life, Margaret foremost in his mind. They'd been married for over a decade, and yet he often wondered if he knew her at all. He tried to remember what had attracted them to each other in the first place, but the memory remained elusive.

He thought of his neighbors and former coworkers as they prepared for work each morning: dressed in their power ties and corporate-branded uniforms. They were, of course, expected to act accordingly; a perpetual 9-to-5 masquerade ball—costumes and masks required. He also wondered about the people he passed on the streets, in the stores, and throughout the goings-on of his daily life. What lurked beneath their cool exteriors?

He recalled a recent news story about a beloved cardinal in New York who'd sodomized two generations of young boys, and the respected female pediatrician in Maine who was caught torturing infants under her care.

What lies beneath their masks? Or mine?

Rusty Creeter had seen it, and so had Don Henry. And Christ, look what happened to them.

He could feel something dark, twisted, and irresistible growing inside him. It smashed its fists against an invisible wall in his mind. A wave of fear washed over Jonathan, unlike anything he'd ever known.

Something wanted out.

He gripped the sheets defensively, eyes wide, feeling his control slipping away.

Margaret stirred with a soft moan. Jonathan held his breath, praying she wouldn't touch him. He knew he couldn't hold back whatever raged inside. But she rubbed an inviting hand across his leg and whispered, "It's time. I've been waiting."

Jonathan couldn't imagine what prompted this, but then realized that it wasn't him that had aroused her. It was something else. As if possessed, he reached over and tore off her shirt, fully exposing her. She groaned with pleasure as he grabbed and clawed at her soft flesh. She responded in kind, biting his shoulder hard enough to draw blood. She pounded at his chest and let him fill her with his desperate need. They had sex like wild beasts, biting, scratching, and tearing at each other. It was as if a storm had filled the room, whisking away the years of quiet desperation and long-suffered deceptions. In a perverse way, they seemed to be relating for the first time.

Their frenzied session went on and on, until Jonathan's adrenaline waned. The moment he regained control of his urges, he forced himself off of Margaret and tumbled to the floor in a bruised and bloody heap.

Margaret remained naked and sprawled out on the bed as Jonathan struggled to his feet. She smiled at him in a way he'd never seen before. There was a secret anticipation in her eyes. She seemed to know something—*see something*—he dared not imagine. Her unblinking eyes followed him as he limped into the bathroom and fell back against the closed door.

Glancing at the bathroom mirror, he gasped out loud. What he saw in the reflection was far worse than the blood and contusions.

His eyes...*Its* eyes. Whatever it was studied his pale reflection in the mirror with a mixture of revulsion and hatred. It glared at him from behind his own eyes.

And suddenly he understood.

The weight of this realization made his knees weaken. He grasped the bathroom sink to steady himself.

There had never been an *It* trying to take control of his life.

He *was* It.

He stared at his mask in the bathroom mirror as the fingers of his right hand grew talon-like. It began to tear jagged holes into his face. The severed flesh of his right cheek fell into the sink with a crimson plop.

I've been waiting. Margaret's whisper still echoed in his mind.

Yes, he thought. *She was waiting for me to realize what she already knew.*

The last of Jonathan Bailey watched as his scalp was separated from his skull and his eyes were ripped from their sockets. The metamorphosis was torturous but blessedly quick; Jonathan's bodily remains littered the floor like the sodden scraps of a slaughterhouse. Wet, jagged shards of skin from his legs and arms hung from the sink like laundry washed in blood.

It took a deep, rasping breath then, breathing freely for the first time. A female voice called out from the bedroom, and It grunted with feverish expectancy. Glancing into the mirror, It was pleased with the reflection staring back. It flashed a savage smile, tearing away the final strips of Jonathan's flesh with Its prehensile tail.

Entering the darkened bedroom, It saw a nude silhouette standing motionless—watching It from the shadows. It heard a squish and looked down to see the fleshy remnants of Margaret Bailey lying under Its feet: a lacerated ear, a mangled breast, and chunks of indistinguishable meat spread across the crimson-soaked carpet.

The thing that was once Margaret slithered out of the darkness with welcoming arms and a blood-soaked smile.

About Taylor Grant

Taylor Grant is a professional screenwriter, filmmaker, author, actor and award-winning copywriter. He has written for both animated and live action TV series, as well as acclaimed music videos that aired on MTV and VH1.

Most recently, he wrote and directed a psychological thriller entitled "The Muse," currently on the film festival circuit. Taylor's fiction can be found in the horror anthology *Box of Delights* from Aeon Press, featuring stories by award-winning authors such as Steve Rasnic Tem, Kristine Kathryn Rusch and Mike Resnick; the literary anthology *Stories from a Holiday Heart,* the critically acclaimed UK magazine *Terror Tales,* and *Horror for Good: A Charitable Anthology* featuring stories by horror legends such as Ramsey Campbell, Jack Ketchum, Joe R. Lansdale, and F. Paul Wilson.

Taylor is currently working on his first collection of stories due out in 2013, tentatively titled *The Dark at the End of the Tunnel*.

You can find out more about Taylor and contact him at TaylorGrant.com.

CORN

by K. A. Opperman

The crispness of the autumn air was scarlet on John's cheeks. He was driving on a meandering country road through an endless sea of farmlands and faintly stirring grasses. Lonely oaks stood sentinel throughout the landscape, keeping their silent watch over the wild hayfields which lapped, wavelike, at their ponderous roots; and pumpkin-headed scarecrows stood vigilant over their corn. Off in the distance, beyond the cornfields, rose a solitary windmill and a rust colored farmhouse. Clouds scudded and crows circled in the rich, evening sky.

John was a youngish man—old enough to look back at his past, yet still young enough to look ahead and not see what was coming. Maybe that's where he was driving , perhaps towards what was coming: the future. He wasn't sure. He knew only that travel—even aimless travel—felt like progress, and that was what he wanted to feel right now. The wind tumbled in his tangled hair as it poured in through the rolled-down window, and the sun flashed in his keen, wayward eyes.

A ways down the road, sheltered beneath an oak hung with an old tire swing, stood an old farmer selling produce. Shelves, baskets, and wheelbarrows overflowed with pumpkins, squash, yams, and corn—the bounty of the fall harvest. Evidently the horn of plenty had been full this year for the venerable farmer.

John would have taken no notice of the old farmer and driven right past him, had the old man not just spilled a basket of pumpkins right across the road. He punished the brake pedal, skidding to a gritty stop hardly a yard before the pumpkin avalanche. The thud of his heart mingled with the heavy rolling of the pumpkins. His lungs sucked in air, thick with tire-thrown dust. He coughed, and a sudden sweat of adrenaline iced his brows.

The sooner the road was cleared, the faster he could be on his way. John pulled over to help.

"Dear me," said the old farmer in a high, croaking voice. "Clumsy, I'ma gettin'." He was hunched over as he gathered up several small pumpkins from the dirt, though not from the weight of them; they weren't heavy. His hair was a wheat field with a circle harvested out of the middle of it, and his face, the weathered side of a wheelbarrow. Surely his clothes were lent him by a scarecrow.

"Here, let me help," said John, stepping out of his truck. He gathered up the remaining pumpkins with ease and put them back in the righted wicker basket.

"Thank yeh, young man," said the old farmer.

John turned briskly to go on his way, but a surprisingly firm hand caught him by the arm.

"In such a hurry, young man?" said the old farmer. "Hurryin' only hurries yeh tuh the grave. Stay an' chat awhile with a lonesome ol' man. And let's have sumthin' nice fur yer kindness."

"It was really nothing," said John. "Happy to do it."

"Oh, but it was!" protested the old farmer. "Hurts my back tuh be hunchin' over aftuh spilt pumpkins. Please, young man, I'd like yeh tuh try sum o' my corn, free o' charge. 'S the best around, I promise yeh that."

John noticed that he was really quite hungry, so the old farmer's offer was a tempting one. He hadn't seen a restaurant—let alone a building that wasn't a dilapidated farmhouse—for miles, and here was free food!

He accepted.

"'Course, we'll need tuh cook it first," said the old farmer, lighting a fire pit beside his stand. "Butter it up nice, too. That way the pepper'll stick real good-like." He hung two ears of corn over the lighted kindling.

Butter and pepper, thought John. *Even better*. He and the old farmer sat on upturned vegetable crates, warming their hands while the flames licked at their corn. John reflected that for the first time in many months, sitting beside this fire with its promise of warm food, and even with this unlikely company, he was content. The revelation settled like a feather in his being as he watched the lanterns of evening begin to wink in the vast, darkening heavens. In this cozy little moment in time, not even the cold pincers of the moon with its melancholic venom could poison him.

"So where yeh headed tuh, young man?" asked the old farmer.

"Nowhere in particular."

"Nowhere, eh? Well, this'll be the place."

"Yeah, I guess it is. I'm a little surprised to have met another human being out here."

"Well, ye'll find all sort o' unexpected things in the middle o' nowhere." An odd smile flitted across the tan, white-whiskered face. "It's ready."

The old farmer took their corn behind his stand and buttered and seasoned it as promised.

John's ear of corn was fat and plump—very, very healthy looking. Its well-nourished yellow hue was nicely browned by the fire. It was delicious, the best corn John ever had. And yet, under the butter and pepper, did something taste slightly off?

If it did, John didn't care; his stomach burned and hollered for food. He dug in, making a buttery mess of his hands and face. The juicy kernels warmed his insides as they went down.

Having devoured every last corn kernel from its patch on the cob like a tornado, John rose stiffly to leave and thanked the old farmer. "That was delicious, sir. The best I ever had. But I've really got to be on my way." He took a tentative step backward.

"No, no," crooned the old farmer. "The fire's warm, an' I'ma lonesome ol' man. Please, young man, stay a little longer?"

His aged face looked old and pitiful in the soft light of the fire. The shadows played on his deep-lined cheeks and forehead in such a way as to pluck at John's heart-strings. The old farmer reminded him of a grandfather he had been fond of who had passed away not long ago.

John realized that his legs felt cramped—probably from driving all day. Standing there, indecisive, he bent wearily downward, stretching and massaging his legs. Perhaps he could keep the old man company for just a bit longer. He would lighten the farmer's burden of loneliness just long enough for the fire to melt some of the fatigue from his heavy limbs.

"I suppose I could stay on just a bit," said John, slumping back down upon his makeshift seat.

The old farmer's blue eyes sparkled with joy. "That's a good lad!" He rubbed his withered and callused hands together with a sound like rubbing corn husks.

John put his legs close to the fire, letting the warmth creep in to relax his muscles. "So, do you do this for a living?" he asked, making small-talk. "Awful weird time and place to be selling a product. Just saying."

It was now full dark, and not a trace of another human being could be seen anywhere. A crow cawed desolately in the distance. A strange wind hissed in the wall of cornstalks across the road, sounding eerily mingled with whispering voices.

"Aye," said the old farmer. "An' I s'pose it is a right curious place an' time fur business. Course, it was different when my whiskers weren't yet so white as they are, before they built that ugly interstate highway oe'r yonder, an' this here little road was the only one what could take yeh through this country. Used tuh be, peopl'd come from all around tuh buy my corn—I'm right famous fur it—an' the kids'd be swingin' on the ol' tire there."

John's eyes followed the arthritic finger to the tire swing. It hung pendulous and empty, creaking as it twisted slowly back and forth, with none but the wind and firelight to ride it. For an instant, John saw a bright-faced young boy laughing as he swung on the tire, his parents smiling as they watched. But just as soon as they had appeared the tire went still again, and they were gone.

"Doesn't anyone come around anymore?" asked John, heavily under the spell of the old farmer's past.

"Naw, not so much, lad," sighed the old farmer like a bellows into the fire. "Most o' the folk in these parts moved on. Died, or went tuh the city. I guess them folks wanted tuh buy their corn at a store, 'stead of visitin' this old farmer. Nowadays," he continued softly, slowly swiveling his fraily supported head to point his ancient face at John, "it's mostly only them come around that get a little...lost." His head swung back into position like a door on rusty hinges. He peered deeply into the fire, perhaps divining some vision in the glaring embers and lurid flame.

"That's too bad," said John. His legs, he noticed, felt even stiffer than before, pulling him into the shallows of his nostalgic reverie. He massaged them vigorously, glad that he hadn't rushed off to confine himself to his truck on this dark back road. He realized that for the moment, at least, he was glad to be sitting by the fire, listening to the stories of this kindly old man. "I'll buy some of your corn before I go."

"Will you?" The old farmer's face lit up strangely, longingly, for some lost chapter of his life. "You'd be makin' an' ol' farmer feel proud agin, proud o' what he works so hard fur."

CORN

John wondered if he would be the old farmer's only customer for the rest of the season. Perhaps nothing, save the cornstalks pressing close across the road, would be here this year; no one would buy any produce, and no parents would bring their children to the tire swing. Probably all of his vegetables, save for whatever John took away with him, would rot and be picked over by the crows.

Sitting there, John found the road beginning to lure his gaze from the fire. Though it stretched off interminably through dark, moon-haunted fields, the future lie down it. His future. And it waited only for him to go to it. Besides, it was getting late, and there might not be an inn for a hundred miles or more; he had no idea where this quaint country road would lead him. The old farmer had provided food, and he had gratefully accepted it. But the old man, for all his friendliness and stories, could not provide shelter.

John rose stiffly, with some effort, and determined now to leave the forlorn old farmer and his corn. "I've really enjoyed your company, sir, and the corn was delicious, the best I ever had. But now I really must be going. It's late, you see, and there might not be another inn for a hundred miles. I'd sleep in my truck, but my legs are really quite stiff, and I'd like to sleep it off in a proper bed."

The old farmer protested, as John knew he would. "Leg cramps, eh? Wouldn't yeh like tuh wait jus' a bit longer, by the fire—jus' until yer legs feel a bit better? Warm 'em by the fire, an' I promise they'll feel better 'fore long."

No, thought John. *I've been here much too long, and I must be getting on my way...But there's sense in the old farmer's words...just a bit longer...just a bit longer...*

"Just until they feel a little better," John agreed at last. "Then I'll take some of your corn off with me, have people try it...tell everyone I meet to...come and buy some." Why was he short of breath? *Tired, that's all,* he thought.

The old farmer's face shone through the fire with an infantile delight, his blue eyes widening with joy, his mouth wrought with silent laughter.

John thought he heard him murmur, "But it's too late," into the fire. *What's too late?* he wondered. But he decided to let the old man be alone in the warm silence of his memories. Oddly, John's legs still did not feel any better and now even his arms were starting to cramp.

"Corn," chuckled the old man, slack-jawed, showing teeth like a picket fence missing half its planks. "Corn, corn, corn, corn, corn.... Funny story 'bout corn: one year, sum corn stalks sprouted up in the community graveyard, jus' beside my field, right where someone'd jus' been buried. Seeds mustha' blew over on the wind or somethin'. They was the healthiest, juiciest corn I ever saw. That's how I learned it."

The question *Learned what?* quivered on John's lips, but he could not ask it. A vague sickening feeling was stirring up deep inside him, uncoiling like a waking serpent. Sweat bloomed uninvited from his pores. For some reason it was difficult to speak and to breathe.

"Bodies," chuckled the old farmer, answering the unvoiced question.

John's cramps were growing even more painful. He clutched helplessly at his chest, which rose and fell in a frantic, crazy tide. His pulse hammered chaotically against his uneven breathing.

"Bodies," repeated the old farmer, lost in the fire, his chest jumping with short bursts of juvenile laughter. "Fresh ones. They make the best fertilizer!"

John felt violently ill. The corn festered in his tightening stomach like the rotting human flesh it had been nourished on. Visions of cannibalistic horror racked his panicked mind; pain and stiffness racked his chest and limbs harder still.

"But there weren't enough folks bein' buried there," continued the old farmer, "on account o' that fancy interstate. Made everyone forget about this here road an' everythin' on it...the ol' buryin' place...my corn..."

He hesitated, his eyes twinkling with flame. His face contorted demoniacally, yet with a bizarre touch of youthful innocence. In the throes of his gasping and spasming, John was nearly oblivious to the farmer's words as he continued, "So I had tuh git my own bodies. I'd git 'em fresh, like fresh-picked corn. It was easy..."

Clenching his teeth, squeezing every last drop of will out of his rioting muscles, John bent over the vegetable crate, grasped it with shaking hands, and pushed. The night spun around him. Stars and fire flashed. Somehow he found himself in a standing position, but he was tottering on legs that felt like numb stilts. He staggered for his truck, breathing heavy, He collapsed at the door, his hand clutching the handle as he slumped down.

The old farmer never lifted his gaze from the blazing fire as he continued his confession. The chuckling, crackling voice of the flames, like a demon priest, bade him to continue; but without promise of absolution.

"I'd do it late, in the evenin', jus' before dark," the old farmer went on, speaking in low, measured tones. "I'd spill a basket o' pumpkins across the road, make 'em git out o' their trucks. It was easy..."

With a final burst of adrenaline, with fumbling fingers and twitching arms, John half crawled, half pulled himself up into the truck. For a moment, the pang of unutterable horror charged his limbs enough to allow them bursts of half-controlled jerking motions. With a desperate effort, slicing several crazy scratches in the dashboard with the key, he started the ignition. But even as the vehicle roared to life, John's own engine sputtered and stalled. His hands, with a sweaty squeal, slid down the side of the steering wheel. The headlights disappeared into the endless corn.

"I'd have 'em try some o' my famous corn, stay an' chat awhile, 'till it started workin'. Just one drop, an' within the hour, they'd be limp as the snakes whose heads I cut off tuh git the poison from. 'Course, they didn't know it were poison! It was easy..."

John fell sideways across the passenger seat, the stick-shift sticking painfully in his side. His lungs were constricting, and he could scarcely twitch his arms or legs. His head hung backward over the passenger seat. His panic-widened eyes stared upside-down at a horribly warped version of the kindly, innocent old man that had somehow reminded him of his late grandfather. Beside his lungs—which were fast constricting under the influence of the snake venom—his eyes were all he could move now. All the movement in his very being burst out through the frantically darting twitches of his eyes. His heart beat erratically.

"I'd jus' put em' in the wheelbarrow, roll 'em right out into the field. Put 'em in the hole what I had dug fur 'em, still awake, still breathin', still fresh. It was easy..."

The lurid firelight played sinisterly on the old farmer's face, on the empty tire swing, and on the shelves of corpse-nourished corn. He rose from the fire, a demon from the mouth of Hell, and approached John's paralyzed body as it lie slumped across the front seats of his truck, its engine roaring wildly into the night. The nerve toxin had immobilized him completely.

With preternatural strength, the old farmer gripped John under his limp arms and dragged him from his truck. Dirt collected in the back of John's shoes as he was pulled, plow-like, across the ground.

John felt himself being slumped rag doll-like into a wheelbarrow. He saw the wall of the cornfield moving closer, livid, under the voyeuristic moon. It enveloped him. Swallowed him alive. The leaves on the cornstalks felt greedily over him, caressing his face, his side, his legs, his chest...The hideously overgrown stalks quivered in the wind, with the countless lives of those who lay buried beneath them.

The last thing John ever saw was the corn, leering down at him as the chuckling farmer shoveled damp dirt over his face.

About K. A. Opperman

K. A. Opperman is a twenty-four year old writer of weird fiction and formalist poetry living in Anaheim, California. His fiction has been published in *The Absent Willow Review, Dark Fire Fiction*, and others. He is the Poetry Editor and Fiction Sub-Editor of *Dark River Press*.

SCREAM QUEEN

by Ed Gorman

Allow me to introduce myself. My name's Jason Fanning. Not that I probably *need* an introduction. Not to be immodest but I did, after all, win last year's Academy Award for Best Screenplay.

Same with my two friends, Bill Leigh the Academy Award-winning actor. And Spence Spencer, who won the Academy Award two years ago for Best Director. People with our credentials don't need any introductions, right?

Well....

That's the kind of thing we talked about nights, after Vic's Video closed down for the night and we sat around Bill's grubby apartment drinking the cheapest beer we could find and watching schlock DVDs on his old clunker of a TV set. Someday we were going to win the Academy Award for our respective talents and everybody who laughed at us and called us geeks and joked that we were probably gay....well, when we were standing on the stage with Cameron Diaz hanging all over us....

We had special tastes in videos, the sort of action films and horror films that were the staples of a place like Vic's Video.

If it's straight-to-video, we probably saw it. And liked it. All three of us were on Internet blogs devoted to what the unknowledgeable (read: unhip) thought of as shitty movies. But we knew better. Didn't Nicholson, Scorcese, DeNiro and so forth all get their start doing low-ball movies for Roger Corman?

That's how we were going to win our Academy Awards when we finally got off our asses and piled into Spence's eight-year-old Dodge Dart and headed for the land of gold and silicone. We knew it would be a little while before the money and the fame started rolling in. First we'd have to pay our dues doing direct-to-video. We were going to pitch ourselves as a team. My script, Bill's acting, Spence name-above-the-title directing.

In the meantime, we had to put up with working minimum wage jobs. Mine was at Vic's Video, a grimy little store resting on the river's edge of a grimy little Midwestern city that hadn't been the same since the glory days of the steamboats Mark Twain wrote so much about.

Even though we worked different gigs, we all managed to go hang at Bill's, even though from time to time Bill and I almost got into fistfights. He never let us forget that he was the normal one, what with his good looks and his Yamaha motorcycle and all his ladies. We were three years out of high school. We'd all tried the community college route but since they didn't offer any courses in the films of Mario Bava or Brian DePalma, none of us made it past the first year.

I guess—from the outside, anyway—we were pretty geeky. I had the complexion problem and Spence was always trying to make pharmaceutical peace with his bi-polarity and Bill—well, Bill wasn't exactly a geek. Not so obviously, anyway. He was good-looking , smooth with girls and he got laid a lot. But he was only good-looking on the outside...inside he was just as much an outcast as the seldom-laid Spence and I...

Do I have to tell you that people we went to high school with smirked whenever they saw us together? Do I have to tell you that a lot of people considered us immature and worthless? Do I have to tell you that a big night out was at GameLand where we competed with ten and twelve year olds on the video games? If Spence was off his medication and he lost to some smart-ass little kid, he'd get pretty angry and bitter. A lot of the little kids were scared of us. And you know what? That felt kinda good, having somebody scared of us. It was the only time we felt important in any way.

And then Michele Danforth came into our lives and changed everything. Everything.

Spence was the first one to recognize her. Not that we believed him at first. He kept saying, "That little blonde chick that comes in here every other night or so—that's Michele Danforth." But we didn't believe it, not even when he set three of her video boxes up on the counter and said, "You really don't recognize her?"

Michele Danforth, in case you don't happen to be into cult videos, was the most popular scream queen of all a couple of years ago. A scream queen? That's the sexy young lady who gets dragged off by the monster/ax-murderer in direct-to-video horror movies. She screams a lot and she almost always gets her blouse and bra ripped off so you can see her breasts. Acting ability doesn't matter so much. But scream ability is vital. And breast ability is absolutely mandatory.

The funny thing is with most scream queens, you never see them completely naked. Not even their bottoms. It's as if all the seventeen-year-old masturbation champions who rent their videos want their scream queens to be pretty virginal. Showing breasts doesn't violate the moral code here. But anything else—well, part of the equation is that you want your scream queen to be the kind of girl you'd marry. The marrying kind never expose their beavers except in doctors' offices.

Couple quick things here about Michele Danforth. She was very pretty. Not cute, not beautiful, not glamorous. Pretty. Soft. A bit on the melancholy side. The kind you fall in love with so uselessly. Uselessly, anyway, if your life's work is watching direct-to-video movies. And those sweet breasts of hers. Not those big plastic monsters. Perfectly shaped medium sized good-girl breasts. And she could actually act. All the blog boys predicted she'd move into mainstream. And who could disagree?

Then she vanished. Became a big media story for a couple weeks and then some other H-wood story came along and everybody forgot her. Vanished. The assumption became that some stalker had grabbed her and killed her. Even though she always said she couldn't afford it—scream queens don't usually make much more than executive secretaries—she had to hire a personal bodyguard because of all the strange and disturbing mail she got.

Vanished.

And now, according to Spence, she resurfaced 1500 miles and three years later. Except that instead of dark-haired, brown-eyed and slender, she was now blonde, blue-eyed and maybe twenty-five pounds heavier. With very earnest brown-rimmed glasses sliding down her nose.

We had to admit that there was a similarity. But it was vague. And it was a similarity that probably belonged to a couple of million young women.

The night the question of her identity got resolved, I was starting the check-out process when the door opened up and she came in. She went right to the Drama Section. I'd never seen her go to any of the other sections. Her choices were always serious flicks with serious actors in them. Bill and Spence had taken off to get some beer at the supermarket, the cost of it being way too much at convenience stores.

I'd agreed to the little game they'd come up with. I thought it was kind of stupid but who knew, maybe it would resolve the whole thing.

It was a windy, chill March night. She wore a white turtleneck beneath a cheap, shapeless thigh-length brown velour jacket. She was just one more Midwestern working girl. Nothing remarkable about her at all. She always paid cash from a worn pea-green imitation-leather wallet. Tonight was no different. She never said much, though tonight, as I took her money, she said, "Windy."

She went under the name Heather Simpson.

"Yeah. Where's that warm weather they promised?"

She nodded and smiled.

I rang up the transaction and then as I handed her the slip to sign, I nudged the video box sitting next to the cash register out in front of me. *Night of the Depraved* was the title. It showed a huge, blood-dripping butcher knife about to stab into the white-bloused form of a very pretty girl. Who was screaming. The girl was Michele Danforth. The quote along the top of the box read: *DEPRAVED to the Max...and scream queen Danforth is good enuf to eat...if you know what I mean! —Dr. Autopsy.com*

"Oops," I said, hoping she'd think this was all accidental. "You don't want that one." I picked up the box and looked at it. "I wonder whatever happened to her."

She just shrugged. "I wouldn't know. I never watch those kind of movies." She took her change and said, "I'm in kind of a hurry."

I handed her the right movie and just as I did so she turned toward me, showing me an angle of her face I'd never seen before. And I said, "It's you! Spence was right! You're Michele Danforth!"

And just then the door opened up, the bell above it announcing customers, and in came Bill and Spence. They'd left the beer in the car. Video Vic would've kicked my ass all the way over into Missouri if he ever caught us with brew on the premises.

She turned and started away in a hurry, so fast that she brushed up against Spence. The video she carried fell to the floor.

Bill picked it up. He must have assumed that I had played the little game with her—bringing up Michele Danforth and all—because after he bent to pick up the video and handed it to her with a mock-flourish, he said, "I'm pleased to present my favorite scream queen with this award from your three biggest fans."

She made a sound that could have been a sob or a curse and then she stalked to the door, throwing it open wide and disappearing into the night. My mind was filled with the image of her face—the fear, the sorrow.

"She'll never be back," I said.

"I told you it was her," Spence said. "She wouldn't have acted that way if it wasn't."

"I wanna fuck her," Bill said, "and I'm going to."

Spence said, "Man, she's nobody now. She's even sort of fat."

"Yeah, but how many dudes can they say they bopped Michele Danforth?"

"Wait'll we get to La-La Land," Spence said, "we'll be boppin' movie stars every night. And they won't be overweight."

Our collective fantasy had never sounded more juvenile and impossible than it did right then. In that instant I saw what a sad sham my life was. Shoulda gone to college; shoulda done somethin' with my life. Instead I was just as creepy and just as pathetic as all the other direct-to-video freaks who came in here and who we all laughed at when they left. Video Vic's. Pathetic.

"Hey, man, hurry up," Bill said to me. "I'll get the lights. You bag up the money and the receipts. We'll drop it off at the bank and then tap the beer."

But I was still back there a few scenes. The terror and grief of her face. And the humiliating moment when Spence had spoken our collective fantasy out loud. Something had changed in me in those moments. Good or bad, I couldn't tell yet. "I got this sore throat."

"Yeah," Bill said, "it's such a bad sore throat you can't even swallow beer, huh?"

Spence laughed. "Yeah, that sounds like a bad one, all right. Can't even swallow beer."

I could tell Bill was looking at me. He was the only one of us who could really intimidate people. "So what the hell's really goin' on here, Jason?"

I sounded whiny, resentful. "I got a sore throat, Lord and Master. If that's all right with you."

"It's when I said I'm gonna fuck her, wasn't it?" He laughed. "In your mind she's still this scream queen, isn't she? Some fucking virgin. She's nobody now."

" Then why you want to screw her so bad?" I said.

"Because then I can say it, asshole. I can say I bopped Michele Danforth." He looked at both me and Spence. "I'll have actually accomplished something. Something real. Not just all these fantasies we have about going to Hollywood."

"I shouldn't have done it to her," I said. "We shouldn't have said anything to her at all. She had her own reasons for vanishing like that."

"Yeah, because she was getting fat between movies and they probably didn't want her anymore." He laughed.

Hard to tell which rang in his voice the clearest—his cruelty or his craziness. Bill was climbing out on the ledge again. Sometimes he lived there for days. Times like these, we'd get into shoving matches and near-fights.

Spence's attitude had changed. You could see it in his dark eyes. He'd thought it was pretty funny and pretty cool, Bill screwing a scream queen like this. But now I could tell that he thought it was just as twisted as I did. Bill always got intense when he went after something. But this went beyond intensity. He actually looked sort of crazy when he talked about it.

"Maybe Jason's right, Bill," Spence said gently. "Maybe we should just leave her alone."

The look of contempt was so perfectly conjured up, it was almost like a mask. So was the smirk that came a few seconds later. "The Wuss brothers. All these fantasies about what great talents you are. And all the big times you're gonna have in Hollywood. And then when you get a chance to have a little fun, you chicken out and run away. We could all screw her, you know. All three of us. A gang-bang."

"Yeah," I said, "now there's a great idea, Bill. We could kill her, too. You ever thought of that?"

"Now who's crazy? All I was talking about was the three of us—"

I was as sick of myself just then as I was of Bill. I was already making plans to go call the community college again. See when I needed to enroll for the next semester. I knew that maybe I wouldn't go through with it. But right then with Bill's mind lurching from a one-man seduction to a three-man rape...Prisons were filled with guys who'd had ideas like that. And then carried them out.

"I got to finish up here," I said, working on the cash register again.

"Yeah, c'mon, Spence, let's leave the Reverend here to pray for our souls. We'll go get drunk."

Spence and I had never been very good about standing up to Bill. So I knew what courage it took for Spence to say, "I guess not, Bill. I'm not feeling all that well myself."

He called us all the usual names that denote a male who is less than masculine. Then he went over to a stand-up display of the new direct-to-video Julia Roberts movie and started picking up one at a time and firing them around the store. They made a lot of noise and every time one of them smashed into something—a wall, a line of tapes, even a window—both Spence and I felt a nervous spasm going through us. It was like when you're little and you hear your folks having a violent argument and you're afraid your dad's going to kill your mom and you hide upstairs under the covers. That kind of tension and terror.

I came fast around the counter and shouted at him. Then I started running at him. But he beat me to the door.

"Good night, ladies." He stood there. "Every time I see you from now on, I'm gonna punch your ugly faces in. You two pussies've got an enemy now. And a bad one." He'd never sounded scarier or crazier.

And with that, he was gone.

《《—》》

It was misting by the time I got back to my room-and-a-bathroom above a vacuum cleaner repair store. I had enjoyed the walk home.

The mist was dirty gold and swirling in the chilly night. And behind it in doorways and alleyways and dirty windows the eyes of old people and scared people and drug people and queer people and insane people stared out at me, eyes bright in dirty faces. This was an old part of town, the buildings small and fading, glimpses of ancient Pepsi-Cola and Camel cigarette and Black-Jack gum signs on their sides every other block or so, TV repair shops that still had tiny screens inside of big consoles in the windows for nostalgia's sake, and railroad tracks no longer used and stretching into some kind of Twilight Zone miles and miles of gleaming metal down the endless road. There was even a dusty used bookstore that had a few copies of pulps like The Shadow and Doc Savage and Dime Detective in the cracked window and you could stand here sometimes and pretend it was 1938 and the world wasn't so hostile and lonely even though there was a terrible war on the way. It was a form of being stoned, traveling back in time this way, and a perfect head trip to push away loneliness.

296

To get to my room you took this rotting wooden staircase up the side of the two-story stucco-peeling shop. I was halfway up them before I looked up and saw her sitting there. The scream queen. If the misting bothered her, she didn't seem to mind it.

She smoked a cigarette and watched me. She looked pretty sitting there, not as pretty as when she'd been in the movies, but pretty nonetheless.

"How'd you find me?" I wondered.

"Asked the guy at the 7-11 if he knew where you lived."

"Oh, yeah. Dev. He lives about three down." I smiled. "In our gated community."

"Sorry I got so hysterical."

I shrugged. "We're video store geeks. We can get pretty hysterical ourselves. You should've seen us at our first Trekkie convention in Spock ears and shit. If you had any pictures of us from back then, you could blackmail us."

She smiled. "That's assuming you had any money to make it worthwhile."

I laughed. "I take it you know how much video store geeks make."

"LA. I must've done three hundred signings in video stores." The smile again. It was a good clean one. It erased a lot of years. "Most of you are harmless."

"We could always go inside," I said.

After I handed her a cheap beer, she said, "I didn't come up here for sex."

"I didn't figure you did." She glanced around. "You could fix this up a little and it wouldn't be so bad. And those Terminator posters are a little out of date."

"Yeah. But they're signed."

"Arnold signed them?"

I grinned. "Nah, some dude at a comic book convention I went to. He had some real small part in it."

She had a sweet laugh. "Played a tree or a car or something like that?"

"Yeah, you know, along those lines."

She'd taken off her brown velour jacket. Her white sweater showed off those scream queen breasts real real good. It was unsettling, sitting so near a girl whose videos had driven me to rapturous self-abuse so many times. And I had the hairy palms to prove it. Even with the added weight, she looked good in jeans.

"I'll make you a deal, Jason."

"Yeah? What kind of deal? I mean, since we ruled out sex. Much to my dismay."

"Oh, c'mon, Jason. You don't really think I just go around sleeping with people, do you? That's in the movies. This is straight business, what I'm proposing. I'll clean your apartment here and fix it up if you'll convince your two friends not to let anybody know who I am or where I am."

"Spence won't be any trouble."

"Is he the good-looking one?"

"That's Bill."

"He looks like trouble."

"He is."

She sank back on the couch—one night Spence and I managed to get a couple of girls up here and we all played a game of *Guess the Stain* with the couch—and covered her face with her hands. I thought she was going to cry. But no sounds came. The only thing you could hear was Churchill, my cat, yowling at cars passing in what was now a downpour.

"You ok?"

She shrugged. Said nothing. Hands still covering her face. When she took them down, she said, "I left LA for my own reasons. And I want to keep them my reasons. And that means making a life for myself somewhere out here. I'm from Chicago. I like the Midwest. But I don't want some tabloid to find out about me."

"Well, like I say, Spence won't be any trouble. But Bill—"

"Where's he live?"

I was thinking about what Bill had said about screwing a scream queen. Even if she wasn't a scream queen anymore. It didn't make much sense to me but it sure seemed to make a lot of sense to him.

"Why don't I talk to him first?"

She looked relieved. Good. I'd appreciate that. I'm supposed to start this job next week. A good job. Decent bennies and from what everybody says, some real opportunities there. I want to start my life all over.

"I'll talk to him."

She was all business. Grabbing her coat. Sliding into it. Standing up. Looking around at the stained and peeling wallpaper and all the posters, including the latest scream queen Linda Sanders. She's a nice kid. Had a real shitty childhood. I hope she can beat the rap—you know, go on and do some real acting. I saw her at a small playhouse right before I left LA. She was really good.

I liked that. How charitable she was about her successor. A decent woman.

Churchill came out and rubbed his head against her ankle. She held him up and gave him that smile of hers. "We both need to go to Weight Watchers, my friend."

"The cat stays up late at night and watches TV and orders from Domino's when I'm asleep."

She gave him a kiss. "I believe it."

She set him down, put out her hand and shook, that formal, forced way people do in banking commercials right after the married couple agrees to pay the exorbitant interest rates. "I really appreciate this, Jason. I'll start figuring out how I'm going to fix up your apartment. I live in this tiny trailer. I've got it fixed up very nicely."

《《—》》

"You didn't screw her, did you?" Bill said when he came into the store.

He'd been hustling around the place, getting the displays just so, setting up the *50% OFF* bin of DVD and blu ray films we hadn't been able to move, and snapping Mr. Coffee to burbling attention. When I told him she'd come over to my place last night, he stopped, frozen in place and asked if I'd screwed her.

"Yeah. Right on the front lawn. In the rain. Just humping our brains out."

"You'd better not have, you bastard. I'm the one who gets to nail her."

At any given time Bill is always about seven minutes away from the violent ward but I couldn't ever recall seeing him this agitated about something.

"She isn't going to screw *anybody*, Bill. Now shut up and listen."

"Oh, sure, he said, "now you're her press agent? All the official word comes from you?"

"She's scared, asshole."

"Listen, Jason. Spare me the heartbreak, all right? She's been around. She doesn't need some video geek hovering over her." Then, "That's how you're gonna get in her panties, isn't it? Be her best friend. One of those wussy deals. Well, it's not gonna work because she'll never screw a pus-face like you. You checked out your blackheads lately, Jason?"

I swung on him. When my fist collided with his cheek, he gaped at me in disbelief, then sort of disintegrated, started screaming at me real high-pitched and all, as he stumbled backwards into a display of a new Disney family movie. Most surprisingly of all, he didn't come after me. Maybe I'd just stunned him. He'd always seen Spence and I as his inferiors—we were the geeks, according to him; he wasn't a geek; he was a cool dude who pitied us enough to hang out with us—and so maybe he was just in shock. His slave had revolted and he hadn't had time to deal with it mentally yet.

"She's afraid you'll tell somebody who she is," I said. "And if you do, you're going to be damned sorry."

And then I couldn't believe what I did. I hit him again. This time he might have responded but just then the front door opened, the bell tinkled, the first customer of the day, a soccer-mom with a curly-haired little girl in tow, walked in with an armload of overdue DVDs. Mrs. Preston. Her stuff was always overdue.

I had just enough time to see that a pimple of blood hung from Bill's right nostril. I took an unholy amount of satisfaction in that.

«« — »»

Michele didn't want to see me. She was nice about it. She said she really appreciated me talking to Bill about her and that she really appreciated me stopping by like this but she was just in a place where she wanted to be alone, sort of actually *needed* to be alone and she was sure I understood. Because that was obviously the kind of guy I was, the understanding kind.

In other words, it was the sort of thing I'd been hearing from girls all my life. How nice I was and how understanding I was and how they were sure, me being so understanding and all, that it was cool if we just kind of left things as they were, you know being just friends and all. Which is what she ended up saying.

As usual, I'd gotten ahead of myself. By this time, I had this crush on her and whenever I get a crush of this particular magnitude I start dreaming the big dream. You know, not only having sex but maybe her really falling in love with me and maybe moving in together and maybe me getting a better job and maybe us—it could happen—getting married and settling down just as the couples always do in the screwball comedies of the Thirties and Forties that Bill and Spence always rag on me for liking so much.

Over a three day period I must have called Spence eight or nine times, always leaving a message on his machine. He never called back. I finally went over there after work one night. He had a two-room apartment on a block where half the houses had been torn down. I was just walking up to the front door when Spence and Bill came out.

They were laughing until they saw me. Beery laughter. They'd both been gunning brew.

Bill was the one I watched. His hands formed fists instantly and he dropped back a foot and went into a kind of boxer's crouch. "You got lucky the other day, Jason."

"I don't think so, Bill. I think *you* got lucky because Mrs. Preston came in."

Spence's face reflected the disbelief all three of us were probably feeling. I couldn't believe it, either. I'd stood up to Bill the other day but I think both of us thought it was kind of a fluke. But it wasn't. I was ready to hit him again.

The only difference between the other morning and now was that he was half-drunk. Brew makes most of us feel tougher and handsomer and smarter and wittier than we really are. Prisons are packed with guys who let brew addle their perception of themselves. Or dope. Doesn't matter.

He came at me throwing a roundhouse so vast in scope it couldn't possibly have landed on me. All I had to do was take a single step backward.

"I don't want to fight you, Bill. Spence, pull him back."

Whatever Bill said was lost in his second lunge. This punch connected. He got me on my right cheek and pain exploded across my entire face. He followed up with a punch to my stomach that doubled me over.

"Kick his ass, Bill!" Spence said.

Even though I was in pain, even though I should have been focused on the fight I was in, his words, the betrayal of them, him choosing Bill over me when it should have been Spence and I against Bill—that hurt a lot more than the punches. He'd been my friend since third grade. He was my friend no longer.

Bill hit me with enough force to knock me flat on the sidewalk, butt first. If this had been the other night, I would've jumped to my feet and started swinging. But I was still hearing Spence say to kick my ass and I guess I didn't have enough pride or anger left to stand up and hit back. I just felt drained.

"You all right?" Spence said to me. I could hear his confusion. Better to stick with Bill. But still, we'd been friends a long time and to see me knocked down—

"He's just a pussy," Bill said. "C'mon."

I didn't stand up till they were gone. Then I walked home slowly. I took the long way so that I'd go past Michele's place. The light was on. I turned off the sidewalk and started moving toward the house but then I stopped. I wasn't up for another disappointment tonight.

«« —»»

Video Vic's real name wasn't Vic, it was Reed, Reed Patrick; and when I called him next morning and gave him my week's notice, he said, "You don't sound so good, kiddo. You all right?"

"I just need to be movin' on, Reed. I enjoyed working for you, though."

"You ever want to use me for a reference, that'll be fine with me."

"Thanks, Reed."

That night, I surprised my folks by showing up for dinner. Mom had made meat loaf and mashed potatoes and peas. I figured that was about the best meal I'd ever had. They were surprised that I'd quit my job but my Dad said, "Now you can start looking for something with a future, Jason. You could start taking classes again out to the college. Get trained for some kind of computer job or something."

"Computers, Honey," my Mom said, patting my hand. "Jobs like that pay good money."

"And they've got a future."

"That's right," Mom said, "computers aren't going anywhere. They're here for good."

"You should call out there tomorrow," Dad said. "And my buddy Mike can get you on at the supermarket he runs."

I pretended to be interested in what he was saying. I'd never seemed interested before. He looked happy about me, the way he had

302

when I was a little kid. I hadn't seen him look this happy in a long time. He also looked old. I guess I hadn't really, you know, just *looked* at him for a real long time. The same with mom. The lines in their faces. The bags under their eyes. The way both my folks seemed kind of worn out through the whole meal. When I left I hugged them harder than I had in years. And all the way back to my little room, I felt this sadness I just couldn't shake.

Over the next week, the sadness stayed with me. I'd realized by then that it wasn't just about Mom and Dad, it was about me and everything that had happened in the past couple of weeks. I tried Michelle a couple more times. The second time she was real cold. You know how girls are when they aren't happy to hear from you and just want to get you off the phone. After I hung up, I sat there in the silence with Churchill weighing a ton on my lap. I felt my cheeks burn. It was pretty embarrassing, the way she'd maneuvered me off the phone so fast.

The next night, no longer gainfully employed, I walked over town to the library. I was reading the whole run of George R.R. Martin fantasy novels. He was one of the best writers around.

Even though they'd bought six copies of his new hardcover, they were all checked out. I picked up a collection of his short stories. He was good at those, too.

On the walk back home, I saw them coming out of a Hardees. He had his arm around her. They were laughing. I was ready to fight now. Just walk right up to him and punch him in the fucking chops. He'd be the one sitting down on his butt this time, not me. And I'd remind her that she still owed me an apartment cleaning.

Good ole Michele and good ole Bill. That's the thing I've never understood about girls. Hard to imagine a guy more full of himself than Bill, but she obviously thought he was just fine and dandy or else she wouldn't let him have his arm around her. He was going to sleep with her and then he was going to tell everybody. I wondered how she'd react if I told her.

But I couldn't. Much as I wanted to go over there and tell her what was really going on, I couldn't make my legs move in that direction. Because I could live with my self-image as a geek, a loser, a boy-man but I could never live with myself as a snitch.

SCREAM QUEEN

A few days later I signed up for computer classes at the community college. I gave up my room on the rent-due day and moved back home. The folks were glad to have me. I was being responsible. Dad said his buddy Mike could get me on at his supermarket and so he had.

What I did for the next few nights, after bagging groceries till nine o'clock, was glut myself on the past. I still had boxes of old *Fangorias* and *Filmfaxes* in my old closet and I hauled them out and spread them on the bed and just disappeared into my yesterdays, back to the time when there was no doubt that I was going to Hollywood, no doubt that I'd be working for Roger Corman, no doubt that someday I'd be doing my own films and no doubt they'd be damned good ones.

But my time machine sprung a leak. I'd get all caught up in being sixteen again and grooving on *Star Wars* and *Planet of The Apes* and *Alien*, but then the poison gas of now would seep in through those leaks. And I'd start thinking about Michele and Bill and Spence and how my future seemed settled now—computer courses and a lifelong job in some dusty little computer store in a strip mall somewhere—and then I'd be back to the here and now. And not liking it at all.

On a rainy Friday night, my mom knocked on my door and said, "Spence is downstairs for you, Honey."

I hadn't told my folks about the falling out Spence and I had had.

I just said OK and went down to see him. He was talking to my dad. Dad was telling him how happy they were about my taking those computer courses.

I grabbed my jacket and we went out. I hadn't so much as nodded at Spence. In fact, we didn't say a word until we were in his old Dodge Dart and heading down the street.

"How you been?" he said.

"Pretty good."

"Your Dad seems real happy about you being in computer classes."

"Yeah."

"You don't sound so happy, though."

"What's this all about, Spence?"

"What's what all about?"

"*What's what all about?* What do you think it's all about? You took Bill's side on this whole thing. Now you come over to my house."

He didn't say anything for a while. We just drove. Headlights and neon lights and street lights glowed like water-colors in the rain. Girls looked sweet and young and strong running into cafes and theaters to get out of the downpour. His radio faded in and out. Every couple minutes he'd slam a fist on the dash and the radio would be all right again for a few minutes. The car smelled of gasoline and mildewed car seats.

"He's getting really weird."

"Who is?"

"Who is? Who do you think is, Jason? Bill is."

"Weird about what? "

"About her. Michele."

"Weird how?"

"He's really hung up with Michele. He won't tell me what it is but somethin's really buggin' him."

So, I'm supposed to feel bad about it?"

"I'm just telling you is all."

"Why? Why would I give a shit?"

He glanced over at me. "I shoulda stuck up for you with Bill. The night he knocked you down, I mean. I'm sorry."

"You really pissed me off."

"Yeah, I know. And I'm sorry. I really am. I—I just can't handle being around Bill anymore. This whole thing with Michele. She's all he talks about and she won't let him do nothin'. He says it's like bein' in sixth grade again."

I wasn't up for just driving around. I'd done enough cruising in my high school years. I said, "You seen that new Wes Craven flick?"

"Huh-uh."

"There'll be a late show. We could still make it."

"So you're not still pissed? "

"Sure I'm still pissed. But I want to see the Wes Craven and you're the only person I know who's got a car."

"I don't blame you for still bein' pissed."

"I don't blame me for still bein' pissed, either."

«««—»»»

I didn't hear from Spence until nearly a week later. After the Craven flick, which was damned good, he started talking about other things we could do but I just told him I was busy. Sometimes, friendships, even long ones, just end. One thing happens and you realize that the friendship was never as strong as you'd thought. Or maybe you just realize that you're one cold, unforgiving prick. Whichever it was, I wasn't up for seeing Spence or Bill or Michele for a long time. Maybe never.

I went my glum way to computer classes and my even glummer way to the supermarket.

He was in the supermarket parking lot waiting for me when I got off work. I walked over to his car. It was a warm, smoky October night. Big ass harvest moon. I wanted to be a kid again in my Halloween costume. I could barely—just quite—remember what it had been like to go trick or treating before the days when perverts and sadists hid stickpins and razor blades in candy apples.

I walked over to the driver's side of his car. I wanted to walk home. October nights like this were my favorites.

"Hey," he said.

"Hey."

"You doin' anything special?"

"Yeah. Nicole Kidman called. She wants to go get a pizza with me. She said she'll pay for it. And the motel room afterward."

"Remember to bring a condom."

"She's got me covered there, too. She bought a big box them."

We just looked at each other across an unbreachable chasm of time and pain. He'd been a part of my boyhood. But I wasn't a boy anymore. Not a man yet, to be sure. But not a boy, either.

"He's pretty fucked up."

"We talking about Bill?"

"Yeah. Had the day off. Drinking beers with whiskey chasers."

"Good. We need to drink more. Make sure we're winos before we hit twenty-five."

"I think maybe we should go over to Michele's place."

"Why?"

He stared at the passing cars. When he looked back at me, he said, "You better get in, Jason. This shit could be real bad."

《《—》》

It was one of the little Silverstream trailers that are about as big as an SUV. Except, given its condition, this one should have been called Ruststream. It sat between two large oak trees on a corner where a huge

306

two-story house had been torn down the summer before. The rest of the neighborhood blazed with laughter and throbbing car engines and rap music and folks of both the black and white persuasion filling porches and sidewalks, most of them trying to look and sound like bad asses. Her trailer was a good quarter block from its nearest neighbor.

A motorcycle leaned against one of the trees. No lights, no sound coming from the trailer.

"Maybe he's getting the job done," Spence said.

"Maybe," I said.

The door was open half an inch. I opened it wide and stuck my head in.

"What the fuck you think you're doin'?"

I couldn't see him at first, couldn't see anything except vague furniture shapes. Smells of whiskey and cigarettes. A cat in the gloom, crying now.

"Get out of here, Jason."

"Where's Michele?"

"Where you think she is, asshole?"

"I wanna talk to her."

"I told you once, Jason. Get out of here. I knocked you on your ass once. And I can do it again."

"No, you can't."

Two steps led up to the trailer floor. I was about to set my right foot on the second step when he came at me. My mind had time to register that he was wearing jeans, no shirt, no socks, and he had a whiskey bottle in his hand.

Bill tackled me and drove me all the way to the ground. He meant to hit me with the whiskey bottle but I had the advantage of being sober. He smelled of puke and booze and sex and greasy food, maybe a hamburger.

As the bottle arced downward, I rolled to the right, moving slowly enough to slam my fist hard into the side of Bill's head. The punch dazed him but not enough to keep him from trying to get me again with the bottle. This time I didn't have time to move away from it. All I could do was grab the wrist and slow the bottle as it descended. It connected but not hard enough to knock me out. Or to stop me from landing another punch on the same side of his head as before. This one knocked him loose from me. His straddling legs loosened enough to let me buck him off. He went over backwards. He was drunk enough to be confused by all this happening so quickly. Now it was my turn to straddle him. I just wanted to make his face bloody. I hit him until my hands started to hurt and then I stood up, grabbed him by an arm and started dragging him to his motorcycle.

"Go get his stuff from inside, okay?" I said to Spence.

He nodded and ran over to the trailer. He didn't need to go inside. Michele was in the doorway, dropping Bill's shoes, socks, shirt and wallet one by one into Spence's hands. She wore a white terrycloth robe. She had a cigarette going. "You stay with me for a while, Jason?" she said.

"Sure."

Bill was on his motorcycle, roaring it to raucous life. Spence handed him his belongings. Spence said, "Looks like her nose is busted, man. You do that?"

"Shut the fuck up, Spence," Bill said. Then he made his bike louder than I'd ever heard it before. Bill glared at Spence for a long time and said, "I don't know what I ever saw in a pussy like you, Spence. Don't call me anymore."

"You beat her up, man. You don't have to worry about me callin' you."

He roared away, grass and dirt churning from beneath his back wheel.

"Wait'll you see her, Jason. He beat the shit out of her," Spence said, then walked back to the street and drove away in his old car, leaving me alone with Michele.

The light was on in the front part of the trailer now. She was gone from the door. When I sat down at the small table across from her, she pushed a cold can of Bud my way. I thanked her and gunned an ounce or two. My head hurt from where he got me with the bottle. She'd fixed up her trailer just the right way—so that you forgot you were in a trailer.

Her delicate nose didn't look broken, as Spence had said, but it was badly bruised. She had a black eye, a bloody, swollen mouth and her left cheek was bruised.

"Maybe you should go to an ER," I said.

"I'll survive." She made an effort to laugh. "I let him sleep with me but that wasn't enough for him."

"What the hell else did he want?"

308

"Well, he slept with me but I wouldn't take my bra or my blouse off. I said I had my reasons and I wanted him to respect them. In some weird way, I'd started to like him. Maybe I was just lonely. I never could pick men for shit. You should've seen some of the losers I went out with in LA. My girlfriends always used to laugh and say that if there was a serial killer on the dance floor, he'd be the one I end up with for the night."

"So you made love and—"

"We made love. I mean, it wasn't the first time. The last couple weeks, we'd been sleeping together. And he tried real hard to deal with me not taking my top off. I wouldn't let him touch my breasts." She smiled with bloody teeth. "My scream queen breasts."

She shook her head. Or tried. She was halfway through turning her head to the left when she stopped. She had a bad headache, too, apparently. "It was building up. His thing about my breasts. And tonight, afterwards, he just went crazy. Said if I really loved him I'd be completely nude for him. I liked him. But not enough to trust him. You know, with my secret."

She lit a cigarette with a red plastic lighter. I'd never seen her smoke before this night. She looked around a bit and then back at me and said, "It's why I left LA."

"What is?"

"I don't have breasts any more. I had this really bad kind of breast cancer. I had to have both of them removed." She exhaled through bloody lips. "So how would that be? A scream queen known for her breasts doesn't have them any more? I went to Eugene, Oregon to get the diagnosis. I kind've suspected I had breast cancer. I didn't want anybody in LA to know. I paid cash, gave a fake name, they didn't have any idea who I was. I had the double mastectomy there, too. I had some money saved and I used it to disappear. I just couldn't have handled all the publicity. All the bullshit about my breasts inspiring all these young boys—and then not having them anymore. You know how the tabloids are. And then do a couple weepy interviews on TV. So I've just been traveling around. And I'll be doing more traveling tomorrow. Because I know Bill will call some reporter or tabloid or somebody like that. I just don't want to face it."

Then she said, "C'mere, Okay?"

I stood up and walked over to her. My knees trembled. I didn't know why.

She took my right hand and guided it to her chest and then slid it inside the terrycloth so that I could feel the scarring from the mastectomy. I wanted to jerk my hand away. I'd never felt anything like that before. But then a tenderness came over me and I let my hand linger and then she eased my hand out of her robe and kissed my fingers, as if she were grateful.

Then she started sobbing and it was pretty bad. I said everything I knew to say but it didn't do any good, so I steered her into bed and just lay with her there in the darkness and we held hands and she talked about it all, everything from the day she first felt the tiny lump on the underside of her left breast to being so afraid she'd die from the anesthetic—she'd had an uncle who died while being put under, died right there on the table—and how she went through depression so bad she lost twenty-five pounds in three months and how that then turned around and become the opposite kind of eating disorder, this relentless urge to gorge, which she was battling now.

In the morning, I helped her load her car. She didn't have all that much. I told her I'd pay the rent off with the money she gave me and return the key. She kissed me then for the first and only time—the kind of kiss your sister would give you—and then she was gone.

The story hit one of the supermarket papers three weeks later. She'd been right. The whole thing dealt with the irony of a girl who'd been made into a scream queen at least partly because of her beautiful breasts—and then losing them to cancer. A minister somewhere said that it was God's wrath, exploiting your body for filthy Hollywood money, and then getting your just desserts. You know how God's people like to talk.

As for me...tomorrow I'm flying to LA. My Dad has a friend out there who owns a video company that produces training films for various companies. Not exactly Paramount, or even Roger Corman. But a start. My folks even gave me five thousand dollars as seed money. They're pretty sure that in a year I'll be back here. And maybe they're right....

It's funny about Michele. I watch her old videos all the time. That's how I prefer to remember her. It's not because of her breasts. It's because of that lovely girly radiance that was in her eyes and how her smile shined back in those days.

I still watch them and I'm sure Spence does, too. He got a job in Chicago and moved there a couple months back. Bill joined the Army. I wonder if he still watches them.

But most of all I wonder if Michele ever watches them. Probably not.

Not now, anyway. But maybe someday.

About Ed Gorman

Ed Gorman has been a writer for nearly three decades. Gorman's work has appeared in numerous newspapers and magazines such *The New York Times, Redbook, Ellery Queen* and *The Writer.* He's the author of more than thirty novels and six collections of short stories. His work has been translated into eleven languages and two of his books have been made into movies.

When the British magazine *Million* called him "One of the world's great storytellers," they were joining other publications such as *The New York Times, The Washington Post, The Los Angeles Times, The London Sunday Times* and *Publisher's Weekly* in acknowledging Gorman's skills.

Booklist called his novel *Ticket To Ride* "An absorbing mystery that offers an insightful portrait of small-town dynamics and has plenty of deadpan humor."

Of his suspense novel *The Midnight Room,* the magazine *Fiction* said "A stunning and sometimes shocking new approach to the serial killer novel."

Gorman's awards include The International Horror Writers award as well as the Shamus and nominations for the Edgar, The Stoker and The Silver Dagger (UK).

REACHING OUT

by Christian Riley

The Gothic Volunteer Alliance is an action league of individual volunteers who conduct humanitarian acts for the betterment of the local and global community. By exposure, people abandon their fears and accept that while people are different and have different lifestyles, they are people nonetheless, and there is value to everyone's existence and individuality.

Man, I certainly hope they mean all that. I hope these guys are for real. Because if they're not, all this preparation will be for shit. That said, I know I should at least try and reach out to these folks. To this "Gothic Alliance."

I'm considering volunteering because...well...truth be told, things have been rather difficult for me lately. I've never really had any friends to invite over to my place for a couple of beers. Never been much into entertaining people, really. I guess you could say I've always been something of a hermit.

But this lifestyle of mine needs to stop, because I can see from the look in Melody's eyes that it's begun to take a toll on her. She doesn't complain, but I can tell.

Well, I suppose Melody just needs to be exposed to something other than what the limits of my trailer and property will allow. I suppose she just needs to be around other people again. And who knows, maybe it'll even help me a little bit as well.

Oh, but don't go getting me wrong. Even though I'm as reclusive as a black widow, and Melody herself is rather unique in her own way, we're certainly no sticks-in-the-mud, that's for sure. For the past few months that I've known her, we've managed to keep ourselves entertained quite well, actually.

My trailer sits smack-dab in the center of a four-hundred acre stretch surrounded by a national forest. Beauty itself can't even hold a flame to the sights and sounds we experience around here. On most mornings, Melody and I pass the time away by simply watching countless butterflies as they flutter about, drunk-like through the air. That's how we often begin our day, actually; sitting on the picnic table in my front yard, drinking coffee, spotting butterflies. What could be better?

After breakfast, we usually watch the woods, and rave about our undying love for each other. We think about our future plans of marriage and having a family. We're constantly surrounded by such magnificent treasures of nature, such God-fearing tapestries of artistry all teeming with life, that I often find myself weeping in joy from it all.

We see squirrels as they scamper across the yard, chattering their approval of our presence. Deer stand in the meadows before us, chewing on pine cones, and staring with admiration. Birds are always whistling in the trees above, singing the gospel of nature as we canter along through groves of oak and hickory. Even bears and bobcats don't seem to mind us being around.

I swear, before I met Melody, it amazes me how much of my life slipped past without the glory of love being so close to my heart, as it is now. How much of this world around me, with its overabundance of life, and its delectable juices of tranquility as found from a single caterpillar on a leaf, to the flowers growing right outside my kitchen window—how much of it I have taken for granted for so long, all up until Melody came into my life? But I'm not missing anything now, that's for sure. Shoot; it's almost as if I'm at one with the universe. Like I'm a little Buddha, or what have you.

For months now we've lived this life of ours, Melody and I. And if we're not watching the animals in the forest in the early morning, taking it all in, lovers lost in love, then most likely we'll still be sitting at that picnic table, where I'll be reading some of my favorite books to her.

In the afternoon, I like to play horseshoes at the pit next to the barn, and Melody just sits there, smiling in her chair as she watches me bend over with my cackling laughter, hair flopping against the jerks of my uncontrolled excitement as I stomp my feet, and score ringer after ringer after ringer. I know I look like a fool out there, tossing those horseshoes and laughing the way I do, but damn if it ain't a blast. "You've always been the best at this game, sonny," my Momma used to say.

Oh, but if Momma could only see me now.

Sometimes Melody and I just lie on the grass and hold hands while we stare up into the sky, dreaming. Seems like we dream about everything, really. And of course, we share the same dreams also. We'd like to own a big ranch one day, with sheep and cattle. Horses, definitely. And I'll build us a big ol' house with huge bay windows overlooking a daisy-spotted green pasture, with grass rolling in the wind like distant waves heading for the shore. That's where we'll have the wedding. But sometimes our dreams get a little ambitious, also. With my portable radio next to us playing country music, I often like to sing the day away as I think about becoming a famous musician. Melody believes in me.

In the evening, I give Melody a hot bubble bath, and scrub her back with a sponge, because I know she just loves that. Afterward, we sit in front of the television while I brush her long black hair, sometimes for what seems like hours on end. Who doesn't like to have their hair brushed, right? And for dinner, it's always our favorite: a steaming bowl of chili with honey and cornbread for dessert. Melody just loves my chili. And of course, we wash it all down with a case of PBR.

I'll admit, sometimes I get a little rowdy later in the night, with all that beer in me. Sometimes I think I hear stuff outside, and that'll get me all jumpy and shit, such that I take to running out there in the front yard, blasting away into the surrounding darkness with my shotgun, drunk as a hillbilly in a rooster fight. But once again, Melody never seems to mind.

And how do I know this? Because when I finally come straggling back into my trailer, ears ringing from all that shooting, greasy hair stinking of sweat and gunpowder, looking like the dumbass that I am, I always find Melody sitting right there on the couch wearing nothing but lingerie and silky panties. But I'll skip past the details on what happens next. "A gentleman never brags about his woman." Once again, as Momma used to say.

Yet things are changing.

Despite the glory of our relationship, I know Melody now needs something more. And so that's why I've contacted this Gothic Volunteer Alliance. I'm hoping these people will be as committed to their pledge of acceptance as they claim. I hope they'll accept us, me and Melody, just the way we are. I don't see why they wouldn't.

"Well, what do you mean you guys are strange?" asked the GVA representative over the phone.

"Like I said, I'm something of a hermit. I don't get out much. And of course, without me, Melody can't go anywhere."

"And why can't she go anywhere?"

"Huh?"

"Do you mean to say, she *won't* go anywhere?"

"No. I mean she can't go anywhere."

"Well why not?"

"Oh, I don't know. It's like she's depressed or something. Maybe she's sick. Her hair's been falling out by the handfuls, and her skin has begun to peel away a little bit...well, a lot actually. And she can't really move much either. In fact, she can't move at all, now that I think about it. And then there's that...smell. I think she's embarrassed to go out in public, really. She hasn't said this of course, but I think she is."

We must've gotten disconnected somehow, 'cause the phone just went dead after that. But that guy seemed to be pretty understanding.

Anyways, I certainly hope these Gothic characters mean what they state on their website, because quite frankly, I've been a nervous wreck about taking Melody out and away from here. Taking her out there, with everyone else. And I think she's been a little bit anxious herself, as she wasn't quite...cooperative with getting ready this evening. She seemed so stiff.

But I know in the end, it'll do her good to get out. I hope it helps to bring back that color in her face. Or that liveliness in her eyes, like she had when we first met. We can certainly use the company of other people, if nothing else.

Well, she's in the truck waiting for me now, so I guess I should get going. I'll make sure to bring the hairbrush and a blanket just in case these people turn us away. There's a park around the corner from where they meet that I know of, and I think Melody would like it there. She'll definitely enjoy the slide. And I should bring the radio too, now that I think about that. I've never sang the night away to her before. Perhaps that'll be the ticket to cheering her up, if these Gothic folks can't.

About Christian Riley

Beginning at 5 AM, Chris spends the only available lot of solitary time he gets in a day feeding his addiction to writing. If he's lucky, he'll get two hours in before "they" wake up, after which he lives a wonderful life as a family man. His stories have been accepted at a number of publishers including *Short Story Me, Bete Noire, The Absent Willow Review, Residential Aliens, Bards and Sages Quarterly* and *Underground Voices.* You can reach him at chakalives@gmail.com, or at his static blog at frombehindthebluedoor.wordpress.com.

ME AND MY SHADOW

by Sandra Crook

I knew immediately that the newcomer would be a problem. It's never easy when a new child joins halfway through a school term; by that time friendships have been forged, coteries and pecking orders established, and social norms adopted. It's an unusual child that can be assimilated into the network without teething problems, and though Monica was, in fact, an unusual child, it was immediately clear that her social skills were sadly under-developed.

She had chosen a seat in the corner of the classroom, from which she could observe her schoolmates and also look out of the window. As I entered, that was exactly what she was doing, gazing intently at someone or something in the bushes, her arms folded defensively across her narrow chest. I turned to see what had captured her attention, noting a fleeting impression of a flash of russet red, something moving quickly enough to cause the bushes to toss this way and that.

"Good morning everyone," I greeted them, their freshly-washed young faces turning expectantly towards me.

"Good morning Miss Crook," they chorused in return.

"And we have a newcomer in our midst," I said in a cheerily welcoming manner. "Monica Jacy, I believe."

Monica dragged her gaze unwillingly away from the window and stared blankly at the sea of faces now turned in her direction. Her hand reached for one of her long black braids, which she slipped between her teeth, before raising her eyes to mine. She said nothing, waiting for me to continue.

"Welcome Monica, would you like to tell us something about yourself?" I said.

Panic flickered across her face, before she shook her head firmly. The other children tittered.

"Well, maybe your classmates should tell you something about themselves instead, and we can come back to you later?" I said. "We'll start with Tommy Flynn, shall we?"

Tommy, who had been smirking at Monica, pulled a face, flushed and stood up unwillingly.

"My name is Tommy Flynn and I live in Ripley Hollow and I like baseball and I have two big brothers and my Dad is the local sheriff and my Mum works at the hospital and my best friend is Joe Walker and..."

"Thank you, Tommy," I said. "Complete sentences, remember? And draw breath in between each, but well done."

Drawing inspiration from Tommy's efforts, the rest of the class followed, each child careful to give their parents' occupations and the name of their best friend.

Attention focused on Monica once again, and I felt my spirits sinking.

"Come along Monica," I said encouragingly.

"My name is Monica Jacy, I ain't got no folks. I live with my gramma and my best friend is a secret," she said.

The class erupted in howls of laughter, and Monica blushed unbecomingly.

"That's very unkind," I shouted at the rest of the class. "*I don't have any folks,* Monica. *Ain't got no folks* is a double negative."

She wriggled uncomfortably.

"Tell me about your best friend," I said gently.

Monica's gaze shifted to the window again. Following her gaze, I strolled to the table near the window, ostensibly to pick up some chalk and a duster. As I did so, I saw a flash of red in the bushes once again.

"He don't like me talking about him," she said, defiantly. "He's a secret."

The other kids sniggered loudly, and I sighed.

"*Doesn't* Monica. He *doesn't* like me to talk about him. Now let's get started then," I said. "Monica can sit next to Tommy. Let Monica share your book, Tommy, just for today."

Tommy looked distinctly underwhelmed, and grudgingly slid his book across the desk, leaning his body well away from Monica. She didn't look particularly clean, and I wondered whether she might smell, though I wasn't close enough to tell.

The morning passed quickly and at lunchtime the children spilled into the yard where they secured benches under the trees for their own particular group, piling lunchboxes of every shape, size and color onto their laps. The contents were laid out, each child eyeing theur neighbor's lunch with curiosity and in some cases, envy.

I was on supervisory duty, so I made my way to an unoccupied bench where I opened up my own pink lunchbox. Scanning the yard for Monica I saw her sitting alone on a tree stump, clutching a brown paper bag. With downcast eyes, she almost secretively drew a wedge of white bread, spread thinly with jelly and peanut butter, from the bag and took a bite. My heart went out to her—peanut butter, and no one to talk to. There was always one.

Sighing, I put my sandwich back in my box and strolled casually round the tables, pausing to have a word with each group as I made my way over to where Monica sat, still alone.

"So how did your first morning go, Monica?" I said.

I heard the bushes rustle behind her.

She slid her hunk of bread surreptitiously back into the crumpled brown bag and twisted it shut.

"Fine," she whispered.

"Where was your last school, dear?" I asked.

"Oh, someplace out west," she said, giving nothing away.

"And what brought you to Ripley Hollow?"

"Gramma said we had to come here."

"Does she have friends here?" I asked.

"She don't have friends nowhere," she said in a matter of fact voice.

"*Doesn't*, Monica, not *don't*. And *anywhere*, not *nowhere*. You're using a double negative again there."

"Whatever," she sighed.

I examined my lunchbox with studied regret. "Oh dear, I just really don't feel hungry at all today," I said. "I wonder whether you might like to eat these for me, Monica."

She looked up, and I detected a quickly masked look of eagerness.

"If you want me to," she said, hesitantly.

"Thank you Monica," I said, wondering whether I had enough change to raid the snack machine in the staff room before the afternoon session.

As I left, I looked back in time to see her passing the hunk of bread behind her into the bushes, where, amongst much rustling, it disappeared. Then she withdrew a sandwich from my lunchbox and, pulling the two slices apart to check the content, smiled ecstatically and bit into it. My mouth watered at the memory of the roast chicken, liberally laced with mayonnaise and I headed quickly to the staff room.

At four o'clock, the children teemed out of the classroom, and were soon reunited in the schoolyard with parents or elder siblings. Monica was in no hurry to leave, slowly putting her notebook and pencils into the paper bag which had contained her lunch.

I was marking homework when I became aware of her close by my desk. My suspicions had been correct; she did smell, but not the pee'd-and-dried smell most teachers recognize. It was something earthy, musty, almost animal-like.

"See you tomorrow, Monica."

"Here's your box back," she said pushing my empty lunch box across the desk to me.

"You keep it Monica, for your lunches."

Her eyes widened, surprised.

"Thank you."

Turning as she reached the door, she smiled for the first time that day. "And my friend says thank you too."

I went to the window, curious to see if her grandmother had come to meet her. There was no one left in the schoolyard, and Monica let herself out through the school gate. She glanced across at the shrubbery on the opposite side of the road and jerked her head.

I watched in shock, as a red wolf loped out of the undergrowth, and bounded excitedly down the road behind her, occasionally nudging her hand with his nose.

《《—》》

"About the wolf, Mrs Jacy," I began nervously, perched on the edge of a packing case outside her trailer, which was parked right on the perimeter of the local trailer park.

Her brows puckered. "What wolf?"

"The red wolf that follows Monica around wherever she goes," I continued.

She'd been leaning back on two legs of her chair, propped against the side of the trailer, but she snapped forward immediately.

"You seen it then?" she said, surprised.

"*Have* seen it," I corrected, before remembering I was not talking to class at this moment. "Yes I have seen it, Mrs Jacy."

"You ain't s'posed to," she said, half to herself, absently rubbing her chin between her thumb and forefinger. "You part Indian then?"

"No, Mrs Jacy," I said, "English."

"Weird."

"Yes it is weird, and worrying."

"For you, p'raps," she said grinning and displaying a gap in her front teeth.

"I mean, it would be worrying for the other children at school if they saw him. It's no place for a wolf, around kids. This has to stop."

"Other kids can't see him," she said, "and ain't no one gonna stop him going where he wants to."

"Is he tame?" I asked.

"'Til she's hurt," she cackled, "then he ain't. Then he's real wild."

She gave that kooky, gap-toothed grin once again, and I left the trailer park.

«« — »»

The bullying started fairly soon after Monica's arrival. At first it was just an apparently accidental push, a casual tripping up as she passed by, but like all bullying it quickly escalated, and I couldn't be everywhere to intervene.

Tommy Flynn appeared to be a ringleader in these activities, and disappointed, I asked him to stay after class one afternoon. There were four other boys I had identified as being involved, but I decided to tackle Tommy first.

"Why are you bullying Monica Jacy, Tommy?"

"Because she's weird," he said, and then added hopefully, as though it may exonerate him from any further blame, "and she stinks funny."

"*Smells* funny," I corrected, and instantly regretted it.

"You noticed it too?" he said brightening.

"No," I lied, "I was correcting your language."

He shuffled uneasily on the spot.

"It has to stop. It's unkind, it's not civilized and..." Why did the word *dangerous* spring immediately to mind?

"Okay," he said cheerily, in a way that clearly indicated he had no intention of obeying. "C'n I go now Miss?"

"You *may* go now, Tommy. And remember, I wouldn't want to have to talk to your father about this."

321

"Wouldn't matter none," he confided obligingly, "he don't like Injuns neither."

Before I could correct him, he was off out the door, galloping across the schoolyard with his hood over his head, the rest of his coat flying out behind him like a cape, flicking away at his flank with imaginary reins.

Hunting '*Injuns,*' no doubt.

«« — »»

Some weeks later, I was awakened by the sound of distant sirens, getting closer, and slipping quickly out of bed I went to my window. There was a full moon that night, and the street was reflected in silver, casting long shadows across the sidewalk. An ambulance and several police cars, some of them from over the county line, hurtled along the road, lights flashing furiously and sirens wailing like banshees as their tail-lights disappeared up the road to the ridge.

I went downstairs to heat some milk, pacing the kitchen anxiously, wondering what disaster had befallen at the other end of town. Out in the moonlit yard I detected a movement under the trees, and a few seconds later I heard a muffled thump at the door. I cautiously opened the door a couple of inches, seeing nothing, yet sensing a presence.

Unhooking the chain, I stepped out onto the porch. As I did so, the red wolf stepped into the light spilling from the open doorway, and settled down a couple of yards away, watching me. His yellow eyes flickered in acknowledgement. I stood transfixed with....what? It wasn't fear, though I knew it should have been.

I held out my hand, and he rose to pace slowly forward, his fur gleaming in the moonlight. His damp, earthy nose nudged the palm of my hand, and then he tilted his head to rub his cheek and ear against my fingers.

Then he bounded backwards, elongated his neck, and gave a long desolate howl that faded after a several seconds, whilst from the ridge east of the town came an answering chorus of eerie howls, echoing around the valley. With one last look at me, he ducked under the fence and streaked silently into the night.

Disturbed, and with a sense that disaster was all about me, I hurried back indoors to dress. As I reached for my jeans, I realized that my hand was sticky. I turned on the bedside light and saw that my fingers were smeared with blood.

Retching, I rushed to the bathroom to wash my hands.

Once dressed, I set off in the general direction the emergency vehicles had been heading. I was joined by others who had been awoken by the activity. At the bridge crossing the creek, about half a mile short of the ridge, our progress was halted by a cordon of police officers.

"What's happened?" one of my neighbors asked.

"You need to go home, folks," said the cop. "Lock your doors and stay inside."

We turned back towards our homes, but not before I had seen Sheriff Flynn, seated half in and half out of a police vehicle, his head in his hands and shoulders shaking with violent sobs.

I turned back with the others, needing company for the short journey home, although somehow I didn't feel to be in any personal danger. There was just an overwhelming sense of horror and loss, a sense that some chapter was now over; some course had been run.

«« —»»

The country's press descended on our sleepy town that week, reporters taking a quote from anyone who would oblige. And there were plenty who would.

Over three hundred sheep had been slaughtered that night of the full moon, their throats torn out and carcasses ravaged. They said that the farmers were ruined, none of them insured, and most having no other livestock to fall back on. It didn't escape my attention that the slaughtered sheep belonged only to the families of those four boys who had helped Tommy Flynn to torment Monica Jacy.

But the real horror was the mangled body of Tommy Flynn, found close to the sheep pastures, his throat torn out as well. No one knew what he was doing out in the fields, and someone said his bedroom window had been forced off its hinges, his bed covered in mud and animal hair.

Hunting parties scoured the woods for days, and many small animals perished as nervous hunters reacted to every movement. But there was no sign of anything that might have wreaked such havoc in the course of one night.

School was closed for a week, and when it re-opened, the sons of those farmers who had been ruined did not immediately return.

Monica Jacy did not ever return.

I checked the school records to see which school she had attended out west. The name sounded familiar, but I couldn't immediately recall why. I phoned them to see if Monica had returned there.

"We had no Monica Jacy here," said the headmaster. "Around that time we had a Monica Jolon. Could her name have been changed?"

"She was a small, thin girl," I said, "with long dark hair."

"Well Monica Jolon was certainly small, thin and dark," he said. "I remember that much. Quiet girl, didn't really fit in."

"Was she bullied?" I asked.

"Sadly, yes, as I remember. She was part Indian and there's still a lot of distrust and resentment about half-breeds round here. Shame really, she had a very sad background. Both parents killed when their cabin was torched by some hooligans a few years back. She and her younger brother were taken in by their grandmother, and then the boy died of meningitis. He'd worshipped her apparently, followed her everywhere, and she was devastated when he died. Sometimes it seems like tragedy kinda follows some folk about. It can't have helped what happened here, either."

Suddenly, I knew why the name of the school was familiar. There'd been a shooting incident, and six boys had been killed. Some kid with a shotgun, wearing fancy dress, an Indian outfit, had managed to break through security. He'd targeted one classroom and had never been caught. Someone said he just faded out of sight, right in front of them. Shock, they said.

"Did Monica see what happened that day?" I asked, already knowing what the answer would be.

"No, thankfully. It was her class that was attacked. Her grandmother had called her in sick that morning, and Monica never returned to the school afterwards. Quite a few kids were withdrawn from the school at that time, but most of them did come back eventually."

I thanked him, and ended the conversation.

Later that week I drove to the trailer park where I had visited Monica's grandmother. As I had expected, the trailer was empty, looking as though they may have left in a hurry. There was a heap of rubbish round the back of the trailer, and I kicked through it, not really knowing what I was looking for. Eventually I caught a glimpse of something pink, and I sorted through the rubbish to pull my sandwich box out of the rubble.

Inside there was a photograph of Monica hand in hand with a young boy, obviously taken at a children's party. Monica was dressed as a fairy. The boy was proudly wearing a full Indian outfit complete with a feathered headdress. Printed on the back of the photo were the words *Me and Red Wolf.*

"*Red Wolf and me*, Monica," I whispered, turning to leave.

About Sandra Crook

Over the last twenty years, Sandra Crook has lived and/or worked in South Africa, Germany, England, Spain and France. She now divides her time between cruising the French waterways in a Dutch barge with her husband and fostering rescue dogs at her home in Cambridgeshire, UK. She loves animals, Formula 1 motor racing and her husband, though not necessarily in that order. Like most short-story writers, she has a half-finished novel lurking on her hard drive.

Her recent work has appeared at *Every Day Fiction, Every Day Poets, Microhorror, Eclectic Flash, Backhand Stories, The Pygmy Giant, Shine Journal, The Short Humour Site, Long Story Short, Apollo's Lyre, Bewildering Stories, 5 Minute Fiction* and in several *Static Movement* anthologies. Links to these and other published works, photos from her travels, and cruising reports can be found at www.castelsarrasin.wordpress.com.

LITTLE GIRL LOST

by Trevor Denyer

Though it didn't seem right, Ben was becoming bored with the news coverage of the abduction of five-year-old Mandy Jacobs. Every day there were pages of newsprint devoted to it, most of which summarized and repeated what had already been printed.

In fact, it was annoying him now and he wondered why he bothered to continue buying a newspaper each day. Force of habit, he supposed, and something to read on the train journey to work; something undemanding.

But there was another reason, one that he didn't like to admit. Since the abduction two months ago, he had started to feel uncomfortable when by himself, as though he *wasn't* by himself. It was a feeling, no more, but unsettling and irritating.

Ben lived alone. He preferred it that way. His mum had been the center of his universe and when she died two years ago, he had fallen apart for a while. At forty years of age he had been vulnerable. He'd never had a dad, certainly not a man who had been present at any time. He had no memory of him and had summarily dismissed the idea of a father figure existing. It was a time in his life when he had begun to think about what his future might hold.

He was not unattractive; only slightly overweight at thirteen stone, mainly due to an expanding belly, which he felt that for his 5'10' height wasn't too bad. He wasn't completely sure of his sexual orientation. He enjoyed the sight of young good looking females (with tight, tidy arses) and young, good looking males (with tight, tidy arses).

He'd never had sex with anyone other than himself and hadn't really ever desperately desired it. 'What you've never had you never miss' was his philosophy.

At forty, he'd begun to reassess that philosophy. He'd started to examine himself more critically, noting the lines on his face, the way his skin was becoming drier and how tiny grey hairs were beginning to

326

show amongst the slightly receding, though still abundant shock of wavy brown hair adorning his head.

Just as he was starting to come to terms with himself, his mum died of a heart attack. He hadn't been there when it happened and he hadn't found her. He had been away in Scotland for a short break. A neighbour had seen his mother lying on the kitchen floor and called the emergency services. She had tried to contact him, but he hadn't got the message until he returned from the wilds of Sutherland to the austerity of Edinburgh. Only then had he checked for messages on his mobile phone. In a panic, he had returned the hire car and flown home to Heathrow, picking up the shuttle bus from there to Woking.

When he arrived home, there was no sign that anything had happened, just a hastily repaired lock on the back door.

What had distressed him more than anything was the lack of continuity. Mum was just *gone*; that was that. Despite her efforts to impress upon him the certainty of an afterlife, stressing the significance of an omnipresent God, when she died he had felt as if she had vanished. She hadn't 'passed on' anywhere, she had just vanished.

«««——»»»

In the dream he stands on the small flowered green in front of the house. There is a triangle of flowers, edged in orange, with pinks and yellows forming a heart in the centre. The triangle is within a diverging path that appears to present the house to him. The bright colors of the flowers offer sadness, like flowers on a grave.

The house is a demon, staring through windowed eyes, the blackness behind the net curtains hiding secrets he dare not contemplate. The door is blood red, with a square of glass above a golden letterbox, flashing reflected sunlight. Two smaller squares hover ephemerally above the light, glinting in the afterglow.

Between the two gabled sides of the house is a tower. The door is recessed within an archway and above it is a rectangular window on the first floor. Above that are two smaller windows with cream colored lintels like thick eyebrows, presenting a startled appearance. The sentient effect chills him. The house is alive.

The roof resembles a wizard's hat, scaly grey and rising to a point on top of which a weather vane rises; a cross with a grey ball hanging from each arm. It reminds him vaguely of the Old Bailey, weighing the prospect of justice against the hopelessness of faith. He knows he is there to bring together the two ideologies, but something stops him from moving forward.

There is an elusive presence that holds him back, despite the towering rage that fills him, from the depths of his toes to the miasma of his mind. The rage is white hot, melting all memory of its cause. There is a whispered plea that forces him to focus on the beauty of the flowers.

He cannot be distracted for long, though. Inside, the rage swells and he takes a faltering step forward, feeling the presence torn away by an overwhelming need to confront the demon. Sadness fills him and fuels the rage. Behind him he senses a figure standing forlornly, but he cannot turn. The demon beckons and he walks towards the house.

«« — »»

Ben folded his newspaper and laid it on his lap. He felt tired and the constant reporting of the abduction of Mandy Jacobs didn't help. The train was busy at this time in the morning. He observed his fellow travelers, mainly business people on their way to the City. They were either napping, some snoring with mouths hung open, or busy metaphorically chasing their tails. Newspapers were flourished and unnecessarily loud impenetrable conversations duelled for prominence over mobiles that buzzed and sang tinnily. Ipods and Ipads absorbed concentration, heads bowed to the electronic highways as the train slid smoothly towards Waterloo.

Ben sighed. The thought of another week of tedium depressed him and he closed his eyes, trying to shut out the sounds and thoughts of the working world.

He decided that in September, he would go on holiday somewhere. That was a nice time of year, less than two months away, and the weather was often good. Best of all, in September there were very few kids around. He considered his options. Would he go abroad?

He preferred England; if he headed North where the roads were clear, there would be fewer people, things were cheaper and the quality of life was better. Move away from the seething masses in the South, like cornered rats, biting, scratching, killing, spreading disease...

He jolted awake, finding himself still on the train. He had been on the verge of...verge of...and then there was Scotland...

He felt himself sinking into a semi-conscious state that felt uncomfortable. His teeth ached and his body became heavy. He felt like a stone sinking into a drowning pool and deep down in that pool, she waited. Her presence drew him down as his discomfort increased.

He couldn't see her or hear anything, but he knew she was there. He felt her anguish suffocating him, her insistent silent plea filling his mind; a ball of sadness that leached into his soul.

He awoke again with a gasp like a drowning man finding air. He had slid down in his seat, and he pulled himself upright, looking around. The drones on the train feigned disinterest or pretended not to have noticed anything untoward.

His heart pounded and he was sweating despite the air conditioning in the train carriage. His white shirt would be drenched, he realized, but that seemed to be fairly inconsequential. The predominant thought that throbbed and pounded dully through his head was insistent:

Little Girl Lost...Little Girl Lost...Little Girl Lost...

«« — »»

In the dream the red door swings open. It isn't locked and that seems strange. He hasn't had to knock and he can hear the sound of the radio coming from the kitchen. Someone is moving around, dancing to the music. He knows who she is and he moves into the house.

He thinks he speaks but his lips don't move:

"You have the girl."

She turns, alarmed. Her long brown hair frames a pale, weather-worn face that appears older than her thirty years. Her large brown eyes widen in surprise.

A flood of emotions ripple across her face, then anger steals the softness from her eyes. Her lips part, exposing startlingly white teeth. She growls at him, "What the fuck are you doing in my house?"

He hears a noise behind him and turns. Little Amy stands forlorn, her brown hair hanging in straggly, tangled profusion, needing a comb. She holds a naked doll in one hand and a piece of her cot blanket in the other. She brings the thinning, greying fabric to her mouth to suckle upon it and smell the safety of her fading babyhood.

"Daddy," she mumbles from behind her comforter.

«« — »»

The next day, Ben dozed on the way to Glasgow. The early morning flight was scheduled to land at 7.30 am. He hadn't managed to sleep much during the night. There were too many thoughts crowding his mind. The question remained: why was he traveling to Scotland? Why was he not going to his job?

The truth of it was because of a feeling that the dream was reality; a haunted, uncomfortable and insistent voice that he could not hear yet understood subliminally. The Little Girl Lost remained hidden, just out of sight behind a veil at the edge of consciousness. The Little Girl Lost *insisted* and he knew that if he ignored the voice he would never be free of her. She told him to go to Loch Lomond. There he would find Mandy Jacobs.

As he drove the hire car onto the M8 out of Glasgow, he knew nothing beyond the Little Girl Lost's insistence that he head towards Loch Lomond. He mused as he drove, wondering where all the other drivers were going. The idea that they were all heading towards annihilation unsettled him, but that was the truth of it. Death was the ultimate destination, but what lay beyond that? Once again, the memory of his mum overwhelmed him and the emptiness he'd felt when she died saddened him.

From that sadness, she came: the Little Girl Lost. For the first time, he saw her in the rear view mirror, sitting in the back seat and the shock of her corporality caused him to swerve, eliciting urgent, panicked hooting from his fellow travelers. He recognized her from the photographs in the newspapers. She was Mandy Jacobs.

His heart hammered in his chest, threatening to burst. He pulled onto the hard shoulder and turned towards the back seat. It was empty, but her presence remained. He heard her voice now. It whispered from the space where she had been: *Daddy.*

«« —»»

In the dream the house gloats. The Demon waits patiently as he turns to the woman.

"What I want," he says through grim lips, "is to take care of my little girl."

The thirty-year-old woman laughs at that; a raw, animal sound like a hyena's baying. "It's a bit bloody late for that," she says.

"No! It's never too late. I'm taking her."

She bristles. The Demon feels her contempt like a furnace radiating heat that sears him.

330

"Never!" she screams, grabbing a carving knife from the kitchen rack. He can hear Ken Bruce in the background, his Scottish brogue introducing the next record.

The Demon's rage ignites once more and he pulls the shotgun from inside his coat.

Amy screams.

《《——》》

The A98 took Ben to Loch Lomond. The Wednesday morning traffic was easing now as people settled into work. The sun was bright and warm in a blue summer sky. A few wispy cirrus clouds streaked icily across the troposphere. The loch sparkled and rippled in the light as the breeze gently ruffled the wide, deep expanse of water. Inchmurrin Island and the hills beyond were sharp in the clear air.

Ben pulled off the road and waited. His mind was a confusion of conflicting emotions. Why had the Little Girl Lost called him Daddy? Why did she look so much like Mandy Jacobs? He didn't have any children. He was certain of that because he'd never had sex with anyone.

One thing was certain, his dreams had compelled him to come here in search of her. Why Scotland? Mandy had disappeared at Covent Garden in London after her parents were distracted by a street performer – a mummer miming being trapped inside an invisible box.

It had been quick, the distraught parents claimed. One minute she was there, standing next to them, enjoying an ice cream and the next she had disappeared.

There were no witnesses as the crowd was focused upon the mime show. It seemed impossible that no one had noticed a small child being led away from her parents, or that Mandy had not protested. It was as though she had disappeared into thin air.

Had the abductor been someone the child knew? Did he or she discreetly cover Mandy's mouth to stop her raising the alarm and whisk her away? Mandy would only have needed to be constrained for a few seconds until she could be bundled into a vehicle or a nearby building.

She interrupted his thoughts: *Hello Daddy.*

He could see her in the rear view mirror. She sat on the back seat, a diminutive figure, slight and pale with...*brown hair hanging in straggly, tangled profusion, needing a comb*...the description echoed within his mind, a last gasp from the dreams.

331

He didn't turn this time, but stared at her in the mirror. She stared back, her clear brown eyes studying him. She raised the cot rag to her mouth and suckled.

"My little girl," he sobbed. He didn't understand how, but felt the certainty within, welling up and overwhelming him. He wanted to comfort her and take away the sadness. "I'm sorry, so sorry..."

Find the Lodges, she whispered in his mind. Her eyes were hard and resentful, nurturing something malevolent that seemed to seep into the air around him. He shivered, feeling cold despite the July heat. He started the car and pulled onto the highway.

«« — »»

In the dream he screams, "Carol, don't!" but she launches herself at The Demon. There is a massive detonation and Ben watches her face disintegrate and explode through the back of her head, drenching the cupboards behind with blood, brain and skull fragments. She is flung backwards and sinks to the floor like a broken doll. Stillness fills the house, absorbing the horror. The sound of the gunshot rings in his ears.

He knows he's dreaming and can't understand why he hasn't woken before this point.

The sound of something solid hitting the floor behind him makes him turn. Amy stands there, the naked doll lying at her feet. She clutches her comforter, sucking hard, hoping to elicit sweetness.

He wants to turn the clock back, to try again, to make amends, but the house locks him into the nightmare. There is no escape and only one solution.

«« — »»

'The Lodges' was a drive off the main road that led towards the edge of the loch. A profusion of shrubs provided privacy for the residents who occupied the small, grey stone buildings set back from the drive. The rhododendrons and azaleas were no longer flowering, but buddleia and abelia were in full bloom, maintaining the natural screening in a blaze of colors from bright pinks through grades of white and yellow to deep blues and purples.

Here, she whispered and he stopped the car. When he looked in the mirror, she had gone.

Ben got out of the car and began walking towards one of the lodges. Its grey stone block walls rose up to a gabled end and slated roof. Small wooden framed sash windows were inset into the walls. He could see one rectangular window on the ground floor next to an arched doorway and a smaller window on the first floor. The door was set back in the shadow of the arch, its deep brown wood forbidding entry. The waters of the loch sparkled in the background, bathed in sunlight. As he approached, Ben noticed that heavy curtains had been drawn across the windows.

He turned to check that the Little Girl Lost had not followed. She was nowhere to be seen and her presence was gone. In its place came a deep sense of foreboding and he felt like a trapped animal, set upon an irreversible course. He did not know whether he should be cautious as he approached the lodge or boldly announce himself by knocking on the door. In the absence of any better idea, he decided on the latter.

The door was opened by a grey haired man, balding on the crown and bearded. His beard was as grey as his sparse hair and had been clipped, leaving a grey curtain of hair that extended a couple of inches from his chin. Ben estimated that he must be in his late seventies. He wore small, black framed glasses that perched upon a thin nose. He smiled at Ben, though this belied what his deep brown eyes betrayed. There was something dark and hateful in the eyes, making Ben flinch.

"I...um...felt I had to come here," Ben stuttered.

"Yes," the old man said, his voice thin and dry. "Come in."

It took a couple of minutes for Ben's sight to adjust to the darkness inside the lodge. Gradually chinks of light became visible where the deep orange curtains were not fully drawn. An orange glow pervaded the space and it felt hot. Sweat pricked Ben's forehead as he followed the stranger into the living room.

"Sit down, please," he said.

Ben sat down, sinking into the tired fabric of the large sofa. In the gloom, it appeared to be black, matching an armchair where the old man seated himself.

"I don't know where to start, really," Ben said.

"I know why you're here. Amy brought you, didn't she?"

"Amy? No, it was Mandy—Mandy Jacobs. I saw her, but then she wasn't there..."

He ignored the question. "You've come to find her."

"Yes. Is she here?"

"Perhaps."

Ben felt annoyance, rising like a tide within him. He stood up. "Look, if you know where Mandy Jacobs is, you have to tell me. I don't understand how or why I came to be here but now that I am here, I have to find her."

"Sit down, Ben," the old man said quietly, "or should I say, Robert. I need to explain some things to you."

«« —»»

In the dream there is only one course to follow. He knows that there is no hope of redemption for what he's done. The horror of it will stay with Amy forever and he cannot bear the thought of that.

There is movement in the living room. He briefly wonders why. Then he turns the gun upon Amy and pulls the trigger. In the split second before she dies he sees a shadow pass across the doorway. There is someone else here.

He hears a young boy's voice yell above the percussive sound of the gunshot: "Robert!"

He realizes that James is in the house. He should have thought of that. He should have remembered. Somehow he knows that his stepson will be all right. The horror will impact upon him, but he's tough. He'll have to be.

Robert stuffs the warm gun barrel into his mouth and pulls the trigger.

«« —»»

They stood by the edge of the loch. Its vastness spread away to the hills beyond. Under the sun, the water sparkled in the clear air and lapped against the bank. That and the sound of birdsong calmed him.

"So where is Amy, or should I say Mandy Jacobs?" he asked.

James smiled, his eyes bright and no longer haunted by the past. "She's living happily with mum and dad."

Ben was still trying to digest that James was his stepson from a horrific past life. "So I was Robert. And the things we do in any life, past or present, never go away."

James had survived the trauma of what Robert's internal demon had done, and the Little Girl Lost – Amy then and Mandy now – found him and brought them together. Ben accepted the reality of what James, now an old man, explained to him.

And so time reset itself.

Ben turned away and gazed across the loch. He wondered just how deep the deceptively calm waters went.

About Trevor Denyer

Trevor Denyer has been published in magazines including *Scheherazade, Nasty Piece of Work, Enigmatic Tales, Symphonie's Gift* and *Night Dreams*. He received an Honorable Mention in the *Year's Best Fantasy and Horror* and has appeared on-line at *Time Out Net Books* and *Gathering Darkness*. His work has appeared in several anthologies including *Nasty Snips* and *Gravity's Angels*. He has recently been published in the Evil Jester Press anthology, *Help! Wanted: Tales of On-The-Job Terror* and *Estronomicon* from Screaming Dreams Press. His own collection titled *The Edge of the Country* is available through *Midnight Street Magazine*.

Trevor is the creator and editor of the critically acclaimed *Roadworks, Legend* and currently *Midnight Street* magazines.

Visit the website at: www.midnightstreet.co.uk

This story, "Little Girl Lost," was written by Trevor exclusively for The Horror Zine.

THE STORY OF MY FIRST KISS

by Jeff Strand

"Who did this?" asked Ms. Tyrone, picking up the severed head by the hair. Some drops of blood spattered on her desk as she looked around the classroom.

None of us responded. I noticed Joey trying to stifle a giggle.

"I know you all think these pranks are oh-sooooo-funny, but they're not, and I expect them to stop immediately," Ms. Tyrone informed us in a very stern voice. She held the head up in front of her to examine it more closely. "Who is this? Can anybody identify her?"

Melissa, who sat in the front row, raised her hand.

"Yes, Melissa?"

"It's Daphne Ridge."

"From Mr. Pendleton's class?"

Melissa nodded.

"So one of you decapitated an honors student. Well, class, we're going to sit here until the guilty party confesses. No recess, no lunch, just sitting here with your heads down until I find out who's responsible."

The entire class groaned.

"And if anybody says a word except to fess up, they'll find themselves staying after class. I'm not kidding around." She set Daphne's head back down on her desk. "This is completely unacceptable."

Ms. Tyrone did indeed make us sit there through lunch and afternoon recess, but at two-thirty she made us take our spelling test. She couldn't keep the entire class after school, I guess, so when the dismissal bell rang we all got to leave.

I caught up with Joey in the hallway, as he quickly walked toward the exit. "Jerk," I said, punching him on the arm.

"What?"

"Why'd you leave the head on Ms. Tyrone's desk?"

"It was funny."

"You're gonna get me in trouble."

"Then you shouldn't be killing people."

"The next time I do, I'm not gonna show you. You know I'll never get that head back, right? You're always doing stuff like this to me."

"You've still got her torso."

"The torso's no fun. First Michael steals her legs, then Adrienne steals her best arm, then Michael's dog steals her other arm, and then you get her head taken away. It's not fair."

"Wahhh wahhh."

I wanted to hit Joey again, but Principal Smith was standing right by the main doors, so I didn't. We walked out of the building and Joey ran over to his bus.

Stupid Joey. He was always doing these pranks. One time, I was going to try out cannibalism, and I cooked an arm on my dad's grill. I would've gotten in so much trouble if he caught me, but I did it anyway, and I grilled it absolutely perfect on my first try. I invited Joey over, and do you know what he did? He put sugar in the salt shaker, just to be funny. The arm tasted terrible.

Another time, I was going to wear human skin as a mask, and when I had the flesh tanned exactly the way I wanted, he drew a great big mustache on it, with permanent ink. I had to just throw the face away.

I don't know why I was even friends with him. I guess part of the reason is that when you have an uncontrollable desire to kill, a lot of the other kids are mean to you. Joey drove me crazy sometimes, but he never judged me, and he never tattled.

I was pretty mad about Daphne's head, but I had too much homework that evening to go out and claim another victim. I thought about setting the alarm for an hour early so I could get one before school, but that never worked. I always kept hitting the snooze button until it was time to get up for real.

When Joey and I walked into the classroom the next morning, there was another severed head on Ms. Tyrone's desk. "Aw, man," I said.

I knew who did it. Oscar was sitting at his desk, trying not to giggle. I couldn't stand him, because he was a copycat killer. He could never come up with any cool ideas of his own. If I killed somebody with a corkscrew, Oscar would do the same thing the next day. He wouldn't even change the profile of the victim. I didn't recognize the head, but knowing Oscar, she was an honors student.

"I'm going to tell Ms. Tyrone that it was you," I told him.

"You'd better not."

"I mean it."

Oscar looked at me carefully, and then his lip began to tremble. "Please don't," he said. Yeah, Oscar wasn't just a copycat, he was a crybaby. I hated him.

Of course, I didn't tell on him, even when Ms. Tyrone made us sit with our heads down most of the morning. She was really mad this time, but there's a code of honor: even if somebody is a whiny little copycat baby like Oscar, you don't tell on him.

After school, I went down to the bus station and killed a vagrant with a pitchfork. (I don't even know why the pitchfork was in the garage. It wasn't like we ever scooped hay with it.) He was light from malnutrition, so I got him into my wheelbarrow and pushed him home along the railroad tracks where not many people could see me.

"What are you gonna do with him?" Joey asked as I lay the vagrant's body out in my backyard.

"Dunno."

"What about something to raise Satan?"

I shook my head. "Satan sucks."

"Then what are you gonna do?"

I shrugged. "Maybe I'll beat him with a hammer and see how much I can flatten him. If I took a piece of gold, I could flatten it out until it filled this whole yard."

"Let's do that!"

So we did. A corpse doesn't flatten out like gold, though. Some of the organs flattened out okay, I guess, but by the time we gave up the vagrant was "scattered" but not really "flattened."

"That was lame," said Joey.

"Yeah."

Joey picked up a big red chunk and threw it at me, just barely missing.

"Stop it," I said.

He grabbed a whole handful of muck and let it fly. Most of it missed, but not all of it.

"I said stop it!"

"Food fight!" he shouted, scooping up as much of the vagrant as he could. Laughing like a complete loser, he ran toward me. I think he was going to dump it all on my head, and I raised the hammer to defend myself, but then Joey slipped on a coil of intestine and hit the ground.

He let out a whimper. "I can't feel my legs."

"That's what you get," I told him.

"No, I mean it. I think I broke my back."

"Too bad for you."

"Call an ambulance."

I figured I had two options. I could call an ambulance, or I could beat him to death with the hammer. I weighed the pros and cons, and then I beat him to death with the hammer.

I got in so much trouble. My mom came home and yelled, and then Dad yelled, and then Joey's mom and dad yelled, and...well, let's just say that the rest of the day was pretty bad for me.

Then I discovered girls, which were way better than killing people. Seriously. When Monica's brother held me down on the ground next to the swingset so that she could kiss me, I barely tried to break free.

And that's the story of my first kiss.

About Jeff Strand

Jeff Strand is the three-time Bram Stoker Award-nominated author of *Pressure, Dweller, Wolf Hunt, Fangboy*, and a bunch of others. He is also a three-time Bram Stoker Award loser, but that rarely keeps him up at night, twitching and vowing revenge against all who wronged him. Visiting his website at www.JeffStrand.com is mandatory for all who read this.

This story, "The Story of My First Kiss," was written by Jeff exclusively for The Horror Zine.

THE DEAD WALL

by Michael Wolf

I get a kick out of it, you know? No one ever gets onto me, no one that matters, anyway, and I'm making a hell of a living. I perform a live stage show of "talking to the dead," using a form of sleight-of-mind called cold reading. Some of these poor bastards actually believe they're talking to their croaked grandfather, aunt, puppy, or whatever—and that's okay. They seem happy. Happy enough to unbend their wallets, so everyone's prancing in daffodils.

So this girl came on to me after the last show. She was a cute brunette with three short lengths of beaded hair on the left side of her head and a killer body. She learned of my "supernatural abilities" from the television commercials I run before arriving in each town. She couldn't have been more than twenty-three, but these were the fruits of being a celebrity.

I started in 1973 and now it's 1988 and I'm just cruising the profiteering band-wagon. Women throw themselves at me like I'm a rock star or something. I have lost count in the last couple of years.

She wanted to talk to her deceased brother. My assistants ran her credit card information to find the funeral industry had recently bilked her for an extremely expensive burial. Looking through the obituaries of her hometown, they deduced her brother had committed suicide.

My well-oiled lines for this kind of thing soothed her pleas for details of why he killed himself. She gave me his name and he "spoke to her through me." He assured her he was in a joyous place surrounded by loved ones at peace with happy memories of her.

Yeah. And all good dogs go to Heaven.

Later, I have her backstage for a private reading. Hey, if the mortuary business can take advantage of her grief, why can't I? It's amazing what a little fame can do for you.

«‹‹—››»

So I'm heading to a gig on Texas Highway 37. Out of nowhere, the engine begins making this clanging sound like a monkey wrench in a laundromat dryer. Dammit. I just dropped a sultan's salary on this rig.

I need to get off the road so I take the next exit where a bent and shot-up sign announces the town of Finnigan, Texas. It didn't say Finnigan was seven more miles off the highway.

By the time I limp into town, the wind is picking up and I'm stuck while the local mechanic—Goober, I could swear his name was—looks at my ride.

I shield my face from blowing sand and see the only place I can wait is a bar named Gary's. I walk into the place noticing it is like an Army barracks, a lot deeper than wide, and deceptively large. I'm feeling a little nausea lately like I have the flu or something, so I figure I might get something to eat to settle my stomach.

About a dozen good-old-boys are lolling in cheap rotting upholstery to the sound of outdated country music. They tend their interests from dominoes to two tired pool tables and the liquor bar.

A wall of plaques with photographs hanging from them run to the far end of the building. There, the light bulbs are unlit, leaving the long wall fading down into darkness.

Avoiding a broken stool, I sit. At the other end of the bar is a slight, girlish form in a mocha tan sundress billowing with white flowers. Her back is to me and slight movements reflect a shivering luster off her satin black hair. She is transfixed to a TV wedged above the bar.

I had to see her face, so noticing her empty drink I ask, "Can I buy you a refill?"

"Hi." She turns and flashes a youthful smile. "You surprised me."

My surprise far outweighs hers. Her crystal Caribbean-blue eyes offset by lavish indigo hair staggers me to the core. She is a diamond amongst the dirt clods in this drunk-hut.

"I think I might get in trouble for buying a drink for an underage cutie," I say, because she is definitely a minor.

She blushes and takes a stool closer to me. "S'ok, I'm eighteen, nobody cares I'm here—I'm just drinking pop." She glances across the room. "That's Dale, the chief of police, over there." She tilts her head toward a chubby, uniformed man absorbed in a game of dominoes.

I motion to the bartender, point to her drink, and look around. "So this is the local hotspot, huh?"

"Hotspot? More like a warm stain."

I smile and offer my hand. "I'm Ricky. Ricky Peterson."

She takes it with a cool softness. "I know who you are. I seen your commercials on the TV."

She pronounces it "Tie-Vie" but that's the way they talk around here. I couldn't help but notice her being a perfect mark for a psychic reading and old enough for some "quality time" with me.

"You look thinner in person," she says.

I freeze. Time to reroute this seduction. "Well, you know television adds ten pounds." Truth be told, in the last six months I've been dropping pounds like loose change, but I figure I'll gain it back after the stress of the tour. "What's your name, farm girl?"

"Amy."

"Does your Dad live around here, Amy?"

"Used to before he died. Now he's over there." She doesn't look up or down but over my shoulder with a sour expression to the wall covered with plaques.

"No, I mean his spirit—his soul," I say, turning to look at the wall. It shows a variety of small brass memorials. They were all just names with a year inscribed below, mostly men. "What is that, anyway?"

"The Dead Wall," a baritone voice says from behind me.

I turn to see a tall, lean man holding a pool cue straight up by his side like a castle guard's pike. He is dressed in complete Old West attire. All black except for silver filigree around the edges. He has an Adam's apple sticking out like an internal elbow.

"The Dead Wall? What are you saying? I had you all pegged for Christians," I say, "Heaven or Hell, you know."

"Even Hell has its standards," goes the cowboy and spits into a floor spittoon with uncanny accuracy.

Amy snickers sourly, beyond her years. "Besides, I ain't got a post card or phone call from Heaven yet." She hooks her thumb up at the plaques. "Up there, that's something different."

So I turn around and I'm looking especially at a plaque with borders painted red and blue in the sloppy motif of a toddler. The pictures of four young children and a teenage girl adorn its edges. The inscription is simply "Jim Cadistro," dated this year. A distant bell rings from the boundaries of my brain. The name seems familiar somehow.

"This Jim fellow must have been a father or a teacher of some kind," I say as I reach out to touch the memorial. "You have to admire people like this because—"

When I touch the placard, something wonky takes place. My hand goes into the brass, breaking the skin of the metal as if it was perpendicular liquid. Something else happens. Happens to my mind. I am hearing someone.

Someone else. Someone thinking.

Animals. That's all they are.

Someone who is angry.

Yeah, they're the future of the world and all that other crap, but to me they're just life-enders.

Extremely angry.

I'm in this miserable cracker-box home a ways outta town, with a wife who insists on taking in foster children.

We need the money we get for them. I can't think of a better solution, so I shut up and sit in the smell of dirty laundry and cat piss enduring the situation. For now.

Always squalling, bawling and needing. They're like pigeons. Disease infested vermin swimming in bacteria, that's all they are.

There are five. My own two slack-eyed imbeciles, two foster booger factories whose names I can never remember, and Courtney. She started it all.

Courtney. So fresh and nubile. Fifteen years old and she don't have a clue how sexy she is. The way she talks, the way she moves, the lines of her body, all cry for the wild. But when I come to her room at night, she only pushes me away. Why doesn't she want me? And now my wife is getting suspicious.

Been a long time in the thinking and more than a few beers before I am out in the yard at three AM, dousing the siding with gasoline. They're all asleep. I quietly fix long screws in all the doors and windows, sealing them in.

One match is all it takes. The fire embraces the house. The screaming comes a few minutes later. I have my gun in case one gets out, but I'm going listen to the shrieks until they stop before I put the barrel in my mouth.

I stand outside Courtney's bedroom. I laugh while she begs and claws at her window for help.

So I'm there in the light of the fire, thinking of what they've done to me, listening to their pleas, when I see the damnedest thing. A huge image of a sitting woman, overlaid on the flames.

The woman's image competes with the fire for reality. Soon the blaze and the screams are flying away and a different world comes flickering to the forefront.

I'm at that bar. The bar in Finnigan, Texas.

"He's back," booms the cowboy, chalking his pool stick in front of himself. He makes a mocking face. "Did you have a 'ghostly experience?'"

Dizzy and out of phase with plain sight. Covered with the poison film of Jim Cadistro's insanity, I stumble to the nearest stool and accidentally put my head down in the middle of an ashtray. I raise spitting and batting the butts off my face.

Jim Cadistro. Something important about that name. Jim Cadistro. Suddenly I remember. The girl with the three short beaded braids on the left side of her head. He was her brother.

But we're a hundred miles from nowhere. This doesn't make sense, so I point to the memorial and ask, "How did you get a plaque to this guy? Did he live around here?"

Amy shrugs. She looks older somehow.

"Plaques appear all the time," she says, "and the rest just move back down to the end of the building to make room for the new ones. They move by themselves." She points to the blackness swallowing the far end of the lengthy room. "We don't ask questions and we sure as hell don't touch 'em like you did."

I watch her and the cowboy bow in private laughter.

"She had a name, you know," Amy says, who is definitely on the dark side of thirty now, "Do you even remember?"

"What?"

"Her name. The girl with the braids. You spent last night with her."

This is impossible. Amy's hair is now more pewter-grey than sable. She is aging before my eyes, and what's with the mind-reading routine?

"The girl's name is Twila Somers," Amy says into what now looks like a whiskey sour. "She works for a place called Rozer Pharmaceutical. I guess she's some kind of undiscovered genius. In five years, she's going to find a cure for AIDS. Well, she would have if you hadn't killed her."

"What are you talking about?" This is too much. "I slept with her; I didn't kill her!" As I speak, I watch Amy age into her eighties or even nineties. Her skin cracks and I see one of her fingernails fall into her drink. The cowboy by her side, who seemed fine a minute ago, now wears the sagging skin of a dying Basset hound.

"You have AIDS, Ricky Peterson," she rasps while standing. "Why do you think you've been ill lately? And losing all that weight?"

Smiling nervously, I get the shtick. "Oh, okay. This is some kind of mentalism-spook show here. You really had me going," I say, edging away. "You ought to take this on the road."

Amy grins at me, a tooth falling out of her wilting face and rattling onto the bar. Her eyes, dancing in the light of youth not a half hour before, were now milky and blind.

I back toward the door as she speaks, her skin falling away in filthy, decayed rags. "In fact, you will kill dozens because for the last two years, during the most sexual time of your life, you have been spreading this disease. You've been a taker, Ricky. A sociopath who has no empathy for others."

A jolt of 200-proof panic and my wise guy image is gone. I crack. Running back to the door, I fumble for the exit. Realizing it had changed to a realistic mural on a solid cement wall, I slump in disbelief.

I turn and suddenly see living, glistening eyes in Amy's dead skull. "And those dozens you will kill will also kill others, unaware of their condition. The numbers will keep doubling as they infect more innocents."

I look to the bartender for help but he is now only a heap of a darkly webbed substance. Frantically searching the room, I see an emaciated woman eating the guts out of a reclining Officer Dale who is unconcerned; as if he is pondering his next dominoes move.

The cowboy is standing aside with the meat of his body dropping away, splattering onto the floor in slimy chunks. Now a near-skeletal form, he says, "Time for his walk, Amy." He snatches my arm above the elbow.

I try to scream at his cold, wet touch but can only expel a squeaky chirp. Amy's peeled cadaver quickly moves forward. I try to kick at them, but it is like punching marble statues. In a blink, Amy grabs my other arm.

They drag me toward the far end of the building. Toward an inky howling nothingness. Loose paper flies by into the suction of the icy void. I screech and bawl until my face is a sheet of bubbling snot but they only join in clattering laughter. As they pull me screaming to my fate they stop and briefly point me toward something on the wall.

A plaque inscribed "Ricky Peterson" and today's date: July 12, 1988. Attached to its edge hanging sideways is a photograph of Twila Somers, smiling with life's promise.

About Michael Wolf

Michael Wolf was conceived in the 1960s during a heated game of Twister. In the fourth grade, when other children were enjoying *The Hardy Boys* or *Pipi Longstockings*, Michael was reading *The Collected Works of Edgar Allen Poe*. He spent all of his free time and money at theaters being scared out of his mind watching "Count Yorga the Vampire," " The Crimson Executioner," " The Conqueror Worm" and every other Hammer Films monster production possible.

Eventually he became a rock-n-roll guitarist, an Air Force computer technician, comic book letterer, and then a syndicated cartoonist. Returning to his roots, he is now a horror and humor writer, although some people say he achieved his scariest and most bone-chilling efforts when he attempted to sing in his band.

Though his work has appeared in scores of publications in both fiction and non-fiction from "The Washington Post" to "Rip-Off Press," the horror genre is where he finds his home. Michael currently resides in Richland, Washington where he lives in fear of vampires, existing on Pez and hot dog water.

SPICY THAI NOODLE

by Alva J. Roberts

The pounding at the door grew louder, more frenzied. A new, softer sound mixed with the pounding, and it took Kevin a moment to realize that it was his own breath panting with fear. Sweat trickled down his face as he checked his shotgun.

Three shells left.

Two for the bastards at the door and one for himself.

A hand smashed through the door panel. Strips of putrid rotted flesh caught and tore loose against the jagged wood. More hands ravaged the door; shards of withered pine breaking away. There had to be at least two dozen of them.

Kevin lifted the shotgun to his shoulder and waited. *Aim for the head.* It was the most important thing he had learned in the month since the world ended.

The door splintered into fragments and the zombies staggered through the opening. The stench of rancid flesh filled the tiny gas station bathroom as the dead lurched forward. The shotgun roared twice in rapid succession, coating the walls and ceiling with blood and brain matter.

Kevin lifted the gun to his chin, then closed his eyes, waiting for the first sickening touch of decomposing flesh. Tears stung his cheeks, cold and bitter. It was not supposed to end like this.

Before he could pull the trigger, Kevin heard a loud snapping sound. He opened his eyes. Black, fetid blood sprayed across the room as the head of one of the zombies was torn from its shoulders, its limp body falling to the floor. Something zig-zagged between the rest of the creatures, a black and white blur moving too fast for Kevin to see, and all the zombies in its path dropped over in a motionless heap.

Kevin stood with his mouth gaping. Corpses littered the floor of the gas station bathroom in a pile of nauseating, rotting flesh.

A man stood in the middle of the pile of bodies. His black clothes stood out in sharp contrast to his skin, so pale that where it was not covered in blood, it would have looked blue. His eyes possessed a strange, feral light.

Kevin took a step backward, almost more afraid of his savior than of his attackers.

"Who...no...*what* are you?" Kevin asked.

"That is an unpleasant way of thanking the guy who saved your life," the man replied, tilting his head as he spoke. He looked like a cat ready to pounce.

"I...thank you. Are you a superhero or something?"

"Perhaps, in a way. My name is John Lyman. I am a shepherd. And you will be joining my flock."

"What do you mean—" Kevin was suddenly on his back, long fangs glistening a few inches from his face. A thin line of spittle trailed its way down to land on Kevin's cheek.

"Enough prattle. I'm hungry," John said, baring his incisors.

Pain tore through Kevin's neck. It felt as if the vampire's fangs were piercing his soul. He was paralyzed, he could not move, could not even speak as the life drained from his body. The world grew darker, pulling him into a long tunnel. He was cold, numb, and thought he was dying.

«《—》»

Kevin groaned as his eyes opened. There was a worn, wooden ceiling above him, and a hard unforgiving floor beneath him. But he was alive.

"You awake? I thought John might have killed you," a woman's voice said.

As memory returned, Kevin sat up. He pulled away from the voice, not sure if he was getting ready to run away or fight. His hand darted to his neck, finding two small wounds piercing his flesh into his jugular vein. He had started with zombies and ended with a vampire. It seemed impossible.

He was in what appeared to be a shed of some kind. The walls were made from aged, untreated pine, and a few gardening tools lay scattered in the corners. Kevin felt his old fear of enclosed spaces return. He struggled for breath, hating the feeling of being trapped.

"I'm Beth. This is Harry and the one sleeping is Jessica. Welcome to the Pen."

Beth was a pretty blonde woman, maybe twenty-five years old. She wore dirty, tattered sweats.

"The Pen? We're in jail?" Kevin asked.

"Might as well be," Harry replied. He was a short, pudgy man with an unkempt gray beard. He reminded Kevin of Santa Claus.

"Harry, that's no way to talk. John keeps us..." Beth's voice trailed off as they heard a strange, crunching noise, outside of the building.

"They're outside again," Beth whispered, her voice tight with fear.

Kevin grabbed a hoe from the wall nearest him. He recognized that noise. It was the shuffle of the walking dead. The shed shook as something pounded on the walls.

"Oh, God! Not again," Jessica screamed, waking from her sleep. She curled into a ball, clasping her hands tight against her ears. "Spicy thai noodle, spicy thai noodle..." she sang to herself in a hoarse whisper. Kevin recognized the radio jingle to a local restaurant.

"She's totally lost it," Kevin said, grabbing a shovel from the corner. "Is there a way out of here?"

"You don't get it. You just don't get it!" Harry yelled. "You can go out the door, but it's worse if you do."

"He's right," Beth added. "Just leave them alone. They've never gotten in; they aren't that clever."

Great, Kevin thought. *I'm stuck in a loony bin.*

One of the boards on the wall cracked. Splinters flew through the air.

"I thought you just said they can't get in! We need to leave here! Now!" Kevin shouted, running for the door.

"No way. No freaking way," Harry said stepping back. "Look at Jessica. She has three doctorates, she used to be a college professor. She tried escaping and look what happened to her!"

"Spicy thai noodle, get your spicy thai noodle todaaaay..." Jessica sang, rocking on the floor, drool bubbling at the corners of her mouth.

"She's obviously had some kind of break with reality, but if we stay here, we die," Kevin shouted, moving for the door. "I won't be a prisoner in your death Pen."

"It's only an hour till sunset. We'll be fine then," Harry said, sounding unsure. "And besides, John bit you. That means he can track you when he wakes up."

"We have guns," Beth suddenly said.

"Guns?" Kevin asked.

She moved a tarp that sat in a remote corner of the floor. A pile of guns and ammunition lay underneath. It was a motley collection that looked as if someone had gathered all the weapons in the nearby town and thrown them into the pile.

"Why didn't you guys tell me about these? I don't see how John kept you captive with all these weapons."

"They can't hurt Johnny. Can't hurt him. Or his spicy thai noodle..." Jessica started to sing the jingle over again.

Kevin picked up a shotgun and two Glocks, shoving them in the waistband of his dirty, faded, jeans. He stuffed his pockets with more ammunition. Beth looked uncertain, but bent down to the pile and picked up a rifle and an old Colt that looked like a prop from an old western movie.

"You leave and I'm locking that door behind you!" Harry screamed.

Kevin answered by opening the door and running out of the shed. He was surprised to hear Beth following a few steps behind. Zombies were all around, stumbling toward them. The corpse of an elderly woman in a flower-print sundress raised her wrinkled, decaying arms. She shuffled forward on broken, mangled legs.

Kevin aimed and fired the shotgun, the recoil numbing his hands. The old woman's head exploded in a dark red cloud of blood. The shotgun blasted again and again. Beth's rifle coughed in rapid succession, dropping three of the creatures.

When the dead walked, everyone became a marksman.

The shotgun ran out of shells, so Kevin swung it like a club, and heard the satisfying crack of a skull being smashed. He dropped the empty gun, and pulled out both of the Glocks, gripping one in each hand. They were almost through the macabre mob that surrounded the shed. The scene was bathed in an orange light. Harry had been right; the sun was starting to set.

Kevin made it past the last of the creatures and sprinted ahead, risking a glance over his shoulder. Beth was right behind him. Her rifle was gone but she held the Colt with both hands.

It was not safe in the open. They needed a place to hide and to plan their next move. In a world full of zombies and vampires, spontaneity could get you killed.

350

Kevin saw an old farmhouse not far from the shed, but figured it would be the first place John would look. A small forest surrounded the barren fields, next to the house.

"Beth, do you know where we are? Is there a place we could hole up for the night?"

"When we tried to escape with Jessica, we found a road. It must to lead somewhere. If we go east through the woods we should be able to find it," Beth replied. She seemed dazed, and only half aware of her words.

"Okay." He was not sure if going the same route Jessica had taken was the smartest plan, but he did not have any better ideas.

The dark forest was ominous and silent, with shadows stretching long as the sun set. Kevin slowed to a jog as they entered the wooded area. The sweat on his forehead began to dry in the cool breeze of early spring. The forest was alive with new growth, the dense foliage adding to Kevin's sense of security. Maybe they would get away.

Kevin paused when they reached a thick wall of hedges. After a moment of hesitation, he pushed through the green barrier, tiny branches scraping and scratching his exposed skin.

Kevin stopped. "Did you know this was here?"

"No, we didn't notice it the last time," Beth said with a puzzled expression.

In front of them was a cemetery. It looked old; many of the tombstones were broken and cracked. But fresh mounds of earth only partially covered with grass told Kevin that the place was still in use. A huge mausoleum dominated the center of the grave yard.

"If we cut through here, we should be able to find a road. It's a cemetery, after all. There's got to be a road. Watch for zombies, because some of the graves look new," Kevin said. He started to sweat again.

They made their way through the maze of grave markers in silence, moving with soft steps, as if a hard footfall would awaken the bodies resting below the ground.

A pair of hands burst through the soil next to Kevin, reaching for his leg. He aimed his Glock at the jumbled soil. He jumped backwards when the monster's head burst from the ground. Kevin squeezed the trigger and a bullet hole punctured the face between the zombie's eyes.

More filthy, decaying hands thrust upward through the soil, scratching at the dirt. The ground was hard and unyielding, slowing the animated corpses' rise to the surface.

The next thing Kevin knew, he was flying through the air, and smashed into a thick, granite tombstone. A fiery pain burned through his arm and into his shoulder. He fell onto his back, and realized he was staring at John.

John had tracked him, just as Harry had said.

"My foolish sheep, I cannot feed on these rotting corpses. There aren't a lot of humans left in the world any more. What would I do if you had gotten caught by those walking corpses?" He turned his attention to Beth. "Elizabeth, I am quite disappointed in you. There can be some excuses made for our newest lamb but you know the rules."

"It was all his idea!" Beth shrieked.

Kevin sat up, his whole body throbbing with pain. Blood ran down his left arm, flowing from where a jagged shard of bone protruded from his bicep. John hunched over Beth's trembling figure, his head nestled in the hollow where her shoulder met her neck. Beth's fingers twitched and her feet kicked.

"Leave her alone, you bastard!" Kevin shouted, emptying his Glock into the vampire's back.

A hand spouted from the ground near Kevin, dirt spraying into the air. It reached out to grab his injured arm, raking at him with decayed claws. Kevin screamed as he felt the flesh in his arm ripping. He brought down the empty gun onto the zombie's hand, smashing the small bones in its fingers. He jerked away from the zombie digging its way from its grave and leaned against a nearby headstone, his eyes darting back to the vampire.

But John was gone. Beth lay on the ground, unmoving, her long blonde hair splayed out beneath her like a golden fan. Her chest and throat were covered in crimson, and most of her neck was gone.

Where was John?

Suddenly an icy-cold hand gripped Kevin's good arm, answering that question. John had reappeared as if from nowhere; his blood-smeared face was just inches from Kevin's own. Kevin could smell the coppery stink of fresh blood on John's breath. The vampire's eyes seemed to twirl and shimmer in the moonlight, and Kevin could not help but look into the spinning orbs.

Kevin felt John's mind forcing itself into his. He felt icy tentacles grip his soul as the world around him fell away. Kevin's brain felt like it was made of glass, and just a few seconds later it shattered, the jagged shards of his mind tearing through his entire being.

«««—»»»

He felt the hard wood of the shed's floor beneath him. He could not move, could not speak, a prisoner in his own body. A low moan escaped his lips, then nothing.

He could hear John's voice say, "Harry, I am glad to see that at least one of my flock appreciates my protection. See to his needs. Beth will not be returning."

John disappeared in a blur of motion.

"I told you not to go," Harry said, wiping the spittle that dribbled from the corner of Kevin's mouth.

Kevin tried to form a reply, tried to tell Harry to kill him, but could not spit out the words. Instead he heard himself sing in a hoarse whisper "Spicy thai noodle, get your spicy thai noodle…"

About Alva J. Roberts

Alva J. Roberts (pronounced Al-Vee J. Roberts) lives in Western Nebraska with his wife and dog. When he is not writing, he works as librarian and helps his wife with Pill Hill Press. For a full listing of his published works and a few free stories visit: http://alvajroberts.blogspot.com.

THE TIDE CLOCK

by James Strauss

Carper was sitting on his back porch, enjoying the cool breeze of the evening, and wishing he still smoked when it began. That woman's laughter, shrieking from the house next door, reacting to everything her two male companions said. Loud, phony, piercing the night. A large family of summer people owned the house, various groups would stop by for a night, a weekend or a week throughout the summer.

In winter it was silent. He loved winter. Carper had moved to the Grove nine years ago, after a twenty-year marriage that didn't have the will to make twenty-one.

The community was quiet, perched atop a sixty foot cliff at the northernmost part of the Chesapeake Bay. He had fallen in love with the beauty of the place instantly. He found a house for sale cheap on the first gravel road by the bay, not waterfront, but you could see the ships heading for the Chesapeake and the Delaware Canal from the living room. The place was a dump, but it felt like home.

He immediately became seduced by the quiet of the Grove, quiet now being ruined by that cacophonous shrieking laughter. This particular threesome, the two men and the woman came by once a year, always started a fire and drank outside at night. The men would murmur, the woman would respond to everything they said like a laugh track. A loud, harsh laugh track. The men could not possibly be that funny.

He grabbed a leash and checked the tide clock, an extravagant gift from his girlfriend Kimberly who lived in the nearby town of Galena. The clock was custom made with a map of the Grove on its face. He needed a break from the noise and Cruiser would love a walk on the beach.

The tide clock indicated that the tide was low and high tide was beginning. Until high tide fully arrived, there would be enough beach for a nice stroll at dusk. Cruiser, a large Doberman that Carper found marooned in the local SPCA, loved the water and was instantly alert at the sound of the leash.

The beach was the most unusual feature of The Grove. On summer days, there would be almost no place to park a chair or blanket. Families with children would descend on the beach like locusts, but at all other times it was deserted, except for Carper and Cruiser who made daily treks along the rocky shoreline morning, noon and night. The tide clock became a necessity, as high tide would completely engulf the beach and lap against the base of the cliff.

One local told Carper that the cliff lost a foot a year to erosion and he had seen himself how trees at the top would begin to show root, then more, finally tumbling into the water below. The process took years and walking under them always gave him a chill. Once humbled, they would start another descent to the water, held aloft for a time by branches, horizontal and sinking down slowly. The small ones could be climbed over, the larger ones needed to be crawled under as long as there were branches intact to hold the trunk off the ground. The cycle was endless and at any time, once proud maples and sycamores would be in slow collapse, teetering or sinking into the bay.

The thick maple that now blocked the north shore path had fallen six months ago after years of predicting it's own demise. Since it hit the beach, Carper and Cruiser had been first walking, then stooping, and now crawling under the space between the thick branches still supporting the old fellow. Its leaves were full and green, believing themselves still vertical and thriving. Fifty or sixty feet of the tree was submerged in the bay and fifty or sixty feet lay prone and suspended across the beach to the cliff where its roots dangled uselessly.

Carper let Cruiser off the leash and the dog methodically began checking his pee mail and leaving messages of his own. He disappeared under the fallen maple and Carper crawled under to join him, heading north toward the Turkey Point lighthouse, which hovered on a faraway cliff facing the Elk River.

The tide was coming in but there was time for a quick trip north before becoming stranded by the incoming Chesapeake. They picked their way cautiously over the rocky beach and surprised a pair of buzzards eating a beached channel catfish.

After reaching a spot made impassable by the tide, they turned around back south to home. They came to the old tree while an orange sun lit the clouds and began lowering itself into the waterline to the west. Cruiser splashed under the tree and Carper cursed to himself, realizing that he would have to crawl through the rising tide to get by. At fifty-six, he wasn't as spry as he remembered himself to be and awkwardly executed an imperfect split to stay above the water.

His left leg cleared the trunk, pointing clumsily forward; but then his body wedged against the trunk and his right leg extended painfully backward while Cruiser wagged his tail-nub and smiled at his owner's contortion.

A cursing Carper heard a low groan, then a dull crack and the great trunk lowered itself onto his back in slow motion. Something popped warmly in his left knee as the groaning tree settled again on what was left of the broken limb.

His body was pinned in the most painful posture the Devil could sketch and the trunk pushed the breath from his lungs. Every inch of him was achingly stretched, tearing or crushed and an ancient panic began confusing the parts of his brain that weren't dealing with the pain. He could move his head a little, but that was the only part of him responding to his will to move.

He tried to scream as he felt ribs cracking in his chest. No scream would come, just a foamy red gurgle of blood through his lips. He heard the dog wandering off as the gentle tide splashed against his nose. His lifeless arms, extending on either side of the tons of lumber refused to dig or push or pull or make any attempt to free him.

Incoherent bubbling moans escaped his lips and his body felt impaled by thick wires of pain, cutting through flesh and bone, an agony building beyond any he could've imagined. He prayed for death, *please Lord take me quickly, end the pain, I want nothing but death, now, now, please.*

The darkness thickened around him and the slow rising tide began to enter his lungs and return, pink and frothy to the bay. He could feel muscles popping loudly, hotly in his right leg as his body sought relief from the pressure from above. He heard a fish slap the water feeding on night insects. And the pain became fire.

Please Lord, now, please, now! his terrified mind screamed over and over and over. A muscle in his neck popped loudly and a new torment began. The water was ringing his face and receding, surrounding, receding in an arrhythmic dance. He tasted the excrement of fish and crabs, the metallic tang of underwater rock, the bitter funk of algae entering and exiting his lungs. He heard Cruiser splashing in the water a world away and still so close.

Snap, another rib buckled and ripped into flesh and lung. *Please Lord, now, please now.* His breathing was now like gargling and his eyes were underwater. The pain left his right leg and reappeared in his broken hips. Up on the cliff he heard a car crunching gravel. Something alive, brittle, timeless and unseen made small tears in the skin of his neck.

He thought of Kimberly. He thought of his mother, he thought of his son. A dull white light became all of his vision as the water playfully lapped up to his ears and away again. The pain was now unified, indistinct from the water, the air, the sand in his lungs. The pain promised to ease and lied. The huge trunk, rolled slightly by the tide, went over him like a rolling pin on dough. He bubbled, he gurgled, he ached, he prayed.

Somewhere off in the distance he heard shrieking laughter as he bubbled a silent scream into the rising waters of the Chesapeake. Back at home the tide clock inched towards High.

About James Strauss

James Strauss is a retired blues guitarist and unretired biochemist. He's written a lot of music but this is only his second short story. He lives in Earleville, Maryland on the Chesapeake Bay and "The Tide Clock" is a recurring nightmare.

ARTICLES

AND

INTERVIEWS

JOHN GILMORE TELLS US ABOUT HOLLYWOOD'S DARK SIDE

An article from someone who knew Elizabeth Short and Marilyn Monroe Personally

They called her the Black Dahlia the year before she was tortured, murdered and cut in half; her name was Elizabeth Short. I'd see Elizabeth in my dreams: she'd come in and out of like a song you keep hearing after its long-finished playing, just kind of floats around in your head. I remember squatting before my grandmother's upright Underwood, typing a vow: since I'd never be able to marry her because she was dead, I swore to whatever unseen spirit hovering over me that I'd never forget her or the kiss she gave me, no matter that I was only eleven years old.

But what could I do about the secret? I still had to keep it. My grandmother made me cross my heart and hope to die if I mentioned to my father that the murdered girl had visited the house that October afternoon just days before Halloween. She came accompanied by two guys, both gay-blade movie extras and friends of my grandmother's boarder. Elizabeth was dressed all in black, a black veil draped from her black-feathered hat, cheeks rouged but her skin almost white as chalk. She wore very sheer black stockings, a stark seam down the backs of her legs, and high-heels with open toes showing the red nail polish through the dark nylon.

As though it was yesterday, I can see her standing by the dining room table, flexing her fingers in those black kid-leather gloves that went half up her arms, asking my grandmother about a cousin named Adel Short—something like that—a cousin she was trying to find. Half of the family on my grandmother's sister's side had produced a swarm of Shorts populating what seemed like half of Los Angeles.

My grandmother didn't think she knew the girl Elizabeth was trying to get in contact with, and I remember my grandmother on the phone, calling her sister. "Adeline Short?" my grandmother asked. One of the Short girls, but no one named Adel—or whatever it was.

Elizabeth glanced at me as I stood by the dining room cabinets, actually admiring her, and she gave a smile that probably made me blush. Bright red lips, and her pale blue eyes seemed bright as lights. She was the prettiest lady I'd seen—even better looking than some of the movie extra girls often hanging around.

There were always movie people around because my step-grandfather was a head carpenter at RKO. My mother was never around because she'd been divorced from my father since I was six months old, and my dad was a frustrated actor who became an important Los Angeles police officer. Even Adeline Short was pretty, and so were sisters Gladys and Sally, who were blonde, but Elizabeth had a movie star sort of look, and told my grandmother she'd come to Hollywood to work in pictures. My grandmother mentioned that I'd done some radio work as well as giving a magic show. Elizabeth seemed impressed and I invited her to see the magic posters in my bedroom.

I showed her ones of famous magicians I'd seen performing at the Shrine Auditorium, like the great Harry Blackstone who'd made someone disappear right from beside him on the stage. "Magic is fascinating," I remember Elizabeth saying. "It lives in the shadows...It must be a thrill to know you can make somebody disappear right in front of your eyes..."

She told me she wanted to be an actress, but not just an "ordinary actress." She said it was in her heart to become a star. I recall her saying, "That is the only thing that will make me happy."

Smiling, she asked if I had ever seen a Barbara La Marr film? I hadn't. She told me La Marr had been a silent screen star, and Elizabeth said she'd been told she looked like her. La Marr had died years ago, but very young, and Elizabeth said, "My birthday is almost the same date as Barbara La Marr's birthday," though a number of years before Elizabeth's.

She sat on the edge of the bed and I showed her the little printed flyers for my few amateur magic performances. I showed her pictures taken of me in a police safety film made by my father's LAPD group, and told her I too wanted to be an actor and be in the movies. I said my mother, who lived a couple blocks away, had worked in movies at

MGM, and wanted to be a star. I remember Elizabeth's soft, understanding laugh, and I could see her teeth.

I can still see her teeth. That was some sixty-five years ago, and I can still see her teeth.

She said something about having to find her cousin, stood up as if to gather herself and the black handbag that looked like braided material. She said, "Well, maybe we'll all be movie stars," and then leaned forward and kissed me on the forehead. It was like a gentle arrow going into my brain. They drove off in an old Packard, her in the backseat. She raised her hand to wave goodbye to me on the porch, but it wasn't really a wave—she just placed the palm of her black-gloved hand on the glass.

Two and a half months later, her naked body was found in a vacant lot, gouged, cut in half at the waist, the two halves of her corpse displayed face up, legs spread.

My father and his partner in their black-and-white radio car, circled the vacant, weed-ridden blocks, then went on foot, going house to house, asking if anyone had seen anything strange or unusual, or had they heard any screams in the night?

I'd never said anything to my father about the girl visiting the house. He lived in an apartment behind my grandmother's house with his second wife—someone I did not like—so for years I said nothing about the murdered girl, but upon my grandmother's death, I told him. "That girl known as the Black Dahlia," I said, "the victim in what the newspapers used to call L.A's most sensational murder—yet to be solved... She was here at the house, but my grandmother asked me not to mention it."

My father said he understood. See, he already knew. The movie-extra friends of the boarder who had brought her to assist in locating her relative had told him about her visit.

Those two guys have long since vanished or died. I look back to the photo slides of those years and check off all that has disappeared. How many funerals have there been? And still that music circles slowly in my head, but I no longer dream about the suicide bridge in Pasadena, or about Elizabeth approaching me slowly over a hump in the center of the bridge—some hinge that didn't really exist. I'd be walking towards that hump, in slow motion, getting nowhere. The dream would then crumble, disintegrate like old newspaper falling off a plaster wall.

Most people who'd been vital to me in some way are gone—maybe dead, like Elizabeth had said about disappearing…right in front of your eyes. Way back, I sometimes accompanied my father to dinner at Rudy's Italian Restaurant on Crenshaw by 39th and Norton. I remember us walking across the boulevard at night, the headlights almost blinding us, then climbing through weeds in the vacant lot where her body had been found. I'd felt hollowed, scared that I'd see her blood on the ground. I didn't want to see any blood, but there wasn't blood underfoot. Just every so often there'd be a crunching of the spent, blackened flashbulbs from police and news photographers' cameras.

The next six or so years, long after Elizabeth's body was fitted into a coffin and buried in Oakland, her unsolved murder was as cold as when the ice man pushes the big chunk into your ice box. I'd become the young actor—a nightclub hopper from Chasen's to the Trocadero, to Mocambo and Ciro's—a potential star dressed white on white, but with empty pockets. I had mentors in Ida Lupino and John Hodiak, and though I'd done some movies and tested at Fox, both mentors suggested I hit out of Hollywood—get a Broadway play and be brought back a success. Hodiak also introduced me to a neighbor, an odd, young angel named Marilyn Monroe, who told me the same thing: "Go to New York."

I met Marilyn Monroe again at one of Wynn Rocamora's parties. He was my agent at the time, a very powerful figure in the industry. Though she had a few years on me, both of us had been born in L.A.'s General Hospital Charity Ward, both estranged from family situations, and lonely despite the flash of the fast lane racing past. She was like finding a kindred spirit in a pile of busted wood washed ashore. Marilyn told me that if she had the chance—laughed and said maybe if she had the guts—she'd skedaddle her butt straight to Broadway and land a play.

Within a parade of faces back and forth between Hollywood and New York, I found another kindred friend in a young actor named James Dean. We hung out all over New York, and within a year he was on his way to Hollywood to make a movie that'd shake the city. He'd make two more pictures and then die at twenty-four, racing a sports car half across the desert.

Back in New York, Tennessee Williams told me I should be a writer. He gave me a weird pair of lizard-skin shoes from Cuba that he said hurt his feet. At this same time, Marilyn Monroe was in New York after walking out on a movie. She holed up at the Actors Studio where I was transcribing Lee Strasberg's obtuse lectures for a book he planned to publish. A mutual friend was Susan Strasberg, daughter of Lee, the so-called "guru," but a failure as a father to Susan.

Marilyn told me the same thing that Tennessee had told me: "You should be a writer," then followed it with, "I wish I could really write…" Howard Austin—Gore Vidal's secretary and my theatrical manager—said the same thing: I should write instead of "waltzing past the footlights."

After doing theatre and television, I wound up at the Beat Hotel in Paris. William Burroughs introduced me to his publisher who wanted a novel I'd written. I got to know François Sagan—a busy mind, then Brigitte Bardot—busy in other ways.

I went to Egypt on a movie deal—not acting, but writing the script. I met a beautiful Egyptian actress who showed me mummies and monuments, and the back streets of Cairo. The movie became one of many I'd be paid to write—a rollercoaster familiar to many writers: you're paid but the movie is never made. Their cup doth not runneth over.

Hollywood again and I did TV shows back-to-back, a couple of moves at Fox, then starred in the L.A. production of the William Inge play, *A Loss of Roses*. Jerry Wald was producing the film—calling it *A Woman of Summer*. Via William Morris, I was up for the lead, opposite Marilyn who was back in the midst of another picture. We'd meet in the back of a tiny coffee shop in Beverly Hills and talk, or have a conference at Fox with Wald and his associate, my good friend Curtis Harrington. Martin Ritt was supposed to direct the movie.

The film ran into a temporary dead-end the day Marilyn died. She was only thirty-six and disappeared from a drug overdose. Her spirit just vanished. Another friend, Joanne Woodward, did the movie as "homage" to Marilyn, but the production stalled, then revamped and Martin Ritt wasn't doing it, and I was out of it.

It was the last straw, as they say. You're almost at the top of the mountain when the landslide hits. I figured that maybe I had better start listening to people's suggestions about becoming a writer.

I wrote quickie novels to get off the mountain. Didn't call them fine literature, but I was inside my own head, no longer "waltzing past the footlights." I'd started working on a big novel set in those Cairo backstreets, when novelist Bernie Wolfe asked me to do legwork for him on a piece for Playboy. A young guy, Charles Schmid, had murdered three girls and buried their bodies in the Arizona desert. They said he'd also murdered a teenage boy, cut off his hands and buried him as well. We were on our way to cover the first murder trial—for two of the girls—while Schmid was being held in Pima County Jail. Bernie knew I had ways of worming into people, and said he'd pay for whatever I dig out of Schmid's friends. He said, "Promise them anything—just get a scoop."

We flew to Tucson where I wormed into the killer's pals and a legion of young girls who were Schmid's "fans." Many things were told to me in confidence, especially from his almost-teenage wife. Their Mexican wedding had come after the murders. So I had to skirt some issues when I laid the stuff out for Wolfe. I told him there were things I couldn't reveal as I'd sworn silence. I said it wouldn't have been ethical.

He fired me.

I flew back to Hollywood, scraped up enough to complete the job on my own and caught the next plane back. Schmid, labeled "the pied piper of Tucson" in Life magazine and almost every media outlet in the country, had refused to testify. His trial ended with two death sentences. I'd made inroads into Schmid during the trail, and next was a post-trial meeting at the jail. He was to make me his personal manager and gave me his story on a platter—not blood-stained since his victims were strangled.

Soon as the Pied Piper was sent to sit on Death Row in Arizona State Prison, awaiting murder trial number two, I moved temporarily to Tucson and spent the next two months involved, at the killer's request, in piecing together his life story—more a task of sorting the fact from the fiction. Again at his request, I brought F. Lee Bailey into the case. Bailey did a lot of fussing over money with Schmid's parents, but the bucks weren't to be had. He nonetheless took the case, gave a good show since the body of the third girl had never been found, but bailed out soon as he realized the prosecutor wasn't the "desert hick" he'd imagined. Bailey saw himself headed nowhere, not a pretty picture, and since Schmid already had two death sentences, a fight wasn't going to make a whole lot of difference. They'd gas him anyway.

When it was all over, Schmid showed the law where he'd buried the third body—a beautiful teenage girl. He even helped dig up her skeleton. A kind of good will gesture. The rumored fourth body was never found, and Schmid was shanked in prison. Despite being stabbed repeatedly in the chest and head, one thrust directly into an eyeball, it took Schmid ten days to die.

I began work on the book, slithering and slipping in a legal swamp and a killer's wild flights of imagination. And then it happened. Tom Neal, star of the noir classic, *Detour*, called me about the Black Dahlia.

My stomach twittered. She rushed back into my head. He had "a sweet deal," Tom said, to do a movie with himself as the lead detective on the case, and with connections via my father's LAPD bigwigs, we'd "cinch it up" and "come out smiling."

Elizabeth was once again in my life, once more in my dreams. I could smell the same perfume; hear that rustle of her stockings when her legs brushed together. I didn't like the idea of writing a movie about her, seemed wrong, but once I read the autopsy report that pointed up her inability to bear children or fulfill herself sexually, and after I got to know a couple girls she'd roomed with briefly, the lure to know more drew me in so deep I wondered if I'd ever get out. I just didn't want it to turn to quicksand.

I liked Tom—he could've been truly a big star, along with Barbara Payton. But the heady indulgences between the two somehow birthed a third form like a kind of freak shadow that destroyed them both. She became a wino whore after washing out a $5,000-a-week movie contract, though Tom at least began managing a Palm Springs hotel restaurant, and had married a pretty girl with class.

I was way into it with cops and cops' pals and those living in L.A.'s gopher holes who wouldn't even give you a name, when Tom got all wired, said it had nothing to do with me or the project, and raced off to shoot his pretty wife in the head with a .45.

Prison, of course. His so-called backer, who no longer wanted to make a movie, was a reclusive wacko sitting on three-million bucks in Barstow, California. I visited him. He wanted to touch the bottoms of my feet because I'd walked on the ground where the Black Dahlia's body had been found. He said, the Black Dahlia murder was a dead issue—an "antique" unsolved that nobody cared about. Nobody'd want to see a movie about Elizabeth Short, and nobody'd read a book about her.

I went on to publish *The Tucson Murders* with Dial Press in New York, my first major hardcover, following a commitment with another publisher to explore the life and crimes of Charles Manson and his so-called 'Family.' That resulted in *The Garbage People*.

Apart from talking to Manson himself, though crazy as he seemed, and others in the case, it was pin-pointedly Susan Atkins who sort of telescoped into the heads of these walking or crawling monsters. Susan was only too eager to talk murder—the bloodier it was the better she liked it. She gave me a sense of true horror the way her eyes glowed, and that slow-motion flickering of a smile as she spoke about of her desire to cut the unborn baby from Sharon Tate's womb for a barbeque with Charlie.

No sooner was *The Garbage People* published than Manson's right-hand killer, Bobby Beausoleil, the handsome ex-star of Kenneth Anger's *Lucifer Rising*, contacted me to visit him on San Quentin's Death Row.

We spent two days skirting the details of the smothering and stabbing murder for which Bobby had received a death sentence. His strange tale served me to rewrite for a later, updated edition: *Manson: The Unholy Trail of Charlie & the Family*.

Next, my Hollywood literary agent contracted for a novelized book on the Zodiac murders. It was signed for hardcover but the publisher decided to rush it in paperback. I opted out. I wouldn't have done if I knew they were going for a mass-market paperback instead of a hardcover. I didn't return the advance—no waltzing past footlights.

I settled back to work on the Egyptian novel, but my agent had a deal for a memoir on James Dean. A publisher had a book on Dean by another writer, but hadn't contracted yet. They'd throw that out and do mine because I'd been a friend of his. I didn't want to write it. I'd never even wanted to talk about Jimmy. But the offer was good: I was married, I had a daughter. I did the book and it sold one-hundred-fifty-six-thousand copies.

The money didn't sew up a tear in the marriage. We divorced and I realized I had nowhere to go, except to get out of L.A. Head back to New York? San Francisco? Cairo?

I took an apartment briefly behind Grauman's Chinese Theatre, thumbed through offerings from art colonies and decided once again to "Get the Fuck Out of Hollywood." Years would go by before I'd appreciate the stupidity of that point-of-view.

I'd been born and raised in Hollywood, a native son with the bitch goddess forever offering me the sweet nectar of her Jayne Mansfield-like bosom.

It would take a while to go home. In fact, two more marriages, another child—a son—a heavy two year live-in romance with a stand-in Marilyn; a life in Louisiana and gathering all I could about Bonnie and Clyde (her middle name Elizabeth, and like Marilyn and Elizabeth Short, Bonnie could never have children). another life in New Mexico with a third wife and after that divorce, the journey home—to Hollywood, but then to find the love/hate relationship I'd carried for Los Angeles was missing.

I could say to myself I no longer have to say I yearn to be home but there isn't any home to go to: I am home. Doesn't matter whatever else, and not to look at all that's passed in some light other than is bright. The memories are delicious.

Seventeen years ago I finished my book on Elizabeth, *Severed: The True Story of the Black Dahlia*, the first ever book on the real case, about the real person. The hack bandwagon followed (of course), and since then the world has become decorated with the Black Dahlia. There are many editions of my book, translations, and it has never gone out of print. I do not have an exact count of how many copies have sold. *Severed* is one of more than a dozen I've written, including one I said I'd never write—*Inside Marilyn Monroe*. Too close to the belt, and so, so radically different from the general mindset on anything "Marilyn."

Movie star Mamie Van Dorn, who I've known since the late 50's at Universal, once asked me if I was in love with a dead woman. I was so "locked up with it," she said, the same as she thought about my "forty year silence over Marilyn...after she died." Mamie said she loved the book I'd written on the Black Dahlia, and then the memoir about Marilyn, but said both were "heavy with implication..." Of course I said no, no, that wasn't it. But I didn't believe myself, and had to ask, if Mamie's wrong, then what was it?

I'm a guest speaker at the Marilyn Memorials, and have been the past four years. And then there's the big one: the 50th. Everybody is coming from everywhere; can you believe that Marilyn has been dead fifty years? I will not be doing any more Memorials after that. My outward participation will have come to an end. So now, it's back to the

Egyptian memoirs, to the mummies and monuments and the backstreets of Cairo...

About John Gilmore

Described by the Sydney Morning Herald as the "quintessential L.A. noir writer," and "one of America's most revered noir writers," John Gilmore has been internationally acclaimed for his hard-boiled true crime books, his literary fiction and Hollywood memoirs. *LAID BARE: A Memoir of Wrecked Lives & the Hollywood Death Trip*, has been called, "one of the best books ever on Hollywood," (Marshall Terrill). His memoir, *Inside Marilyn Monroe*, based on his friendship with the screen legend, candidly reveals her unhappy background and her struggle to the pinnacle of movie stardom, while laying the groundwork for her premature demise.

Gilmore's following spans the globe from London to Tokyo, from Hong Kong to Hollywood. Son of a former actress, and a Los Angeles police officer father, Gilmore was born in Los Angeles and raised in Hollywood. He has traveled the road to fame in many guises: kid actor, stage and motion picture player, painter, poet, screenwriter, low-budget film director, journalist, true crime writer and literary novelist. He has headed the writing program at Antioch University, and has taught and lectured extensively, having made an incomparable contribution in true crime literature. Gilmore now lives in the Hollywood Hills where he is at work on two more books.

JOE R. LANSDALE TALKS ABOUT WHEN HE LEARNED TO FIND HIS SOUTHERN VOICE

And Ardath Mayhar showed him how

I loved Ardath Mayhar like an aunt. We knew each other for years...thirty-five or thirty-six, I think. She was the first writer I ever met.

I read a story of hers in an Alfred Hitchcock anthology, and it took place in East Texas and was written in East Texas vernacular, and at that point my life changed. I was already writing, but I was trying to write like a New Yorker or someone from Los Angles, and in that moment, when I read "Crawfish," my brain switched and went South where I belonged. I've always thought career-wise that there were some major turning points for me, and my reading of "Crawfish" was in some ways the second most important.

The most important was that growing up, I read everything I could get my hands on, and that was pretty much everyone. Twain and London and Kipling made me want to write, and Edgar Rice Burroughs (who isn't the writer the others are, but is an eleven year old boy's greatest writer) set me on fire and *made* me have to write.

And then along came Ardath's story and I knew which way to go as a writer. It took me a little longer to get there than I expected, finding my own voice, I mean. Southern writers like Flannery O'Conner, Faulkner (a little), Carson McCuller, Capote, and Harper Lee bumped me over even more. I warmed myself in their smoke, then built my own fires from my own native materials.

Back then, I was living with my wife in a rundown farm house out in the sticks, and doing farm work to survive. I was reading and writing in a journal, now thankfully lost, about our time doing truck cropping and trying to survive. I planned for that to be my first book, a non-fiction book. I sold a few articles that I would have incorporated into it, but that book never happened.

369

What I really wanted to do was write fiction. I was reading a ton of it between getting up at the crack of dawn to do farm work, and then dead tired, I would still come home to more writing and finishing up about eight at night. Karen and I would read in bed until ten thirty, then I would get up and write till midnight, then back at the farm work, repeat and rinse.

Everything I wrote was awful. I had been trying to write about things I didn't know and people who lived in places I had never been, and about things I had never experienced.

And then I read that story, "Crawfish" by Ardath Mayhar, and things changed. Hers was an East Texas voice, at least in that story, and it was not too unlike my own real voice. From then on, I knew what to do.

So here is my advice for new and upcoming writers: write what you know, write what you are, and write where you are. The authenticity will come out, and the *heart* of your story will show.

Anyway, my wife and I met in Nacogdoches, and I had been doing farm work there while she and I went to the University, and then we moved to Starrville to another farm house, and did some serious farm work there, and then we moved back to Nacogdoches, where we both still live.

Without realizing it, Karen and I had moved from the very place where Ardath lived. I think she had been living in Oregon before that, but East Texas was her home, and she had come back. At that time, our paths had yet to cross. Of course, I didn't know that, because I didn't know Ardath back then. I knew that story and I knew that name, but for some reason I thought it was a man's name.

I don't remember exactly how Ardath and I met, but when I arrived back in Nacogdoches, someone told me about her, and I called her, and we met, and have been friends ever since. We founded a writer's club together that lasted for about twenty years. Gone now. Most of the writers moved off, some dead, some no longer writing. But during that time Ardath and I became close friends.

When we met, she had sold a few stories and lots of poetry. She was trying to break into novels. She was one of the most natural writers I've ever known. She had a gift for writing readable, correct prose at the drop of a hat. She was a great aid to me, and is the only one of two writers I can personally give credit to having helped me understand my style and develop it. The other was a friend of mine named Jeff Banks,

370

a literary professor who read my manuscripts and advised me. He wrote articles about genre fiction, and had one novel published under the name Rufus Jefferson.

I remember how excited I was when Ardath sold her first novel to Doubleday. I don't remember what year that was, but I know it wasn't long after that I sold my first two novels a week apart. The first was a pen name novel, the second was *Act of Love*. I had already sold quite a few short stories, but when those two novels were sold, I was able to stop working as a janitor.

Oh! I forgot to mention this one, didn't I? I got that janitor job as soon as we moved to Nacogdoches. Funny how things change in life. I was a janitor in the very University buildings where I now teach creative writing and screenplay courses from time to time. I might also add that I never did get my degree, and long ago gave it up.

I was doing, and am still doing what I want to do, and I have Ardath Mayhar to thank for much of it.

In fact, Ardath was close to my entire family. We went to conventions together, and when we were both working to establish ourselves as writers (she had already been published a little, as I said, both as short story writer and poet) and we grumbled at the publishing world together. We talked at least an hour daily for years. Later, we spoke to each other less due to my raising children, and her husband being ill, but we always kept in contact.

I loved her dearly. She was such an inspiration. I like to think we shared inspiration with one another. She was more like an aunt than a friend.

Ardath passed away in the early morning hours of February 1, 2012.

Her death has been washing over me as I sit here, and it's a sad and painful wash. But she was not in good shape toward the end. She told me just the week before she died that she was ready to go. That she didn't mind at all. She told me she loved me and my family. I told her the same. And I do. And I always will.

About Joe R. Lansdale

Joe R. Lansdale is the multi-award winning author of thirty novels and over two hundred short stories, articles and essays. He has written screenplays, teleplays, comic book scripts, and occasionally teaches creative writing and screenplay writing at Stephen F. Austin State University. He has received The Edgar Award, The Grinzani Prize for Literature, seven Bram Stoker Awards, and many others.

His stories "Bubba Ho-Tep" and "Incident On and Off a Mountain Road" were both filmed. He is the founder of the martial arts system Shen Chuan, and has been in the International Martial Arts Hall of Fame four times.

He lives in East Texas with his wife, Karen.

SINGER KASEY LANSDALE TELLS US ABOUT GROWING UP LANSDALE-STYLE

Much of my life has been a musical.

I grew up in East Texas as "a Lansdale," and from an early age was surrounded by art, music, writing, you name it. I've been asked since I can remember what it was like growing up Lansdale, having a famous daddy and all that entails. To most people's disappointment, I had a normal childhood. Normal being that I had two parents who loved me, a brother, and any pet that I could take home within a twenty-mile radius.

I guess certain aspects wouldn't be considered typical. The art we had hanging on the walls was not that of Rockwell, but of skeletons and cemeteries. The house guests we hosted were directors, actors, and all sorts of folks, rather than cousin Tilly.

I don't recall ever thinking anything was out of the ordinary or what it all really meant until I got a little older. As time has passed, I realize the impact my father has had on literature and his readers, and it's nice to be a part of that legacy. Also, his hard work and following helped in the early stages of forming my own career.

Although I do read a lot, I was always a fan of music. My earliest memories are of me singing and dancing around the fireplace to *Reba's Greatest Hits 2* with the family German Shepherd in tow behind me, and listening to the Contours singing *Do You Love Me* with my dad in the hallway. I was always the kid in the neighborhood who was writing, directing, starring in plays, and dabbling in songwriting as a child.

When asked what I was gonna be when I grew up, the first answer I ever gave was "dazzling." I felt a passion and a fire inside me since I was born. I knew singing was my first and truest love, and somehow, I was gonna do something with that, and I hoped, something big.

My first gig came about by accident. I had graduated high school and come to the realization that the labels weren't going to be beating down my door, so I thought I had better do something to get this ball rolling. I put up flyers and spread the word for my need of a guitarist. I got a call from a guy who had seen my ad in the local music store, and we met, and he played for me for a few gigs, but he was a lead man, and I needed a rhythm player. A friend of mine worked with a woman who had once dated a guy who played...(Let that process). I got his number and called him up, told him what I was up to and his response was that he wanted no part of it, that he had done the band thing and he was out. I told him meet with me, to give me fifteen minutes, and I was sure he would change his mind. Reluctantly, he said he would later in the week.

A few days later, I was with my current guitarist, the lead man, and he and I were practicing a few songs at my house and we took a break and walked down to the mailbox. Down at the pool some of my neighbors were having a party of sorts, maybe more a gathering, and a man approached me and told me he was Danny, and I had called him. I had no idea what he was talking about. Turns out, the guitarist I had spoken to and asked to hear me sing was my next door neighbor. True story.

By the end of that week, we were all down at the pool hanging out, his guitar in hand, me singing a song here and there, and one of the other neighbors offered us a gig. Turns out he was new in town, and had just bought Banita Creek Hall. That's how it started "officially." I had sat in other people's gigs, and played with tracks at a few places, or at the high school show, but this was money promised, and hopefully an audience.

Maybe I was too optimistic. We spent the first couple months playing at Banita, applauding for each other, and generally garnering no more attention than a fly you swat at on your otherwise lovely picnic. Eventually though, people started really listening.

I also had a call from my father who was teaching a short course at the college for screenwriting during this time about a student in his class who played keyboard. Nothing more impressive to someone than your daddy talking you up and saying how good you are, huh. Needless to say, Chris, the keyboard player, did not have high hopes.

We met out of courtesy and turns out we were both wrong. We held an audition that night, he called his friend Bill the bassist, who in turned called his friend Jeff the drummer, and a band was born. *Kasey Lansdale and the Daletones.* These days it is just *Kasey Lansdale.*

374

I got real lucky with all this. When people started paying attention, they started talking, then other people called and more word of mouth spread, and I started booking regularly. As time passed, I started going to Nashville and now the band rotates, but I always call these guys first. I learned a lot, and had a real legit band first crack out the box. Never had to go through the trials most people do when starting a band. It all came about pretty easy and I got more than I deserved from it early on. I just kept learning and talking to people, and soon realized that most people will do whatever they can to help someone who is helping herself.

I am proud to say that I have lived my life this way ever since, and have had so many amazing experiences, that I couldn't even begin to list them all. Singing has taken me all over the world, and introduced me to some amazing people. I've gotten to do all sorts of things that I feel lucky for every day. I've played festivals, arenas, bars, weddings, theaters, had my music on TV, radio, film...and I wake up each day hoping that it continues and that someone isn't gonna give me a good shake and tell me to wake up and quit daydreaming.

I recently attended the CMA and BMI Awards and met my idol, Reba. That was a life-changing moment, and gave me a little sense of "I have arrived." I of course am only at the gate, and I still have to get through security, but by golly, I met Reba. The good news is, upon meeting Reba, I played it very cool, if cool is bursting into the ugly cry.

Currently, I am recording and writing for my first "real" album. I had recorded an album years ago, and it was a trial and error venture. I wrote a lot for it, but I was experimenting with so many things, my sound, my "brand," my overall package as an entertainer. I've since done two EP's and the last one sort of segued into the upcoming CD. I've been so lucky to work with the caliber of people that I have. Half the project is produced by Mike Clute, who in his own right had a lot to do with Faith Hill's early career, and still works with Diamond Rio and some other acts, the other half with Grammy nominated hitmaker, Derek George of the *Wide Open Music Group.*

I took some outside cuts for this project, and have been writing for it as well. They say you keep writing and listening to songs until the day you go in, constantly trying to top the songs you already have.

This new album I am working on, I am really excited about! I feel it really reflects me as an artist, and I know my team is going to do great things with it.

Those are the good things, but some things aren't as nice as others. Being a singer is so much more than just getting up on a stage and belting out some tunes. When you're little, you don't think much about it. You think you will just perform your songs, people will love them or not, and your hard work will pay off.

Unfortunately, it doesn't always work like that, especially these days when the music business (and so many other creative businesses) is in such financial hardship. Every day I hear of layoffs and mergers of labels. It's a scary thing on one hand, but a lot of people look at this as an opportunity to go the independent route. That, I think, is up to the individual artist. Being an artist is about presenting yourself as a product, or a brand if you will. I never thought of myself as a brand, (nor did I hear the words "let it happen organically") as much as I did when I moved to Nashville.

One thing to know is: it's not always about talent, but having talent sure doesn't hurt. People ask me sometimes if what I do is hard. The answer is yes. But I will tell you it's not hard like other jobs I have had. I was lucky in that I never had to worry where my next meal was coming from, but I did the waitressing thing, the retail thing, and odd jobs here and there, and those were no fun. So sure, there are obstacles in what I do, naysayers, and disappointments, but it sure beats having to do a job you hate.

Being a singer is more than just showing up at the gig, though. People don't think about all the little details that go along with it. You have to orchestrate your band, and that's at least five people for whom you are responsible and have to keep in line. The gigs have to be booked. The set list has to be created. I put a lot of thought into a set list. The songs have to flow, and you have to be sure there is a proper mood set. You have to be sure what you are doing fits the venue you are performing. Equipment has to be set up, someone needs to run sound, and you need to be there early for a sound check.

Then, you have to know that you can sound check all night, but when that room fills up with people, the dynamic will change, and you have to be willing to roll with it. Sometimes, you don't even get a sound check, or a monitor.

Here's something important: Singers need to hear themselves when they sing. Helps with that pesky staying on pitch thing. People who aren't singers sometimes don't factor in how big of a deal that is. They think if the audience can hear you, then that's is all that is needed...wrong.

I've had it happen where I show up to a gig that has "all the sound equipment," and no monitors. It's all fine and dandy to have the speakers set up for the audience, but what about the person baring there soul up there on stage? They like to hear themselves too. I've also had times where I've done sound-check, everything is in order, and then the fella (or lady) introducing you will go over and take it upon himself to adjust the levels, cause for those two sentences he's saying, he needs to know he sounds good, and then the main entertainment is just out of luck. It's never malicious, but sometimes it makes you want to grind your teeth to sand.

The way I see it though, if that is the worst it gets, you are doing all right. Live music is a hard one to figure. Musicians are notoriously known for being late and unorganized. I do not have this affliction, therefore making it sometimes difficult in an environment where everything is often done by the seat of one's pants. Truth is, when you get up onstage and the audience responds to what you are doing, there is no bigger high, and monitors be dammed, 'cause it doesn't matter anymore.

Trying to explain what being on stage feels like to me is like trying to explain the nature of the universe. It can't be done, and it's different for everyone, but for me it's amazing, terrifying, gratifying, exhausting, exciting, and downright euphoric.

To get up there and give it your all, to really let loose, and to have someone tell you that your song, a song you wrote, that came from your heart meant something to them...that's a feeling akin to what I think you might feel when your child is born. It's your baby, and you want to show it off and hope people love it as much as you do, and when they do, it just ignites the fire all over again.

It's terrifying. too. You constantly think, "Am I gonna forget the words? Is my voice gonna crack? Will they throw garbage at me this evening?"

The more established you become, the better the venues and gigs will be. The best gigs are nowadays, when I can show up, everything has been set up, the band is prepared, (sometimes my own, or sometimes a group I sent the music to ahead of time) and I do a quick sound-check. I talk to the mic and get my levels in my monitor correct and make sure everyone sounds the way I need them to. Then I go back

377

to the dressing room, lounge area, or wherever is set up for the entertainment, have a quick bite, and do a mental checklist of everything.

As far as behind the scenes, we have a lot of fun. The band guys become like family, and you joke, and do things on stage and little musical licks that are for y'all. When you play the same songs over and over, you have to keep it fun and interesting.

I do get tired after a show, but I love staying after and talking to as many people as I can. These are the people putting food on my table, and inspiring me every day with new ideas and hope, and so I want to meet as many of them as I can.

My fans are amazing and so supportive, and they just remind me how worth it all of this is. I am in a lot of hotels, gone a lot away from my friends and family, and that's a tough thing, but when I get in the studio or on the stage, I'm not thinking about anything but the music. I learn something every time I play. I like to go different places vocally on a song just to mix it up, and sometimes, I even surprise myself with some of the things I do.

All of this energy just sort of trickles down into other projects too. I love the singing and songwriting, and have always considered being onstage a kind of persona, so I guess being involved in acting isn't too far a stretch. I grew up doing commercials and theater and little things like that, but I really started getting into acting after being asked to do some music videos, and most recently, my first feature film.

Other than singing, writing has been around from the beginning. As I said, I've been writing songs for a long time, and wrote short stories and was even published by age eight at Random House along with my father and brother, Keith, so making the transition from songwriter to editor and writer just felt so natural. My *Impossible Monster* anthology book is coming out this year from Subterranean Press and I feel grateful they took a chance on lil' ole me! Being first and foremost a country singer, monster stories may not be the first correlated project that pops into one's mind, but, I am a Lansdale after all!

It's just that I feel like I've got so much inside me that I want to put out there in the world, that it manifests wherever there is an opportunity: singing, acting, or writing.

I believe all the arts are connected, and that we all ought to support one another because we all want the same thing: to do what we love and to share our stories and hope that someone wants to hear it or read it. I sure thank you for listening to mine.

About Kasey Lansdale

Kasey Lansdale is a published author of short stories and articles. She is also known for her career in music as a vocalist and songwriter. Kasey is the editor of the new Subterranean Press anthology *Impossible Monsters*, as well as various other projects. She is currently writing a novel, and appears frequently as a book cover model and in music videos. You can visit Kasey at www.kaseylansdale.com

GRAHAM MASTERTON WRITES
A TRIBUTE TO HIS WIFE

Wiescka Masterton 1946 - 2011

The first time I realized that Wiescka and I had a fateful connection was when I stepped out of my office at Penthouse Magazine one September morning in 1973 and saw her standing in front of her desk in a black dress with the zipper at the back still two-and-a-half inches undone.

I came up behind her, lifted up her hair and zipped her dress up to the top. I was very matter-of-fact about it and didn't do it with the deliberate intention of being flirtatious. I was the editor of an international men's magazine and even though I was only twenty-seven, I thought that I was being mature and helpful and (dare I say it) cool. You know. Very Tom Selleck.

But I felt the softness of her skin with my fingertips, and how silky her hair was. In those days she had very long brunette hair, thick but fine, and everybody used to say that she looked like a young Sandie Shaw. She turned around and looked at me and that was the moment that the Van der Graaf generator crackled between us. We said nothing more at the time but our future was already determined.

In those few seconds, the time it took for me to fasten that zip, we were destined to become lovers, and then husband and wife, and then parents, and then, eventually, grandparents. When I fastened that hook-and-eye at the top of her dress, I was fastening US together for the next thirty-eight years—thirty-eight years of love and laughter and adventure and almost unbelievable events.

In mid-December we held the magazine's Christmas party at the Penthouse Club. Stirling Moss was there; Kingsley Amis was there; Humphrey Lyttleton was there; John Steinbeck's son was there. I found that I was introducing Wiescka to all of our celebrity writers and photographers, and doing it with pride. She wore an evening dress that she had borrowed from our receptionist, and she looked beautiful.

380

That night we became lovers and we were lovers every single minute after that for the rest of her life.

What was extraordinary about Wiescka was not only her distinctive Polish looks but her personality—her moral courage and her refusal to accept cant or hypocrisy or dishonesty. But all of these qualities were combined with remarkable shyness, and warmth. She always told me that she would support me in my writing career and do everything possible to promote me and to back me up, but she never wanted to step into the limelight herself.

She didn't have to. Wherever she went, whoever she met, she was received with the kind of affection that most celebrities can only dream about. She could be sharp-tongued, certainly. She could be highly critical of pot-bellied middle-aged men in shorts that they had dug out of the bottom of the wardrobe for the summer and if a woman walked into a pub looking like mutton dressed up as lamb she would always nudge me and say "I don't like yours much." But she was a naturally sympathetic person, a person who would help anybody if they needed help, and a person who would talk to anybody who looked lonely.

Wiescka was born in Cologne, in Germany, in 1946, the daughter of Janina Niconchuk and Kazimiz Walach. Wiescka is short for Wieslawa, which means "great glory." She came to live in Wales when she was three years old and she was educated at Bedwellty Grammar School. After working for Butlins in Minehead and taking a secretarial course, she came to London and eventually found a job as editorial assistant at *Penthouse*.

Then...I zipped up her dress.

We had three sons together: Roland, Dan and Luke, and now she has a grandson Blake, from Luke, and a new baby on the way from Roland and his wife Millie.

In 1999 we moved to Cork, in Ireland, for four years, for tax reasons. They loved her in Cork, and several of our friends openly wept when we left. But last week I found one of the diaries she had written when she was there. Over and over again, she had written, "Gosh, I miss my boys."

She was constantly supportive in my career, helping me to secure some amazing publishing deals, not only because she was so strong and determined, but because publishers found her so enchanting. Probably her greatest achievement was getting my books published in Poland even before the collapse of the Communist regime. We visited Poland in 1989—the first time she had ever been there—and even the grumpiest of publishers couldn't resist her. Over the years she has become something of a heroine in Poland, appearing on the covers of magazines and on popular Polish websites.

She insisted on reading all of my books before I sent them off for publication in case I had made some ghastly mistake. In one early book, she spotted that a woman who had lost her leg in Chapter Three was running around again by Chapter Seven.

One of her greatest talents, though, was for interior decoration. She had a wonderful eye for making a room look welcoming and distinctive. She was clever, and funny, and impatient, and stubborn, and lovely, and there was no one like her, and never will be.

I have had messages of grief and sympathy from America, from France, from Belgium, from Germany, from Greece, from South Korea, and tearful phone calls from Poland – all from people who had met her and had recognized the same Wiescka magic that first electrified me on that September morning. I could write a whole book about her. Maybe I will, one day, when I can do it without crying. Meanwhile, I will just have to leave you with the lines that I wrote to her seven years ago, in my Christmas card:

There are no accidents in love.
We open doors; and there they are
Our lifelong companions
Standing by a window; sitting in a chair.
Not even turning round, or looking up.
They do not recognize us yet.

But the smallest gesture
A fastened dress; a hand held, crossing the street
Will join our destinies forever:
Turn both our faces to the same warm wind.

About Graham Masterton

Graham Masterton has published over one hundred novels, including thrillers, horror novels, disaster epics, and sweeping historical romances.

He was editor of the British edition of *Penthouse Magazine* before writing his debut horror novel *The Manitou* in 1975, which was subsequently filmed with Tony Curtis, Susan Strasberg, Burgess Meredith and Stella Stevens.

After the initial success of *The Manitou*, Graham continued to write horror novels and supernatural thrillers, for which he has won international acclaim, especially in Poland, France, Germany, Greece and Australia.

His historical romances *Rich* (Simon & Schuster) and *Maiden Voyage* (St Martins) both featured in The New York Times Bestseller List. He has twice been awarded a Special Edgar by Mystery Writers of America (for *Charnel House*, and more recently *Trauma*, which was also named by Publishers Weekly as one of the hundred best novels of the year.)

He has won numerous other awards, including two Silver Medals from the West Coast Review of Books, a Tombstone award from the Horror Writers Network, another Gravestone from the International Horror Writers Guild, and was the first non-French winner of the prestigious Prix Julia Verlanger for bestselling horror novel. The *Chosen Child* (set in Poland) was nominated best horror novel of the year by the British Fantasy Society.

Several of Graham's short stories have been adapted for TV, including three for Tony Scott's *Hunger* series. Jason Scott Lee starred in the Stoker-nominated *Secret Shih-Tan*.

Apart from continuing with some of most popular horror series, Graham is now writing novels that have some suggestion of a supernatural element in them, but are intended to reach a wider market than genre horror.

Trauma (Penguin) told the story of a crime-scene cleaner whose stressful experiences made her gradually believe that a homicidal Mexican demon possessed the murder victims whose homes she had to sanitize. (This novel was optioned for a year by Jonathan Mostow.) *Unspeakable* (Pocket Books) was about a children's welfare officer, a deaf lip-reader, who became convinced that she had been cursed by the Native American father of one of the children she had rescued. (This novel was optioned for two years by La Chauve Souris in Paris.)

Ghost Music is a love story in which a young TV-theme and ad-jingle composer discovers that his musical sensitivity allows him to see and feel very much more than anybody else around him—but with horrifying consequences which only he can resolve.

Other novels recently released from Leisure Books: *Descendant*, an idiosyncratic vampire novel; *Petrified*, that includes Nathan Underhill, the zoologist introduced in *Basilisk*; *The Pariah*, a ghost story; and *Mirror*, about a looking glass that has witnessed death of a very young Hollywood star.

Graham Masterton's website: www.grahammasterton.co.uk

DEBORAH LeBLANC

Deborah gets a visit from her deceased grandfather...maybe?

When I started delving into paranormal investigation years ago, my adventures were done alone and with little more than a disposable camera, compass, flashlight, and a set of brass balls. Over time, I collected more sophisticated tools of the trade, like an EMF detector, infrared cameras, etc. The set of brass balls remained a constant. Eventually, I joined professional paranormal investigation teams, began traveling to purported haunted locations throughout the country, and even did some scouting for MTV's Fear program.

Over the years, I've visited hundreds of cemeteries, and my camera's caught flying orbs near Poe's grave in Baltimore, squiggly strings of white light that wove through tombs in old family plots in Nebraska, and child-size shadows perched atop two headstones in Atlanta, Georgia. Oddly enough, the cemetery known as the most haunted in America, Big Woods Cemetery, offered nothing but hungry mosquitoes.

The most fascinating experience I've had in a cemetery came from a small town of Mire, Louisiana, where my maternal grandfather is buried. One evening I took my youngest daughter and two of her friends out for burgers. While we were eating, my daughter decides to tell her friends about the weird things her mom does for fun...like ghost hunting. They grow wide-eyed, of course, and ask a million questions, their last one being, "Can you take us to a cemetery and show us how to hunt for ghosts...like now?"

My daughter then gives me that, "You've gotta, Mom, 'cause they'll think I'm so cool" look. Geez...

Before long I had three fourteen year-olds (two girls, one boy) begging—loudly—to ghost hunt. Although I envisioned angry parents pounding on my front door later that night, insisting I be taken away to a mental ward, I couldn't resist those cherub faces. That, and the fact

385

that they pooled their money and bribed me with a slice of chocolate cake did me in.

Wanting to minimize any risks, I thought of the most benign cemetery I knew—St. Theresa's in Mire. The cemetery sits on a corner lot in the middle of town. Beside it is a church and across the street is a gas station and Mire City Hall. Streetlights line both sides of the street, so in truth, the spookiest thing about the place is the creak of the cemetery gate when you open it.

So, armed with a digital camera and a flashlight, both of which are always in my car, we head for the cemetery. Once there, the kids stayed glued to my side, whispering to each other, looking over their shoulder every few minutes as we walked amongst the graves. A car backfired in the distance, and the boy gasped so loudly, I thought he'd swallowed his tongue. We had a good laugh over that, which helped the kids to relax and eventually wonder off on their own to different tombs. All the while I'm snapping pictures, hoping for an orb or two, but getting absolutely nothing.

It wasn't long before I spotted my grandfather's grave. I was three when he passed away, so my daughters never knew him.

As I drew closer to the tomb, I got a sudden, overwhelming urge to 'introduce' my grandfather to my youngest. So I called my daughter over, showed her the tomb, then said aloud, "Pop-pop, this is your great-granddaughter, Sarah." No sooner did the words leave my mouth than another urge hit. Take a picture...now! So I did.

And this is what showed up:

The image, which stood at the foot of my grandfather's tomb, wasn't physically seen by any of us. Had it not been for the camera, we would have never known it was there. Is this my grandfather stopping by to say hello?

About Deborah LeBlanc

Deborah LeBlanc is an award-winning, best-selling author and business owner from Lafayette, Louisiana. She is also a licensed death scene investigator and has been an active paranormal investigator for over fifteen years.

She was the president of the Horror Writers Association, president of the Writers' Guild of Acadiana, and president of Mystery Writers of America's Southwest Chapter. In 2004, Deborah created the LeBlanc Literacy Challenge, an annual national campaign designed to encourage more people to read. Two years later, she founded Literacy Inc, a non-profit organization dedicated to fighting illiteracy in America's teens. Deborah also takes her passion for literacy and a powerful ability to motivate to high schools around the country.

EARL HAMNER TALKS ABOUT CREATING "THE WALTONS," AND HIS FRIENDSHIP WITH ROD SERLING

He wrote eight scripts for the original The Twilight Zone series

"Prepare for landing," came the voice over the PA system. "Make sure your seat belts are securely fastened and place your seat back in the upright position."

It was twilight when the landscape softens and the light begins to fade. From my window I looked out on purple mountains that gently sloped down to an endless expanse of sparkling lights. The plane glided in to a gentle landing and I stepped out into the softest, warmest air I had ever experienced.

I arrived in Los Angeles on January 4th, 1961. I had been a professional writer, living in New York, writing novels and radio scripts and live television. Surely within days I would have assignments from major studies to write screenplays or pilots for television. Right?

It wasn't to happen—at least not right away. My agent, Ben Benjamin, one of the best in the business, had arranged meetings with all the right people. But one after the other "all the right people" had the same response: "We've read your books and know of your work in live TV, but you haven't written film."

It was as if writing film was some talent you could possess only after breathing in a certain amount of smog or to have been baptized in the Pacific surf. All the Hollywood studios were telling me the same thing: I was a leper.

With a family to support, no income, and desperate for work, I decided to "enter" The Twilight Zone. I had never written fantasy or suspense type stories. Most of my work had been of a folkish nature, focused on the family, set usually in a rural locale, often in the past...another minus in fast paced, glamorous, slick, suspense-laden stories so typical of Hollywood.

I had originally met Rod Serling in New York City in 1947. Each of us had won awards in a radio script-writing contest and was invited to come to town to be interviewed on the radio by the host of the show. We were both students at that time. Rod was in Yellow Springs, Ohio and I was a student at the University of Cincinnati.

After graduation, I became a staff writer at Station WLW in Cincinnati. Once I saved enough money to take time out to write a novel, I resigned the job, which by an interesting coincidence was taken by Rod Serling.

Eventually Rod left Ohio for Hollywood and started writing and producing "The Twilight Zone." So when it turned out that I was unqualified to write film, in desperation, I decided to contact Rod.

I had a script in mind that I had written about a hunter and his dog. Both the hunter and his beloved hound die on a hunt and try to enter Heaven. Hell tries to get them first, but the dog is the one who can see through Hell's lies and leads his master to the real pearly gates.

I sent that script along with a second script idea to accompany a letter that said:

Dear Rod:

Having been a fan of The Twilight Zone for a long time, I was happy to hear from Ray Bradbury that you might be on the lookout for new stories. I am enclosing two that might interest you.

Best Regards,
Earl Hamner

And as a result of that letter, "The Hunt" was aired as a "The Twilight Zone" episode on January 26, 1962 and starred Arthur Hunnicutt, the first of eight scripts that I was to write for the series.

During that time, I came to know Rod Serling and to develop a friendship. I remember our first meeting in his office at the MGM Studios in Culver City. He greeted me warmly and recalled some of the friends we had worked with back in Ohio. He was smoking, and so was I at the time, and we lit up—part of the ritual of the day.

We spoke about our first meeting in New York and exchanged some accounts of our personal lives. I remember that our meeting was interrupted from time to time by phone calls that would cause Rod to roll his eyes Heavenward and occasionally raise his voice. After hanging up, he would explain, "Network!" and we would continue the meeting.

He did not offer any notes on my story outline. He just said, "Go write it." After that first script meeting when I delivered my finished script he would simply say, "What would you like to do next? I would describe a new idea and he would say, "Go to it!" At long last I was writing film!

In those days, writers were almost never invited to the set to see their scripts being filmed. This practice changed as the industry came to recognize more and more that the whole process began with THE WORD and the producers came more to recognize where those words came from.

Even though I was not on the set to observe the filming, I did become friends with many of the actors who appeared in my scripts or on "The Zone." Nancy Malone who appeared in my episode, "Stop Over in a Quiet Town" is still a good friend. I see Mary Badham from time to time. She was Sport in "The Bewitching Pool."

And Anne Francis who played Jess Belle in that hour-long episode was a good friend until her untimely death this past year. Jeanette Nolan, who did such a fantastic job as the witch in "Jess Belle," later did a guest star role on "The Waltons" playing a nun for Lord's sake! And even though he was never in an episode I wrote, it is always fun to run into Earl Holliman at one of our local restaurants or even at the super market.

My favorite script will always be "The Hunt." Not only was it my first assignment in Hollywood, but also in addition the characters were mountain folks and the setting was my beloved Blue Ridge Mountains of Virginia. But most especially, by giving me that assignment, Rod opened the door to a career in film that has been richly rewarding to me and I hope to the audience.

People often ask me how I could write for shows like "The Twilight Zone" when I am primarily a "soft writer" for shows like "The Waltons" and "Apple's Way." I received that question especially after the TV series "Falcon Crest" began.

The answer is, of course, that I am a professional writer. I can write about the lives of many kinds of people; hopefully with objectivity, understanding, and compassion. "The Waltons" and The "Falcon

Crest" characters were people, and any good writer should be able to write about people, no matter what their walks of life.

Now we're going to get a little melodramatic here, so I'm warning you that I was never shot at during World War II and the most discomfort I endured was suffering severe acrophobia while climbing over the side of a troop ship and down a rope ladder to a landing craft at Omaha Beach.

But the invasion of Normandy was well underway and while I was in no immediate danger, I had to face the fact that I had been trained to diffuse land mines and that the life expectancy on such an assignment could be very short on the battlefield.

And it was this realization that prompted me to start thinking seriously about my life, trying to find meaning, and to evaluate how my family and the village where I had grown up had made me the man I had become. And so while trudging forward through the hedgerows of Normandy by day, at night I started making notes and those notes became the basis for my novel *Spencer's Mountain*.

Spencer's Mountain became a best seller, and then a Warner Brothers film starring Henry Fonda and Maureen O'Hara. Its sequel *The Homecoming* became the basis for my series "The Waltons."

Each character in "The Waltons" was based on a member of my own close-knit family and our lives during The Great Depression of the 1930s. So the characters in that show were very real people. "The Waltons" ran for eight years in first run, and even today is seen all over the world in syndication and here at home on three different cable channels.

In the parlance of Hollywood, stories that deal honestly with character and the human heart are considered "soft." While I attempt to be objective, I remember one occasion when I became emotionally involved in the project. I wrote the script for the animated movie "Charlotte's Web" based on E B White's book. I was near the end of writing this film when the phone rang and the caller said, "You sound all choked up."

I answered, "Yes I am. A spider just died."

About Earl Hamner

The author is best known as the creator and producer of two Emmy Award-winning series, "The Waltons" and "Falcon Crest."

He is also the producer of many other television series and specials, and has written for "The Theater Guild on the Air," "Wagon Train," "The Twilight Zone," "CBS Playhouse" as well as "The Today Show."

His short stories have been published in *The Strand, Dark Discoveries, The Twilight Zone Anthology* edited by Carol Serling, and *The Bleeding Edge* and *The Devil's Coat Tail* from the publishers of *Dark Discoveries Magazine.*

He is the author of eight best-selling books. His latest book, *Odette, a Goose of Toulouse* was inspired by his reaction to seeing a goose who seems destined to become pate, but who becomes an opera singer instead. One reviewer called it a "minor classic."

Earl Hamner and Jane, his wife of fifty-seven years, live in Studio City and Laguna Beach, California with a bossy pug named Peaches. Their son Scott, who lives in Vermont, is Co-head writer for the daytime series "The Young and the Restless." Their daughter Caroline is a family therapist and lives with her husband in Laguna Beach, California.

INTERVIEW WITH TIM LEBBON

The New York Times bestselling author Tim Lebbon tells how he got his start and what he is doing now. Tim also shares tips for new writers.

JEANI: You've been a best-selling author since 1997, with your first novel Mesmer. What made you decide to become a writer?

TIM: I don't think I really decided; it just happened. It wasn't a case of me sitting down and thinking, right then, what shall I do with my life? Airline pilot? Plumber? Guitar manufacturer? Writer...yeah, writer.

I've always loved writing, from a very early age—I guess I was writing my first stories when I was still in single digits. It progressed, and the love of writing grew in my mind and is still growing. Doing it full-time, there are different stresses and tensions, and the business side of it comes to the fore sometimes. But I still love it, and I'm always thankful that I can do what I do and make a living from it.

JEANI: How did you begin the process? (For example, did you submit short stories to magazines, or did you start out with a complete novel, etc).

TIM: I wrote short stories for the UK small presses of the 1990s. These were magazines—sometimes with covers and artwork, sometimes just photocopied and stapled—that rarely paid, and had circulations of a couple of hundred, run by people passionate about short stories. The editorial input was sometimes good, and at other times there was barely any. The magazines had names like *Peeping Tom, Psychotrope, Grotesque, Black Tears, Dreams from the Stranger's Cafe*...I'm sure some people reading this now are nodding nostalgically. I guess I had maybe forty stories published before my first novel *Mesmer* was picked up by Tanjen.

Following on from that were more short stories and novellas, then more novels, and over the past few years I've been writing only a couple of short stories per year.

393

JEANI: All writers receive rejection notices when they first start out. Did you get your share of rejections in your early days? And what advice can you give to new writers who are feeling discouraged over their own rejection notices?

TIM: Hell, I got hundreds of them, and I still get them now. Everyone gets rejection letters. They should make you stronger—I wrote dozens of stories trying to get into the magazine *The Third Alternative*, and eventually got there, and I think I improved immensely doing so. Take positive comments from rejections, and don't let them grind you down. They're as much a part of the learning process as anything, and a good writer never stops learning.

JEANI: You were once quoted as saying: "Gradually over the years I've become more serious about [writing] until now it's an obsession: it's no longer that I want to write, I have to." Can you expand on that?

TIM: I think most writers will communicate a need to write. I need to write, both from a psychological perspective—it's the way my parents put my hat on—and now from a professional perspective too, so that I can earn a living and so continue doing it. But if I wasn't making money from my writing, I'd still write. It's what drives me, and what makes me able to function as a (relatively) normal human being.

I believe that storytelling is one of the most important aspects of being human—it requires empathy for others, appreciation of different outlooks, and an ability to think beyond your own self-contained world. And all of that is very, very healthy. I'm very lucky to have made many life-long friends through what I do, and though writers can be amongst the strangest people I've met, they're also the nicest.

JEANI: Your newest best-selling novel, *Echo City*, is a fantasy about an ancient city in a vast, empty desert. How do you shift between the fantasy and horror genres so seamlessly?

TIM: Well, I wouldn't say it's best-selling just yet, but I keep my fingers crossed. As for shifting between genres, I really don't see it like that at all. It's not a shift, more of a drift, and sometimes it's barely noticeable to me. I'm tackling some of the same ideas, the writing is the same; the only real difference is setting.

With my horror novels, they're generally set in a recognizable world. Fantasy novels are set somewhere else. There are challenges to both, of course, and that's why I enjoy being able to drift back and forth. Lines are blurred, if there at all. That's a good thing.

JEANI: I understand there are two (not one, but TWO!) films in progress, one based on your short story *Pay the Ghost* and the other on your novel *The Secret Journeys of Jack London: The Wild*. Can you tell us how it feels to move from novels to the silver screen?

TIM: It's fantastic. Writing screenplays is something I've dabbled in over the past few years, and I really enjoy it—a very different process, but still storytelling. So when Fox2000 optioned the *Secret Journeys of Jack London* series (which I'm writing with my mate Chris Golden), and hired us to write the script, I was thrilled. From dabbling to writing for a major studio in the blink of an eye.

It's been a thrilling process, and my learning curve has been steep. I'm sure it'll lead on to more projects, and I see screenwriting becoming a larger part of my future. I'm already writing another screenplay of my own, collaborating on one with Steve Volk, and developing a couple of TV series ideas with other collaborators.

Pay the Ghost is still in development, but it has slowed down somewhat.

The perfect situation is that both movies start shooting, but film-making involves a series of hurdles. I have high hopes for both, and I think the *Jack London* series especially could turn into a series of major blockbusters.

JEANI: Who have been your influences?

TIM: Many and varied. Arthur Machen, Stephen King, Willard Price (from my pre-teens), Clive Barker, Algernon Blackwood, Graham Joyce, China Mieville...I think any writer picks up influences, but the older he or she becomes, the greater and more defined his or her own voice.

JEANI: How do you discipline yourself about your writing? Do you spend eight hours a day at your computer, or do you write when inspiration hits?

TIM: My writing is shaped around my family—two kids in school, and my wife who has just returned to work after a few months off. So I write for a few hours through the day, then often do more work in the evenings, which usually involves talking to people I'm collaborating with (Chris Golden, Mark Morris, some people I can't mention), emailing, or working on proposals or new ideas. I usually try and hit 3,000 words in a day when I'm working all-out on a new novel.

JEANI: What advice would you give to a new writer about coming up with ideas for a novel?

TIM: Take something that really interests you, that feels like a proper, fully rounded idea, and don't worry about how other people will perceive it. Write through difficult parts of the book...coming out the other side will often give you what you need to go back and fix the problem part.

JEANI: What suggestions would you give to a new writer about finding a literary agent?

TIM: Research who you're approaching, and find out what they ask to see as a submission (usually a proposal, cover letter, and first three chapters). Don't pay a reading fee. Give them a couple of months to respond to you before querying them a second time. Send to three or four agents at a time.

JEANI: All new writers want to know what they can do to make their work stand out from the slush pile. Any advice?

TIM: Get an agent. Seriously, submitting stuff unagented means it will end up on the slush pile. An agent is the first quality filter, and a good agent is worth his or her weight in gold, as they'll often know the editors on a personal level and will be able to talk to them directly about the project.

JEANI: Of all the books that you wrote, do you have a favorite?

TIM: Eek. Well, there are lots that stand out for different reasons. I think *Echo City* is my most accomplished dark fantasy novel yet. I think Chris and I did something special with *The Map of Moments*, and the *Jack London* novels are something I'm so excited about. My novella *The Reach of Children* is perhaps the most personal thing I've written, based very heavily around my mother's death. And my horror novel *Coldbrook* is, I think, probably one of the most action-packed and exciting novels I've written.

JEANI: Tim, can you please tell us something personal about yourself? Your hobbies, recreational activities, and your favorite vacation spot? How about your favorite movie?

TIM: My hobby is writing. My life tends to revolve around that, and my family.

We walk the dog a lot (a donkey-sized monster called Blu). At the beginning of 2011, I started exercising a lot more, and have completed various 10k and half-marathon races.

This year it's on to a couple of marathons, and perhaps an adventure race or two (running, biking, kayaking long distances).

My favorite TV program ever is *The Shield*; I think that series was fantastic and the final three or four episodes are simply sublime.

Movies...I love movies, picking favorites is very difficult. But fave horror movies would include *The Thing, Jacob's Ladder, The Haunting*...the list is long.

JEANI: How much fan mail do you get? If one of The Horror Zine readers wants to send you a fan letter, to where can he/she send it?

TIM: I get quite a few emails, and that's very nice. Always makes my day. Best to send an email to my address which is lebbon1984@yahoo.com. I have had letters, but not so many these days.

JEANI: Is there any more advice you can give to struggling writers, poets, and artists who haven't yet made it to your level of fame?

TIM: Fame? Ha! My advice is to carry on. If it's something you love doing, you'll carry on anyway. And if you carry on and you're good at it, aim to continuously improve, and you'll be noticed.

About Tim Lebbon

Tim Lebbon is a New York Times-bestselling writer from South Wales. He's had over twenty novels published to date, as well as dozens of novellas and hundreds of short stories. Recent books include *The Secret Journeys of Jack London: The Wild* (co-authored with Christopher Golden), *Echo City, The Island, The Map of Moments* (with Christopher Golden), and *Bar None*. He has won four British Fantasy Awards, a Bram Stoker Award, and a Scribe Award, and has been a finalist for International Horror Guild, Shirley Jackson, and World Fantasy Awards.

Fox 2000 recently acquired film rights to *The Secret Journeys of Jack London*, and Tim and Christopher Golden have delivered the screenplay. Several more of his novels and novellas are currently in development, and he is also working on TV and movie proposals, solo and in collaboration.

Find out more about Tim at his website www.timlebbon.net.

PAUL DALE ROBERTS

Forget Dan Aykroyd and Bill Murray. Here is a real-life ghostbuster!

My name is Paul Dale Roberts, and I perform paranormal investigations with my partner, Shannon McCabe. In fact, I belong to a company called HPI (Haunted and Paranormal Investigations), an international company based in Sacramento, California.

The purpose of this article is to tell you the why's, what's, and how's of a ghost hunter. A real ghost hunter, and not an actor on television.

I will even give you an example of one of my paranormal investigations!

First the WHY: One of the reasons why I do this is because it's my high. I get an adrenaline rush when I witness true paranormal activity. It doesn't happen very often, but when it does and I can witness the events with my own senses and not just with machines, it is the ultimate high.

Now the WHAT: HPI International is a ghost hunting company with affiliates across the globe. HPI helps home owners and businesses deal with their paranormal needs. This part of the company is run by its General Manager (that's me, Paul Dale Roberts) along with a core team of seasoned paranormal investigators.

And finally, the HOW: When we get a call for a possible investigation, I listen to the client's story. I listen for inconsistencies and contradictions in the statements. If the story sounds plausible, I will then obtain information on how old the residence is, do they know of any history about the residence, and what are the 'symptoms.'

I then provide the address to our researcher in London, England, who is Laurie Rutledge. Laurie has the ability to find anything on anyone and anybody. She has the ability to obtain information on any residence address I provide to her. She is somewhat mysterious, but I do know that she has a very extensive legal background.

How investigations are performed:

I will go through bios of my thirty-five investigators to decide which ones would be more adept for this particular investigation. It's like the way Jim Phelps of *Mission Impossible* would select his agents for an assignment. After choosing the investigators, we all meet up at the address of the potential haunted site. My videographer John Shue always records the events, but owners have the option of staying anonymous or allowing HPI to publicize the investigation.

Before the investigation, there is an initial briefing. I learn what areas of the residence needs to be investigated. I break up the group into three teams. The teams will go into different areas of the home. Each team will have a lead investigator.

The teams will be in communication with base camp (me, the audio analyzer, and the video monitor) via walkie-talkie. Each investigation has a duration of forty-five minutes.

Afterwards, we have an evidence briefing, and this is where we actually allow the homeowners to assist in our investigation. In the evidence briefing, the homeowners actually get to see videos and hear audios, the evidence we have collected. We show them any anomalies.

Then comes the decision! Is the residence (or business or property) haunted or not?

We always look for the logical explanations first. A real haunting is somewhat rare and so we may give them a reasonable explanation for what they may have considered to be a strange event.

We explain the McCabe Method of obtaining EVPs (Electronic Voice Phenomenon). With a digital recorder, we say something simple like: "Is there anyone here?"

We pause for a while, allowing the entity to respond, then play it back and sometimes you may hear a voice say: "Yes, I am here!"

We call it the McCabe Method, because Shannon came up with this quicker way of collecting EVPs. Most ghosthunting groups leave their recorder on all night and analyze the recordings all day the next day. But logically thinking, if these are intelligent ghosts and if you asked the ghost what his or her name is, wouldn't they respond immediately and not wait two or three hours to tell you their name?

By the end of the night, we know if the home is haunted or if there is a reasonable explanation.

But if the residence really is haunted...then what?

If the entities are benign, we generally just try to ask them to leave. If the entities are malevolent, we will do a cleansing. We call in Catholic, Wiccan, Voodoo, Native American cleansers or metaphysical cleansers, depending upon the circumstances and the wishes of the homeowner.

After the investigation, the homeowners have open communication with me via my cell phone. I listen to follow-ups, their thanks, or if the activity has started back up again. It is very rare after a cleansing that activity returns, but if it does, we send out a second team for another investigation and another cleansing.

A real haunted house:

The home at Brougham Way was a strange home because rumors of hauntings abounded. When HPI Paranormal Investigators got wind of it, Shannon sent two teams of seasoned investigators on a scouting mission.

When she got the results back from the scouts, Shannon told me that Brougham Way was definitely haunted, because the first preliminary investigation resulted with eight EVPs captured at the home. Since most incidents can be explained as logical instead of paranormal activities, I knew this was an exceptional opportunity and would be a great experience.

So I decided to pay a visit to this home myself.

When we set up at Brougham Way, we conducted a séance that produced amazing results. These results included the sounds of a little girl giggling and saying "Hi." We didn't even need instruments because we could hear the child with our own ears.

Then came the sounds of the walls echoing with a ripping effect, and later a series of knocks. We could hear someone walking down the hallway towards us. It was a séance that really produced results; this house had ghosts.

The outcome:

When faced with proof that Brougham Way was indeed inhabited by actual ghosts, the owners gave us a surprising conclusion to the investigation. Unlike most homeowners that are faced with this situation, these homeowners were not afraid, and actually embraced the existence of the entities in their home.

Instead of asking that their residence be cleansed, the owners told us that they had gotten used to their spirit "friends," and had actually grown to like their presence. They felt it was a unique situation, and if the ghosts had made the decision to stay in the house, who were they to question it?

Therefore, no efforts were made to send the ghosts away. To this day, the house on Brougham Way is still haunted, although not in any malicious manner. In fact, the ghosts have the permission of the owners to share the house, which is why this particular case stands out in my mind.

About Haunted and Paranormal Investigations (HPI):

HPI International began as a paranormal investigative group in 2004.

HPI has a select core of investigators and a large group of members (or Ghosties as they are called) who perform scouting missions and cleansings.

The owner is Shannon McCabe, who has a background in promotions, event planning and paranormal investigations. Paul Dale Roberts is the General Manager.

Together they have been on television shows such as History Channel's *Monster Quest, Conversations With A Serial Killer, Penn & Teller's Bullshit,* TV's Pay Per View Special *Off The Hook,* UK's Sky 1 Network's *Michael Jackson: In Search of His Spirit* and a documentary about angels and demons.

HPI respects and honors requests for confidentiality from clients and conduct themselves in a professional manner at all times.

If you have unusual activity in your home, on your property, or in your workplace and would like to get to the bottom of what's going on, feel free to contact HPI at 1-888-709-4HPI.

POETRY

DESPAIR
Artwork by Paula McDonald

STRAW MAN
Artwork by John Richards

POETRY BY G. O. CLARK

ALL IN THE FAMILY

His mom and dad
never told him about their
alien abductions.

His sister never shared
her stories about being part of a
college vampire clique,

and his brother
kept silent about his wartime
run-ins with zombies.

He learned these facts
later from his bohemian uncle,
the family artiste,

their keeper of secrets,
who one night over steak and ale
divulged quite a few,

including a most startling one,
which convinced him to become a
vegan, and avoid full moons.

INSOMNIA

Haunted by the tapping
of cat claws upon a hardwood floor,

he finds sleep impossible to come by,

this side of his silk lined coffin,

and wanders the night like a homeless
ghost wrapped in cardboard solitude,

a creature of dark alleys and dim light,
the hunger ever present,

the pulsing of jugulars
dark music to his sonar-sensitive ears,

the tapping of cat claws, that ticking
of a clock by one's death bed

THE STRANGER

The stranger sets off
car alarms when he stalks
the midnight streets, a shrill
warning to some.

Passing through
the cemetery, he pauses to
sharpen his long, black nails
on granite tombstones.

Each night he seeks out
darkened bedroom windows,
avoiding those still lit by
late night TV glow.

His prey is always the
same. Young, female, asleep
and dreaming of prom dresses
and athletic young men.

Come the morning,
a parent's worst nightmares
become real, sheets stained red
with shattered dreams,

the stranger come and
gone. Dead batteries, angry
commuters, death and sirens
left in his wake.

About G. O. Clark

G. O. Clark's writing has been published in *Asimov's Science Fiction, Talebones Magazine, Strange Horizons, Cinema Spec: Tales of Hollywood and Fantasy, Tales Of The Talisman,* and many other publications. He's the author of nine poetry collections, the most recent *Shroud Of Night,* 2011, and a fiction collection, *The Saucer Under My Bed and Other Stories,* 2011.

He won the Asimov's Readers Award for poetry in 2001, and has been a repeat Rhysling and Stoker Award nominee. He retired from the University of California, Davis in 2008, where he worked in the library for many years.

POETRY BY DENNIS BAGWELL

IF FRANKENSTEIN'S MONSTER WERE ALIVE TODAY

If Frankenstein's monster were alive today...

He would sue the doctor for malpractice and a jury would award him millions
The doctor would blame it all on the pharmaceutical companies and plead not guilty by reason of insanity
He would enter some kind of rehabilitation program
Congress would enact new laws prohibiting mad scientists from constructing humans from the dead tissue of other humans and regulate the use of lightning for scientific research

The monster would change his name to Steve or Ron and Oprah would have him on the show to tell his story
Dr. Phil would get to the bottom of his abandonment issues
How his heart is filled with rage because his daddy doesn't love him
The monster would cry and the audience would cry with him

He would work for charities to raise awareness about monsters, or as he likes to call them, "Reanimated Tissue People" or RTPs
He would run for mayor of a small town to show other RTPs that you can do anything you set your mind to
He would write a best selling book entitled, "I Am Not a Monster"
He would go on Larry King Live to promote it and Larry would ask the "tough questions"

A made-for-TV movie about his life would draw the highest ratings in TV history
His Halloween mask would be the must have costume for several seasons

By day he would bask in the glory of his new found celebrity, but he would spend his nights alone, grunting and moaning in an alcohol soaked stupor trying to drown the monster inside of him
He would drive drunk and crash his car into a pole on Sunset Boulevard and suffer serious injuries
But with a face like his, who could tell?

Time magazine would have his police mug shot on the cover with the caption, "Man or Monster?"
He would go to the Betty Ford clinic and emerge humbled
Maybe he would have plastic surgery to make himself feel better
He would go on Barbara Walters and apologize and tell the public, "I am a man, not a monster!"

He would wisely invest his riches and marry a hot former playboy center fold

His fifteen minutes of fame would come and go like the flash of lightning that brought him into being
He would die in relative obscurity

Despite his philanthropic work, a best selling book, a made-for-TV movie, a popular Halloween mask, raising millions of dollars for Reanimated Tissue People, dozens of schools and plastic surgery hospitals named for him, hundreds of Steve or Ron Frankenstein scholarships for underprivileged inner city youths,

Obituaries the world over will remember him simply as "the monster"
R.I.P.

YOU'RE NOT A VAMPIRE

You work the night shift
And have a graveyard tan
You're thinking about getting a real coffin to sleep in
But you're not a vampire
You've read every *Twilight* book twice
And never miss an episode of True Blood

Your girlfriend is a hot Goth chick named Mina
But you're not a vampire
You write poetry about cemeteries
And have a tattoo of Bela Lugosi
And a poster of *Interview with a Vampire*
But you're not a vampire
You have an appointment next week to get your eye teeth sharpened
into fangs
You hang out in dark clubs on weekends with other "Vampires"
But you pass out at the sight of blood
Because you're not a vampire

SUICIDE NOTE FROM A
DISTRAUGHT JACK O' LANTERN

To whom it may concern:

I can't take it anymore
I hate my job
I'm burnt out
My wife has shriveled away
My little pumpkins have all grown and left the patch
I don't have the guts to go on
I feel hollow, just a shell of my former self
It's time for me to roll
Goodbye cruel world...
Love,
Jack

P.S. – Donate my remains to a bakery

BUCKETHEAD

Every night
Before he went to bed

The old man unscrewed
His old wrinkled head

He put it in a bucket
Of putrid, rusty water
And hid it in his closet
From his unsuspecting daughter

Then early one morning
We heard an awful shout
His daughter found the bucket
And threw the water out

The neighbors all gathered
And watched with horror and dread
While his body stumbled aimlessly
Looking for his head

"What have you done?"
Her father's head exclaimed
"Throwing me so hard,
Could damage my old brain!"

"Oh Father!" she cried
"Forgive me for this!"
"I found that putrid bucket,
And though it was your piss!"

About Dennis Bagwell

Dennis is a politically incorrect, mad at the world, X-Generation, heathen, musician, and writer originally from Orange County, California. Dennis moved to North Georgia in 2007 and is quietly preparing for the inevitable zombie apocalypse. He has been writing in one form or another since high school. His warped rantings and observations about the cesspool of a world we are surviving in keeps his spiraling descent into madness at bay.

Dennis has had his poetry published by the *League of American Poets, the American Poets Society, 63Channels, Black Petals, Death Head Grin, Word Salad Poetry Magazine* and *Tree Killer Ink*. He has released two spoken-word CD's, *A Random Litter of Thought* (2006) and *Paid in Full* (2007) on Batteryface Records. A short film of Dennis' poem *Hollywood* was made available to coincide with the release of *Paid in Full*.

Visit Dennis at www.dennisbagwell.weebly.com

POETRY BY IAN HUNTER

WHERE THE DEAD GO

Get used to that coffin
Those dimensions
That cramping
Definitely not enough room
to swing a cat
Let alone stretch your arms
Flexing toes will have to do
Tensing calf muscles
Relax
It's not as if you are going
anywhere
Just drowse
Bask in the comfy whiteness
Padded cushions all around
Once, or twice, when
he gets round to you
The keeper of the dead
will pull you out
Ask how you are doing
And if you have a mind
feel like resisting
You could always try and sit up
Rise against those protesting hands
And look at all those other drawers
That stretch into infinity

THE OSSUARY

The ground does not need them
It has taken its fill
Fleshy pieces are no more
He imagines the earth

taking a deep breath, a deep sigh
that pushes up these bones
These gifts
He is always grateful
as he digs a new grave
Stacking the remains of limbs
in little piles, strange kindling
Mere diversions, adornments
Guardians of his greater endeavor
The pyramid of skulls
No mere pile
Each one nestling,
nuzzling against the other
Placement is a matter of precision
Carelessness means disaster
The loss of a lower jaw,
a cratered skull, or worse
With a steady hand
he lights the candles on the floor
and steps back
to watch the dead talk

CALLING THE PAST

Press 1 to hear the taunts of playground bullies

Press 2 to hear your neighbor's threats if you tell anyone what he did

Press 3 to hear the doctor say your mother will never regain
consciousness

Press 4 to hear the life-support machine being switched off

Press 5 to hear your demented father accuse you of stealing

Press 6 to hear the shriek of the smoke detector going off in the middle
of the night

Press 7 to hear the sermon beside the open graves

Press 8 to hear her say there is no reason to stay together

Press 9 to hear the doctor's prognosis which chills you to the bone

Press 0 to hear what's left of your future

About Ian Hunter

Ian Hunter lives in Scotland where he writes stories and poems and edits anthologies as well as being the poetry editor of the British Fantasy Society's journal *Dark Horizons*. His work has appeared in magazines and anthologies in the UK, the USA and Canada, and a collection of some of his previously published poems appeared under the title *Second Hand Poems*. More about his adventures can be found out at www.ian-hunter.co.uk.

POETRY BY WESLEY DYLAN GRAY

THE SKITTERING

On his skin they crawl;
as he sleeps they dominate
his flesh. He's aware of them
in the deep corridors of
his dreams, running the gauntlet
of twisted nightmares.
The skittering sensations
penetrate his pores
as tiny legs tickle the hairs.
They scour across his eyes
and loom in the hot moisture
of his snoring mouth.
They find rest upon the
soft tongue, as dew from
slumbered breath settles on
the hard-shell frames of
their black bodies.
When morning comes, and he
rises from the abyss
of hellish sleep, there is no
sight of them, for with the
breaking dawn they find retreat.
But he knows they've been; he
feels the impressions left behind—
all the pulsing echoes of
The Skittering across his skin.

HERE FOR NOW

I'm in the house,
large and cluttered;
the dead body is
beginning to stink,
smelling like the water
once home to my pet fish.

The girl is there,
trying to eat a sandwich,
but the rotting smell
is getting too strong
for her appetites.

In the basement,
there's another body,
and we must dispose of it
before it starts to decompose.

I'm handed something
like a black plastic sack,
or perhaps a tarp.
I could drag the
bodies with this,
but I swear they should
have placed them on the
plastic first!

Of course, they are
gone, and so these
bodies must remain—
here for now.

FROZEN

Behold the bitter bite
Of winter's hollow bark.
Hunter's wolf is starving,
Lone in sheltered wood.

Catch a solemn scent
Upon a gentle wisp;
Sense the crimson drops
Sinking in the snow.

Rivers run through flesh,
Calm now with fading form.
Fair maiden rests,
With lover's rose in frozen stone.

About Wesley Dylan Gray

Wesley Gray resides in Florida with his wife, Brenda and daughter, Ellie Jadzia. He drinks his coffee strong and his wine from the box. In his spare time, he writes poetry, prose, and things in-between; with these words he attempts to exude a disposition of resplendent contrast, writing things of darkness and light, things beautiful and grotesque. Such writings can be found in various small press magazines and anthologies. Find him online: www.wesleydylangray.com.

POETRY BY
JORGE BALDOMERO VALDES JR.

RAIN DROPS IN HELL

A dark and lonely cloud
Sat outside my house
Dark and lonely me
No one to touch me
Please say my name
I need to at least feel pain
Something instead of a vein.

OUR SKY UNDER THE INFINITE SPOT

Remember our place
Out in the woods
Down some country roads
Quiet, lonely, ours.

I remember the tree
In the backyard it lay
Broken out of the earth
The limb where we'd lay

I can smell your hair
The scent, your soft white skin
Enhanced by the moon light
Memories that stab.

We sat on that tree at night
Your lips, your sweet kisses
Surrounding me, fulfilling my senses
Your lotion, Eucalyptus.

Sweet salivations
Our lips hugging each crevice
My legs gripping the tree
Your legs gripping me.

That was long ago, all is gone
The lonely place, the tree
The moon and my heart
Will be forever apart.

Still I wander for that spot
Those nights, where we'd kiss
In the dark, a bit lonely
But our moment under the sky, forever mine.

ROMANTIC BRUISE

The world may never know.
I wish I didn't. And I know you do.
We both denied it. These masks, our hot hides.
Sometimes, at night I sit up and remember your face.
I can see it, staring at mine. Both dying in just one spot.
Love sickens the soul and hate bleeds through our hearts.
So I took a knife,
And kissed you goodnight.

About Jorge Baldomero Valdes Jr.

Jorge Baldomero Valdes Jr. was born in Lufkin, Texas, on August 28, 1984. His interests have always been an observer of the arts; he likes to look at things and to ponder them for a while.

Jorge decided to write in 2007, and his direct influences have been his professors, including Joe R. Lansdale who teaches Creative Writing at Stephen F. Austin State University. Jorge graduated in 2009 with his major in Spanish and double minors, Ceramic Arts and of course, Creative Writing.

Today Jorge is a graduate student majoring in English. If he happens to feel the need to paint, draw or write about how he feels, he does! To keep up with himself, he drinks lots of coffee.

POETRY BY ANDREA LAHAM

A CHILD THINKING TO HIMSELF AT BEDTIME

There is nothing under the bed
There is nothing under the bed
There is nothing under the—!
That means
They are in the closet!
But Daddy checked…
They're so sneaky, they can fool him.
I wish I could do that, then I wouldn't get caught
When I try to sneak a cookie before dinner.
What's that growling noise?
Quick, under the covers!
There's something crawling on the sheets
But They'll get me if I call out.
I can't move,
I can't fight them,
I can't catch them.
They'll always come back
Night after night
Year after year
In different forms
The coworker who places the blame
The media who twists the message
The wife when you find her untrustworthy
And in the neighbor's bed.
They are all waiting to catch me
And break me in my weakest moment.

WONDERLAND DRIVE

A straight and narrow county road
Off highway fifty-nine
Leads to who-knows-where
Under the half-open eye
Of a waxing crescent.
Two rabbits appeared onto the road
And began a game of chess in the dirt.
The white one sat straight
Analyzing his opponent's erratic movements
Both on and off the board.
The brown one jittered and twitched
In aching anxiety.
He said to the white rabbit if he would please give up a piece.
"You have to earn it," the white one replied as he moved his pulpy red queen,
"You recall what happened to the last challenger."
The brown rabbit's eyes squeezed shut, hearing the red piece squelched into place
Leaving a fresh puddle of blood around her.
The brown one lost his bone-white knight and his stomach growled.
Immediately, his move was made clear:
The chunky bishop, lined with fat
Lay helpless against his other knight.
The white rabbit conceded with a sneer
And the brown rabbit gnawed at the meat.
Suddenly, the raw red knight moved into position
And the brown rabbit slowed his chewing.
"Checkmate," the white rabbit grinned with calm red eyes
And yellow canines.

JUDGEMENT FROM BEYOND

"Sad way to go," she spoke through smoke and musk
And hovered beside me as we watched the end
Of the buildings twist and break and bend
"Even though I've seen it all, this sucks."
I choked and asked her what would happen now
Her answer caught my throat, "You ought to know."
I never understood 'Reap what you sew'
But she took it to heart and raised her brow.
I saw her glance at me before she ripped
Her sickle through the smoky sky and turned
To take me in. I quaked like fire and churned;
I could not fight; she pushed me in the crypt
Beyond the broken seam. "Your penalty,"
She said and closed me in with vengeful glee.

About Andrea Laham

Andrea Laham was born in Dallas, Texas and now lives in Houston.
She graduated from Klein Forest High School in 2008, and now studies
English at Stephen F. Austin State University in Nacogdoches, Texas
with a focus on Creative Writing. She has published poems in her high
school's literary magazine, *Aquilae Stilus*. Her favorite horror short
story is "For All The Rude People" by Jack Ritchie. Her favorite horror
movie is *The Haunting*, but she also has an affinity for dark comedy
and comic books.

POETRY BY BENJAMIN BLAKE

THREE YEARS OF NIGHT

A lengthy affair with the nocturnal sky
Carried out on near-empty trains
And cracked sidewalks, beneath towering city blocks
In the seat of a swing-set alone
The houselights of the suburban set
Flickered to life simultaneously with the stars
A crackling recording of lonely piano keys
With an aging monologue
Played as momentum was gained
I swung higher and higher
Until I parted ways with the wood and chains
And floated towards the heavens
Passing bats in flight
In the chill of the winter air
But I awoke on the parks dew-covered grass
In the wee hours of the morning
And carried on my way home

That night stayed with me like an infatuated scar
And swiftly took over my conscience
Until my mind was almost totally cloaked in darkness
It clung to me like cancer
Enveloping every cell
I would wake in the dreaded afternoon
Seeking solace in the shadows
Eventually rising from wine-stained bath-tubs
When the sun had finally sunk
Well below the horizon

I took an international flight
Back to my crumbling home town
And found it falling into the emerald ocean
I sat back and smoked a stolen cigarette

In company of sirens
And watched the buildings disappear
With the rising tide

Aboard another lengthy plane journey
This time to the city of fallen angels
Sipping an unfortunately petite whiskey
To play distraction to agitating thirst
I sighed, and flirted with a pale reflection
In the cell like window
I watched the sun come up at around 3 AM
While the other passengers
Got lost in dreams

Time has passed
One hundred broken clocks
With one thousand silent alarms
I've shown lovers their graves
And shallowly buried them in despair
I've grown absent from the Gentlemen's Clubs
And I have burnt a handful of carefully hidden photographs
The chemical drenched paper
Burns so strong and bright
These days my whereabouts is relatively unknown
(Apart from a select few that can be trusted)
To the rest of them
I have become a faded memory
Much like a late actor
From an almost forgotten silent movie
Although from time to time
My name is whispered on dead cold frosted nights
It carries in the haunted air
Through dying trees
And crooked tombstones
Drowning in the grounds
Of local Catholic churches

WE ALL FLOAT DOWN HERE

Pry open the casket, smile framed by the light of the spirit lamp
On the early evening of her funeral day, she looks as pretty as always
Sophie rides shot-gun as you drive the long way, one hand rests atop of hers
Her flesh now as cold as her wedding ring, but her heart stills burns like a ravenous furnace
Once home, pour two glasses of cheap Merlot and raise hers to Arden-smeared lips
Twin red rivers trickle from the corners of her mouth
Glenn Miller serenades by moonlight as you entwine throughout the night
And as the morning sun begins to yawn, let the blade caress your wrists in one last goodbye kiss

HELLO DEER

Headlights caught you by surprise
Roadside pity pouring from your eyes
There's only the furs to witness this
And the guilt and glass sticking in your skin
Bathe in new born blood on the dented grille
Your alibi fell through with your fractured legs

Insomnia suggested a late night drive
Gloved hands in death-grip on the steering wheel
Snow drifts alongside troubled thoughts
Down empty streets and vacant routes

Flashlight shone through thin disguise
Slackened mouth spilling disjointed lies
It's only you and me, kid
And the torn fabric and perfume reeking potently of sin
Bask in the light of a tell tale moon
Your dignity died next to the 'Welcome' sign
That should have read

"So who was it, the boy on the track team, or the man with the tire iron?"

About Benjamin Blake

Benjamin Blake was born in the winter of 1985 (in a hospital that is now demolished) and grew up in a small town named Eltham, where he spent a lot of time playing in the woods that sprawled behind his house, and living inside of his head. His work has been published by various magazines and online in Australia, USA and England.

He is currently at work on his first novel as well as a collection of short fiction. He believes in ghosts.

POETRY BY ELISE R. HOPKINS

CRICKETS

They fly out of a passage of Exodus
to blacken the football field.
They swarm around the stadium lights
in a dark cloud and light upon the bleachers.

A small girl's scream
rivals the intensity
of the cricket's cries.
Some spectators tuck their pants into their socks
or flee to the safety of their cars,
but the marching band has no such luxury.
For the sake of uniformity, we stand tall
as dark shapes crawl over our jackets.

As the clock on the scoreboard ticks toward halftime,
the percussionists
flick the insects off their mallets
and knock them off the crotales.
I kick my stick bag and twitch
as bugs come creeping out on jutting legs.

I cringe as we crunch
through crickets on the track.
My hands shake, and my best friend cries
into her clarinet, but once the conductor counts off,
none of this matters.

From the bleachers, no one can see the horror in our faces,
but they can hear lovely melodies soar from the black-speckled earth,
see our shapes spiral on the field in formations
that meld softly with the sounds of our instruments.
Somehow, our music becomes something we are not.
Somehow, it makes us strong.

By its mercy, I can hold my tears until I am alone
in my quiet bedroom, and a single cricket wails outside my window,
plaguing me with a thousand memories that chirp through the night.

GOLDEN GATE BRIDGE IN THE FOG

Two ruddy arms grope toward heaven and disappear.
Cars rush past me into a premature horizon.
I let my eyes glide up the suspension cables,
which grow ever longer at my side,
only to fade into white obscurity.

I pause.

The vibrant arches that should sweep across the sky
are shrouded so completely by droplets of water
that eerie shadows replace any hint of orange.

It is as if ghosts hover all around me.
Perhaps they do.

The chill seeps through my shirt
as I lean across the railing and stare
at the grey water swirling in the bay.
I shiver to think of all the souls
who have passed beneath those opaque depths;
of how the waves hid the bright world
from their unseeing eyes;
of how long they were blind to all but grey
before they could look no more,
and they came to this bridge where I stand now
and sought solace from the ashen sea
alone.

Glad to be so high above
those teasing waves,
I lift my gaze
to the mist that cloaks the bridge

and I race back toward land
lest I lose myself in the sky.

THE DIAGNOSIS

When she woke up, her hand was fine,
but as the day wore on, it turned blue-grey,
the skin rotting to black around her fingernails.

She waited in the ER for six hours
before a doctor would see her.
By then, the grey was traveling
up her arm and her fingers
were completely numb.

She showed the doctor her hand,
the fingers withered and dark.
"You're perfectly healthy," he said.
He smiled and waved her out the door.

About Elise R. Hopkins

Elise R. Hopkins graduated from Stephen F. Austin State University
with a BFA in creative writing in May 2011. Her work has appeared in
HUMID, *The Colored Lens*, and *Travel by the Books* and has been
listed in the Honorable Mentions section of *Allegory*. She maintains an
online presence at www.onlivinginabox.com.

About the Artists

I'LL PROTECT YOU FROM THESE TEARS
Artwork by Lauren Nash

AUNT IMADDER
Artwork by John Frazee

ABOUT THE ARTISTS

Ignacio Bernácer Alpera
Page iii

Ignacio Bernácer Alpera was born in Valencia, Spain, and still lives there today with his wife Pilar and their twin sons. Ignacio is influenced by the master H. R. Giger, whom he met in a Valencia Exposition three years ago. Giger gave Ignacio the inspiration to work hard at his craft.

Ignacio creates artwork from his imagination, and his favorite medium is graphite and pencil. Ignacio is currently working on his own exhibits for the next Valencia Exposition.

Ignacio is beginning a collaboration with his friend Avencio who has created a new global website for artists, musicians, authors, and independent filmmakers. Currently contributors come from Argentina, Brazil, and Spain, but creative people from all countries are invited to participate.

You can see more of Ignacio's work at
http://ignaciobernacer.wordpress.com.

Ester Durães
Page vi

Ester Durães is a Portuguese artist born in France. Always being passionate about art, Ester would not follow her passion until she was nearly sixteen when she drew her first portrait.

One hundred percent self-taught, she started creating celebrity portraits and joining online art communities as her drawing skills improved. As she started mastering graphite, she began exploring her imagination by creating more personal artwork while using color.

Ester loves mainly traditional art and her favorite mediums are graphite and color pencils. The inspiration for her drawings comes both from realistic and fantasy artwork.

She recently started selling accepting commissions, selling her artwork as tubes for digital art and sharing her art on YouTube through speed drawing videos.

You can see more of Ester's work at
http://esther-duraes.deviantart.com.

John Frazee
Page 433

John Frazee was born and raised in New York City, pursuing art his entire life. He Graduated from the High School of Art and Design and Pratt Institute, both in New York City. His work has been exhibited in well over one hundred solo and group exhibitions world-wide by both juror and invitation by curator, including the Biannual International Contemporary Art, Florence, Italy; Art Basel, Miami, Florida; the Museum of Natural History, Invitational, New York City; the Boca Raton Museum of Art, Boca Raton, Florida; the Bruce Museum, Greenwich, Connecticut; and at the Florida Atlantic University, Jupiter, Florida.

You can find more of John's work at www.frazeefinearts.com.

Larkin
Pages 18 and 439

Larkin holds an Associates Degree in Applied Sciences from Onondaga Community College in Syracuse, New York, where he graduated with honors in 1993. At OCC, he majored in illustration with a minor in figurative painting and drawing.

His early work is characterized by isolated nude figures in brightly colored, yet desolate interiors and landscapes.

In later years, his obsession with detail led him to create larger more complex works. He often represents combined biological forms to create new symbols and features small sculpture and fibers techniques in tandem with two-dimensional media. Elements of dark Surrealism and Victorian formality permeate Larkin's recent work.

Larkin's work has been published in *Cthulu Sex Magazine, Pentacle* (UK), *Greatest Uncommon Denominator*, among many others. He is also featured in the book *Imagine the Imagination: New Visions of Surrealism.*

Now living in Washington state, Larkin shows throughout the Puget Sound region, nationally, and internationally.

ABOUT THE ARTISTS

Lauren Nash
Pages viii and 432 and 438

Living in Las Vegas, Nevada with her husband and two sons, Lauren Nash paints and draws in a traditional genre for a living. She grew up in the Rocky Mountains and that was where she found a deep love for crows and ravens.

Lauren records herself making almost all of her art. She edits it together into a vlog and posts it to YouTube as a series called *Transient Art*.

She takes inspiration from her dreams, but she has found that books and music can play a large role. She enjoys the mundane in life, and is constantly looking for new and exciting creations to make and try to bring out emotions in her works.

Visit Lauren's gallery at http://www.transientart.deviantart.com.

Paula McDonald
Pages xvii and 404

Paula McDonald is predominantly a pencil artist who was born and still resides in Central Scotland. She has always been passionate about art and expressing herself though creative means. Upon leaving university after studying Graphic Design, Paula's career path took a different avenue and only recently has her passion for art began to dominate her life once more; alongside her family life and enjoying her two young children.

Self-taught, she began to refine her drawing skills in order to create photo-realistic drawings. The aid of online communities and trial and error has, and still is, aiding her in achieving her growing goals. She is a lover of traditional art in all forms and finds inspiration in anything and everything surrounding her.

Paula draws for personal pleasure and also accepts commissions for her graphite works. She is currently working in collaboration with her sister in writing and illustrating a children's book.

More of Paula's work can be found here:
http://pbird12.deviantart.com.

John Richards
Page 403

John Richards was born in Milwaukee, Wisconsin. His older brother Kerry was an avid fan of the classic black and white horror films, and was instrumental in the development of Johns' artistic interests. A major point in this influence was the year 1975 when Kerry purchased a copy of *The Fantastic Art of Frank Frazetta*. The stark use of black and white ink drawings that Frazetta utilized was the call that John has since answered.

At the age of twelve, John and his family moved from the city to an antiquated farm-stead on the edge of the Kettle Moraine State Forest. It was during this time that he would explore the dark and unfamiliar surroundings of this rural environment, at first the mysterious structures on this seven acre plot, then later into the nearby hills and dark woods.

His current project is the culmination of many years spent amongst those shadows of imagination. He knew what lived in those out-buildings, the bogs and the endless forests. And this is his work.

John is a self taught illustrator, and aspires to establish an art center for talented children and young adults who think and dream beyond what they have been told.

THE
EDITOR'S
CORNER

DETERMINED
Artwork by Lauren Nash

POSSESSED
Artwork by Larkin

THE GOLEM

by Jeani Rector

It was the time of the Blood Libel.

Rabbi Loew felt uneasy. Tensions between the gentiles and the Jews were rapidly increasing. What made this particular night so much more significant than the other stressful evenings was the fact that Passover had begun, and part of observance included the baking of unleavened bread.

Judah Loew heard the rumors. Despite the ridiculousness of the content, the rumors persisted and were believed by the gentiles on the other side of the gate. *Of course the Christians believe the rumors*, Loew thought, *because they are the ones who started them.*

On his side of the gate, Rabbi Loew was afraid for his people. The Jews in the ghetto of Prague were increasingly becoming the object of Christian persecution. Why, only that very afternoon, a gentile had stood at the ghetto gate and shouted, "You Jews murdered Christ! We ought to crucify all of you!"

And what could the Jews do? By law, they were not allowed to leave the gates of the ghetto. Nor would they want to, because to leave the security of the ghetto community would be to risk one's life at the wrath of the gentiles.

And now there was this new rumor. The Christians were accusing the Jews of baking the unleavened Passover bread with an additional ingredient other than the water of *matzoh* and flour. The additional ingredient was supposed to be the blood of murdered Christian children.

Rabbi Loew shook his head sadly. No matter what went wrong in the Christian community, it was always the fault of the Jews. Christians blamed Jews for everything. If a child went missing, a Jew had snuck out of the ghetto in the middle of the night and committed murder. If that same child turned up floating face down in the Vltava River, well then, the Jews had committed murder by drowning the victim. If a

440

disease spread through the Christian community, then the Jews were poisoning all the wells. If the weather turned bad, then the Jews were incurring the wrath of God.

Loew wondered, *How can anyone believe that Jews are murdering Christian children to use blood in bread? This is the year 1580, and in these modern times, people should be more tolerant of others. It is not like a hundred years ago when superstitions abounded. In God's glory, Jewish people do not murder children to bake bread.*

Rabbi Judah Loew was an aging man; his beard was gray and his posture stooped. He had lived a long time and had been devoted to his people during his entire life. He could not forsake the Jews living in the Prague ghetto now.

But what could he do to help his people? Instinctively Loew understood that very soon, all the tensions would come to a head and the gentiles would burst through the gates of Prague to destroy the Jews.

Somehow he would save his people.

He sat in a chair in his front room, watching the fire that warmed the cottage. Deep in thought, Loew almost didn't hear the faint knocking at his front door. When he did hear the knocking, Loew's first thought was that his wife would answer the door. But then he realized that his wife was fast asleep in the other room.

So he stood, stretched, and walked to the door. "Who's there?" he softly asked without making any moves to open the door. These days, one couldn't be too careful.

"It's Itzak," came the voice of Loew's son-in-law. "Open up, Father, I have news."

Loew let Itzak inside. "Warm yourself up by the fire," Loew invited.

But Itzak only stood inside the door, closing it behind him. "There's no time. A child has been found dead. Father, the child was found inside the ghetto gate. And the child is a gentile."

"What!" Loew sputtered. "That's impossible. It's only another rumor, Itzak."

"No," the son-in-law said, "I saw the dead child myself."

There was silence for a moment.

"Then it begins," Loew finally said.

"Yes, the slaughtering of the Jewish people of Prague begins," agreed Itzak. "I think the Christians put the dead child within our gates."

"We don't know that," Loew said.

"It is a set-up!" cried Itzak.

"That is not the problem," Loew said.

"What are you talking about?"

"The problem is to figure out what we can do to protect our people."

The words sunk in. Itzak asked, "What can we do? The gentiles will be storming the gates by morning to kill us all."

"I will pray," Loew said.

Itzak's face grew scarlet. "You will pray! You will pray! And all of our people will be slaughtered like cattle."

"God will protect us."

"Father, you are a Cabalist."

"Cabalism is a mystical interpretation of the Scriptures that is communicated only in an appropriate setting and in discreet ways," Loew said.

"No Father, you know what I mean."

"I seek religious and mystical experiences through Cabala. I seek truth through the divine interpretation of Cabalism."

"Cabalism has two sides. Two interpretations."

"Itzak, what are you saying?"

"You know what I'm saying." Itzak was grim. "The *Sephir Yetzirah* is the Book of Creation. Only a righteous man, a pure and just man, can use Cabala to achieve the power of Genesis."

"It would be an abomination!" Loew cried. "It would be a monster!"

"Father, you must create a monster to save your people."

Loew rubbed his eyes with shaking hands. He and his son-in-law remained standing in front of the door, neither of them speaking. Loew gazed into the fire, deep in thought. He felt apprehension and dread. But most of all, he felt resignation.

His son-in-law was right. The Jewish people of Prague could only be saved by a monster.

"It may be just legend," Loew whispered.

"No, it is not legend," Itzak said. "It is Cabala. It is the other side of Cabala, the dark side. It is dark magic. It is no legend."

"We will need three people," Loew said.

"Does that mean you'll do it?"

"Do I have a choice?" Loew felt a hot tear trickle down his withered cheek. "Can I in good conscience allow my people to be slaughtered? But on the other hand, can I in good conscience be so arrogant as to pretend I am God?"

"No," said Itzak as he opened the front door, "you don't have a choice. I'll fetch Yakov, and then we'll be three."

Loew shut the door as his son-in-law walked into the night. He knew that in order to prepare to use the power of the Cabala, he must be ready. He must be pure. He must be cleansed.

He began to heat water on the cookfire, then got his nail clippers. The primordial protection that Adam had in the Garden was the shields of the finger and toenails. The cleansing and paring of the nails was vital in order to be open to Cabala's power. Carefully Loew clipped his fingernails and his toenails, and then threw them into the fire to be burned.

When the water on the cookfire was warm, Loew poured it into a glass. With his right hand symbolizing Hesed, he poured the water on his left, and then reversed the process. The left hand symbolized Din. Now his hands were clean.

He undressed and then carefully chose his ritual garments. He put on clean clothes that had been purified from washing. Finally Loew was ready, and he sat in a chair, patiently waiting for his son-in-law's return.

He didn't have to wait long. He heard a knocking on the front door. Again Loew questioned who it was before he opened the door. He let Itzak inside, and then softly greeted his favorite student, Yakov. Young Yakov desired to become a Rabbi, and Loew felt that the youth had the qualities to achieve his dream.

"I know why I'm here," Yakov said before Loew had a chance to explain.

"Good, then we are all of the same mind," Loew said. "We must go to the river immediately."

All were aware of the risks involved to travel to the river. All understood that it was against the law to go beyond the walls of the Jewish ghetto. But Itzak knew of a secret crevice in the wall where rocks could be removed. It was a way out; an escape into the world beyond.

It was late, very late. By the position of the moon, Loew judged the time to be about one in the morning. He took a deep breath when he walked out his front door, sniffing the air. The air smelled fresh and there was no scent of rain.

Loew and his followers stepped quickly through a deserted, narrow lane of the ghetto. The sky was incredibly clear, and the moon was a tiny crescent. Millions of stars sparkled and shimmered, and the night sounds were beautiful as crickets sang in their search for mates. Loew took another deep breath of the fragrant night air, and felt how wonderful it was to be alive in such a world. God had created beauty, but mankind created hate and prejudice. It was up to Loew to join God and mankind together to achieve peace.

Silently the three traveled through the dark streets of the ghetto. They had no candles and the moon's light was dim. Loew knew when they had reached the right place at the wall because Itzak signaled with his hand to come forward.

All three quickly removed rocks from the wall. The opening was small and it was fortunate that none in the trio were overly large. When all three men squeezed through the space, they reached inside to pull the rocks back into place. It would not do to leave the hole exposed in the wall for any guards to see. If the hole was discovered, then none of the three could ever return home.

It was exhilarating to experience such an adventure, and Loew chastised himself for permitting such an emotion. He saw it as pride, and to be prideful was to sin. Rabbi Loew understood that in order for Cabala to work, he needed to be righteous and pure in thought.

So he focused on the purpose of this dangerous trip. He was doing this for the salvation of his people.

Once outside the wall, the three men were careful as they walked the streets of the gentile city. They crouched and stayed within the dark shadows of the buildings. They walked quickly and with purpose. Loew's eyes darted back and forth as he traveled, searching for anything amiss. His senses were heightened and adrenalin coursed through his veins.

The buildings became sparse as Loew and his followers reached the edge of the city. He smelled water and knew he was close to the river. Soon he heard the water, and felt the slippery mud beneath his shoes. Moving underneath the trees and through the underbrush, Loew found a location that seemed to fit his needs.

The dusky, earthy scent of damp mud filled his nostrils. Mud was what Loew had been seeking. And there was a lot of it here.

"Let's begin our work," Loew instructed.

In the dark of the night, the three men got to their knees. They used their hands as shovels, their fingers as molds. They scooped the rich, fertile mud and began to push it into a mound. They worked together as a unit, shaping the wet earth until it began to resemble something. It resembled a silhouette lying in a prone position, flat on its back.

It resembled a man.

Loew stood erect. His arms and his knees were slick with wet mud. His hands were caked with earth and he held them out in front of him.

"I can create a man, but I cannot create a soul," he said. "That is for God alone."

"What do you mean, Rabbi?" asked Yakov.

"This earthen man shall be mute and without will," Loew explained.

"But you are his will," Itzak said. "This man shall do your bidding, am I right?"

"Absolute power corrupts absolutely," Loew said softly. "I hope you are right and that this abomination will awaken to do my bidding. If he awakens at all. That has yet to be seen."

"What is this thing we are creating?" asked Yakov.

"This is a golem," Loew answered. "I will name the golem Josef, after Josef Sheda of the Talmud. Josef Sheda was half human and half spirit, and saved the Jews from conflict. It is a fitting name for this golem, who is to save the Jews of Prague."

Then Loew said, "We have three people here. Each of us represents the elements of the Cabala. I am air. You, Itzak, are fire. And you, Yakov, are water."

"The earth is the fourth element. Who represents the earth?" asked Yakov.

"Why, the golem, of course," Loew said. "In Genesis it says, *And the Lord God formed a man of the dust of the ground, and breathed into his nostrils the breath of life.*"

Rabbi Loew began to chant, "*Shanti, shanti, dahat, dahat.*"

The surrounding countryside darkened even more as clouds quickly covered the moon. Sudden gusts of wind yanked the leaves from the bushes, and their limbs became horizontal as they yielded to the heavy flow of the strong breezes. Night creatures scurried to the safety of their burrows. The sound of the rushing Vltava River rose to a roar.

Loew raised his voice to be heard, and shouted the Hebrew words of Cabala, "*Ato bra Golem devuk hakhomer v'tigzar zedim chevel torfe yisroel.* Life to the clay man!"

The wind began to howl through the trees at an accelerated rate. Small whirlpools of leaves and debris swirled around the man of mud, who was still prostrate on the ground.

Once again, Loew got to his knees. He leaned forward, bending over the golem's head. He had a thin stick in his right hand. On the forehead of the clay monster, Loew used the stick to draw the Hebrew word *EMET.*

"*EMET* means truth," Loew shouted above the wind as he rose to his feet. "The truth is to be told."

A large tree branch, close by, came crashing down. The wind was relentless in its fury. Nothing was spared. The clothes of the three men were flattened against their bodies as the wind pressed against them. They leaned forward as to retain their balance, unconsciously pushing back at the wind that pushed them forward.

And then the thing made of mud moved.

The golem's huge hand closed into a fist. His knee rose as he tucked his massive foot closer to his body. The monster's elbow bent to prop himself into a sitting position.

The wind suddenly ceased. There was no sound, except the river, and even that became almost quiet. The stillness of the forest was eerie. No owl shrieked and no mouse squeaked. No crickets chirped. There was total and absolute stillness.

"Josef," Loew spoke, surprised at the steadiness of his own voice as it broke the stillness of the forest. "You must awaken now. You must arise and follow me."

It was frightening to witness the golem rise to his feet. The man made of clay seemed to extend nearly into the sky as he stood erect. He was almost seven feet tall and his arms and shoulders were massive. His head was almost square and his eyebrows protruded like that of a Neanderthal. The features on his face were vague because he was smooth and appeared almost unfinished.

The golem looked like what he was: a monster made of mud.

"Rabbi," said Yakov and his voice shook, "how can we sneak such a being back into the ghetto?"

"He is dark like the night," Loew answered.

"But he is so large," Yakov said.

"He is dark like the night," Loew repeated. "He will not be easily seen. And God will protect us during our journey back."

"Have faith," Itzak told Yakov.

"Josef," Loew commanded, "you will follow me."

The lumbering hulk started to walk, his huge feet shuffling. Yet the golem made no noise as he lurched forward. Appearing clumsy and oafish, he nonetheless walked silently and steadily.

This creation will be very efficient at what I will set him to do, Loew thought. *And I am afraid. Deathly afraid.*

Loew was not afraid of the trip back to the ghetto. He was afraid of what he would be forced to do once he got there.

Silently and carefully, they made their way back through the city of gentiles.

Three men had come out of the ghetto.

Four men were returning.

When they reached the secret hole in the ghetto wall, the men had a problem. There was no way that a huge creature like the golem could possibly squeeze through the tiny opening.

"He will climb," said Loew. And the golem mounted the stone wall and then scaled it.

Rays of dawn light were beginning to streak the sky with colors in the east. The men could see themselves more clearly now as they pushed the rocks back into the wall to disguise the escape route. They knew that time was running out for them, and also running out for the Jews of Prague.

The morning sun was rising quickly now, and its light was reflecting off of the slick mud surface that was Josef. The monster could be viewed in all his massive proportions, a hideous caricature of a man. To view the creature was to experience awe mixed with fear. It was very obvious that Josef could be strong and threatening.

Just as they began to head back to the Rabbi's cottage, the three men stopped in their tracks to listen. Josef mimicked the men, making no sound of his own. But then there *were* sounds. Loew could hear a large crowd of people somewhere outside of the wall and they were approaching the gate of the ghetto.

"They've come!" cried Itzak in a panic. "The gentiles have come to kill the Jews of Prague!"

"Rabbi," pleaded Yakov, "send the golem."

Loew hesitated. To send Josef would be fury unleashed. At the last minute when it really mattered, Loew found himself uncertain.

"I can't," he said meekly.

"Send the golem or we die!" cried Itzak. "We will all be slaughtered, every one of us! Think of your family!"

"I don't know what to do," said Loew.

"It is no sin to defend oneself!" shouted Itzak.

"Please Rabbi, send the golem," begged Yakov.

Grimly Loew stood there, his feet planted on the ground as though he were a tree. He could hear the gentiles getting closer, and he could tell that there were many in number, probably hundreds of angry people, all coming to kill.

He needed to decide. Perhaps the golem was an evil being. But nothing was more effective to fight evil than another evil. The gentiles were coming for a spree of mass murder. That was the worst evil of all.

He, Rabbi Judah Loew, would send the golem. He would burn in Hell for this act so that his people could live.

"Josef." Loew spoke to his monster as though the golem were a child. "You must protect the Jews from the gentiles. The Christians are storming the gates of the ghetto. You must stop them." Loew hesitated, and then added, "Josef. Stop them any way you can. Do whatever is necessary so that the gentiles do not enter the ghetto."

"Thank you, Rabbi," breathed Itzak.

Yakov said nothing. He just watched and waited.

The golem turned his square head towards the gate. He straightened his massive shoulders and then began to lurch forward. The monster walked with huge strides, and the earth shook beneath his feet. The immense hands were clenched in anger. The protruding forehead and brow were knitted with rage.

Loew watched with dread. Yes, it was fury unleashed. Because the golem was simply a reflection of Loew's own inner hatred, the hatred that he always denied existed. But the hatred for the gentiles was there, and now the golem would mirror that hate.

A righteous man could possibly create a righteous golem. But a man who secretly hated would create an atrocity.

It was too late. Josef was going to have his way with the gentiles.

And Rabbi Loew was horrified at himself, because he found he had no desire to stop his monster. He had set his evil creation free to do the destruction that he himself secretly wished to do.

The golem ripped the gate off its hinges as though it were a toy. He stomped out of the ghetto, pounding the ground with his feet. His massive arms outstretched, the golem began grabbing the gentiles, one right after another. He ripped them apart, tearing off arms and legs and throwing pieces of people by the wayside. The gentiles tried to run, but Josef also ran in his lumbering but fast gait.

Loew shut his eyes, but the screams of the gentiles could not be ignored. It was horrible, horrible, but the Rabbi was rejoicing in his heart.

Yakov began to panic. "Rabbi, call him off."

Loew just stood where he was, his eyes closed.

"Rabbi, the golem is killing people," Yakov tried again.

"He's right," Itzak agreed. "Stop the golem. The golem has done enough."

Loew did not move. *Absolute power corrupts absolutely.*

"Rabbi!" Yakov began to shout to be heard above the screams of the gentiles, "Stop the golem!"

"No," Loew said.

Yakov stared at Loew in disbelief. The young Yakov hadn't wanted anyone killed. That was not supposed to be part of this. The golem was created to threaten, not to maim and murder. Why was the Rabbi allowing the golem to commit the same mortal sins that the monster was created to prevent?

"Stop the golem or I will," Yakov said.

Loew laughed. "And what could a mouse like you do to stop a powerful monster like Josef?"

"I don't know, but I intend to do something."

With that, Yakov ran to follow the golem.

Passing the ruined gate, Yakov picked up speed. The sun had risen fully now, so he could see the huge monster in the distance. It sickened him to view all of the blood and body parts that were littered on the countryside. Yakov tried to run without seeing what lay everywhere on the ground. He shut his ears to the screams and the moans of the maimed and wounded gentiles.

And finally Yakov reached the golem.

Josef loomed directly in front of Yakov. Without thinking, Yakov leaped and landed on the golem's back. His arms around the golem's neck, Yakov hung on to the monster's back.

Josef stopped moving. Then he reached behind himself and pulled Yakov over his head. The monster literally threw Yakov over his head and the young man landed hard on the ground.

Yakov couldn't breathe for a moment. He lay on the ground, gasping for air. The moment was too long.

Josef approached, and the massive clay man loomed above Yakov.

Yakov was doomed.

Suddenly he heard a voice. It was Rabbi Loew!

"Josef," Loew said, "don't hurt him. Don't touch Yakov."

Yakov turned his head to see Loew standing behind the monster. Loew was breathing very hard. The Rabbi had run after both he and the golem and now he had caught them.

"Rabbi," Yakov said, as he still lay on the ground, "put an end to this."

Loew stood without speaking, his breathing beginning to calm. The monster didn't move. It was waiting.

"Do the right thing," Yakov tried again.

Loew looked around as though seeing the gruesome scene before him for the first time.

"These people have families too," said Yakov. "Let's be the first ones to end the hate. Let's lead by example."

Still Loew did not move. The golem waited for his master's decision.

"You have accomplished what you wanted to do," Yakov added. "It's over."

"Yes, it's over," Loew finally agreed. "Josef, come to me. Bend down. Let me whisper into your ear."

But instead of speaking into Josef's ear, Loew quickly rubbed a letter of the word *EMET* off from the monster's forehead.

The letter was *E*, and once removed, the word *EMET* was then changed to *MET*.

While *EMET* was the Hebrew word for truth, *MET* was the Hebrew word for death.

The golem crumbled, turning to earth once again, and it left a huge mound of mud upon the ground.

Dust to dust.

Editor's note: All of the characters in "The Golem" were real people who lived in the 16th century. It is a fact that in 1580, Rabbi Loew single-handedly saved the Jews of Prague from slaughter by the gentiles. It is legend about how he managed to do that.

The Jewish stories about the golem may have been the inspirations for Mary Shelley's *Frankenstein*.

A GHOST IN THE HOUSE

by Jeani Rector

The old Victorian house loomed ahead of her.

She was here because the owner had called her on the phone, asking for an appointment right away, and telling her that it was an emergency. But in Tara's line of business, all of her calls were emergencies, because all her clients thought they had a ghost in the house.

She pushed past the gate of the picket fence which hadn't been painted in so long that it was gray. Squinting against the sunlight, she quickly scanned the ornate window frames on the second story of the house. The house had a third floor, but it was so tiny, she figured it must only contain an attic.

She saw that some shingles had blown off the roof and now littered the tattered and weedy front lawn, and part of the porch overhang was loose and leaned away from the wind. The overhang was old, but the two columns holding it up seemed strong and freshly painted, and the porch underneath looked new and solid.

Reaching the new and still unvarnished wooden slats that made up the base of the porch, Tara saw a beautiful brass knocker on the door that was in the shape of a lion's head. In fact, the entire front door appeared brand new; a solid, polished oak. She could see that the house was in the process of being restored to its original beauty; and in the meantime it was a collage of the rundown and the fresh, the old and the new, all combined.

So she used the brass knocker, and was satisfied at the noise it made. *Loud enough to wake the dead,* she thought. Of course, Tara knew that if anything dead walked in this house, it would never sleep; not until she helped lay it to rest.

The oak door opened, and a young man stood in front of her. "You must be Tara Sanders," he said, and then beckoned for her to come inside.

452

To say the interior was gloomy would have been optimistic. The inside of the house was worse than gloomy; it was almost dark. All the windows were dirty, preventing most of the light from shining inside. Tara had to wait for her eyes to adjust to the dimness. When they did, she could see a thick layer of dust on the floor, and cobwebs were seemingly everywhere. There was no furniture in the house, but she could see a brick fireplace. In the corner was a staircase that went drunkenly up to the next floor, its steps warped and minus a few boards.

Tara was thinking that if someone had purposely decorated this old place as a Halloween fun house, they couldn't have done a better job than what time did naturally.

"I want to apologize for the condition of the house," the man told her. "I just inherited it, and it's been empty for years. I haven't had time to work on the interior yet, so it's still a wreck. As you can see, I've been renovating the outside, and I've gotten quite a lot done out there. The house is now pretty much structurally sound. But now that I'm ready to start on the inside, I can't, because I found out that this house is haunted—"

Tara held up her hand to interrupt. "Stop; please don't say anything more. I don't want to be influenced by anything you might say. I need a clean slate to work with. My job is to tell *you*, not for you to tell *me*."

"Well, okay," the man said. "Anyway, I'm Michael; so what do we do now?"

"Let me take a tour of the house," she told him, and then added, "By myself. Can you wait outside?"

"Well, I don't know," Michael said with a doubtful expression. "Do you think you'll be all right here, alone in this house?"

She smiled. "I may or may not be alone in this house. But yes, I'll be fine. Go ahead and wait outside, and please don't worry."

He went out the front door, and Tara turned to face the inside of the house.

She ventured further into the large, front room. It looked as though it had been a parlor, probably the area where guests had been greeted and entertained when the house was new. Tara guessed that the kitchen and probably a formal dining room would be on the other side of the parlor, and that the bedrooms would be upstairs.

And then suddenly Tara knew that what she was looking for would be upstairs. She felt a chill, the hair stood up in the follicles on her arms, and she thought, *So it's true; this house is haunted.*

It came to her as a sense of foreboding; a deep feeling of dread. Whatever walked in this house knew evil. But the question was, did it do evil or was evil done to it?

She went to the rattletrap stairs and began to climb, testing every step before she put her weight upon it. The railing beside the stairwell was wobbly, so Tara chose not to use it.

Cobwebs hung from the walls, just like in the movies. Before this, Tara had always thought that movie cobwebs were exaggerations. But here they were, hanging down from practically everywhere. The thought made her uncomfortable—where there were cobwebs, there were probably spiders.

Finally she reached the top of the stairs. She stood at a landing, which led to a hallway. There were five doors, all shut.

She heard a soft murmuring from behind one of the closed doors. It was like a voice, but not loud enough for her to make out the words. Was it a man's voice or a woman's? She wasn't sure. Tara peered down the hallway, and decided that the sound seemed to come from the first door on the left.

She went to the door from where she thought she had heard the quiet, muffled talking; but there was only silence now. Tara's hand touched the crystal doorknob which looked incredibly old-fashioned but was still beautiful. The door opened and she looked inside.

Nothing.

It was just a bare room, no furniture, and full of dust. At least the room was much brighter than the rest of the house. The upstairs windows were not as dirty as they were on the first floor, so the sky sent a little filtered sunlight inside. This room's window was curtained with fabric that was long since tattered and frayed.

Leaving the room, Tara jumped a little as the door swung shut behind her. But old houses sometimes did that and there was often nothing supernatural about it. Old houses tended to lean from their foundations, causing an imbalance in the leveling.

Or there could be a ghost in the house.

She opened the other four doors and peeked inside every one. It turned out to be three more empty bedrooms and a bathroom. The tub in the bathroom was huge and stood on top of clawed animal feet.

Oddly, none of these other four doors shut on their own; only the first door had done that.

And then she heard the muffled voice again. It came from behind her, so Tara left the bathroom and turned back around. The voice seemed to gain in pitch, sounding suddenly urgent. Tara was still unable to make out the individual words, but she thought it was coming from the first empty bedroom which was the only one with the door shut.

She went back down the hallway to that bedroom. Cautiously she pushed open the door again, her hand on the crystal doorknob. Her feeling of foreboding was stronger now.

This time she knew an entity would be waiting for her.

It would show itself.

And when Tara looked inside, there was a dark-haired girl standing in the middle of the otherwise empty room. The girl looked to be about thirteen or so, and her face was thin and drawn, making her dark eyes appear luminously large in her small face. She was wearing a shift-like dress and her hair, uncombed, streamed down her back in tangles.

She was holding out her arm, and Tara could see something shiny in her hand.

The girl spoke a single word: "Stop."

The girl dropped what she had been holding. And then she disappeared.

Tara hesitated, closed her eyes, and took a deep breath. Something had been in the girl's hand. Something shiny. She looked at the floor where she had last seen the ghost before it had disappeared.

There it was, a shining silver object reflecting the sunlight that streamed through the dirty window. Taking a second deep breath, Tara went to the center of the old, dusty room and grabbed the item off of the floor.

It was a silver locket with no chain attached. The locket was rounded on the ends, about an inch and a half long, and an inch wide, giving it a slightly oblong shape. It was engraved on the front with little lines etched into the shape of a flower. When Tara turned it over, she saw that the back was simply smooth silver.

Then she noticed that there was a clasp on the side of the locket. She tried to spring the latch, and suddenly it opened.

There was a tiny black and white photograph of a man inside. The man looked like Michael. But was it really Michael, or could it be one of his forbearers? Could it be a father or a grandfather? Didn't Michael say that he had inherited this old Victorian house?

And then suddenly Tara knew that there were two ghosts in this house, not one. Because she still felt a sense of evil, and it had not come from the thirteen-year-old girl who gave her the locket.

The young, dark-haired girl had given Tara a warning. The warning had been about something else in this house.

She took the locket and made her way back down the rickety stairs. Tara went out the front door, because she was ready to talk to Michael about his haunted house. She found him standing in the weedy lawn, inspecting the unpainted fence. He turned around at her approach, his eyebrows expectantly raised.

"I want to know about a girl," she told him. Tara described the ghost from the second floor of the old Victorian house.

"I only know from family gossip," he said. "The description sounds like Karen, who would be my aunt today; my mother's sister. Karen ran away from home way back around nineteen-sixty-nine or nineteen-seventy; you know, back in the hippie days. The story goes that she ran away to join a commune. So, it can't be Karen, because she's not dead; or if she is dead, she didn't die here."

"Don't you think thirteen is a little young to be running off to a commune, no matter what year it was?" Tara asked.

"Actually, I think she was supposed to be around fourteen or fifteen when she ran away. She probably just looked younger."

Tara studied Michael for a minute. Then she made her decision, and told him, "Karen did not run away. Karen is dead; killed in this house. In fact, she was murdered by this man." And Tara held up the locket.

Michael looked at the locket, and blanched. "That's me. Wait, it can't be me. That locket looks old. And I never had a picture like that taken."

"It's not you," Tara said. "It's your grandfather."

"What!" Michael exclaimed. "Are you trying to tell me that my grandfather murdered his own daughter?"

"I don't know the circumstances yet," Tara said, "but I think your grandfather is dead as well. So, both your aunt and your grandfather are dead, and both of their ghosts are in this house."

Michael stood with his mouth open, appearing stunned.

Tara continued, "There is a second side to the locket, which is supposed to have a photo of his wife. As you can see, the second side is empty. What happened to your grandmother?"

"I don't know. She divorced my grandfather. I was never told what happened after that."

"Another so-called runaway?"

"Maybe, but I don't think so."

"Okay, I don't think so either. I don't feel your grandmother's presence in your house," Tara conceded, "but your grandfather is definitely here. We need to make another appointment. I'm leaving now, but it is imperative that I come back."

"Wait," Michael said, "you're just going to leave now? What about the ghosts? I can't go back inside that house until you get rid of them! You promised to eliminate any hauntings."

"Oh, I'll do that, all right," Tara told him. "I'll be back tomorrow night after dark. Be here."

"What do I do in the meantime?"

"Stay outside. You can paint the fence. But afterwards, spend the night in a motel."

She went through the gate and got into her car. On the drive home, Tara reflected on the house, and what it had done to her. Most hauntings were harmless; and Tara knew that usually she witnessed things that had happened a long time ago. Most hauntings were from a moment in time, captured as though it were on a DVD; the same recording that played over and over again. Those were the easiest ghosts to send back to the grave.

But Tara was sensitive to the afterlife, and intuitively understood when evil was present. And she felt that evil had a presence in that old Victorian house.

She was drawn to the old house. It was as though it was reaching out to her through her subconscious, and Tara had the irrational feeling that the house wanted her presence; needed her participation in something unspoken.

She figured that somehow, this would end badly. But she couldn't walk away. Something compelled her to come back; and she felt that the house was possessing her, but she felt powerless to change anything.

The next evening, the dark sky seemed to set the mood for what was to come. Because it was starting to rain, night came faster, throwing its ebony blanket over the town to change it from a place of friendly familiarity to a maze of menacing shadows. Tara wondered, *Is the weather an omen?*

She left her apartment at eight o'clock. Lightning flashed, and what began as drizzle suddenly changed. The sky opened to release torrents of water that slammed down upon the earth without mercy. Tara ran to her carport and escaped the pelting rain inside her car. The windshield quickly fogged and she turned the blower on to full force to clear the inside glass. The windshield-wipers made an effort to grant some visibility, but the effect was dismal, and the glass was constantly streaked with water.

The feeling that she had to return to the house was very strong now. She was bringing the tools of her trade with her: five white candles, a tiny, round table that only stood ten inches off the ground, and a piece of white chalk.

Tara drove up to the house and looked at it. Through the driving rain, it seemed menacing, looming out of the darkness as though it were a monolith; waiting. She put her car in park and noticed that Michael's car was already there, and he was sitting inside of it.

Together they ran in the rain towards the porch of the old Victorian house. They stood beneath the overhang, watching the rain water run off, splashing into puddles on the ground. Then Michael opened the door and they stepped into the entryway, dripping onto the hardwood floor.

"Bad night, huh?" Michael said.

"Actually, it's a perfect night for a séance," Tara told him.

"A séance? Really?"

"Well," Tara said, "what do you think I do?"

Michael looked at her. "I'm not sure, but I guess I'll find out. That's a pretty big tote bag you've got there. What's in it? The kitchen sink?"

"An itty bitty table," she said. "Here, help me lug this stuff up the stairs. We need to summon the spirits on the second floor, in the first bedroom. My perceptions are pretty strong there."

When they reached the first bedroom, the door was shut once again, even though all the other doors on that floor were open. Michael was holding the tote, so Tara reached for the crystal doorknob. Slowly she turned it, and the door opened.

The room was empty.

"Good thing I had the electricity turned on," Michael said as he flicked on the switch. A soft glow came from the ceiling.

They put the table down in the middle of the room. Tara laid a scarf on it that looked as though it might have come from India, and placed a large, thick candle upon it. She lit the candle and it emitted a pleasant scent. Four other candles were in holders, and Tara placed them upon the floor, all lit now; one in every corner.

She turned off the electric light. Immediately gloom enveloped the room.

The five candles cast long, moving shadows upon the walls. The flickering light made it appear as though the shadows were leaping around the room in some sort of tribal dance.

"Sit on the floor at the little table," Tara instructed. "The room is bare of furniture, except for the table, and that's good, because now we'll have minimum interference. A candle is placed in each corner of the room, to be directions of the points of a compass. The fifth candle on the table is to center the Spirit of Death and to provide a beacon to lead the two entities here."

"What do you mean, the Spirit of Death?" Michael looked uneasy.

"Well, you don't think they are alive, do you?"

Tara took the white chalk she had brought and got down on her knees and began to draw upon the wooden floor, making a large circle around the table. Michael simply watched as he remained seated at the small table.

"We will be protected as long as we remain inside this circle," she informed him. "Under no conditions are you to move outside this circle, no matter what you see or hear."

She sat down next to Michael, and took his hand. She started to speak in an almost singsong voice, "Open, we are open to you from the other side. Hear us speak of our willingness to listen to your communications. Let us know you are with us in this room."

Tara stopped, and became silent. The only sound was the rain drumming upon the window.

The temperature of the room dropped noticeably. She saw Michael's breath forming mist in the air. The candle flame on the short table was flickering wildly and distorted the appearance of their faces until they became grotesque impersonations of reality. She felt a change in the air as though a static charge of electricity was present; the sort of thing that precedes a bolt of lightning.

She knew something had come.

She knew they were now three, not two.

The light from the tabletop candle shined, wavering from some draft that blew cold air into the room. The flickering flames caused the shadow-creatures upon the walls to dance wildly.

And then there was a shimmering orb floating over the table. It was translucent and sparkled as though it was sprinkled with morning dew, except it was night and that wasn't possible. It got stronger until it formed the shape of a person, but still it lacked any details, as though it was unfinished. The form seemed delicate and moved like waves in the ocean.

Tara continued to stare, staying calm. The shape moved and drifted in and out of sight, sometimes appearing easier to see, and other times, almost disappearing underneath the dim light of the candles.

The nearly transparent shape hovered in place, undulating as it shimmered. It resembled lace, having some substance, but thin enough to be able to see through it. It was a specter, a phantom; an elusive apparition that seemed like an impossibility, but it was there all the same.

Suddenly Michael let go of her hand. He started to stand up.

"No! Sit back down!" Tara cried. "Stay inside the circle, where you'll be safe!"

But it was too late. Michael turned to run.

She tried to catch him. She stood and grabbed for his arm. For a moment it was a tug-of-war, and she tried to pull him back. But her grip was unsure. Michael slipped from her grasp and tumbled, falling onto the floor, the upper half of his body lying outside the chalk circle.

There was a keening sound, and the ghostly shape moved to hover over Michael. Tara saw the phantom enter Michael's body.

And then Michael stood up, a horrible expression on his face. He had become the man in the locket photo. "I'll kill you!" he screamed.

As Michael lunged for her, Tara cried: *"L'envoi des morts, the sending of the dead!"*

Suddenly there was a gust of wind in the bedroom; impossible inside a closed building, but happening nonetheless. Small whirlpools of dust and debris swirled around the floor, and then the candle on the table blew out. The wind was becoming relentless in its fury. Their clothes were flattened to their bodies as the wind pressed against them.

The wind pushed Michael away from her, and she stepped back into the chalk circle. Tara shouted again, at the top of her voice: *"L'envoi des morts, the sending of the dead!"*

And then the wind stopped just as quickly as it began.

The house was quiet; empty and still. The ghosts were gone.

She looked at Michael. He looked back at her, blinking, innocent.

"Let's go outside," Tara said, "now. We'll leave the table and the candles behind."

She turned on the ceiling light, and walked around the bedroom, blowing out the four remaining candles that had somehow remained lit. Then together they made their way down the ramshackle stairs and out to the porch.

They walked to their cars, heedless of the rain that still fell. When they reached their cars, Michael asked, "It's over now, right? The ghosts are gone?"

"The ghosts are gone, but it's not over."

"What are you talking about?" Michael began yelling. "If the ghosts are gone, than this is just an ordinary house!"

"Michael, this will never be an ordinary house. The ghosts did not possess the house. This house possessed the ghosts! That's why they haunted this house, because they couldn't leave! As it is, you and I barely got out with our lives. This house doesn't want to let anyone go."

He stared at her, the rain running in rivulets down his face. "You're crazy."

She turned to him in anger. "After everything you've witnessed tonight, you doubt me now?"

"But my grandfather murdered my aunt. The house didn't kill her...he did. You said so yourself."

"Yes, your grandfather physically murdered your aunt. But the house made him kill so it could keep them both. It drove your grandfather insane by possessing him. And this house will do the same thing to anyone else who tries to live here. That's why no one has wanted to live here for almost forty years."

"This house is just wood and nails!"

"For the sake of your very life, you'd better listen to me," she told him. "There is a dimension harboring corrupt forces that would prey upon the living as if a malignancy. This house is a cancer that possesses the people who live here, and the damage it does is fatal."

461

Michael was still angry and scared. "You make the house sound alive!"

"I keep telling you to listen to me! This house has a force that gains strength from the living, which feeds upon energy and negative emotions to gain its foothold in this dimension. The house is usually confined to its personal plane of existence, and cannot cross the barriers to the dimension of the living on its own. So this house waits for an opportunity. It lies in wait for someone to live here. And then it pounces. Please don't be that someone. You can't live here, even when there are no ghosts left inside."

"But this house is worth money!" Michael cried.

"Is any amount of money worth your very life?" Tara countered.

They stood by their cars in the rain, looking at each other, their faces wet. Tara's hair hung in wet ribbons, and her expression was grim as rain dripped from her chin.

Finally Michael gave in. "Okay. I believe you. I inherited this place, so the only money I'm losing is in the repairs I already did. I'm going to walk away from this house. I won't be back."

And without saying goodbye, he got into his car and drove away.

And as Tara also got into her car to drive away, the house watched her leave.

The house was patient. Tara knew that since its outer structure was repaired, it would stand for a long time, waiting; she likened it to a spider weaving its web. Sooner or later, the house would entwine someone.

This time, it had been up against a medium that had powers matching its own. But next time, there would be an unassuming type of person walking through the front door; and next time, Tara knew the house would win.

About Jeani Rector

While most people go to Disneyland while in Southern California, Jeani Rector went to the Fangoria Weekend of Horror there instead. She grew up watching the Bob Wilkins Creature Feature on television and lived in a house that had the walls covered with framed Universal Monsters posters. It is all in good fun and actually, most people who know Jeani personally are of the opinion that she is a very normal person. She just writes abnormal stories. Doesn't everybody?

Jeani has had stories featured in magazines such as *Aphelion, Midnight Street, Strange Weird and Wonderful, Dark River Press, Macabre Cadaver, Ax Wound, Horrormasters, Morbid Outlook, Horror in Words, Black Petals, 63Channels, Death Head Grin, Hackwriters, Bewildering Stories, Ultraverse*, and others. Her book *Around a Dark Corner* was released in the USA on Graveyard Press in 2009.

Jeani Rector is the founder and editor of The Horror Zine.

THE BOND

by Dean H. Wild

"What time did they crap out, anyway?" Mike Bledsoe asked as the last rays of the sun splashed the wall in his office.

Ten years in the mortuary business left him with a nice repertoire of appropriate conversational prompts but none of those were called for, not when his brother was the only other person in the room.

Cameron sat in a corner chair, smoking and nervously bouncing his legs up and down. His eyes were red from jet lag. "I was told it was around lunchtime. Both of them out like a light. And at the same time." He snapped his fingers. "I'm not surprised. Are you?"

"No. What surprises me is that they were taken to Serenity Home instead of here."

"Don't look at me. The coroner had everything handled before my plane landed." Cam snorted, hawked back a mouthful, swallowed.

"Still, two women in their eighties die at the kitchen table before their iced tea has a chance to warm over and nobody thinks to call the nephew who lives in town? The one who incidentally runs a mortuary?"

Cam shrugged. "Maybe they thought you were too close, a family thing, you know? Conflict of interest. When is Ted bringing them over from Serenity, anyway?"

"He'd already gotten a start on Alma, but he said he'd transfer her and Lizzie right over. It's funny, I want to do this, and yet I don't."

"You want me to stay for the whole thing, don't you?" Cam looked up, his cigarette nearly spent.

Mike switched on the office overheads, bathing them both in harsh light. "If you can still take it, yeah."

"I remember those two summers, Bro, and I did appreciate the chance to earn the cash." Cam pulled out a fresh Marlboro from his pocket. "It just wasn't my cup of tea, dressing up what we become after

464

we're dead. I'll stick around tonight as long as I don't have to do any of the grisly stuff."

Mike smiled. "I'll make it as dull as possible for you."

"Just like any other evening with the Aunties, then."

Mike fought back a laugh. His Aunt Liz had spoken directly to him only once in his life that he could recall. He had been ten years old and the family had been paying a courtesy call to the two aunties. The house they shared was small and smelled as if each room had been neatly packed in mothballs until company arrived. He'd wandered outside and pulled a row of stones from a backyard flowerbed, then stacked them one by one into a pail, stopping to check the weight differential each stone brought. It was an act of boredom and he was unaware of the disarray he was causing until Liz came across him and descended on him, waggling one of her craggy fingers and cawing, "How dare you? That's not for you to mess with, you stinking little pup."

He ran inside and stuck close to his mother, waiting for Liz to come in and announce his transgression. Instead, she took her place at the table and picked up the conversation with the adults, no fuss involved. His Aunt Alma was the only one to give him a second glance and he realized from her expression that she knew exactly what he'd done. Liz had shared what she knew with her sister but never spoke a word. It gave him goosebumps back then and a hint of the same feeling was coursing over him right now.

The back door buzzer sounded. "That will be our delivery." Mike said and allowed Cam to go ahead of him.

«« — »»

Ted Wilkes opened the back door of the hearse when Cam and Mike came out with their gurneys. "Sorry about the mix-up," Mike said, "I appreciate you taking the time—"

Ted grunted, "Just get them out of there so I can go home."

"Would you start, Cam?" Mike glimpsed at the two long black bags in the belly of the hearse, and then stepped up to Ted. "Is there a problem?"

Ted did not reply but watched Cam as he loaded one of the bags onto a gurney with marginal grace and success and then reached for the other. "Hey—oh hey. Use just the one gurney. Stack 'em. Stack those bags together. I mean it."

Cam shot them a puzzled glance and Mike shrugged back, "Do what he says."

"How is *that* supposed to work?" Cam said around his cigarette, scratched his head and sighed into the open tailgate of the hearse. "Ridiculous. Bossing me around as if this was still my summer job, for Christ's sake."

"They died in each other's arms, you know," Ted said quietly.

Mike nodded without surprise. Stories had rumbled through his family like constant thunder, sometimes playful, sometimes grim, about the two women who would do practically nothing apart from one another.

"And there's something else." Ted, tall and gray, tugged his shirt collar down to show a pad of gauze taped to his throat. Blood had soaked through in the center.

Mike blinked, "Ouch. What did you do?"

"Not me. It was Liz. There's probably some of my meat still under her fingernails. Motor reaction twitch, I suppose, but it left me with a queer feeling like I'd just pissed her off or something. Unprofessional of me, I know, but take my advice, Mike. Don't follow the regular rules on this one because this isn't regular. Watch yourself."

"Watch myself?" Mike laughed but the other man wasn't smiling.

"You heard me," Ted said as he climbed behind the wheel of the hearse. "Don't doubt it." Then he drove away.

"Hey!" Cam stood under the thin light of the receiving area, the two black bags piled precariously on a single gurney, his hands on his hips. "Do I get a little help with the door here, or what?"

«« — »»

"Stacking up bodies like old duffel bags," Cam grumbled as they steered the stretcher toward the embalming room. "That Ted guy's not all there, is he?"

Mike cut in front to open the door and switched on the work room lights. "Something about our aunties got him spooked."

"Join the club, I say."

"Bring them in here, please."

Cam parked the gurney next to the single embalming table and Mike went to a cabinet on the other side of the work area to prepare the implements he needed for the job ahead. The mutter of a body bag zipper came to him as he sorted his tools. A slow sound. Tentative.

466

Laborious. "I'll help you in a minute, Cam," he said, not looking around. "If you wait for me we can lift—"

"Mike," Cam's rasping voice came from directly behind him.

He turned, bumped into his brother. The zipper sound was coming from the gurney behind them. It became slow, slower. Stopped.

"I didn't, uh…do that," Cam said. A sick look of alarm passed over his face.

Mike glared at the stretcher. The top bag was open a few inches at the head end, gaping like a black mouth.

"They're dead, right?" Cam cast a wary glance toward the heaped bags. His breath sounded small and tight, the way it had sounded when he got scared as a child. "Auntie Alma? Aunt Liz?"

"Knock off that crap," Mike gave his brother a gentle shove and crossed over to the stretcher. He pulled the zipper as far as it would go, his heart slamming in his chest, his thoughts circling around and around—what if the occupant, whichever one is was, sits up, looks at me, waves an old lady finger in my face?—and then he spread the bag completely open. Liz was there. The frailer of the two sisters, she seemed wasted and shrunken in the confines of the bag. She wore the floral dress in which she'd sat down to lunch. Pink beads were clipped to her earlobes. Her tiny hands, delicate and splayed like the claws of a sparrow, were at her sides. He let one of his palms float just above the partially open mouth and sensed no movement of air. Then he set his fingers on the pulse point of the folded neck.

"Nothing," he said. "Help me get her off of there. I want to check Alma, too."

Cam took the foot end of the bag and helped Mike set the small load onto the stainless steel embalming table. Then he stood back and took more of those small breaths. Color had begun to drain from his cheeks.

Alma had been undressed and disinfected at Serenity Home. Her hair, dyed a shade of red that reminded Mike of the sunsets that streaked through his office shades, was wet and tangled, plastered to the doughy face like garish seaweed. The bare chest showed no signs of breath or heartbeat. A droplet of water, cloudy with soap, dribbled down the mound of one sagging breast.

"Motor reaction," Mike concluded. "Liz's hand twitched against the side of the bag. The zipper wasn't caught and it slid open. Same kind of deal that got Ted his trophy scratches."

"Maybe," Cam said and inched closer.

Mike followed his brother's doubtful gaze to Liz's hands. They rested in repose on the floor of the bag, unstrained, undisturbed, limp. He reached out and broke the bags down around both sisters. "Let's switch them around. I want Alma on the table so I can finish what Ted started."

Alma and Liz had gone from adorable childhood sisters eternally hand holding and snuggling with one another to quiet, moody young women ("touched" is how Mike's mother had put it) to cackling old ladies who never married and were continually finishing one another's sentences. He vividly remembered watching them pass looks across a room, never curling a lip or blinking an eye, and yet simultaneously nodding in agreement or bursting into gales of grating laughter—some grim observation or catty old lady joke that had traveled along invisible tethers between them—something the family called The Bond. And he had not merely seen it happen. On a sunny April day of his fifteenth year, while in the aunties' presence, he had felt it happen. He had gotten in the way of it, stood in just the right place between them so that one of their wordless exchanges coursed over him like an eddy of murky water. It threatened to engulf him with a sort of dark electricity, something that seemed intent of flinging him off to the side and at the same time holding onto him eternally. Once he was free of it he felt his way to the sofa and sat there until the awful shaky sensations in his joints dissipated, all the while watching them finish their conversation in smug silence. The family spoke of The Bond often, but he wasn't sure any of them had ever had it surge over them in such a way.

"Are you dealing with this okay?" he asked his brother once they had the bodies switched. His hands did their work, it seemed, by themselves, manipulating trochar and cannula, checking the pumps that stood sentinel near the work table.

"To be honest, those summers were a lot longer ago than I thought," Cam said as he gazed at the pallid form of Alma laid out in front of him. He held an unlit cigarette as if it were a talisman to ward off all that he was seeing. "I don't know if...uh—"

"Go in the back office and make us some coffee," Mike told him with a knowing smile. "I'll be there in a little while."

Once he was alone, Mike stripped Liz's body down and worked the bag out from under her. Covertly spoken family stories played inside his head.

"Probably sit on top of one another all day long," one of the uncles would snort in their randiest voices over beers. "And what do you think happens at night?" They would all have a loud laugh then, passing naughty winks to their wives who traded tight, unsmiling looks that held a randiness all their own.

He opened the cooler and brought Liz's gurney around. A moth-like flutter passed by his ear. He stopped just short of putting her in the refrigerated room with his hands on the stretcher frame, waiting, weighing. All he could gather was the hum of the fluorescents and the smell of brewed coffee drifting from the other end of the basement. He searched Liz's pale face. Another flutter grazed the back of his neck. He was between them, he thought, with Liz in front and Alma behind. He was blocking the path, the frequency.

"The Bond," he grunted and then turned around.

Alma rested on the table a few paces away, ready for his invading tubes and hoses, her horny toes pointing up, ancient and uncompromised nipples almost devoid of color. That put Liz behind him. How could he be sure her bird-like hands weren't ready to drift up and latch onto his shoulders—*How dare you get between us, stinking little pup!* He turned again.

Liz rested undisturbed, dry and white. *This isn't regular*, Ted had said. *No it isn't,* he thought, *it's The Bond and I'm stuck in the middle of it like some damned conductor.*

Cam knocked on the door. He nearly screamed.

《《——》》

"It's freaking you out, isn't it?" Cam asked him.

They were in the small basement office and the air was becoming rank with Cam's cigarette smoke.

"Maybe Ted should have finished the whole damn thing."

"Ted didn't want them, as I recall." Cam drained his coffee cup and then refilled it from the pot on the corner of the desk. "Probably something to do with The Bond, I'm guessing."

Mike thought of Liz's hands and tried to fight the suspicion that they might fly out if he got between the sisters again. He shook his head. "You're not making this any easier."

"Just telling it like it is. Don't think I bring up stuff like this in the bowels of a funeral home for fun."

469

Mike watched him drain his second cup. Cam's hands trembled and that made what he was about to ask seem more difficult, but he said it anyway. "You're still going to stick around, right? At least within shouting distance?" He attempted a half smile as he added, "This isn't quite my cup of tea, either. Not this. Not tonight."

Cam took one of his small, tight breaths and nodded. "I'll stay close, Bro."

《《—》》

"Why in the hell is it so cold in here?" Cam said as they stepped into the embalming room.

Mike didn't answer. Instead he said, "I left Liz by the cooler. I know I did."

The fluorescents above the work table were stuttering on, off, on, off. The aunties were parked side by side, Liz's gurney situated next to the work table beneath the strobing light. Their hands—Alma's left, Lizzie's right—were tangled in a loose clasp. Cam let out a frantic wheeze, "No fucking way."

Mike moved into the room with small, measured steps, barely aware he was speaking under his breath. "There is probably no one else on earth that could be ready for this."

"What are you going to do?"

"Finish it," he told his brother. "I've got to. Would you mind going upstairs and ordering the caskets? There are forms and catalogs on my desk. I don't care what you get but you better make damn sure they match."

"Yeah, upstairs," Cam moved away, staring at the colorless hands that bridged the two bodies. "They'll match. Thanks, Mike."

"Don't mention it."

He stepped into the flickering light. He wanted to be sure the aunties were gone, really gone. That was the first order of business.

He went to the cabinet against the wall and brought back a small scalpel. Heart hammering, he set the arc of the blade against the inside of Alma's wrist and pressed the sharp edge into her skin. When he pulled it away a dark droplet welled, almost black in the stuttering light, but it did not ooze or trickle. Then he gripped the aunties' intertwined hands and turned them to expose Liz's wrist. He made a similar cut there. A gash opened but yielded no fluid at all.

470

"Well then," he tossed the scalpel aside, "let's get busy dressing up what we become when we're dead."

He grasped the women's hands, more confidently now, and pulled. The fingers resisted, their jerky release reminded him of pulling thick roots out of the dirt. And there was something else, an almost magnetic pull in the air even after the hands were apart. He parked Liz's gurney near the refrigerated drawers in the back of the room and tossed a fresh sheet over her. The flickering pool of light around Alma was blinding and disorienting, but he plunged into it and began to work quickly, making his incisions and rude insertions and then sheeted her up to the neck. It was regular work for him now, even if the place was lit like a damned dance club, and once the familiar hum of the pumps began to fill the room, he felt himself relax. He sat down in a chair next to the embalming table and wondered how Cam was progressing, how many cigarettes—

Behind him, the wheels of a gurney squeaked.

He stood up and turned toward the back corner of the room. Liz's gurney moved across the smooth floor. A thin arm jutted from beneath the sheet like a mottled prow in the half light. The arm wavered, the index finger rose and searched the air. Next to him Alma's hand flopped out from its coverlet, the knuckles brushing his pants leg. He let out a small gagging cry and whirled to face her. Her expression was dull and still, as empty as a clay pot, and yet her ashen fingers creaked open. He felt The Bond well up around him—not a flutter but something swift and sudden like a surging river. It sluiced around him, sifted through him, rose and fell like cries of anguish on the air. His clothes shifted and dragged against his skin. Amid it all he could feel their longing. Death had blinded these bonded women, he thought, had deafened them and made them mute. All they had now was touch, all they craved was one another. Their bond was a broken tether, and they flailed their respective ends of it like bullwhips searching for entanglement, seeking a conduit through which they could find the solace of union—seeking, perhaps unaware of their objective, for him.

A cart holding metal tubes and small surgical tools toppled over, its contents chimed across the floor like broken bells. Liz's gurney drifted closer, sheet fluttering with ghostly silence. Mike's breath became a plume of white. The thick door of the cooler clanked and swept open. The door to the upstairs slammed.

471

He found himself taking a stance in the path of Liz's approaching gurney, holding his hands out like a half-back during a Sunday afternoon game. Bottles fell from a shelf across the room and smashed on the floor. He reached out to latch onto the gurney's side rail but Liz's leading hand swayed suddenly and the thick yellow nail of her index finger sliced a neat gap into his wrist. He leapt backward, stunned. Alma's fingers raked the back of his left hand, the side of her thumbnail tearing his skin.

Liz's gurney veered as if to circle him, the peaks and mounds of her face and shoulders joggled beneath the sheet like so much cargo. He was still between them. The Bond gushed through him in uninvited waves and Liz's avian fingers curled toward him—*how dare you.*

Alma's body joggled, too. Her fingers splayed open, perhaps sensing the closeness of her sister. Liz's sheet tangled in her gurney's wheels and was swept down and away, her wasted body exposed in the jittery light. *Here it is,* he decided. *Here is what sisters with The Bond become when they are dead.* It was something desperate and hungry. *Not for you to mess with, stinking pup.*

"Yes it is," he shouted into in the stuttering light. "It's my job to get you ready to go into the ground, you and your goddamned bond!"

Liz's gurney continued to circle. A fluorescent tube exploded above him in a cough of glass shards. He fell into a crouch at the foot of the work table, covering his head, and he realized he was in a perfect position for the gurney wheels to grind over him. Instead it slipped past him, bumped against the side of the work table and came to a halt. The Bond flowed over him in a dark wake, tugged at his cuffs and his hair, slid around his neck like an icy sling and then relaxed. Searching strands had found their counterparts and began to quiet. Alma's sheet drifted to the floor next to him. Hard, cold flesh squeaked against a polished metal surface. A pressing sound came from above him, skin on skin.

Cam yelled from the stairwell, threw open the workroom door and stumbled in. "Why did you slam the door? What the hell happened in here?"

Mike got to his feet. On the work table the sisters were nestled, arms around each other, bathed in the steady glow of cold fluorescents.

"The Bond," he told his brother. "That's what happened."

"Holy Christ," Cam puffed as he glared at the entwined forms. "Did you—"

"No." he said as he dug the car keys from his pocket. "Can you do one more thing for me? Please."

«« — »»

Attendance at the wake was sparse, and he supposed the closed caskets had kept some people away. They had an uncle who likened closed casket funerals to building a model ship inside a crockery jug instead of a bottle. "Sure you can tell folks it's in there, but there's no pay-out if you can't see it." It was the only way around this, he thought as he glared at the identical coffins. He was managing quite nicely to maintain his perfect and polished funeral director's face.

"Tell me once more," Cam said from behind him, keeping it low. "We did the right thing, didn't we?"

Mike checked his fingernails and wished he'd had time to clean them better. There were moons of dirt under them, garden dirt that came off of the stones from the aunties' flower bed. Those stones now rested inside one of the coffins, spread out to make the weight even. The other coffin held two women stacked face to face, bonded forever in contented, peaceful rest. If he stood next to it long enough he could sense the delicate ebb and flow that worked inside, no longer something that flailed desperately but a coursing, restored cycle that moved endlessly, one heart to the other. A family thing. He wondered if anyone else would notice.

"No doubt in my mind at all," he said, patted Cam's shoulder, and went over to shake a few hands.

About Dean H. Wild

Dean H. Wild has been writing for over twenty years, and most of his work is in the horror and dark fantasy genre. Some of Dean's work in print includes "Harm None," published in The Horror Writers Association's *Bell, Book & Beyond* edited by P.D. Cacek, and "The Kid," included in William Simmons' *Vivisections*.

Dean is the Assistant Editor for The Horror Zine.

Made in the USA
Coppell, TX
03 January 2022

70816595R00260